The Scion Princess

THE SCION
PRINCESS

Tovaley B. Kysel

Mellor Publishing House
HONOLULU, HAWAII

Publisher's Note: This is a work of fiction. Names, characters, places, and incidents are a product of the author's imagination. Locales and public names are sometimes used for atmospheric purposes. Any resemblance to actual people, living or dead, or to businesses, companies, events, institutions, or locales is completely coincidental.

Book Layout ©2016 BookDesignTemplates.com

The Scion Princess / Tovaley B. Kysel. -- 1st ed. Paperback.
ISBN-13 978-0-9971587-2-4 • ISBN-10: 0-997-15872-7

for Chelsea,
thank you for your patience.

Everyone is like a moon, and has a dark side which he never shows to anybody.

–MARK TWAIN

Note from the Author:

This book contains mature content (language and minimal sexual content). Possible triggers include domestic violence and rape. Though neither are graphic, please continue at your own discretion.

Mahalo.

1   HOW WILL I KNOW

Beautiful, submissive, silent, and powerless.

That was the only way the high-borns in the scion society wanted the women in their community. They wanted seductresses, who were passive and obedient.

Anything else, and their value went down.

Odette Thomsett had these beliefs ingrained into her memory since she was old enough to understand them.

Do not speak in the presence of a man unless acknowledged and spoken to first.

Do not interrupt.

Do not back talk.

Her mother, Annalise Thomsett, taught her that men were beasts. They needed to be treated with benevolence and compassion. In return, their women would be treated like goddesses.

Their women.

Odette sat on the black stool with her hands in her lap. Dil Watanabe circled her while gripping onto his clipboard. He worked as the auctioneer at the annual Scion Bridal Expo. He was a decently young and slender Japanese man, and the light from the ceiling danced against his thick, greasy black hair with his movements. He was there to critique her appearance, which would decide exactly what Odette Thomsett was worth, and Odette couldn't help but silently critique him right back.

He bent over at the waist to look at her legs. They were barely long enough to reach the metal rim at the bottom of the stool. He stood up straight again, and glowered at her in disapproval.

"Too short," he said as he roughly scribbled down onto the pad of his clipboard. He got in her face as the hairdresser pulled at her blonde locks. Odette gripped the bottom of the stool to make sure she didn't pull back with it. Mr. Watanabe frowned. "Eyes are much too far apart." He shook his head as he pulled away from her and waved his hand, dismissing the stylist. "Stand," he commanded to Odette.

She slid off of the stool and smoothed out the pleated skirt of her forest green cocktail dress. Mr. Watanabe pulled his measuring tape down from around his neck and wrapped it around her waist.

Merely glancing at the number, he whipped it away from her, lashing Odette's arm with the tape.

"Far too skinny," he continued with a dramatic exhale and draped the tape over the back of his neck again. He grumbled to himself while writing on his clipboard.

Odette rubbed at the welt forming on her skin. "Too skinny, too short..."

The more Mr. Watanabe complained about her appearance, the more she worried. But Odette was a professional by now when it came to not letting the distress show on her face. She was very doll-like in appearance. Plump lips, with large green eyes and long eyelashes; her mom and her mom's friends often told her it would work in her favor.

She hoped it would.

"She's a grot, yes? No psychic ability?" Mr. Watanabe asked Odette's parents without looking up from his clipboard.

Mrs. Thomsett nodded as she gripped at her expensive leather purse.

"Yes, just like her sisters, Odette came out *grotesque*."

Grotesque. *Grots*. It didn't matter how it was said. Odette hated the word and averted her eyes at the mention of it. She didn't feel grotesque, and she certainly didn't look it, but being a grot had nothing to do with her outer appearance. Being a grot meant being a high-born scion and having no psychic ability whatsoever. She was often told she was lucky she wasn't mid-born. That neither of her parents were mundane, the normal folk their society co-existed with. Otherwise, if she were, two years ago when she was sixteen, she could have been kidnapped by high-borns and sold into their society as a concubine.

"Virgin?" Mr. Watanabe asked her.

Odette nodded.

Mr. Watanabe scribbled one last thing on his clipboard and tore the bottom half of the page. He handed it to Odette's mother and left the room, the heavy door slammed shut behind him. Odette hadn't noticed until then that the entire make-up team had also cleared out, but she only glanced around before her gaze settled upon her mother.

"Is it good?" she asked hopeful, though the expression on her mom's face was promising.

Odette's smile began to build. Her posture perked up from where she stood and she gently bit down on her bottom lip.

"It's very good, far more than your sister was worth." Mrs. Thomsett nodded. She looked up at her daughter. "Six hundred scripts."

Odette's eyes widened.

In mundane money, that meant sixty-thousand dollars at minimum, with the possibility of a higher bid. Her father smiled in approval and Odette turned to look at herself in the mirror.

She hardly recognized the girl staring back.

Her long lashes were coated in mascara, the smokey eyeshadow only made her large green eyes look larger, and her cheeks were lightly dusted with blush. She looked more like a doll now than ever. Odette sighed and pulled the ringlets of blonde hair over her shoulders as she turned to face her father.

"I don't know why he was complaining so damn much," Mr. Thomsett said, putting his hands on her small shoulders. "I doubt any of the other girls will be going for this amount, or higher."

A slow smile began to spread across her face again as she let out a delicate breath of relief between her parted lips.

His hands slipped from her shoulders and he took his wife's hand just as Odette turned back to face the mirror. "Come on," he said to her mother. "We'll let her have some time to herself before it starts."

Through the reflection, she watched as her parents exited the room; the door opening and closing behind her.

The Bridal Expo was an annual scion event that happened in their communities located all around the world. The one in Honolulu was always rather spectacular, since there was only one scion society in the entire state of Hawai'i. Many, if not hundreds of people, would be there. Dozens of families looking to buy attractive, young brides for their sons.

The backstage halls were mostly empty; young women waiting patiently in their dressing rooms to be called to the stage.

Odette shook out her hands, trying to shake the nerves that began to creep across her skin. She faced the mirror still, and straightened the sweetheart neckline of her strapless dress. It was a tight forest green cocktail dress with a softly pleated skirt that ended just above her knees. She adjusted her silver necklace hanging flat against her chest; it read *Odette* in cursive.

The door flung open, and she almost screamed.

"Oh my god, look at you!" Sophie said as they stepped into the room. Sophie always made a bold entrance; vibrant and worthy of attention, much like their personality. Androgynous in appearance and beautiful copper skin, everyone found themselves falling a little bit in love with them.

Behind Sophie's mass of unmanageable black curly hair, was Midori and Paisley following after them. Paisley's light brown hair was messily tied up in a bun as always, and her worn, faded overalls adorned holes in various places. Only one buckle was clipped while the other hung behind her, broken. Her white crop top only came down to her waist, showing off the Chinese dragon tattoo on her side.

Midori was dressed the nicest of the three people who had come through the dressing room door, but this was nothing new. She could look like a Japanese model in sweats. She delicately pushed her perfectly straight black hair over her shoulder as she entered the room.

Odette had her hand over her chest and let out an exasperated sigh. "You scared me!"

"Damn, Odette." Paisley circled her like a hungry shark. "If I had the money, I'd buy you."

Odette's mouth tugged into a lip-closed smile, revealing dimples everyone seemed to love.

"I can't believe you guys are here." She then glanced at the door and her smile faded. "Where's Shiro?"

"Outside," Midori said, eyes shifting toward the door as well. She tucked her black hair behind her ear. "He couldn't bring himself to come in."

"What I can't believe," Sophie cut in, "is that your parents are *selling* you." They pulled themselves up onto the black stool in front of the mirror. Sophie then crossed their legs and lifted an eyebrow in Odette's direction.

Odette shrugged. "Part of The Scion Order."

"Well, if you weren't a high-born, I'm pretty sure this would be illegal. Actually, I'm sure it doesn't matter. This is illegal."

"Thanks to Mayor Mendoza, it doesn't matter if the country as a whole considers it illegal," Odette informed her. "They'll never know. They'll just manipulate them to forget. You know that, Sophie."

Odette leaned back against Paisley, who was nearly a head taller than she was. "That's why Hawai'i's scion society has the least amount of problems; we live on an island. Easier to keep and maintain secrets."

"Why are you okay with this?" Sophie asked, sitting forward on the stool to readjust in the seat. "You should live in one of the mid-born territories, or even at the Imperial Quarter with us. I mean, I left the city and I'm doing just fine."

"My parents need the money."

"It might not be so bad," Paisley suggested, Sophie nearly killed her with their eyes the second the words left her mouth. Odette tilted her head back to look up at Paisley as she spoke. "I mean, you could end up with someone who loves you."

"Ugh," Sophie groaned and slipped out of the seat. They walked up to Paisley and pushed her face away with their palm and Odette was forced to get up from leaning against her. "Get out of here with your optimism." Sophie tried to push Paisley right out of the door.

"Stop touching my face — Green!" Paisley shouted, pushing against Sophie's arm as she tried to reach for their face. "Control your S.O.!"

Midori laughed and crossed her arms.

"I know better than to get between you two," she said. Paisley managed to pull Sophie's arm down and shoved them away from her. "We should actually leave soon before someone catches us. Oh my god, especially with you two making so much noise," Midori scolded the two of them.

"Wait, you guys aren't staying?" Odette frowned and put her hands on her hips. She almost looked like Tinker Bell, in her green dress and with her nose scrunched.

"I'm sorry, O." Sophie and Paisley separated from each other as they both turned to face her. "You're like a little sister to us," Sophie told Odette with a shrug. "We can't watch you just — you know — get auctioned off like some kind of antique doll or something. We just wanted to stop by to make sure you were okay."

Paisley's eyes began to water, and she forced a smile. "Come visit us at the shop the second you get a chance, okay?" She grabbed Odette and pulled her into a hug. Paisley's arms wrapped tightly around her slender frame. "I'm going to worry about you everyday until you do."

"Please don't cry or you're going to make me cry," Odette mumbled over Paisley's shoulder. She gripped the loose, dangling strap of her overalls.

"Don't cry," Paisley told her. "You don't wanna mess up that make-up." She stepped back and wiped the tears from her own face. She sniffled and forced herself smile again, even though her face was now red and splotchy. "Please take care of yourself, okay?"

"Yeah," Midori said as she grabbed Odette's waist from behind, forcing her to let go of Paisley's overalls. Sophie grabbed her from the front and they both sandwiched her into a hug. "We love you."

They let her go and as the three of them headed toward the door, Sophie turned back around to face her. "Make sure whoever buys you, pays more than whatever they said you're worth. You're priceless, all right? Don't forget that." Sophie grabbed hold of Midori's hand and they left together.

Paisley lingered in the doorway a little longer. "You're gonna be okay, right?" she asked, thumbing the pockets of her overalls.

She leaned her head against the frame.

Odette gave her a reassuring smile and nodded. "And if I'm not, I know where to find you."

Paisley's expression faltered when Odette's bottom lip quivered. She ran back into the room to give her another hug.

"Listen, you're an amazing person," Paisley whispered, not letting go just yet. Odette could hear her sniffling between her words, which only made it harder for her not to cry. "And you're going to make someone very happy, and I hope they make you just as happy, because that's what you deserve. Never forget that. No matter what anyone tells you, you deserve to be happy too." Suddenly, her eyes lit up. She jumped away from Odette.

"Oh, I have something for you," she said, digging into her pocket. "I almost forgot."

Paisley pulled out a small, egg-shaped, papier-mâché doll with no eyes, and handed it to her.

"What is it?" Odette asked. She stared at the little red doll that felt almost weightless. Whenever she tried to knock it over in her hand, by gently flicking it with her index finger, it always returned upright.

"A Daruma doll," Paisley said, thumbing the sides of her overalls. "He'll grant you a wish as long as you promise to provide him with full sight. You paint one eye when you make a wish, and the other will fill in on its own when it comes true. Get knocked down seven times, stand up eight."

"You don't really believe in this stuff, do you?"

"I have to," Paisley said. "And it'll make me feel better, knowing you have one. Mundanes use them for motivational purposes, but in our society, you get to make a wish. Wish for something nice."

The speaker blared with the announcements of the start of the Expo. Paisley grabbed her arm and pulled Odette into one last hug.

"I guess that's my cue to go," she said. She stepped back once she loosened her hold and walked backward slowly, heading toward the door. She didn't take her eyes off of Odette, who stood there with the doll sitting on her palm. "Be strong, Odette."

Paisley closed the door as she left.

Sophie and Midori stopped in the hallway once they noticed her trudging behind them.

"You going to be okay, Pazey?" Sophie asked, and she nodded, but she didn't make eye contact. She knew if she did, she'd cry for sure. Tears still gathered at her bottom lids, damping her lashes.

"Well yeah, I mean, my parents aren't selling me."

Sophie slipped their arm around the back of Paisley's neck once she reached the pair and pulled her close to them.

"She'll be okay. She'll come to the shop in a few weeks once she's all settled in and she'll be happy."

"You don't have foresight, Soapy."

"Neither do you, stop letting the dead people get you down. Come on," Sophie said, dropping their arm down to pat Paisley on the upper back, lightly against her shoulder blade. "We gotta get out of here or we'll be the dead people."

"Hey Paze, remember when you first found out you were a Medium?" Midori asked with a soft chuckle to change the subject and Paisley laughed.

"Of course!"

"I can't believe 'I see dead people' was literally the first thing that came out of your mouth."

"Well, what would you have said?" Paisley asked Sophie.

"Touché."

Odette sat alone in her dressing room, swiveling on the stool, while her friends looked for a way to escape the stadium unnoticed. She slipped off the seat. She placed the Daruma doll down on the vanity in front of her and tilted her head, observing it. Pursing her lips together, she sat back down on the stool again momentarily while trying to think of something worth wishing for. Odette grabbed her make-up bag and dug for her liquid eyeliner. Carefully, she filled in one of the eyes.

I wish... that the one I end up falling in love with, will love me in return.

Odette gently blew against the newly painted eye and dropped both her eyeliner and the doll into her bag before anyone could see it.

It didn't take long for her parents to rejoin her, and an attendant escorted the three of them to the front. Soon she would take the stage, and the bidding would begin.

She would leave the expo as someone's future bride.

Odette Thomsett was about to become property.

She stood patiently in front of her parents as other girls, dressed up much like her, took to the stage after being called up one by one by Mr. Watanabe. He had changed his clothes since she last saw him, or at least finished getting ready. He now wore a black suit with a sparkling silver vest. The illumination of the bright stage lights reflecting against his greasy black hair made it look almost white.

Mr. Thomsett was right, most of the other girls were in the two to four-hundred range. Being a grot gave her a two-hundred script advantage, which came with worry. The girl currently standing on stage had no bids.

What if no one bid on her?

Her father found her shoulder and patted her back, as if he had known she needed the reassurance. Odette looked up at him and he smiled down at her.

"You're next!" Mrs. Thomsett squealed as Odette turned to her. "Are you ready, love?"

Odette took a deep breath and nodded as she exhaled through her mouth. Her mother took her bag from her and Odette shook out her hands as she turned to face the stage.

"Next we have a grot — Odette Thomsett!" Mr. Watanabe announced and a spotlight shone upon her as she crossed to the center of the stage. The lights were so bright that she couldn't see into the audience, which settled her nerves a little as she was unable to see their reactions to her. "The bidding will start at six-hundred scripts."

Men began shouting various numbers, none of which she could understand with Mr. Watanabe's auction chant ringing in her ears, but then came another bid.

Higher than the rest.

"One-thousand scripts."

Air caught in her throat and the entire auditorium went silent.

It even caught Mr. Watanabe off guard.

"Can you repeat that, please?" Mr. Watanabe said into the microphone, looking out into the audience for the bidder. "I'm not sure I heard you correctly —"

"I said, *one-thousand scripts.*"

The voice was louder the second time, carefully enunciating each word as he spoke.

The spotlight found a young man in the audience who sat poised and relaxed; fingers tapping against the surface of the clothed table.

Sharp jawline, angular face.

The long blonde hair that rested over his shoulders and against his chest, was striking against his dark suit. He was elegant in his appearance. When his intense blue eyes caught Odette's gaze, the corner of his mouth twitched. She looked away from him and blushed, catching her breath.

"Going once, going twice, sold! Odette Thomsett for one-thousand scripts!"

Odette walked off stage, careful to hide the bounce in her step. Her mother stood there with her hands clasped over her mouth and her father gaped.

"One-thousand scripts!" Mrs. Thomsett shouted as she pulled her daughter into a hug so tight, Odette found it hard to breathe. "That is amazing, sweetie! Who knew you'd be worth so much?"

Mrs. Thomsett released her and clapped her hands greedily.

Odette turned to her father and started chewing on her bottom lip, suddenly very nervous. "Do you think he's nice?"

"He better be," Mr. Thomsett said, he gently ran the back of his index finger against Odette's cheek.

"Why don't we find out?" Mrs. Thomsett asked, as she nodded ahead. Odette turned around to see the same man approaching her.

"Allow me to introduce myself. My name is Lailoken Baskerville." He bowed to her as he took her hand within his, and kissed the back of her fingers.

"Odette Thomsett," she said softly, a gentle smile spread across her full lips.

Lailoken stood tall, his posture straight. At six feet and two inches, he was about a foot taller than she was without her heels on. "Your name is nearly as beautiful as you are." His gaze wandered over the curves of her body. He lifted her hand in the air and she turned for him. "Normally, I don't come to these things, but I'm glad I did. You are absolutely exquisite."

"You're making me blush so much." Odette fanned herself with her hand; her cheeks were bright red. "I might faint," she squeaked.

"I promise I'll catch you," he said. His voice was smooth and attractive. Lailoken let go of Odette's hand as he turned to face her parents. "I promise I will take good care of your daughter," he said.

Her parents nodded, and Mrs. Thomsett handed Odette's purse back to her daughter.

Mr. Thomsett stepped up to her and took her hands in his. "Be good, Odette."

She nodded. "I will, Daddy." She slipped her hands out of his grasp and threw her arms around him. Mr. Thomsett smiled and hugged his daughter for what he knew would be the last time.

"Be good," he said again and kissed the side of her head softly.

When Odette let go of her father, she turned to find Lailoken's hand awaiting hers. She filled the empty space and walked with him down the hallway.

"I read in here," Lailoken said as he acknowledged the pamphlet in his hand, "that you enjoy things from the eighties. You should know that I came out of the eighties too. 1988, to be exact." Lailoken was nearly a decade older than she was. "You're very young," he continued as he tossed the pamphlet in a nearby garbage can. He stopped in his tracks to turn to face her. "I want you to know that I'd like this to be a long engagement. I'd like you to fall in love me on your own terms, however long that takes."

Odette looked up at him in awe.

"What?" he asked, a look of concern crossed his face, noticing her expression of adoration as though he had just granted her a wish.

She hadn't meant to seem so surprised, but she was, and she couldn't hide it. She bit down on her bottom lip.

"I don't mean to speak out of place, but I've heard rumors." She furrowed her brows. "Horror stories, really. About brides without choice. Near slaves to their husbands, and I —"

Lailoken shook his head and pressed his hand to his chest. "I may be a Pusher, but I promise not to compel or manipulate you. I'll wait for you," he said. "We even have a bedroom for you. My parents set it up, if I ever decided to attend one of the expos. Your comfort and personal space are important to me. Till whenever you're ready to share."

"You still live with your parents?" she asked.

"I saw no reason to move out and live on my own, without someone to share my life with. Hawai'i may be paradise, but what is paradise without love?" His thumb affectionately rubbed against the back of her hand. "You don't think it's weird, do you?" he asked, tucking his chin down.

"I think it's sweet," she said and smiled up at him. He really was beautiful.

She followed Lailoken as he searched for his parents in the crowd before leading her to an elegant looking pair. Both older, the man's hairline receded and the rest of his thinning blonde hair was brushed back. The woman's blonde hair fell perfectly in loose curls against her shoulders. Odette could see traces of both of them in Lailoken's face.

"Mom, Dad, this is Odette Thomsett. Isn't she stunning?"

"I am delighted to make your acquaintance," Odette said and curtsied.

"Well, she certainly has manners, doesn't she, Chardonnay?" Mr. Baskerville raised an eyebrow at his wife before he bowed his head to Odette. "You're a very lovely girl."

"She's a little young, Lailoken." Mrs. Baskerville looked down at her with her very large and owl-like, condescending eyes. She opened her mouth to speak, only to turn her attention back onto her son before doing so. "How much longer am I going to have to wait to have grandchildren? You're almost thirty."

"Mother —"

"Whatever. We'll see you at home, Lailoken. Come, Ahren." Mrs. Baskerville waved her hand as she turned away. She linked her arm with her husband's and pulled him to leave with her.

Odette glanced up at Lailoken. He clenched his jaw, and a small pout crossed her lips. "She doesn't like me very much, does she."

She watched his parents walk away.

"She will." Lailoken turned to her. He gently hooked his finger beneath her chin and made her look up at him. "What matters, is that I do. She'll come around. I mean, how couldn't she? Look at you."

Odette couldn't help but smile at his words. In that moment, she had faith that Paisley would end up right. She could be with someone who loved her.

Lailoken Baskerville was perfect.

2   LET'S WAIT A WHILE

He opened the door for her and helped her into his metallic gray Corvette.

Lailoken took her to a fancy restaurant for dinner, where he told her about his life as a Baskerville, and what he desired out of life. Odette admired his ambition. He spoke with such confidence and passion, she hung onto every word. She didn't take her eyes off of his. Crystal blue, intense.

His face was flawless and smooth. She couldn't find a single thing wrong with him, though she wasn't looking very hard. Even if he wasn't perfect, and she was positive he was, she knew that loving someone meant loving their flaws as well. She wanted to accept him wholly.

He brought her to his home in Kahala. After parking his car beside his father's black Chevrolet Chevelle, he took Odette by the hand and led her down the driveway. "I want you to see it from the entrance," he told her.

Areca palms stood in front of a thick stone wall on either sides of the mahogany gate. They were both surrounded by an assortment of colorful plants, visible by the lit entrance lights. Lailoken unlocked the gate and led her across the stone pathway, over a shallow moat, and to the front porch. She turned around, admiring the beautiful garden and carefully crafted structures that lined the greenery.

"You like what you see so far?" Lailoken asked as she turned to face the main entrance. It was brightly illuminated by the porch lights on the front two columns of the house. Fixed and awning windows bordered the large Mahogany French doors.

"It's amazing," she said, unable to pull her gaze away from the beautiful exterior of his home.

"Wait till you see the inside."

The front door opened, and a hapa haole man named Mr. Wong, greeted the two of them with a bow as he stepped aside.

The entrance hall had black marble flooring and a large pendant bowl chandelier hanging from the polished wood board ceiling. It opened up into a higher ceiling living room, with a beautiful curved staircase leading to the second floor, guarded by black banisters and wooden handrails. Odette stepped in further, and even the second floor opened up to the living room like a balcony. Wood crackled in the stone fireplace, shielded by a black gate. She clasped her hands over her mouth as she turned where she stood. Wooden flooring in the living room, black leather couches, a glass table over a European styled area rug. She was in awe.

"Would you like to see your bedroom?" he asked, offering his hand to her.

Odette nodded, slipping her hand into his. Lailoken led her up the stairs. She couldn't help but look behind her as she followed him.

The upstairs was just as magnificent, and he lead her down the hall and opened the far door.

"This will be your room until you feel comfortable sharing one with me," he said as he stepped back against the door to allow her entry.

The door was in a far corner of the bedroom. The walls were splashed with a light gray paint. Across from where she stood, a queen sized bed was pressed up in a corner against two walls and to her left, a vintage styled rosewood dresser and a matching vanity. Between them, stood a full length mirror. A bench sat at the foot of her bed, and faced a bay window which was beside a walk-in closet.

Odette stepped further in and stared at the door beside it. She turned to Lailoken.

"I have my own bathroom?" she asked.

He nodded. "I want you to be comfortable here."

"Where's your room?"

"Down the hall, to the left. I figured it'd be best for you to have as much space as you need."

The corners of her lips tugged into a subtle smile.

"Thank you."

"There are clothes in the closet and dresser. Whatever doesn't fit, we can have altered tomorrow — or whenever you're ready." Lailoken leaned against the door frame and stuck his hands in his front pockets. "Do you like it?"

"I love it," she said.

"I'll let you rest," he said as he stepped out of the room and rested his hand on the doorknob. "I'm sure you've had a long day."

Odette ran to him and threw her arms around him.

"Thank you so much!" She hung onto his neck, feet lifting in the air. Legs bent at her knees.

"You're very welcome. One last thing," he said as Odette released her hold and dropped back down to the ground. His gaze locked with hers and his pupils constricted. "Please don't leave the property without permission."

"I won't leave the property without permission," she repeated after him in a rather monotonous voice and a blank expression on her face.

"Now, you will forget I told you that, and carry on with your evening like a good little girl." He stepped back. "Goodnight, Odette."

"Goodnight!" she replied cheerily and he closed the door.

She turned around, pivoting on her feet, before running to check out her bathroom, feeling like a kid in a candy store.

A free standing stone bath sat near a corner shower encased in glass. The Carrara marble countertop matched the floor, creating a nice contrast against the rosewood cabinets. Odette ran her hand against the fluffy black towels that hung from the racks before returning to her bedroom.

She put her bag down on the vanity and went to her dresser. The top drawer was filled with types of underwear and lingerie that made her raise her eyebrows. In the second drawer, she found loose fitted pajamas, which she changed into immediately.

Odette hung up her dress and went to the bathroom to wash up for bed.

There was a knock on her door.

"Odette?"

It was Mrs. Baskerville.

Odette opened the door as she put her blonde hair up and tied it with a rubber band.

Mrs. Baskerville had her hair in curlers, and she was dressed in a robe. The woman somehow still looked elegant, even without a spot of make-up on her face.

Would you please come with me?" She didn't wait for a response and walked down the hallway.

"Yes, Mrs. Baskerville." Odette quickly scrambled to follow her, shutting her bedroom door behind her.

She followed her down the stairs and to a part of the house she hadn't yet seen. Through the tight hallway, Mrs. Baskerville pushed open the swinging door and led her into the kitchen. Two uplit chandeliers hung from the ceiling over the center island. Counters lined most of the walls, except for one that seemed to be dedicated entirely to oven and stove space. At the other wall, stood an industrial refrigerator.

But the kitchen wasn't empty. Standing there folding dish towels, was a Japanese woman, no older than forty. Her black hair was pulled back in a tight bun, and she wore a white dress over her slender frame and a white apron to match. Her dark eyes seemed to smile at Odette, but her lips remained pressed together, forming a thin line, like the sight of Mrs. Baskerville put a bad taste in her mouth.

Her hands stopped moving and she stood to the side, and bowed to Mrs. Baskerville.

"This is Mrs. Hamasaki, head of the kitchen staff. You are to assist her daily, and you can start by scrubbing every inch of this disgusting tile until your fingers bleed. When was the last time it was cleaned?" Mrs. Baskerville shot an accusing glare at Mrs. Hamasaki. Mrs. Baskerville grabbed one of the folded dish towels and threw it at Odette, who clambered to catch it against her chest. "You may be my son's future bride, but until you're married, you're nothing but a servant girl to me. Now get to work, *Cendrillon*. Don't make me say it again."

Odette's eyes began welling up as Mrs. Baskerville left the kitchen, the door swinging freely. She turned to look at Mrs. Hamasaki, who waved her hand, acknowledging her to come toward her.

"Come here, child. It's okay." Mrs. Hamasaki wrapped her arms around her, comfortingly rubbing her back as Odette fought back tears. "It'll be okay."

"Who's the Barbie?"

Odette moved away from Mrs. Hamasaki to find another girl standing there, a towel thrown over her shoulder. She had short black wavy hair that hung just over her shoulders, and thick bangs swiped to the side. The girl stood beside a Japanese man who was nearly half a foot taller than her, and she hit him in the stomach to acknowledge Odette. He was lanky, with a bit of a muscular build to him. Odette backed away from the two of them and Mrs. Hamasaki grabbed her shoulders.

"It's okay," she said.

"Oh, did I scare her?"

"Kiko, be nice." Mrs. Hamasaki turned to Odette. "This is my daughter, Kiko, and that's Gentry. There's also Amaris and Jiyun who assist in the kitchen, but they've already finished their shifts for today. Kiko, Gentry, this is Odette."

Kiko took a step toward her and offered Odette her hand. "Pleasure to meet you, Doll Face."

Odette furrowed her brows as she gently shook Kiko's hand, who had a firm grip.

"Doll Face?"

"Unless you prefer Sugar Lips. Mega G — look at her lips!"

"Ignore her," Gentry said. "She gives everyone nicknames. I'm Gentry Yoshimura. I usually work nights, so I might be seeing a lot of you — I overheard Mrs. Baskerville." Gentry stepped up to her and slowly took the dishtowel from Odette's hands. "You should rest. I bet you had a long day."

"Besides," Kiko said as she hopped up onto the counter. "You're gonna wanna go to bed before the ghosts come." She started to laugh and Mrs. Hamasaki threw a towel at her face. "Hey!"

"There are ghosts?" Odette looked up at Gentry and he grinned.

"Don't worry, they're friendly. Mostly." He gently nudged her with his elbow toward the door.

"Go on, go back to bed."

Odette wasn't exactly sure how she was supposed to go to *sleep* knowing there were ghosts roaming about the house. It didn't help that it was her first night there, either. Her room seemed bigger in the dark. More shadows. The house, creakier.

She had the blanket up to her nose once she crawled into bed. Eyes wide open. She listened carefully to every sound that could be heard from where she lay.

Odette sunk further into her bed as her closet door slowly swung open. She frowned.

Pull yourself together.

She pushed her blanket off of her and crawled out of bed, tiptoeing to her closet door. Once she closed it, someone grabbed her and cupped their hand over her mouth as she tried to scream.

"I'm sorry! Don't scream."

As she was released, Odette turned around.

A girl started laughing as she walked away from Odette and headed to the door. She put her hand against her chest as she tried to contain her laughter. "I'm sorry, go to sleep." She brushed her brown hair out of her face and took a deep breath, but she couldn't stop laughing.

"Who are you?" Odette demanded to know as the girl clumsily grabbed at the doorknob.

"Pia Accardo. I'm a concubine — or I was a concubine. I'm a maid now. Now that you're around, anyways. By the way, if you're trying to be intimidating or something, it ain't working for you."

"You were Lailoken's concubine?" she asked. Odette studied what she could see of her in the dark. Pia was very pretty, and unlike the rest of the staff she had met, she wore make-up. Her maid outfit fit her well, most of her height coming from her long legs. Pia winked at her and opened the door.

"Sweet dreams, darling."

Odette clenched her jaw.

TOVALEY B. KYSEL

3   WHEN DOVES CRY

Odette survived through spring in her new home. She ended up asking Lailoken about Pia, and he told her she had nothing to worry about; Pia was nothing more than a maid now.

Sitting up in her bed, Odette twisted the intertwined engagement ring on her left hand. Lailoken gave it to her after her first month with him. The white gold ring encased a round, three carat diamond, with smaller diamonds embedded in the band. He told her it cost half as much as she did.

It was the most expensive thing she's ever worn. It was the most expensive thing she's ever owned, aside from herself. Though she no longer owned that anymore.

Not that she was sure she ever owned herself in the first place.

Odette got up and made her bed before going to her bathroom to get ready for the day.

She ate breakfast with the Baskerville family every morning at 7:15 a.m.   Breakfasts were often silent.

Mr. Baskerville read The Scion Advertiser, when Mrs. Baskerville wasn't on the phone, she was ordering the staff around, Kiko in particular, and Lailoken, he'd flip through his planner, careful not to drop any of his breakfast on the pages. Odette had no choice but to sit there and watch the three of them while she ate. She had no idea what any of them did, but she did know Mr. Baskerville's father owned a brothel that now belonged to him.

But everyone knew they owned a brothel. It was the most popular one among the scions on Oahu.

Everyone knew of the Baskervilles.

Odette took a sip of her orange juice and turned her attention onto Lailoken, who sat across from her at the breakfast table. His intense blue eyes focused on his planner as he shoveled up scrambled egg from his plate. She enjoyed watching him, the way he would bite down on his bottom lip for a second, before bringing the food to his mouth.

She scooted forward in her seat and gently nudged his shin with her foot.

He dropped the egg on his planner.

"Odette!" he snapped as he wiped it with his napkin. She flinched when he said her name. "What the fuck is wrong with you?" Odette sank back in her chair. His glare was like a knife to her throat.

"I'm sorry." Her voice lowered to a whisper.

"Clean this up!" he shouted to Kiko as he got up. Odette flinched again at the sound of the chair scraping against the ground. Lailoken glared at Odette again and grabbed his planner. He walked away with heavy steps.

"No," Mrs. Baskerville said as Kiko reached for Lailoken's plate. She turned her attention onto Odette. "You do it."

But Odette didn't move. Her eyes began to water as she stared at Lailoken's empty chair.

Mrs. Baskerville smacked her palm against the table and Odette flinched.

"Now!" she shouted.

Odette got up from her chair. She trembled as she moved around the table and picked up Lailoken's plate and napkin. The utensils rattled as her hands shook. She approached the kitchen door and pushed it open with the side of her arm, not daring to look back as she went inside.

Jiyun took the plate and napkin from her and Mrs. Hamasaki wrapped her arm around her. She rubbed Odette's arm with her hand.

"Are you okay, sweetheart?" Mrs. Hamasaki asked and Odette's bottom lip quivered. She struggled to fight back tears, but couldn't hold it in any longer. Odette turned in toward Mrs. Hamasaki and cried against her shoulder. "Aw, sweetie, it's okay."

"One of these days, I'm gonna fight that guy," Kiko announced as she made her way into the kitchen, shaking her head. She came to a sudden halt when she spotted Odette wrapped in her mom's arms. Her expression fell. "Oh no, she's crying! No, Doll Face! Don't cry!" Kiko put down the pitcher of orange juice and hugged Odette from behind. She stepped back and tugged on Odette's shoulder.

Mrs. Hamasaki slowly let her go.

"It was my fault," Odette said, wiping her cheeks with the back of her hand. She turned to face Kiko. "I feel awful."

"Lai's a giant baby with a temper. That was not your fault. As for Mrs. Baskerville, well, she's just a —"

"Kiko."

"Sorry, Mom."

Amaris slid a bowl of strawberries across the counter. "Have a strawberry, Odette. Abbey got them fresh out of the garden this morning." Amaris gave her a very warm smile. Abbey was her older brother; he managed the garden, the upkeep of the yard, and kept the pools clean. "I promise they're delicious."

Odette looked at Kiko, who nodded at her.

"Go ahead. Popeye's strawberries are the best." Popeye was her nickname for Abbey. Kiko had nicknames for everyone. Some made sense, others, not so much. Perhaps Abbey enjoyed spinach. Kiko reached over and took a strawberry for herself.

"Thank you," Odette said softly as she took one from the bowl as well.

"She's so timid," Jiyun said as she came in through the door again, carrying several plates stacked on her arms. Odette wasn't sure how she managed to carry all of that without dropping it. Jiyun slid them into the soapy water with ease and turned around. "You can't let Mrs. Baskerville know she affects you. She likes that." Jiyun took a strawberry. "But you're doing good."

"Is she still out there?" Odette asked, her eyes were wide.

Jiyun nodded.

Lailoken stormed upstairs and slammed his bedroom door behind him. He groaned at the sight of Pia sprawled out on his bed. "What are you doing in here?" he asked as he put his planner down on his desk and went straight for the bathroom.

Pia sat up.

"Waiting for you, obviously. Someone seems to be having trouble in paradise." She turned over on his bed and lay on her stomach. "Maybe I can help." Pia drug her body against his sheets and tucked in her thighs, lifting her butt.

"I'm gonna be late."

Lailoken didn't even look at her as he came back out. He grabbed his planner and went out the door, slamming it shut behind him, just the same as he had done when he went in.

She groaned and went downstairs.

Pia swung open the kitchen door, keeping her hand pressed against it. "Are you trying to get Lailoken to come crawling back to me?" she asked as she finally stepped in, letting the door swing freely behind her.

"Pia!" Amaris snapped.

"What?" She shrugged her shoulders and reached for a strawberry. She looked at a frowning Odette, all splotchy-faced and puffy-eyed. Pia's lip curled. "You look awful."

"Thanks," Odette said sharply before the two girls parted ways.

Odette did her best to take Jiyun's advice when it came to dealing with Mrs. Baskerville. She didn't get fussy, and she made sure not to cry when the older woman would order her around like Cinderella.

That night, she lay flat on her bed, staring up at the ceiling.

She heard the door creak.

"Pia?" she asked as she sat up, pulling her comforter toward her chest. "Is that you again?"

There was no response.

Odette scooted back on her bed so that she was wedged in the corner between the wall and her pillows. Her eyes were wide as she watched nothing in the darkness. Every single movement in the shadows made her jump.

Then they emerged. It was a masked person, wearing the face of a monster. No eyes, and nothing but a black hole for a mouth with a forked tongue flickering out. They reached their arm out to her as they came closer, and lunged at her.

Odette screamed.

She awoke with a startle and sat up in her bed, chest rising and falling as she gasped for air. Sweat trickled down the sides of her face. She glanced at her clock on her nightstand. Only 2 a.m.

Odette fanned herself with her hand before wiping the sweat around her face with her blanket. She crawled out of bed and quickly ran down the hall to Lailoken's room.

Softly, she knocked on his door near the knob.

Within a few seconds, he opened it. Sleepily, he leaned against the frame. His blonde hair was messily pulled back into a bun.

"What?" he asked, his tone was flat.

"Lailoken," she said and inhaled deeply, averting her gaze. "I wanted to apologize. I'm really sorry for what happened this morning. I'm sorry —"

He wrapped his arm around Odette's wrist and pulled her toward him. His long arms wrapped around her frame. "It's okay," he whispered and kissed the top of her head. "I know it won't happen again."

"Can I stay in here with you? For tonight?" she asked. She took a step back and looked up at him, hopeful. A small smile peeked at the corner of his lips and he nodded.

But much to her dismay, the nightmares didn't stop. Only a few nights had passed until she was jolted awake again in her own bed. Her lungs felt like they were being restricted of air as she struggled to catch her breath.

Once she managed to calm herself down, Odette got out of bed and tiptoed down the creaky stairs to the kitchen.

Gentry was at the sink, scrubbing the inside. His hair was down, long enough to cover his neck and rest against his shoulders and back. Kiko was sitting on the counter, gently tapping her heels against the cabinet. She looked up when Odette opened the door and raised her eyebrows.

"Did you guys lie to me about the ghosts?" Odette asked. "That night I first came here?"

Gentry turned around, a little startled by her sudden appearance.

"Oh no, there are definitely ghosts here. Just ask Quinlan," Gentry said, wiping his hands with a dishtowel. "She's a Medium."

"Why? Did something happen, Doll Face?" Kiko asked as she slid off of the counter.

Odette pressed her lips together, and bit down gently on her bottom one.

"I just — I keep having this nightmare but I'm sure it's nothing."

Gentry and Kiko exchanged glances.

"Nightmare about what?" he asked.

Odette shook her head. "I'm sure it's nothing. I just wanted to be sure that it wasn't —" she cut herself off and shrugged. "I don't know."

"You can stay down here with us for tonight if you want," Kiko suggested as she looked up at Gentry. "We'll keep you company."

He nodded. "We'll keep the pretty girl safe."

"You think I'm pretty?"

Kiko laughed at Odette's question.

"All of the scion brides are pretty," Gentry said and turned to Kiko. "Isn't that like — a qualification or something?"

She shrugged. "I don't know how you expect me to know," Kiko said. "I've barely been outside of this house my entire life."

Odette frowned. "You've been here your whole life?"

Kiko pulled herself back up onto the counter and nodded as she hooked her ankles.

"My mom had me in this house. But I mean, it could be worse." Kiko glanced at Gentry who had walked away from them.

Odette pressed her lips together. "You haven't been here your whole life, have you."

Gentry shook his head. He tucked his long, black hair behind his ear as he turned around to face them again and leaned back against the counter near the sink.

"I was kidnapped by Shadow Crawlers when I was nine. Sold to the Baskervilles by the age of ten." Gentry wet his lips and crossed his arms tightly over his chest. "Not a day goes by that I don't miss my little sister. She was deaf and I just — I hope nothing bad happened to her."

"What do you mean?"

"As an older brother, you know, you just feel like you're supposed to be there to protect your family, and I couldn't do that." He forced a laugh. "I couldn't even protect myself." Gentry shrugged it off. "But I mean, it is what it is. No one's really here by choice except for Mr. Wong and Mrs. Hamasaki."

"Was everyone kidnapped?" Odette asked. "I thought only —"

"Whatever you thought or were told, was probably wrong." Kiko gently tapped Odette's butt with her foot and Odette turned around. "Shadow Crawlers kidnap a lot of mid-borns. Not just for concubines anymore. Servants, maids. It's not like it's been horrible though. We still get to do things we enjoy as long as we don't leave the property. You follow the rules and nothing bad happens."

Odette knew she had been sheltered her entire life, but she wondered why there were things she was told, and things she had been left in the dark about. Growing up, her mom had only told her how lucky she was to be a high-born grot and not a mid-born grot, or she'd be kidnapped and sold. But it seemed they were kidnapped and sold, regardless.

Gentry wasn't a grot. He and Kiko were both Animators, they could bring inanimate objects to life, and they did so with the silverware and plates. They had them dance around the kitchen singing Be Our Guest to Odette in attempt to distract her from the nightmares she was having. Caught up in the moment, it worked.

The dishes were putting themselves away when Quinlan swung open the door. She stopped in her tracks, her fingers still pressing against the wood as she stared at the animated dishes. Quinlan was inches taller than Odette. But everyone was taller than Odette, including Mrs. Hamasaki who was no taller than five feet and four inches. Quinlan's long, slender brown fingers didn't move from the door as her large eyes scanned the kitchen.

She looked surprised.

"Wow, full house this morning." She finally stepped into the kitchen and let the door swing shut behind her. She moved to the refrigerator and turned around as she pulled the door open. "Is it my birthday? Must not be or all ya'll wouldn't be in here." She waved her free hand and brushed her thick black hair out of her face.

"Quinlan, this is Odette." Gentry bumped into Odette and forced her to take a step forward.

Quinlan pulled the orange juice from the fridge. "Oh, so you're the girl Pia doesn't like," she said as she grabbed a glass from the cabinet. "Good."

Odette furrowed her brows.

"Good? What do you mean 'good'?"

"They hate each other." Kiko shrugged, sitting on the counter again. She swung the cabinet door shut after Quinlan got her glass.

"*We* do not hate each other," she said as she poured her drink. She pressed her hand to her chest. "*We* don't do anything together. I loathe her. But when that girl tries to sleep with your boyfriend, you'll know what I'm talking about." She put the juice back and got out a slice of bread, which she stuck in the toaster.

"Who's your boyfriend?" Odette asked.

"Abbey. I try not to make a fuss about it though," Quinlan continued, tapping her fingers against the counter while she waited for her toast. "Because I know if one of us gets in trouble, it's gonna be my ass, not hers. Not Lailoken's precious mundane concubine."

"She's mundane? But that's illegal!" The three of them broke out into laughter and Odette frowned. "What's so funny?"

She didn't like being laughed at.

"That you think the high-borns really follow the rules of the scion society. The high-borns have their own constitution that they honor first and foremost. Everything else, they'll try to get away with whatever they can. Including manipulating mundanes. Pia has no idea where she's even from. Ask her one of these days."

Odette's expression softened. "That's so sad."

"Speaking of asking," Kiko said as she tilted her head to the side toward Quinlan, while staring at Odette. She nodded.

"Oh, Quinlan?"

"Yes, babe?" she answered as her toast popped out of the toaster. She spread the butter on and she looked up at Odette.

"Is this house really haunted?" she asked.

A smile began to travel across Quinlan's dark face. She then turned her attention to Kiko and Gentry. "Are you two scaring this poor girl?" she asked and the both of them shrugged. Quinlan returned her attention onto Odette. "Don't worry," she said. "They're harmless."

"Us or the ghosts?" Kiko asked.

"Both," Quinlan said without even looking at her. She reached out to rub Odette's shoulder. "They won't hurt you, I promise."

Kiko slid off of the counter again as Quinlan put the butter away.

"Come on, Doll Face," she said to Odette. "I'll walk you back to your room."

As soon as Kiko and Odette left, Quinlan shot Gentry a glare.

"What is the matter with the two of you?"

"What?" he asked, trying to shrug innocently.

"Why would you tell her about Autumn and Stasi?"

"We didn't!" he said. "We just said the place was haunted and it is. We never said by who."

"You two are unbelievable." Quinlan tore her toast and popped a piece into her mouth.

"Pia actually hid in her room to scare her the first night she was here."

"Ugh, I hate that girl."

"What do you think though? Odette?"

Quinlan glanced at the door and sighed, dusting the crumbs from her hands onto her plate. She looked up at Gentry. "I think it's going to be an interesting year. Things are already different, and Autumn and Stasi... Something's going to happen, Gen. I just hope it's not gonna be bad." Quinlan started backing up toward the door. "This is exactly why I stay away from all ya'll. Causing trouble." She continued to mutter to herself as she left the kitchen with her orange juice.

Gentry stared at the swinging door. He sighed.

He started gathering his hair to put it up as Kiko came back.

"What'd she say?" she asked.

Gentry pulled the rubber band from his wrist and tied his thick black hair up as he turned around to face her. He shrugged. "Quinlan being Quinlan." He stared at the door. "She thinks something's gonna happen."

Kiko pursed her lips together and turned around to look at the door.

"I hope not. Doll Face is growing on me."

"Yeah, but what are we supposed to do?"

Kiko shrugged. "Try to keep her happy, I guess. I mean, what else can we do? All we're supposed to do is our jobs."

He nodded. "How's the search going? About your dad?"

Kiko groaned and rolled her eyes. "My mom still won't tell me anything. Mr. Wong claims he doesn't know anything. You know, what if he was my dad? Mr. Wong."

"That would explain so much."

Kiko crossed her arms. "What are you trying to say?"

"You're both just so... approachable."

She could just hear the sarcasm oozing from his words. She hit him in the arm and jumped onto the counter again. "By the way, Odette has a Daruma doll. I saw it on her dresser."

"So what?"

"So what? She's not Japanese, Mega G. She's white. That girl is full white. Someone cares about her, and —" Kiko shrugged, leaning back against the wall. "I doubt the Baskervilles will be able to pay it off this time. Or compel *everyone* to forget."

4   HERE I GO AGAIN

It was a scorching summer day on O'ahu, with pavement hot enough to fry eggs. Paisley Eversley probably would've tried too, if Sophie actually let her. She was hardly allowed in the kitchen, and never allowed to use the stove by herself. Not after the fire she started last time.

'We live in a wooden building, Paze, stop trying to burn the house down.'

'I was distracted by the spirit!'

'All the more reason you shouldn't cook!'

Paisley Eversley was one of the strongest Mediums of their generation. Ever since she was a little girl, she knew the spirits were there. She could hear them, she could see them. She could even interact with them. She just didn't know they were spirits until she got older.

The older she got, the scarier they became.

Her childhood home was in Kaukolu, nearly an hour away from the scion society, with the Imperial Quarter sitting in the middle. Paisley's father, Taliesin Eversley, was a high-born scion, which meant noble blood, everyone in his bloodline dating as far back as records had, were scions. They were also white.

Her mom's side, Evaline, were Japanese and Chinese, with deep immigrant roots in Hawai'i. Most kama'aina, or local scions, tended to be mid-borns, considering the ethnic diversity found in the islands. Typically with one scion parent and one mundane. Mid-borns abandoned the original Scion Order that controlled the high-born societies throughout the world. By high-borns, mid-borns were considered lesser, dirty mongrels.

Evaline was a mid-born, and Taliesin left the scion society for her.

Paisley struggled with her identity with a mixed background. As a child, Evaline would often dress her and her older sister, Phoebe, in cheongsams for Picture Day at school, while full Chinese mothers of her classmates would often stare at her.

The same thing would happen when she'd sit with Phoebe outside of their Japanese school. The whispers that surrounded them.

Why were two white girls trying to learn their language?

Paisley grew ashamed. She stopped trying to learn Japanese and she stopped wearing any type of cultural dresses her mom tried to put her in. She focused on her European ancestry, and she idolized it. At least she did, until she visited a small city on the East Coast with her father, and realized quickly she didn't belong there either.

She wasn't white enough, and she wasn't Asian enough.

She didn't belong anywhere.

Paisley was ten years old when she found comfort in spirits. Most Mediums didn't have true contact with the spirits until they were in their late teens at the earliest. Even then, rarely full manifestations. They often had to use objects, or perform séances at certain times when spirits were known to be at their strongest.

Ones who did it for monetary means, advertised to the mundane, were usually fakes or low-borns, or really weak scions who cared more about the show they put on than the actual contact with the dead.

The dead were to be respected.

The spirits of little girls and boys would often follow her home. They appeared just as real as she did. Feeding off of her energy, they were able to pick things up, and affect the mundane world. Paisley sunk further into a hole of what she believed was strictly imaginary. Talk of scions and mid-borns always seemed like grown-up business, and something she never cared to pay attention to.

She usually kept herself locked up in her room; her family believed she played alone and there were ideas planted into the heads of her parents by her aunties and uncles that it were possible she could be a grot. A person with scion blood, but no apparent psychic connection.

To high-borns, grots were considered an abomination. But the attractive ones went for high prices at the Bridal Expos because *they couldn't fight back.*

The Eversley family wouldn't sell their daughter though.

Most mid-borns believed the Constitution of the Scion Order was nefarious.

It was Phoebe who found out first that Paisley was a Medium.

She had walked in on her, playing alone. At least for years, they *thought* she played alone. Being a Telepath, it was easy to tap into an untrained mind, and one by one, the dead children began to materialize around her little sister. A moment that haunted Phoebe for weeks.

Paisley currently sat at the table in the two-bedroom place she shared with Sophie, and Sophie's girlfriend, Midori, and Midori's little brother, Shiro, who lived in the attic.

Their place was situated above the Apothecary in the Imperial Quarter, and she bit furiously at her pen while tapping her jagged and uncut nails at her laptop. Her bright, fiery orange hair was messily thrown up in a bun. Thanks to Sophie, who 'accidentally' spilled a potion on her, her hair started to change colors with her mood.

"I'm not helping you right now, I have to finish my draft," she seemed to tell no one, as there was not another living creature in the room. Instead, a ghostly figure sat in the chair across from her. They made no noise, they just stared at her with the darkness of their shadows for eyes.

Not that she even had a draft to finish. Paisley barely knew what to write about.

Stories were never about her.

At least, not about people who looked like her.

She threw her pen across the room. It smacked against the wall and she muttered expletives under her breath.

"Still writing?"

Paisley looked up as Midori emerged from her bedroom. She yawned and scratched the side of her head, messing up her thick black hair as she pulled the door shut behind her.

"If by 'writing', you mean sitting here, staring blankly at a cursor that mocks me while I play with my baby hair and talk to myself, then yes. Still writing."

"Oh, you look — stressed." Midori stared at Paisley's bright orange hair as she put a cup of instant coffee into the microwave.

Paisley sighed and leaned forward, resting her forehead down against the mousepad of her laptop. "I feel like I'm wearing a mood ring — mood hair," she grumbled.

"Sophie hasn't figured out how to fix it yet?"

"I doubt they're even trying," Paisley said as she sat back up. "You know this wasn't an 'accident'." She lifted her hands in the air to make finger quotations. "They did this to my hair on purpose."

"Well, you should stop keeping things bottled in."

"I'm not keeping anything bottled in," Paisley said with a shrug. "I'm fine. I'm over it."

"But it's okay if you're not."

"I know." Her words came out soft as the microwave beeped.

"Were you up all night?" Midori asked and took a set across from Paisley, cupping her mug as she placed it on the table.

Paisley looked up and her eyes widened. Her hand shot out in front of her as she jumped forward in her seat, bumping into the table. "No! Don't sit —" the spirit began to dissipate, disturbed by Midori's presence. Paisley sat back. "There."

She shot up from the chair and started dusting her face and the front of her shirt like the remains of the ghost were cobwebs she sought to get off of her.

"Geez, Paze, warn a girl when you've got dead company."

"Not company. It's the one I've been trying to get to leave me alone."

"The same one?"

Paisley nodded.

"Can't they find someone else to help them?" Midori asked, taking her seat again. "It's not like they're aren't other Mediums."

"I don't think they're strong enough yet. They still haven't spoken to me. Barely materialized. You sure there's nothing your psychic shield can do to stop this?"

Midori shook her head.

"What you see are real, physical manifestations. It has nothing to do with the mind. If someone was manipulating you into seeing things, then yeah, I could block that, but this isn't in your head. Like you've said, you know? You see dead people."

"I used to think they were imaginary." Paisley pulled the hairband from her bright, orange hair and ruffled the messy strands with her fingers. "I admit, I miss that innocence."

When you're young, all you want to do is grow up. When you're growing up, all you want is for it to stop.

"Soph's not up yet?" Paisley asked as Midori pulled the mug away from her mouth.

She shook her head.

"As if they ever get up before noon. Has Shiro come down at all?"

"Haven't seen him since last night." Paisley chewed on the inside of her cheek and frowned suddenly. "I can't believe he has better legs than I do."

"You don't even wear skirts."

"Maybe I would if I had legs like his — no, I probably still wouldn't but that's beside the point." Shiro looked better in a skirt than the three of them combined. "He has better make-up skills than me, too. Who taught him?"

"Not me," Midori said. "His winged eyeliner is better than mine too."

"Wait, if Shiro's not home and Sophie's sleeping in, who's going to open the shop today? What if Odette comes today?"

Midori sighed.

"It's been months, Paze. The Bridal Expo was in February. It's already August. Do you really still think she's coming to visit us?"

"I have to."

Midori formed a line with her lips, showing visible concern and Paisley closed her laptop.

"Does this have anything to do with —"

"No," Paisley said quickly. "I just — I just have to, okay?"

"Okay."

Paisley gathered her bright orange hair as it began to fade into purple and tied it up again with the black hairband.

"Wait, shouldn't you get some sleep?" Midori asked.

"I'm fine," she insisted. "I'm going to grab a mocha ice blend and I'll be just fine. Did you want anything?"

Midori shook her head and held up her mug. "Instant black coffee is good enough for me," she said.

She got up from the chair and went back into her room as Paisley went downstairs. She put the mug down on the nightstand and climbed back into bed with Sophie.

"Did she take the potion last night?" Sophie asked in a mumble.

They felt Midori's arms wrap around them.

Midori shook her head. "It was still on the counter. Smells horrible, I don't blame her."

"I have to keep making it stronger," Sophie said as they rolled onto their back. "The energy surrounding Paisley is too strong. I don't know what else to do."

Sophie had to keep coming up with new brews just to keep the spirits at bay so Paisley could get some sleep. Each brew, stronger than the last. Each brew, clumpier than the last.

Paisley was part of the reason Sophie renounced being an Empath. They could feel the weight of the pain she carried, and the suffering of the spirits that followed her. Not that Sophie would ever actually tell her that. Paisley felt guilty enough over too many things that were out of her control. They weren't about to add to the list.

"She's still seeing the same static spirit. Do you think it has anything to do with —" Midori gasped. "You don't think it's Odette, do you?"

Sophie dropped their arms back over their mass of curly hair to see their girlfriend better and narrowed their eyes upon her. "Maybe that's why she didn't take it. She's probably trying to get a stronger connection."

"I hope she's okay."

"Hey, look at me," Sophie said, and reluctantly, Midori did as she was told. Her small dark brown eyes met Sophie's hazel ones. "I'm sure she's fine. I'm sure they're both fine."

Midori nestled in against Sophie's body and Sophie's gaze turned up to the ceiling.

The Imperial Quarter was located deep within the walls of the Ala Moana Shopping Center. Paisley passed by the many doors that still had their closed signs up. Unless the place was open twenty-four hours, most of the Imperial Quarter opened after Ala Moana, and closed after too; staying open way into the night. So those, like mid-borns, belonging to both worlds, could get things done without anyone ever noticing they were gone.

The Imperial Quarter was unbiased territory, shared by both high-borns and mid-borns. The high-borns had their own area, The Royal Sector, where mid-borns didn't dare go, in fear they'd be kidnapped and sold. Paisley quickly ran past the dark alley way and ran up the stairs just beside it. The coffee shop was located just to the left of those stairs. She climbed over the yellow caution tape and slipped into the coffee shop to order her drink.

By the time she returned to the Apothecary, her hair had changed into a cool blue color. She got out her keys and unlocked the door.

From the outside, the door of the Apothecary looked like someone had rested the remains from a shipwreck up against the wall — like the wooden board Rose wouldn't share with Jack in The Titanic — than an actual door.

The Apothecary kind of was a hole in the wall. It was hardly bigger than a walk-in closet and if you weren't paying attention to where you were going, you'd miss it completely. Various potions in different sized bottles and vials sat on the high shelves, while cauldrons were stacked on the ground beneath the tables. The staircase was in the far back, behind the counter, leading up to their makeshift apartment.

Paisley nearly dropped her drink when she saw the spirit waiting for her.

"Oh, it's *you* again." She sighed and put her drink down. "I really don't have time for this."

"Give to—err."

Paisley turned around. This was the first time the spirit had bothered to say anything. The voice was distorted, and she could barely understand it.

"What?"

"Give to!" the spirit shouted at her and Paisley's hair started to turn red.

"Give to who? Give what to who?" she asked, growing frustrated. "I don't know what you're trying to tell me."

A coin clattered onto the ground. "Give to her."

"To her? Who's her?"

"HER!" the spirit screamed. Papers flew off of the desk and tables, and a vase shattered as a small, black tornado began to grow in the shop. "Her!" it said again, knocking several things off of the shelves, including a picture of Odette, before it disappeared entirely.

Everything was back on the tables and shelves like nothing had happened. The vase hadn't broke either. But the coin on the ground remained where it was.

Paisley crouched down in front of it and almost fell backward when she lost her balance, after realizing what it was. A Dreamweaver token.

Dreamweavers were once considered part of the scion society, until one day, they weren't. Thought to weave out nightmares and consume them, they were painted as demons who would also consume hopes and dreams, leaving the person a shell of what they used to be.

Nearly three-hundred years have passed since they were eradicated and believed to be extinct.

But Paisley knew differently. She knew they still existed, in their own version of the world; almost like a dreamscape.

The Woolgathering.

She had ancestral ties to it; it was what made her such a strong Medium.

"Paze? You okay?" Sophie's voice questioned her from the top of the stairs. Paisley quickly grabbed the token and stood up.

"I'm fine!" she shouted back, and slipped the dreamweaver coin into her pocket.

But even after all those months, Odette wasn't a spirit. She wasn't dead.

In fact, she was very much alive, and *mostly* living comfortably in the house of the Baskervilles. There were servants waiting on her every need, except for when Mrs. Chardonnay Baskerville was home.

Disgusted with the fact that her son chose a grot at the Bridal Expo, Chardonnay made Odette's life as much like a living Hell as she could manage, considering she could not *do* anything about her son's seemingly rash decision.

Not only did Odette cost her a thousand scripts, but she found her to be irritating.

Odette was very polite without manipulation, which only frustrated Chardonnay further. She did everything Chardonnay asked of her, without back talk. Without question. She listened. She obeyed. It was infuriating. There was no room to punish her and it was near unbearable that this perfect princess was living in her household, under the rather watchful guard of her son.

Chardonnay was an older woman; thin white blonde hair in a rather old fashioned blown-out style. She had condescending eyes that Odette often felt were always watching her. Chardonnay didn't want her son with someone who had no fight in them. Who came submissive.

She wanted someone to break. But there was nothing to break in Odette. She was raised to know her place. Odette was just about as hostile as a newborn puppy.

Today was one of the rare days that Lailoken was off from work. Mr. and Mrs. Baskerville had made plans to go to the Imperial Quarter, when Lailoken suggested they go with him, much to Chardonnay's displeasure.

"Shouldn't you stay here and get to know your future wife a little more?" she asked, speaking about Odette as if she weren't even in the room.

"She hasn't left this house once since she got here, Mother."

"She is rather pasty looking — fine." Chardonnay walked up to Odette. The older Baskerville woman towered over her; she was at least five feet, ten inches tall, if not six feet. Lailoken was only a little shorter than his father, who stood at six foot, four. They all towered over her. "No funny business," she warned Odette, and poked her in the nose with her long, manicured finger nail.

Odette turned to Lailoken once his parents left the room. He nodded once, acknowledging her desire to speak.

"I'm going with you guys? To the Imperial Quarter?" she asked, a smile spreading across her face. Lailoken grinned at her happiness. He nodded, brushing his long, blonde hair out of his face with his fingers.

"I'm glad it makes you happy," he said.

"I feel like I haven't been there in ages," she said, then frowned, She chewed on her bottom lip. "I actually can't remember the last time I went — but so much has happened these last few months. I'm so excited!" Odette squealed happily and clapped her hands as she bounced where she stood. "I'm gonna go change! I'll be back down in a minute."

Though she wanted to run upstairs, she made herself walk, albeit rather quickly. When she got to her room, she shut her door and went straight for her dresser. Digging through her clothes, nothing seemed good enough for her first day out of the house in months.

When she pulled out a blue top, something fell on to the floor and hit her foot.

Odette brought the shirt toward her and looked on the ground. Standing on the floor was a red little one-eyed doll. She picked him up and placed him on the top of her dresser. She recognized it as a Daruma doll, but she had no idea where he had come from. Odette folded her shirt and put it back in the drawer before moving to her closet.

Her closet was full of clothes bought for her by the Baskervilles, all sized and altered perfectly to fit her body. Odette pursed her lips together as she moved through the dresses before deciding on a vintage 1950's blue cotton sundress. She pulled the thin straps over her shoulders and ran her finger along the scoop neckline. Odette turned to her full length mirror as she reached behind her to zipper the back.

Her eyes fell upon the necklace that rested against her chest. It was her name in silver, written in cursive. It was something she always had and she never took it off.

She couldn't remember where she got it though — probably from Lailoken. She glanced at the engagement ring on her finger and smiled.

"Odette?" a voice came from the other side of the door as they knocked. It was Lailoken. "Are you almost ready?"

"Yes!"

She grabbed her small white purse from the vanity and ran back into her closet for a pair of white sandals. Odette slipped on her heels and finally answered her door.

Lailoken gave her a once over and he smiled.

"Wow," he said, and extended his hand to her.

Gracefully, she took it.

Mr. Baskerville drove a black 1970 Chevrolet Chevelle with a beige leather interior. Lailoken opened the door and pushed the seat back for Odette to get in. He moved around the car to let himself in through the other door, near where his metallic gray Corvette was parked. Mrs. Baskerville shoved the seat back and sat down before slamming the door shut, but Odette was too excited to notice her rude behavior.

Lailoken placed the back of his hand down on the leather seat and Odette pressed her palm against his, lacing their fingers together. She only briefly glanced at him, before turning her attention to the window. She spent a lot of mornings out on the patio in the backyard, admiring Hawaii from the house she now lived in, but she hadn't been able to see it up close in months. It was to get to know the people who would be her family, to get to know the staff, though she was sure Lailoken wasn't going to live at home forever. Mrs. Baskerville claimed she made her work in case they have less servants then they do once they moved out.

A wife needed to be capable of taking care of the household and her husband, after all. Odette didn't argue. Mrs. Baskerville knew more than she did, and Odette sought to make Lailoken happy. But in that moment in the car, she kept her eyes fixed out on the world around her.

A monstrous face appeared in the reflection of the window and Odette sat back.

It was gone, disappearing as fast as it had appeared.

"Everything okay?" Lailoken asked. He squeezed her hand, but Odette couldn't take her eyes off of the window.

"Lailoken asked you a question," Mrs. Baskerville said from the front.

"Right," Odette said. She shook her head. "I'm fine. I just — I thought I saw something but it must've been my imagination," she told him. Odette glanced over at him and gave his hand a reassuring squeeze back.

Odette returned her gaze to the window and frowned at the buildings while they passed. She couldn't get the image out of her mind; what freaked her out the most was that it was the same face from her nightmares. Odette often had trouble remembering her dreams when she awoke, but lately she had been waking in a startle, sweat trickling down the sides of her face.

She sighed. It was gone now; it couldn't hurt her.

The parking lot for the Ala Moana Shopping Center wasn't too crowded, as it was August and many people were back in school, not bothering with the shopping malls. Mr. Baskerville drove toward the marked off construction site, the bit of the parking lot that just never seemed to be finished but was really marked that way for scions only, and parked his car deep in its darkness.

Odette got excited again. Giddy in her seat, she waited patiently for Lailoken to open the door. He helped his mother out first, and then pushed the seat back, offering his hand to Odette.

She took it and stepped out, and he closed the door behind her.

Odette let go of his hand and looped her arm around his while they followed his parents through the dark, enclosed passage way that would lead right into the Imperial Quarter, skipping over having to deal with any mundane folk, should they use any of the other entrances.

Odette rested her head against Lailoken's arm, considering he was about a foot taller than she was, and observed all the shops as they passed them. The walls were made of stone, with shop signs painted on or engraved.

Lailoken came to an abrupt stop which brought Odette back from her daze as she stood up straight. Jacinta Valentine, Jac for short, stood in front of them. One of Lailoken's old friends. Odette had been surprised by their friendship, considering Jac wasn't a high-born, but she might as well have been. She may not dress like one, always dressed in scrappy and ripped attire with things tied here and there all over her body, but she acted like one.

She was a Shadow Crawler, and she certainly acted like she was better than Odette.

"I see you brought your little mate out to play," Jac said, giving Odette a once over. Odette took a step back behind Lailoken. Jac snickered as Odette's arm slowly slipped from around her fiancé's. "She's so timid," Jac commented and Lailoken shrugged.

"Not always," he told her.

"She acts like I'm gonna take a bite out of her or something."

Odette didn't take her eyes off of Jac. They were about the same height, but Jac seemed so threatening, and the way she stood made it seem like she was always ready for a fight. Odette's eyes wandered over Jac's ripped clothes. She was sure there were knives hidden in there somewhere.

"I think she's checking me out," Jac said with a grin and Odette looked away. She could hear Jac laughing, but it soon dissolved as she spotted a small shop she hadn't noticed before. Sophie's Apothecary. She took a step forward, away from the two scions and walked toward the shop. Odette was positive her closet at home was larger than the store.

She wondered if maybe there could be something in there to help with the face she saw.

"Hey!" Paisley said, a large smile crossing her face as Odette entered the Apothecary. She moved around the front counter. "It's about time you stopped by. What took you so long? I was getting worried about you."

Odette frowned and took a step back. "You know me?"

"Oh," Paisley said as she stepped back too, bumping into the counter. Her expression faded from excitement to dejection. "My mistake. I thought — I thought you were someone else." She knew better than to make a big fuss about it though. She stuck out her hand. "I'm Paisley."

"Odette," she said, shaking her hand. "So what is it you sell in here?" Odette asked as their hands slipped away from one another. Her large green eyes scanned the many vials on the shelves. "Do any of them help with nightmares?"

"Hey Odette!"

"I'm sorry, do I know you?"

'Wow,' Sophie mouthed as their eyes widened. They turned right back around, shaking their head, the large mass of curly black hair shook with it.

"Your friend goes off and starts a new life and suddenly they don't know who you are!" Sophie told the wall as they started rearranging bottles on the shelf. They continued to mutter angrily.

"So, you're having nightmares?" Paisley asked, ignoring Sophie.

"Yeah," Odette said, staring at the shelf in front of her. "I keep seeing this person in a mask — or at least I think I do — but I don't know who it is. I have trouble remembering when I wake up but I know they want to hurt me — is this really full of bat tongues?"

"*Please* don't touch that," Sophie said, taking the jar from Odette, who had grabbed it from the shelf. "Please don't touch *anything*."

"I'm sorry," she said and her face flushed.

Paisley glared at Sophie, who glared right back at her and stuck their tongue out at her. Sophie moved back behind the counter, keeping their jar of bat tongues beside them.

"*Anyway*," Paisley said, hissing through her teeth, returning her focus back onto Odette. "Ignore Sophie. Tell me about your nightmares. Maybe we can help."

"Fat chance," Sophie muttered.

"Will you be quiet?" Paisley snapped and Sophie humphed. She looked back at Odette. "You said there's a masked person? Who wants to hurt you?"

"It's the same every night," Odette said, tucking her hair behind her ear. "I see them and they're coming toward me and then... they hurt me."

"Have you tried fighting back?" Paisley asked.

Odette nodded. "I want to, but there's nothing I can do. I can't move, or run, or scream. I just endure it. I just want it to go away. Dreams used to make me feel safe, I think." She frowned. "I miss it."

Paisley dug into her pocket and pulled out the token she had gotten from the spirit. This must've been what they were telling her to do.

"Do you know what a Dreamweaver is, Odette?" she asked, holding the token out in her palm.

She nodded, staring at the small coin.

"They're demons," she said softly.

Paisley curled her hand up, covering the token.

"Actually, they aren't. The high-borns just want you to think that. You see, hundreds of years ago, there was once a small boy who people say was the son of a Dreamweaver and a high-born. This little boy was having nightmares and his father tried to help him by eating his nightmare. But when his son awoke to find his father in his true form, it scared him. He grew up hating them and once he was in a position of power, he had the Dreamweavers eradicated. But some still live. People claim they exist in another realm called The Woolgathering. You can summon one with this." Paisley opened her hand. "Stand in front of a mirror, and say, *'Dreamweaver, consume my fears.'* When one comes, and one will, they'll be asleep. Steal their necklace so they can't return home. Then they have to do whatever you ask them to do until you let them go."

"It's just a story," Odette said, staring at the coin. "They're all gone."

"Odette, we live in a world full of psychics and witchcraft and magic, and you don't believe in this?"

Paisley grabbed her hand and put the token against Odette's palm. "Just take it, you may change your mind."

"But I thought they also consume hopes and dreams?" she asked.

"Only if they're here for too long. Thanks to the scions who employed witches to curse the land. But I promise your nightmares shouldn't last forever."

"Odette?" a voice streamed from outside. "Where did you go? Odette?"

Her eyes widened.

"I have to go!" She tucked the coin into her bag. "Thank you!" Odette didn't waste another second, and slipped out of the Apothecary. Paisley followed and went to the door just as it began to close. She watched as Odette ran up to a tall and slender man with long blonde hair and a sharp jawline. Lailoken Baskerville.

She stepped away from the closing door just as he looked up. Paisley's hair began to turn orange and she turned to Sophie.

"Make a memory conveyor."

Sophie almost dropped the jar of bat tongues.

"What?"

"You couldn't see it?" Paisley asked, approaching the counter.

"See what?" they asked, putting the jar down between them.

"Behind her eyes, Sophie. Her soul is dying."

Sophie rolled her eyes. "Paze —"

"Just do it, please," she said. "If nothing happens, I'll drop it. Fine. She forgot about us, we don't matter. We aren't part of her new high-born lifestyle and she can continue pretending like we don't exist. But there's a chance I could be right, and we have to take that chance. No matter how small it is."

Sophie rubbed their face and groaned at Paisley's words.

"Do you have any idea how complicated recovering memories can be?"

"You can do it," Paisley assured.

"How are you so sure?"

"Because I remember when you did it for me. Don't think I forgot. You're a better witch now than you were back then so I know you can do this. Please, Soapy."

"Don't use cute nicknames with me." Sophie moved around the counter to glance out the small dirty window and watched as Odette happily looked up at her fiancé. "You're sure it's not a façade?"

"Only one way to find out. It's just — I had nightmares too. About something similar. The signs are there, we just have to prove it."

"And then what? They bought her."

"I don't know yet but maybe she'll summon a Dreamweaver all on her own."

"If she's convinced it's not going to consume her hopes and dreams."

"Which is why we need a back up plan," Paisley said just as Midori and Shiro came down the stairs. "Please, Soph."

"All right, I'll do it. But it's going to take all of us," Sophie said, pulling their gaze from Paisley and onto Midori and Shiro. "To gather the ingredients. I can't get in trouble for this again, or they'll cut off my hands this time. Anything that messes with a Pusher's manipulation —"

"What's going on?" Shiro asked.

"Paze thinks O's being manipulated. She came in here, and she had no idea who we were."

The siblings exchanged glances.

"We'll help," Midori said. Shiro and Midori both moved by Sophie and looked out of the window. Odette walked off, hand in hand with her future husband, Lailoken Baskerville.

"We're going to mess with the Baskervilles?" Shiro asked, looking back at Paisley. "This is going to be nasty business, Paze. They're one of the richest families in the society — in Hawai'i — did you see that rock on her finger?"

Paisley remained leaning against the counter. She didn't dare move to the window. She didn't want to see the shell of the girl who was once her friend. "Manipulation is nasty business," she said. "People don't deserve to be treated that way."

TOVALEY B. KYSEL

5   WIND BENEATH MY WINGS

The nightmares always seemed to come when Odette felt at peace. When she was calm, and for once, truly happy. Her subconscious seemed focused on making sure she wasn't. The masked person always appeared at the worst of times, and she was shaken from her sleep. They kept her from a state of bliss.

And they only seemed to get worse. Odette could hardly remember the last time she had a good night's sleep, or the last time she had woken without a jolt.

Lailoken would sometimes come into her room early in the morning after he knew she was awake. His mother often sent him to check on her, to make sure she wasn't up to anything. To make sure she wasn't hiding anything.

Odette had only come with one bag.

She wasn't sure what exactly she could be hiding.

"What's this?" Lailoken asked, staring at the small red doll sitting on the top of Odette's dresser. He picked it up, and it was lighter than he expected. He threw it up in the air and caught it in the same hand. It almost felt like it were made of paper.

"A Daruma doll," she answered quietly.

"What?" he asked, peeling his eyes away from it to look at her. "Why's it only got one eye?"

She shrugged, not getting up from where she sat on her bed. Her hands slipped between her knees. Odette couldn't remember why she had it, or what it was for. All she knew was that she wanted to keep it.

"I don't know," she said. "I think it's special to me, though. I just... I don't know why. Can I keep it?" she asked. "Please?"

"I guess," he said. "Even though it's a little —" he made a disgusted face and shrugged it off. Lailoken placed it back down on the surface of her dresser. He sat down beside her and took one of her hands within his own. "Are you sure you don't want to share a room with me yet? I mean, it's been a few months — and it'd be nice to not wake up alone."

Odette smiled at his words and she squeezed his hand. But she shook her head and averted her gaze. "I'm just not ready yet," she said, glancing back at him. "You won't make me, will you?" she asked, scanning his face.

He sighed.

"Never," he said, and kissed her cheek. "I promised you I wouldn't do that to you and I intend to keep that promise. I want you to love me, on your own terms. It's not the same if you don't."

"Thank you." She smiled sweetly.

She knew how lucky she was. Odette had heard many of the brides bought at the Expo didn't get much say in what happened to them.

Lailoken was kind to her. He was patient.

It was his mother who wasn't.

Odette had trouble understanding why Mrs. Baskerville wasn't pleased with her. She did everything she asked her to, without making a fuss. She worked just as hard as the people who actually served the household; but nothing she did was ever good enough.

The following morning, after Lailoken had gone to work, Chardonnay's screechy voice filled the hallways. "Odette!" she shouted from somewhere in the mansion. "The rugs won't beat themselves!"

By this time, Odette was already up. Though still in bed, her eyes were fixed on her ceiling. The nightmare had returned. Sweat trickled down the sides of her face, and though she wanted nothing more than to stay in bed, she forced herself to get up and get dressed, having already missed breakfast again.

'Men want wives who are capable of cooking and cleaning,' Mrs. Baskerville had told her not long after they had bought her.

Odette no longer minded, though. In fact, it humbled her. She knew her place in the household, and it was okay that Mrs. Baskerville felt the need to remind her. Sometimes people needed to be reminded, or they'd forget.

She put on a loose gray shirt and black yoga pants. She tied up her shoes and then her hair, before walking down the stairs.

'Never run. If you're late, there's nothing you can do about it now. Maintain composure.'

She tried.

I am in control of myself. I am in control.

Though the words were of little true value, they made her feel better.

She found Mrs. Baskerville and her husband in the living room. It was usually the same with those two, Mrs. Baskerville yelling about something or another, while Mr. Baskerville pretended to listen. Mr. Baskerville was more tolerant of his wife than most were.

Odette had been told if she stepped out of line, she would be punished. She knew the Constitution for the Sion Order. Whatever punishment Chardonnay had up her sleeves, she didn't want it. Perhaps the Baskervilles just had a different arrangement than the marriages she was familiar with.

"I'm here," she announced at the doorway. The pair looked up at her. Ahren almost looked relieved at the sight of her.

"Well? Why are you just standing there?" Chardonnay asked, her fists moved to her hips. "Go beat the rugs!" she snapped. "All of them!"

"Yes, Mrs. Baskerville," she said and turned around.

"Quickly!" Chardonnay shouted from the room and Odette quickened her pace.

She was barely over five feet tall, and she struggled with the longer rugs, but one by one she managed to pull them outside in the backyard and hit them over the railing.

Odette used her shirt to cover her face, but it hardly made much of a difference once the dust lifted in the air.

She coughed and turned away, her eyes still shut tightly.

"You need some help?" Abbey asked as he approached her. He rose his arm to cover his eyes as she struggled with beating the rug.

She dropped it against the rail and leaned back on the pillar to catch her breath.

"No," she said quietly. "But thank you."

"You sure?"

Odette looked over at him. Amaris was dark in comparison to her, but Abbey was even darker. Though he did spend all day in the sun. His unruly, shoulder length hair was bound back with a rubber band. They had the same kind faces, him and his sister. He raised his eyebrows, waiting for a response as he glanced at the rugs.

She nodded. "I'm almost done."

"All right, kiddo. Don't work too hard."

Her entire body ached by the time she was finished. Her fingers were rubbed raw from the burns of the rugs. Hours had passed, and she ate between pulling rugs, even though she wasn't supposed to. Mrs. Hamasaki made sure that she did. Odette had her doubts she'd be able to join Mr. and Mrs. Baskerville for dinner, since Lailoken wouldn't be home yet.

She finished the rugs, and she desperately waited for her soon-to-be mother-in-law's approval.

But Chardonnay was never pleased with her.

"Go take a shower," she snapped, looking up at Odette from where she sat in the dining room. "What are you doing standing around? You're filthy!"

"Yes, Mrs. Baskerville," Odette said before leaving. She trudged up the stairs, dragging herself with each step. She didn't dare touch the railing, in fear Chardonnay would know and yell at her for getting it dirty.

She went into her room and shut the door behind her, and briefly rested against it. Odette looked around and a frown crossed her face when she spotted the Daruma doll on her dresser. She picked herself up from the door and went to look at it. It still only had one eye. For a moment, she pondered the idea of giving him a second eye, but decided against it.

If he was supposed to have two eyes, he would have. Odette put him back down and disappeared into the bathroom.

The hot water temporarily soothed the aches and pains, and although she could probably stay in there all night, Odette couldn't stop thinking about the Daruma doll Lailoken had pointed out, and the people at the Apothecary she had wandered into.

She hadn't thought something was wrong with her memory until that moment. The way they looked at her; you don't look at strangers like that.

Especially the one with blue hair. Paisley. Her expression had burned itself into Odette's mind.

She got out of the bath and went to shower.

She wrapped the towel tightly around her body and slipped out of her bathroom to approach her vanity.

In the top drawer was the token Paisley gave her. It had an unusual shaped hole in the center.

She sat in the chair and stared at the small coin that rested in her palm. As much as she wanted the nightmare to stop, summoning a Dreamweaver just seemed like too much of a risk. She closed her eyes and dropped the coin back into the drawer.

Odette put on a thin, loose tank-top, underwear and pajama shorts which she rolled up at the waist, and climbed into her bed. Her body ached against the softness of the mattress, and no matter how she tossed and turned on her bed, she couldn't get comfortable.

Nor could she shake the fact that someone had messed with her memories. Why would Chardonnay do this to her? Odette didn't understand. She did everything to try to please her.

Her stomach growled.

Odette slipped out of her bed and walked down the hall. The stairs were too creaky to walk to the kitchen for something to eat, so she didn't bother and simply walked past them.

She knocked on the door at the other end.

"Come in," a voice said.

Odette opened the door and peered into the room.

"Is something troubling you?" Lailoken asked, sitting up on his bed. He put his book down on the nightstand. He frowned when she wiped her cheeks. "Are you okay, Odette?"

"Can I just stay in here with you for a little while?" she asked as she stepped further into the room and let her hand drop from the doorknob.

"Of course," he said. Lailoken got up to close his door. He wrapped his arm around Odette's waist and leaned forward to kiss her cheek. "What happened?"

She just shook her head. She couldn't tell him what she thought of his mother. Odette knew she'd be furious if someone spoke to her about her mother the way she wanted to speak to Lailoken about his. She knew Mrs. Baskerville was a Pusher like Lailoken. The last thing she wanted to do was offend him.

She bit her bottom lip and followed him into his bed, where he wrapped his arm around her again. "I just want to lie here with you for a little while, if that's okay?" she asked, tilting her head back to look at him.

"Stay as long as you need," he said. His hand slipped beneath the helm of her shirt, and he brushed his fingers against her skin.

She woke in a startle. It was the same thing, sweat trickling down the sides of her face, but this time she remembered the masked face she saw in the window. It had its hands on her neck, and it hurt her. Choking her.

Odette slipped out of her bed, Lailoken must've carried her back to her room, and went right to her full length mirror that hung on the wall beside her vanity.

Her eyes widened and a gasp left her lips as she stared at the bruises on her throat. She lifted her tank-top and they were on the sides of her body, her wrists, and even her thighs. She cupped her face with her hands and took a step back. Her eyes began to water.

She sat back on her bed, her hands slid down from over her mouth to cover the sides of her neck. She took deep breaths, trying to calm herself so her crying wouldn't turn into sobbing hysterics, but the hiccups still came.

Her long, deep breaths turned jagged and rough and she wiped her dampened face with her hand and covered her mouth to soften the sound. She reached for the cell phone Lailoken had bought for her, but then dropped it on her bed.

Odette knew she had to tell him, but she didn't know how.

Her whole body ached; and now she wasn't sure whether or not it was from the rugs or the possibility of being beaten herself.

She slid off of her bed and went to the bathroom to run a bath.

Odette pulled off her shirt and stared at the bruises on her slender body, but she didn't stare for very long. She looked away and stepped into the tub as it filled with warm water, soothing against her skin and aching muscles. Odette sat down and pulled her knees up. She wrapped her arms around her legs and rested her chin on her knee, before tucking her chin in toward her chest, to rest her forehead down.

She cried to herself, the sound muffled by the running water.

When she looked up again, resting her chin on her knee, her large green eyes were puffy and red. She took shallow breaths, and though she was calmer now, she didn't feel the least bit better.

Odette got up from her bath and took a shower as the water drained from the tub. She carefully ran the washcloth over her body, softly against the bruises, trying not to wince. But showering was hardly the worst of it. Drying herself off and putting clothes on was far worse; but once she was dressed, all she wanted to do was lie in bed. But she couldn't, not today.

Today was one of the rare days when none of the Baskervilles were home and she didn't want to spend it in her room by herself with nothing to eat.

She opened her door as quietly as she could manage and peered into the hallway. Min-Jae was in the hall, and he gave her a nod at the sight of her. She returned it and smiled, while trying to subtly move her hand over her neck as she passed him.

"Is something wrong, sweetie?" Mrs. Hamasaki asked as soon as Odette entered the kitchen. Odette tugged on her sleeve and shook her head.

"Just tired," she said. She sat at the counter while Mrs. Hamasaki was preparing food for tomorrow. "Any leftovers for me to eat?" Odette asked.

"I'm sure there's something in the fridge," she said. "Give me a second and I'll get it for you."

"That's okay, I can get it."

Odette slipped off of the stool and walked around the counter to the stainless steel refrigerator. She pulled open the door, and to her surprise, there was still roasted chicken and some rice left over from dinner last night. Odette grabbed them from the refrigerator, dumped them both onto one plate and stuck it in the microwave.

She turned around and rested against the counter edge while she watched Mrs. Hamasaki marinate the meat. Odette rubbed at her neck.

"Is — is Mrs. Baskerville —" Odette frowned, unable to get the words out.

"Is Mrs. Baskerville what, dear?" Mrs. Hamasaki asked without looking up from her work.

"Is she a good person?" Odette asked.

Mrs. Hamasaki's hands froze. She glanced up at Odette, and furrowed her brows.

"She's not the best high-born I've met," she said, "but she's not the worst, either. She pays me, gives me a raise every six months, she's never used her Pusher ability on me —"

"How would you know?" The microwave began to beep. Odette ignored it. "How would you know if you were being manipulated or not?" she asked.

"Gaps in the memory, things not making sense. The more you're manipulated, the more you forget about your past. But Mrs. Baskerville wouldn't do that."

"Why not?"

"If that woman is mean to you, she'll want you to remember it. She won't compel you to forget." Mrs. Hamasaki glanced down at the bowl of liquid and pulled the meat out. "Mr. Baskerville though, has asked his son to manipulate people for him." She frowned then, and looked back at Odette. "Is someone hurting you?"

Odette fixed her collar and shook her head.

"It's nothing," she said and turned around. She pulled her plate out of the microwave. "I was just wondering, because Mrs. Baskerville — you're right." She frowned. "She's never made me forget a moment of it."

She left the kitchen as soon as she was able. Odette ate alone in the large dining room. The table was made of mahogany, with chairs to match. It was a solid table, and a large, exuberant chandelier hung above it, with two large candles sitting on each end of the bowl of flowers that sat in the center.

She ate quietly, hoping no one would disturb her or realize she was there; especially not Kiko or Gentry. Even worse, Pia. Odette couldn't stop thinking about what Mrs. Hamasaki said, that she often found herself staring blankly at the flowers sitting in front of her.

'The more you're manipulated, the more you forget about your past.'

Those people from the Apothecary seemed to know her. The Daruma doll had special meaning, but she didn't know why.

Instinctively, Odette touched the silver necklace that read her name. She couldn't even remember where she got it from, she just assumed Lailoken gave it to her, like everything else she owned.

Odette cleared her plate and put her dishes in the sink.

The doorbell rang.

"I'll get it," she said quietly, to no one other than herself. Mr. Wong was out helping Mrs. Baskerville with the shopping and she doubted Mrs. Hamasaki heard her. Not with the water running. Odette turned it off and went into the hallway.

Odette opened the door.

"Oh, hello," she said and smiled, recognizing the face before her. Odette remembered them from the Apothecary. The curly hair especially. She wondered how Sophie managed to keep it so neat, considering Odette had trouble with her own hair, which was in fact easy to maintain in comparison to theirs. "Can I help you?" she asked, leaning against the door frame.

"I —" their words dropped when their gaze did, at the sight of the bruises on Odette's neck. Paisley was right. Sophie's eyelids fluttered as they turned their attention back onto Odette's face once they realized they were rudely staring. She even adjusted her collar, uncomfortable by Sophie staring at her neck. "I came to give this to you." Sophie handed her a vial.

"What is it?" Odette asked before she took it.

"A tonic, to help you with those nightmares you mentioned when you stopped by the other day."

A small smile started to appear on her face, but then she looked up in confusion.

"How did you know where to find me?" she asked.

"Sorry, I, uh, I saw you with the Baskervilles. Everyone knows where they live. They're like, one of the richest families on the island."

"Right, of course. Thank you."

"Be sure to take it before bed — and don't eat or drink anything after. It won't taste very pleasant, but it works. I promise."

"Okay, but I haven't gotten any money to pay you."

Sophie just shook their head at her words.

"On the house," they said. "You look like you could use it."

"Oh." Odette tried to readjust her collar again, pretending her collarbone itched. "Thank you so much," she said.

She took a step back and closed the door as Sophie stepped off the porch. They ran across the street and opened the door of the van that was parked there, waiting for them.

"You were right, Paze. She's got bruises all over here," Sophie said, patting their throat and the front of their own chest. They glanced out the window. "Someone's doing something to her."

Paisley closed her eyes and sighed.

Her hair had been a constant orange since Odette came into the shop.

"What do we know about the Baskervilles?" she asked as she opened her eyes again.

"Nothing really, except that they own a brothel and they're rich enough to practically *buy* one of the Hawaiian Islands."

"What are we going to do, Soapy?"

"I don't know, but once she drinks that, hopefully she'll do something. We kind of did all we can do. She's a high-born grot, there's not much else we can do that's legal in the scion society."

"The things some people do for their parents."

"The Thomsetts don't deserve it, if you ask me. None of them do. Who can just sell off their children like that? Especially grots? It's not fair."

"Life's not fair," Paisley mumbled.

"I hate when you say that. I'm the only negative one in this car."

Paisley sighed and glanced past Sophie to look out their window and at the mansion of the Baskervilles.

"Do you think she's going to be okay?" she asked.

"At this point, I don't even know, Paze. I don't want to lie to you. But whatever's happening to her, it's going to hit her like a bag of bricks to the face. I really — I really do not want to say this so please forgive me but — think about how you felt."

I do, she thought. Every day.

"Yeah, we should go," Paisley said and started the engine. The whole car rumbled and shook. Paisley owned a purple, white, gray, and black 1991 Toyota wagon which she was quite proud of.

"Are you sure this piece of junk is going to get us back to the Imperial?" Sophie asked, holding onto their seatbelt.

"Of course," Paisley said and pet the dashboard. "It's a MasterAce, just like —"

Sophie rolled her eyes.

"Just like you," they finished for her.

Paisley wiggled her eyebrows as she looked over at Sophie.

"See, you know."

Being asexual had its perks; for Paisley, bad puns were one of them. Sophie knew that all too well.

She managed to start the van and drove away from the house.

"You gonna send one of your spirits to watch out for her?" Sophie asked.

"Believe me, if I could, I would."

"Why can't you?"

"There are spirits around the house," she admitted. Paisley kept her eyes on the road. "They've a Medium working there. They'd know."

"You probably should've given her that vial instead of me."

"I probably would've kidnapped her."

"Or maybe not."

"Besides, it was your potion," Paisley added. "You should've been the one to do it. I just hope she stays safe."

"Now that she'll be aware, that could be really dangerous but Odette's smart. She'll figure it out."

"I hope so," Paisley said, tightening her grip on the wheel. She clenched her jaw and the rest of the car ride was silent while she forced Sophie to listen to country music. They didn't bother trying to change the station like they normally would.

Paisley needed it.

As much as Sophie wanted to rip off their own ears, they didn't fuss.

6   WHERE DO BROKEN HEARTS GO

Odette placed the vial on her vanity and sat on her bed, staring at the dark liquid it contained. Though Sophie told her not to take it until she was ready for bed, she couldn't stop staring at it.

Part of her *was* already for bed, even if the day was hardly half over. She wanted to sleep, she wanted to pretend that this was all a bad nightmare, and when she'd wake, the bruises would be gone like they were never there to begin with.

She couldn't look away from the vial; Odette wondered too much about what exactly it would do. How would it work? Was it only just for one night or would it be continuous?

Would the demon finally leave her alone?

There was a knock on the door, and not even that could peel her gaze away from it

Though it did scatter her thought process a little.

"Odette? Are you coming down for dinner?" Lailoken asked. She shook her head, only to then make the realization he couldn't see her.

"I'm not feeling well," she said, making sure she spoke loud enough for him to hear through the cracks of the door.

He didn't answer right away. There was a long, drawn out pause. Or at least it felt that way. Odette readjusted herself in her seat as she waited for him to say something else. She could see his shadow still lingering at the bottom of her door.

"Do you want me to get you anything?" he asked then.

"No, thank you," she said, her gaze returned to the vial. "I just want to rest."

"Okay, I hope you have a good night."

I intend to, she thought.

Odette didn't look away from the vial again, except to only glance at the door when she heard his footsteps walk away. She checked the bottom of her door to make sure his shadow was gone. The last thing she needed was someone to burst in and catch her drinking this — whatever it was.

Odette slid off of her bed and walked up to her vanity. She grabbed the vial and uncorked it. Glancing at herself in the mirror, she watched herself as she took a deep breath.

"No more nightmares," she said.

Putting the rim of the glass to her lips, she drank the liquid and tossed her head back to swallow it down in one gulp.

It was disgusting. Probably the worst thing she had ever tasted in her life.

She started to cough and dropped the vial, which shattered on her vanity. Odette ran to the bathroom and turned the water on. She cupped water with her hands.

*'Be sure to take it before bed — and don't eat
or drink anything after.'*

Odette dropped the water back into the sink and gagged. She covered her mouth, trying to keep herself from throwing it back up. She closed her eyes and continued to try to swallow whatever was left lingering on her tongue, trying to get the taste out of her mouth. For the most part, it worked. Only a subtle taste lingered. Her thoughts crossed to the bat tongues she saw in the Apothecary and she just shook her head.

She'd rather not think about the ingredients that went into that, but she could've sworn there were some kind of fibers, or tiny hairs.

She stuck her tongue out in disgust and shuddered at the thought.

She brushed her teeth over and over again to get the taste out of her mouth and continued to swish around mouthwash until she could no longer taste the tonic.

Odette grabbed a washcloth and dampened it beneath the water before turning the faucet off. She cleaned up the mess she made from dropping the glass vial and wiped up her vanity before throwing the cloth and the broken glass into the trashcan.

"No more nightmares," she said again to her reflection. "You're going to wake up tomorrow, and there will be no more nightmares. It'll all be over."

Her gaze dropped down to her neck.

She moved away from the vanity and crawled into bed. Drowsiness hit her almost as quickly as her head hit the pillow. Odette could hardly keep her eyes open.

"This is for you, Odette. Look, it even says your name." Her mom showed her the shiny, silver necklace that read Odette in cursive. *"Wherever you go and wherever you may end up, I hope you never forget us."* Mrs. Thomsett put the necklace on her daughter, and smiled at her reflection in the mirror.

She was only six years old.

The memory of her mother faded out as the masked person made a subtle appearance. He stood in the background, watching with no eyes. He made no other movement.

It was almost like he were waiting for his turn.

"Are there luaus often?" Odette asked Paisley, who pursed her lips together and nodded.

"Kanaka Maoli mid-borns tend to have them whenever they can. It's a real treat, with hula dancing, all the kalua pig and laulau

you can eat, both made the Hawaiian way, so ono, and ancient Hawaiian tales you won't hear anywhere else." Paisley ran her fingers through her light brown hair as she pushed it out of her face. Her fingers were manicured with French tips, but the bottom was black, not clear. "Kawika said I could bring some friends. Come on, it'll be fun. I think Miss Kalama is going to talk about Pele tonight."

Sophie, Midori, and Shiro came stumbling in. "You need to come out," Shiro said. "You could use a little fun from your strict high-born lifestyle."

The memory quickly switched to another.

"Don't cry, Odette!" Sophie said, wiping their nose as they pouted. "You're going to make me cry. I hate seeing people cry, don't do this to me!"

She knew them, she knew all of them, and she had forgotten them.

The memories kept coming while she tossed and turned in her bed. Her head was spinning, until suddenly, everything stopped.

The masked person stepped forward. The closer they came, the more their demonic facial appearance began to fade until they were fully in view.

Long hair, cool blue eyes.

It was Lailoken.

He reached out to grab her neck.

Odette woke, gasping for air, like someone had tried to smother her with a pillow while she slept. She quickly crawled out of bed and went to the bathroom to splash her face with water. When she shut her eyes, another memory hit her.

> *Lailoken kissed her neck; his lips left a trail of bruises as they traveled along her skin. "Tell me you won't scream," he said, when he pulled away. He looked right into her eyes as his pupils constricted. Cruel and uncaring. He was manipulating her.*
>
> *"I won't scream," Odette's voice came out robotic and cold, but she obeyed.*
>
> *"You want this," he said, trailing his hand up her inner thigh.*
>
> *"I want this," the same voice came from her mouth before a soft gasp escaped her lips.*

She pressed her palms against her temples and squeezed her eyes shut tightly as she fell against the wall. "Stop, stop!" she mumbled, smacking the side of her head with her palm, as if the force would knock the memories back out. "Stop."

Tears began to flood from her eyes. She ran out of the bathroom and started opening and slamming drawers trying to find the coin that Paisley gave her.

'I would never use my ability on you.'

Liar.

'I want you to love me, on your own terms.
It's not the same if you don't.'

Her tears began to blur her vision as she searched for the token. How could she think it was Mrs. Baskerville? Mrs. Hamasaki was right, Mrs. Baskerville wanted Odette to remember when she was cruel, or she wouldn't have thought the things she had. She would've been clueless.

The more her thoughts traveled, the more she wondered how long it had been going on, she began to grow increasingly frustrated with herself as she searched for the Dreamweaver token.

She should've known. Lailoken told her everything she wanted to hear. He got inside her head, he made her think the best of him. That he was perfect.

Odette dropped into the chair at her vanity and cried. She rested her arms against the edge of the table and put her head down.

She couldn't stop.

She should've known.

Odette pulled one hand down and covered her mouth to muffle the sound of her whimpers.

All those nights she climbed into his bed, looking for comfort after being yelled at by Mrs. Baskerville. All those nights she couldn't remember falling asleep, or how she got back to her bedroom.

How many times? How many nights?

She sat up and wiped her face.

Odette looked up in the mirror as her body trembled from the staggered breathing.

"How could you forget?" she asked her reflection. "How could you let him —"

Odette closed her eyes and took a deep breath.

When she opened her eyes, she didn't look at her reflection again. She needed this pain to be taken away. She had to find that stupid coin.

The memory of Paisley's face was burned into her mind when she realized Odette didn't know who she was. The way Sophie just accepted the idea she didn't want them in her life.

She slammed the drawer of her dresser and the Daruma doll fell onto the ground. Odette picked him up and put him in the drawer knowing he would never fully gain his sight.

She stopped abruptly.

The token was in her vanity drawer.

She yanked the drawer open and dug for the coin. As soon as she found it, she started pacing her room, trying to focus on what Paisley had told her to do. She clutched it tightly in her hand.

"Dreamweaver, eat my dream? No, that's — Dreamweaver, consume my nightmare?" she said and turned to her mirror, but nothing happened.

It wasn't working.

She couldn't remember it.

Odette could remember everything else now, but the one thing she needed most, was clouded in her mind. In front of the full length mirror in her bedroom, Odette collapsed to the floor while still gripping tightly onto the token.

"Please," she whispered through her rough breaths. "Dreamweaver, just consume my fears." Her hand cupped over her face as she cried against her bed frame. "Please," she begged. "*Please.*"

The Woolgathering had been sealed to scions since the high-borns managed to convince powerful witches into cursing the land. Mundanes could still summon them if they needed, assuming they knew how. But for a scion, it was especially difficult. For a grot?

Near impossible.

The little hope Odette still had left, began to fade. Her pain remained, and it seemed to double in strength as she remained on the ground, smothered by the weight of her memories. She felt dirty and disgusting. Unclean.

No amount of soap would wash this feeling away.

She remained leaning against the wooden frame of her bed as she cried. Odette pulled down her sheet to bury her face, having no energy to stand up. She almost wished she never drank from that vial.

She was better off not knowing. Better off wondering. The nightmares were better than the pain that began to consume every bit of her.

She couldn't stop crying.

Odette looked up when something sparkled in her mirror.

It shone at her feet, and a young man began to manifest on the ground in front of her.

Startled by his sudden appearance, Odette crawled over her bed and scooted back against the wall, while she pulled her comforter over her body. She peered over the blanket, not sure what to expect. But he didn't move.

He was asleep.

She got up from where she sat, and slowly slipped off of her bed and crawled toward him. He had long dark hair, small eyes, and a dark, even tan; wearing nothing but a black pareo wrap tied around his waist. He looked Hawaiian; at the very least, mixed, possibly Asian also, and looked peaceful in his slumber. Something she longed for.

'You have to steal their necklace, or they'll immediately return to the Woolgathering.'

Odette stared at the skeleton key hanging around his neck, resting against his bare chest, just beside letters inked onto his skin beneath his left collarbone. *KEAHI.*

She looked back at the key. The beautiful blue gem centered at the top, between two folded wings that coveted the key.

She wiped her face and leaned forward. Her hand shook as she outstretched her arm.

He stirred, adjusting himself on the floor, and she jumped back.

But he was still fast asleep. He even snored a little as he draped his arm over his face.

Odette tried again, outstretching her arm, her hand shook a little less this time. If she didn't grab that necklace, he'd leave. Her fingers wrapped around the key and she tore it from his neck just as he opened his eyes. Quickly, she scooted away from him as he sat up.

"Where am I? Who are you?" he asked upon seeing her. His hair was longer than she thought, much longer than hers, hanging far past his shoulders and halfway down his chest. His gaze dropped to what she was holding in her hand. "Give that back."

She curled her fingers over it, tightening her grip on the skeleton key.

"Please," she said, slowly getting to her feet. "I just want the nightmares to go away. I just want them to stop — please — take them away."

"I said to give me my key!" he snapped.

"Please." She collapsed back onto the floor, still gripping onto it tightly. She pulled up her knees and cowered in the corner, burying her face into the crook of her elbow. "Please, Dreamweaver."

"Dreamweaver?" he repeated after her. "You think I'm a — oh. I'm —"

He stared at the sobbing girl on the ground. She hadn't bothered to look up at him again. He watched as her back rose and dropped with the jagged breaths she took.

He sighed.

"Okay, okay." He knelt down on the ground beside her and placed his hand on her shoulder.

She rose her head from her arms; her arm and cheeks both damp from crying. Her eyes were bloodshot, puffy and still watery as more tears threatened to fall.

Odette looked up at him, eyes growing wider as she waited; she wondered what he was going to do. She didn't know how it worked. She slowly shrank away from him as he came closer.

"I'm not going to hurt you," he said as she leaned away from him. "I have to — I have to kiss your forehead for your fears to pass to me."

She stared at him with wide eyes, and finally nodded. He leaned forward and she closed her eyes as he kissed her forehead.

"You want this," a blonde-haired man told Odette as he unbuttoned the front of her top.

"I want this," she repeated after him like a scratched record, as if she had no choice but to agree with him. He held her arms down and kissed her forcefully.

Keahi pulled away from her.

"What's your name?" she asked, wiping her face with her fingertips. She still gripped the skeleton key tightly in her hand. "Is that your name?" She pointed at the letters on his chest.

He nodded as he sat back against the frame of her bed, resting his arms against his knees. He didn't look at her.

"How do you pronounce it?" she asked, staring at his collarbone.

"Kay-ah-he."

"Thank you, Keahi. I'm Odette."

"I know," he said. He ran his finger back and forth against the front of his neck, still turned away from her. "That's what your necklace says."

"Oh, right." Her bottom lip quivered. "You don't see the — you know — do you?"

"No," he lied. Keahi finally turned his head to look at her. He outstretched his hand to her. "Can I go home now?" he asked.

Odette opened her hand and looked down at the skeleton key.

"But I need you," she said softly, so soft that he almost didn't hear her.

"People have nightmares every day. People who don't know we exist. What makes you think you're special?"

"I don't," she said. "I just can't handle my dreams being as awful as my li —" Odette bit down on her bottom lip as she averted her gaze. "I mean, I just can't handle it, I guess." Her eyes slowly found their way back to his. "Sometimes we just need a safe place, to keep hope. Even if it's only in our heads."

"This isn't some kind of trap?"

"Trap?" She frowned. "Why would I trap you?"

"You know what they did to the Dreamweavers. You know what they'll do if they knew what you know now. That we still exist."

Odette shook her head.

"Like I said, I need you. I need your help. I promise, I won't. I won't tell anyone."

Keahi chewed on the inside of his cheek. Despite his better judgment, he agreed.

"All right," he said. "I'll stay for a while. But when you no longer need me, I'm leaving." He looked down at his necklace in her hand. "Can I at least fix my chain? You broke it when you ripped it from my neck," he said, rubbing the back of his.

She started to hand it to him, then stopped.

"This isn't a trick, is it?"

"I just want to fix the chain," he said. "It's going to bother me."

Reluctantly, she handed it to him.

He stared at the metal loop that was stuck to the other side now, torn from the chain. He glanced up at Odette before looking down at the metal piece. Keahi bit down onto the next loop and forced it open to conjoin the two. He shoved the small metal back together.

"How long have you been a Dreamweaver?"

Keahi frowned and looked up at her. She was standing up now, leaning against her vanity. Her arms were crossed over her chest, blonde hair messily draped over her shoulders. She tucked a few stands of hair behind her ear as she waited for an answer.

"My whole life? It's not a profession. You can't just choose whether or not you want to be one. Did you choose to be a scion?"

"Are you all assholes or did I just get lucky?"

He threw the skeleton key back at her, which she caught against her stomach.

"Go back to sleep," he grumbled. He twisted his body so that he laid on the floor. Keahi stared up at her ceiling. Over his stomach, he laced his fingers together.

She ignored his grumbling. Odette turned toward the mirror of her vanity and unhooked the necklace to put it around her neck.

"Are you hungry?" she asked as she wiped her face, trying to make herself look a little more presentable. "You need a proper place to sleep —"

He sat back up, staring at her reflection in the mirror.

"You know, I'm not some lost dog that followed you home."

"I'm just trying to be a decent person!" she snapped as she turned around. "Maybe you should try it. Don't they teach you manners in the Woolgathering? I'm trying to be polite."

"What would you know about the Woolgathering? Perfect little high-born scion princess."

"I am not a princess!" She tightly crossed her arms over her chest. "If you're not a dog, then why are you going to sleep on the floor? Where dogs sleep?"

"Dogs sleep on the ground?" he asked as he stood up. "Well, my dog sleeps in my bed, so." Keahi sat down on her bed and laid back, pulling the sheet halfway over his body. He turned toward her. "Coming, princess?" he asked, patting the spot beside him.

Her face flushed.

"Get out of my bed," she demanded. "*Now.*"

Keahi kicked the sheet off and sat up. He stood up and walked right up to her. She didn't step back. "I said I'd stay for a while," he said, his face inches away from hers. "But I don't need you coddling me."

There was a knock at her door.

"Odette?" a voice came from the other side, seeping through the cracks. "Are you all right?"

"I'm fine, Lailoken."

She turned back to face Keahi, but he vanished.

Odette turned around in a circle.

He was gone.

She pressed her hand against her chest to make sure his skeleton key still hung around her neck.

Odette sighed and climbed back into her bed, her hand still fumbling with the new chain. She turned on her body to face the wall, and pulled the sheet over her. Biting down on her bottom lip, she frowned. She hadn't realized it at the time, but she no longer felt sad. She hadn't since Keahi kissed her forehead.

The pain and the fear, it was gone.

Just like him.

Still, she remembered.

It just didn't hurt anymore. For some reason, she felt safe. She closed her eyes.

Sweet dreams, Odette, she told herself.

Keahi was far from gone, though. He had only vanished from her sight, drawn by the voice that came from the other side of the door.

The voice he recognized from Odette's nightmares.

He dissolved into smoke when Lailoken had knocked, and slipped through the crack beneath the bedroom door. Keahi stood behind the man, but Lailoken wouldn't be able to see him even if he were to turn around.

Long, blonde hair tied back in a bun, and shallow blue eyes.

It was the same man.

Keahi clenched his jaw. His hands curled into fists, but he remained where he was.

Invisible. Undetected.

He glanced at Odette's door as Lailoken turned away and descended down the hall. Keahi had half a mind to follow him, but he didn't move. Instead, he leaned back against her door and slid down to the ground. He would wait in case Lailoken came back.

Keahi didn't move from that spot all night, where he sat, guarding her door.

There were things he never wanted to witness.

He was never going to get the look in her eyes out of his mind. It wasn't just fear hidden behind the green in her eyes. It was agony. The result of trauma.

If this was what Dreamweavers had to deal with whenever mundanes summoned them, he was far from jealous.

Keahi glanced down the hallway, in the direction Lailoken had disappeared to. He didn't like scions, he didn't much like mundanes either. But some were worse than others, and their actions weren't victimless. His fingers curled in and he clenched his fists.

If Lailoken laid a hand on her again, he'd kill him.

He was sure of it.

TOVALEY B. KYSEL

7   THAT'S WHAT FRIENDS ARE FOR

Things were mostly quiet in the Apothecary after the four of them found out the truth about Odette. It was a surprise if Paisley ever came out of her room.

She'd often claim she were writing if someone came knocking, but there were doubts between the rest of them on whether or not it was true.

She did sit in front of her laptop quite often, her fingers running through her blue and orange hair, as she tried to write about something. Spirits flooded her room as her negative energy increased, all but the one she wanted to talk to.

The one who told her to give the token to Odette.

Some days, most days, she laid in bed, with her pillows pressed up against her ears. She just wanted the chattering to stop. She wanted the buzzing to stop. Paisley wanted everything to stop.

"I'm worried about her," Midori said, frowning at Paisley's closed door.

"She'll be fine," Sophie said as they dropped something into a cauldron. "Paisley needs time to deal with things on her own, but she'll be fine."

"What if she's not?" Midori asked.

"She'll be fine," Sophie repeated. "She knows when she needs to take care of herself." They threw another leaf into the thick, boiling liquid that looked something like mud. "Did Shiro find out yet if Odette has a Dreamweaver?"

Midori shook her head as she looked up from her book.

"He went by their place this morning, but Mr. Baskerville is too strong of a Shield. We should just be lucky that they don't have a Telepath in their house. If they know what she took, if they find out who gave it to her —" Midori put her book down. "You didn't have to do it, you know."

"How can you say that?" Sophie asked, nearly dropping the vial in their hand. "She's like our little sister, Green."

"But did you do it for her or because Paisley asked you to? I know Paisley's your best friend but you don't have to do everything she asks."

Sophie slammed the vial down on the counter, so hard that the bottom cracked. They pulled their hand away from the broken glass and Midori got up to help them.

But Sophie pulled away from her.

"I did it because Paisley was right, and it was the right thing to do. I did it for both of them, okay? Paisley already went through this shit with someone, and now she has to think about Odette going through the same thing? What kind of friend would I be if I didn't do something? If I didn't do the only thing I could do to help?"

Sophie's eyes began to well up with tears as they pushed back their curly mess of thick black hair in frustration. They turned away from Midori, who stood in the kitchen with them now. She started to clean up the broken vial with a dish towel as she glanced at Sophie.

"Maybe Paisley's not the one who should stop keeping things bottled in."

"Ugh, I can't talk to you right now!" Sophie snapped. They turned off the stove and ran down the stairs to the Apothecary.

Midori sighed and wiped up the glass. She threw it in the trashcan and stared at her book sitting on the table. Glancing at Paisley's door, she went downstairs.

When the room was silent, Shiro came down from the attic and grabbed a glass of water. He could clearly hear the argument between the two of them, and what was being said without actually coming out of their mouths.

He could hear Paisley's thoughts too, but he tried extra hard to stay out of her head. Especially right now, she didn't need that kind of invasion.

In her room, Paisley stood just on the other side of her door. She had heard the two of them arguing and she couldn't help but think Midori had a point.

Sophie kept things bottled in; they always had since turning off their empathy. They stayed strong when others fell apart. Clear-headed, Sophie never made emotional decisions.

Paisley sighed and opened her door.

"I know you're worried about her," Shiro said when Paisley finally came out of her room. He was the only one in the room. He sat at the window, looking out at the Imperial Quarter, his glass of water rested on the windowsill. He didn't have to look away from the window to know it was her. He knew all of their footsteps individually.

Paisley walked with heavy steps and long strides, like she was tired of carrying the weight of the world, but somehow, found reason to keep going.

"I will never not be worried about her," she said, taking a seat beside him. She put a bottle down on the nearby table. "Especially knowing what we know now. After what Sophie saw? She should be here, with us. Safe. Away from those monsters."

"I know," he said, glancing at her. "Do you have anymore information on that spirit that contacted you?"

Paisley shook her head.

"I still haven't fully seen them. I see other spirits, and it's just overwhelming. They all come at once, they all talk at once. I've been taking so much Hypnolin-Z lately just to get some sleep that I'm not even sure what's real anymore and what's a dream. They never want to leave me alone. I'm just glad it wasn't Odette, you know?"

"Why'd you stop taking Sophie's potions? Weren't they helping?"

"Because it's not fair."

"What? What's not fair?"

"That they have to worry about me all the time. That they feel responsible for taking care of me and making sure I'm okay. It's not fair. I feel so — so — weak," she grumbled.

"If it makes you feel better," he started, returning his focus to the window without really looking out of it. "I was bullied this morning. Almost got dragged into the Royal Sector. I felt like my life flashed before my eyes."

"What? By who?"

Paisley's hair began to turn a bright red.

"Of course that doesn't make me feel better."

"It's okay," he said. "I'm fine. It's just, you think you have safe places to be yourself, you know what I mean? And all it takes is a few people to ruin it for you, and suddenly, you don't feel so safe anymore."

Paisley glanced down and noticed he wore baggy pants now. She frowned as her gaze moved up to his face and saw his bottom lip quiver before he turned away from her.

She rested her head against his shoulder.

"I'm sorry, Shiro," she whispered.

He sniffled. "It's okay," he said, though a tear rolled down his face.

"I can't believe you thought that would make me feel better. You know I can't stand when anyone hurts you."

"I feel like I deserve — I feel like —" he sighed. "I never know what to say when you bring up — what happened to you. I just — I don't want you to think I don't care — I just — I feel like it was my fault."

Paisley lifted her head from his shoulder.

"She was my friend," he continued. "And what she did to you was —"

"Not your fault," she told him sternly. "She chose to manipulate me and victimize herself. She chose to pressure me. She decided 'no' wasn't an acceptable answer. *She* did that, Shiro. Not you. I can't believe you've been blaming yourself. Have you been blaming yourself this whole time?"

He shrugged.

"Shiro."

"Okay, yeah. It's just, you wouldn't have met her if it wasn't for me. None of that would've happened if it wasn't for me."

"Look at me."

He shook his head at first, but slowly he finally turned to her.

"You aren't a Pusher. You can't control her. No one can control her actions but her. What matters to me? Is that I had friends to fall back on. I had you, Sophie, and Midori help get me out of a toxic situation I didn't even know I was in. It doesn't matter how she came into my life, okay? What matters is my friends noticed something was wrong. What matters? Is I have friends who cared enough to get me out of there. Who didn't give up on me when I kept falling into her self-victimizing trap. When I kept giving her a chance even though I knew better. Shiro, I don't blame you, so please don't blame yourself."

Her hair began to turn blue, but there were strands of red still woven between.

He nodded, and turned to face the window again.

"I'll try," he promised.

"She was a bitch anyway," Paisley said, nudging his side with her elbow. "With an ugly haircut."

He laughed.

"There's no one like you, Paze. Is that why so many girls like you?"

"It's my charm," she said, wiggling her eyebrows and a smirk cursed her lips. "Though honestly, I really wish they wouldn't. I'm sick of it. I don't get why everyone tries to make things romantic or sexual. What's wrong with being friends?"

"Nothing," he said. "Friends save lives."

"Then why are friendships always seen as lesser?"

"Because that's what society wants us to believe. Nothing's more important than sex. If you're not having frequent hetero sex, your relationship must suck. Guys can't wear make-up, or skirts, or show any signs of femininity, or we're weak. The Constitution for the Scion Order just makes all of those things a hundred times worse. But mundanes deal with it too, it's everywhere."

"And people don't talk about it because it's easier to ignore than to believe things are really that fucked up."

"Exactly," he said. "It's safer to do nothing." He pushed himself away from the windowsill and looked down at his clothes.

"It's safer to just — put on pants."

"You know you can wear skirts in here, right? With us?"

"I know," he said, a smile forming on his face. "This is my safe place. With you — guys." He looked out the window and Midori and Sophie were sitting on the wall that bordered the center island of plants in the middle of the walkway. "I want what my sister has," he said.

Paisley looked down at the two of them, laughing. They made up.

"A partner?" she asked.

Shiro shook his head. "Happiness," he said simply. "You don't need a partner to be happy."

"Tell that to Hollywood."

He laughed and nodded, which made Paisley smile. There was no better music to her ears than the laughter of her friends.

"Do you think friends can be soul mates?" he asked.

"I think friends can be anything."

"Do you think Odette's going to be okay?"

She paused. "I have to believe that she will be. I just wish we could do more." She shook her head and brushed her hair behind her ear with her fingers. "I'm lucky that I'm a mid-born. It was an easier situation to get away from."

"I don't think so," he said. "Being with someone who's toxic is always hard to get away from. Just because she didn't buy you, doesn't make it any less severe."

"I just wish I could take her place."

"I think she'll be okay," he said. "Odette's a sweet girl, but she's got some bite in her. Hopefully she's got a Dreamweaver helping her."

"I hope so too," she said. "I'd hate to think we made her nightmares worse."

Paisley turned to the side and reached for the bottle of Hypnolin-Z sitting on the table. She started to uncap it and Shiro frowned while he watched her.

"You're not going to measure it first?"

"Well, this way, every morning is a gift."

"Paisley."

"I know how much to take," she insisted, fumbling with the bottle in her hands. "I've been taking it every day for months."

"But you're not sick."

"See this?" she held out the bottle and pointed to the label. "Nighttime Relief. It does exactly what it says. Gives me nighttime relief."

"You promise you're not addicted to it?"

"Of course not. It's just temporary. You know, when I was seventeen, my dog was sick. We all knew she was gonna die and it felt like every time I woke up, I got bad news. I had major insomnia after that. I figured, if I didn't sleep, I'd have no bad news to wake up to. But I got through it. I'll get through this, too. Even if this time, I just don't wanna wake up."

"I'm going to take it with you, then."

"What?"

"If you're expecting me to be okay with you taking it — without even measuring it — then you should be okay with me taking it too."

"Okay," she said, putting the bottle down. "No Hypnolin-Z tonight, then. But I'm blaming you if I can't sleep."

"Blame away," he said.

Odette managed to keep up her façade that she was ill. As far as the Baskervilles knew, she had no reason to lie about it. None of them seemed concerned enough to call a doctor either, though she assumed it was because Lailoken probably didn't want them to see the bruises on her body.

She didn't want anyone to see them either.

Even around Keahi, she wore long sleeves and long pants. She kept her hair down so he wouldn't see the ones on her neck and most of all, she kept her distance from him too. Whenever he manifested, at least.

He lingered in her room like a shadow, and sometimes, he'd even disappear into them. Odette never knew where he went, if he went anywhere at all, or if he just didn't want to be seen by her. But his presence alone made her feel safer.

Still, she didn't leave her room.

Keahi couldn't protect her out there, from them. She doubted he would if he could. All he wanted to do was go home.

"Are you going to turn into a monster?" she asked him. "The longer you stay here, in the mundane world, I mean." He sat in her vanity chair, staring at her through the mirror while she sat on her bed behind him. He rubbed his face, sliding his hand down to his chin. Keahi dropped it back down against the armrest.

"Not if you let me go home," he said, returning his focus onto her.

She looked down at the skeleton key hanging around her neck and she shook her head.

"I can't," she said softly. "Please understand — I just can't. Not yet."

"When?" he asked. "What are you waiting for?"

"To feel safe, on my own. Do you think I like relying on you? You're not very nice."

"Says the girl holding me prisoner."

"You said you would stay."

"Which is why I'm still here," he said. "But you took me from my home. Literally. You have any idea how that feels, princess?"

"As a matter of fact, I do, and I'd appreciate it if you'd stop calling me that. You don't know me, Keahi, so don't act like you do."

He averted his eyes from the mirror. "I know everything I need to know." Keahi slouched in the chair and leaned his head back. "You high-born scions are all the same."

Odette got up from her bed and stomped over to him. He had his eyes closed, like he was trying to fall asleep. She stood over him.

"No, we are not," she said sternly. He opened one eye. She was inches from his face. "When I was eighteen years old, I was sold at a Bridal Expo. To this family. My parents were given a thousand scripts and I didn't see one bit of it. I was raised to be submissive. Told that what I thought and what I said didn't matter. To anyone. That my appearance was the only thing that gave me any worth." Odette took a step back from him as he sat up and turned to face her in the chair. "You don't know me, Keahi. I don't know what you know about the scions, but you don't know me. And your 'tough guy' act isn't fooling anyone."

"Act?" he asked. "You think I'm acting?"

She pressed her lips together and nodded.

"You care about me, don't you. Maybe not very much, but you do. You wouldn't have stayed if you didn't. Not with what you're apparently risking."

He scoffed and turned to face the vanity mirror again as he slouched back into the chair.

"You wish."

"I know you do," she said, tapping the skeleton key gently with her fingertip. "You don't have to admit it, but I know."

He got up from the chair and turned around.

"What you *know* is pity," he snapped and she took a step back. "I saw a girl sobbing on the floor and I felt sorry for her. If you want to mistaken that for compassion or concern, be my guest, *princess*. It's not like I have any say in anything."

Keahi turned away from her and sat back down. He avoided looking in the mirror again.

Her face flushed with embarrassment and she sat back down on her bed, silenced by his words. But she wasn't going to cry. Not in front of him.

Not again.

Mrs. Hamasaki knocked on the door and Keahi faded into smoke that quickly dissipated. Odette got up to answer it, and Mrs. Hamasaki's thin eyebrows scrunched together.

She knew it was her; Mrs. Hamasaki was the only one who came up to check on her and to make sure she was eating.

Odette hated lying to her.

"How are you feeling?" she asked. She held a tray in her hands, with chicken noodle soup and a glass of orange juice. "Do you have a fever? Your whole face is flushed — you poor thing."

"I'm okay," Odette smiled weakly. "Is Lailoken home?" she asked.

Mrs. Hamasaki shook her head. "But I can let him know you were asking for him when he comes back."

"No! I mean, no, that's okay," she said quickly. "I don't want to get him sick. It's better to wait until I feel better."

"Here, eat." Mrs. Hamasaki handed her the tray. "And feel better! Everyone misses you down in the kitchens. Kiko won't stop asking about you."

A genuine smile crossed her face as she gripped hold of the handles on the tray.

"I'll try," she said.

Odette stepped back and Mrs. Hamasaki closed the door for her.

She turned around.

"At least someone likes you," Keahi said, standing right behind her.

Odette dropped the tray.

He managed to catch it before it could hit the floor; though some of the soup spilled out of the bowl. Keahi put the tray down on the vanity.

"Are you always this clumsy or did I just get lucky?" he asked.

"You startled me," she snapped.

"You should've seen your face," he said. Keahi widened his eyes and dropped his jaw, trying to make the dumbest face he could manage. "It was real ugly. I might have nightmare."

"You're an asshole."

She pushed past him and started making her bed.

"I'm sorry," he said and she stopped. She turned around as he turned to face the vanity. His gaze dropped down to the soup that had spilled over onto the tray. "I just want to go home," he mumbled.

"That makes two of us," she said. Odette walked toward him and grabbed the back of his hand. Keahi turned to look at her. "I promise I'll let you go home before you turn into a monster that eats people."

Her eyes told him she was sincere. He couldn't help but grin at her words.

"Actually, we just start feeding off of hope and dreams," he corrected. "We don't eat people."

She shrugged and let go of his hand.

"You might as well eat the people too, because what's the point of living without hope and dreams? People need to dream," she said as she turned back toward her bed and flattened the sheet. "People need to have faith in something. Or there's just no point."

"What do you have faith in?" he asked, leaning back against the edge of the vanity.

Odette glanced back at him before straightening her posture. She went to her dresser and opened the top drawer and handed him the Daruma doll.

"This," she said. "I have faith in this."

"What is it?" he asked, staring at the one-eyed doll.

"Perseverance."

He handed it back to her.

"Thanks," she said. "For not making a face — or making fun of it."

"Why would I?"

"I don't know," she said, and tucked the doll back into her drawer.

Lailoken did when he saw it.

Her eyes lit up.

"I have an idea." Odette grabbed his hand and started pulling him toward the door. She looked back at him, then down at their hands and let go of his. "Sorry," she said. "Um — I — um — I want you to give him a nightmare. Lailoken."

Keahi frowned.

"I'm a Dreamweaver. I can't give nightmares, I can only take them away."

"Why not? You must be full of darkness, right? Consuming fears and all. And he deserves it."

It wasn't that Keahi disagreed with her, he didn't. But Lailoken's mind was uncharted territory he didn't exactly want to venture into. He hardly knew the high-born, but he already loathed him, knowing what he did to her.

Odette didn't know that he knew, and he preferred to keep it that way. The last thing he sought to do was make her uncomfortable.

How could he tell her no?

"Please, Keahi? Please?" she pouted and fumbled with the skeleton key hanging around her neck. Her bottom lip was already plump enough that it looked like she had a permanent pout on her face if she wasn't smiling. An actual pout just made it worse. It was kind of cute, though. She was kind of cute, in an annoying yet somewhat endearing way.

He rolled his eyes and leaned against the vanity again, seemingly in defeat.

"Okay," he said. "I'll give it a shot."

Odette smiled and bit down on her bottom lip.

She bounced up and down where she stood and clasped her hands together.

"What are you going to do? What are you going to show him? Tell me everything."

"Can you relax? We only just decided this five seconds ago."

"But you must have some idea."

He pulled out the chair in front of the vanity.

"Eat your food," he said. "I need to think."

She sat down on the chair but she only turned around. She slid her elbow over the back and rested her chin on her arm as she watched him pace back and forth in her room.

"I like this better," she said.

"What?" he asked, stopping in the middle of her room.

"When you aren't talking," she said. "You're easier to tolerate. Kind of cute when your mouth isn't messing it all up."

He scowled.

"You'd be easier to tolerate too if you'd sit there and eat your food like a good girl."

"But I'm not a good girl," she said. "I summoned a Dreamweaver. Good girls don't summon evil dream demons."

He briefly widened his eyes to mock her. "Whoa, watch out. High-born scion living on the edge."

Odette frowned and sat up.

She pulled her arm down from the back of the chair and turned to face the soup. "You have fast reflexes," she said, putting her spoon into the bowl.

"I know," he said.

She raised her eyebrows.

Okay, then.

Odette shifted in her chair and crossed her legs as she ate the soup Mrs. Hamasaki had brought up for her. She looked up in the mirror every now and then, and Keahi still paced behind her. "Are you thirsty?" she asked, and he looked at her reflection, then at the juice on the tray.

"No," he said.

"But you haven't eaten anything since I summoned you here."

"While I'm here, I feed off your fears. Why do you think I kiss your forehead every night? I'm not tucking you into bed and kissing you goodnight."

She narrowed her eyes and put down her spoon.

"Oh, right. Because you don't care about me. You're just an angry Dreamweaver who doesn't care about anything." Odette grunted. He frowned. Was she trying to mock him? "You know what I think is manly?" she continued. "Showing emotion."

"You know what I think?" he asked, placing his hands down on the edge of the vanity beside her. He got right in her face. "That I don't care what you think. Now, be quiet and eat your food."

"You're so bossy. Are we sure you aren't a Pusher?"

Keahi narrowed his eyes and she almost sank back in her chair. "Don't you compare me to those scions."

He pushed himself away from the vanity and disappeared.

Odette looked around.

"Really? I didn't mean it!"

She huffed and sat back in her chair.

Keahi went to Lailoken's room. If Odette really wanted him to give him a nightmare, he needed to learn a little more about him, aside from the obvious. His room, for the most part, was kept neat. Though Keahi doubted he cleaned it himself.

He stopped in his tracks when he noticed Lailoken's bed frame. The top was glass, which encased a black woven web, that almost mirrored a veil. It was thin, running along the width of the frame. Keahi flicked the glass with his finger and the webbing unraveled.

Scions were pathetic with trying to ward off Dreamweavers, as if they lingered waiting to attack. Keahi closed his eyes at his realization. That was exactly what he was doing.

He sat down at Lailoken's desk and looked through the papers scattered on top of it before he started opening drawers.

Then he stopped.

The bottom left drawer had dozens of used women's underwear stuffed into it. Did he keep Odette's underwear after each time? Was it some kind of trophy?

Keahi slammed the drawer so hard that it snapped off of the tracks.

The doorknob rattled and he disappeared.

He knew exactly what he needed to do. Now, all he had to do was wait.

Keahi waited in the darkness of Lailoken's room. He hid in the shadows, like predator waiting for prey. He watched the door, and he waited.

Lailoken didn't bother turning on the light when he finally went to bed. He stumbled into the bathroom for no more than a few minutes, before falling back against his mattress.

"I should've just made that brat sleep in here with me," he grumbled, turning on his side. Lailoken buried the side of his face into his pillow and Keahi clenched his fists.

Patiently, he waited for him to fall asleep.

The second he heard the first snore, Keahi emerged from the shadows of his room; only he emerged as a monster. His eyes were pitch black and without eyelids. His skin was taut against his skeleton, blackening in color as he outstretched his wings.

He leapt onto Lailoken's bed, and punctured just beneath his chin and above his throat with the tip of his tail.

"Touch Odette again, and I will rip your skeleton right out of your body, Lailoken Baskerville."

His voice came out deep and throaty, and he vanished into thin air as Lailoken awoke with a startle. He climbed out of bed and flipped on the light.

But he was alone.

He didn't feel alone.

"Did you do it?" Odette asked, as soon as Keahi reappeared in her room. She sat up in her bed. He could see her clearly, her pale face was bright, even in the darkness. "What'd you show him? Tell me! Tell me!"

She was like a child.

"Why aren't you sleeping?" he asked. He looked down at the empty bowl and glass that sat on the tray. At least she finished her food.

"You didn't kiss me goodnight," she said and frowned. "I mean — kiss — err — you know what I mean. Is there like, some kind of term for it?"

"Feeding?" he asked as he turned to face her. "I didn't feed off of you tonight?"

"I prefer kiss," she mumbled.

"Most people do," he said. Keahi kissed her forehead. "Go to sleep."

"You're not going to tell me?" she asked. "Can you at least tell me whether or not you did it?"

"I did it," he said, sinking into the shadows of her bedroom.

Keahi slipped beneath the crack of her door and stood in the hallway in the darkness, folding his arms over his chest.

He stood out there, just in case.

8   CRUSH ON YOU

He grew restless, staying cooped up in Odette's bedroom. There were nights when he wandered around the dark house.   Down the hallway, he'd stop momentarily to observe the portraits of the Baskervilles that hung on the walls. Despite it being the twenty-first century, they were still very aristocratic with their decorum.

He was good when it came to disappearing when someone approached; but maybe he shouldn't be.   He needed interaction.   After being around Odette all day every day for the last week or so, he needed to talk to someone else, or he'd go mad.

Keahi chewed on the inside of his cheek and glanced out the bay window of her bedroom.

It was nearly six in the morning.

He disappeared and went out into the hall, passing the portraits he didn't bother to look at. Keahi went around the corner and stood just on the other side of the master bedroom.

"I'm going to the Royal Sector to see if the Shadow Crawlers have any better help. The kitchen staff is slacking. I don't think Odette is of any real use to them."

"Would you like me to —"

"No," she snapped, in her shrill voice Keahi had grown accustom to hearing. "I'll take myself. I'm not reliant on you, you know."

"I never said that you were, dear."

Keahi turned away from the door and raised an eyebrow.

He'd work for the Baskervilles. Problem solved.

He disappeared just as Chardonnay opened the door.

The Imperial Quarter was somewhere he hadn't gone in a long time. The Royal Sector, was somewhere he had never been.

He knew mid-borns got snatched right where he stood, but how was he going to get Chardonnay to pick him? Keahi looked down at his clothes. Still the same pareo wrap. Still barefoot. Still shirtless. He'd stick out like a sore thumb in here.

He walked to a darkened stairwell in the Imperial Quarter and brushed his collarbone with the back of his fingers.

A white collared shirt began to grow over his frame, and the sarong wrap folded itself around his legs, turning into long black slacks. Keahi looked down at his feet and wiggled his toes. He glanced up, looking at the items in the windows.

A smirk spread across his face when he spotted a pair of charcoal colored combat boots. He stomped his heel and the boots appeared on his feet.

Keahi rolled up his sleeves as he stepped back out into the Imperial Quarter.

It was still too early for any of the surrounding shops to be open, but he took his time walking toward the Royal Sector, trying to come up with a way to get picked by Chardonnay Baskerville. If they needed more help, he doubted she'd go for someone younger than him.

Keahi looked up at the shop signs as he passed them — realizing he should've known he wouldn't recognize any. Things had changed. It was one thing to know, it was another to witness it for yourself.

He bumped into someone.

"Oh, sor —" he stopped mid sentence at the sight of Mrs. Baskerville glaring at him. Her cup of coffee had spilled all over the front of her shirt.

She looked up at him with daggers in her eyes as she dropped the empty cup in her hand.

"How *dare* you."

"I'm sorry," he said and picked up the cup. "Can I buy you a new — shirt? Or a cup of coffee at least?"

"I can afford it myself," she snapped. She whacked the cup out of his hand. "Do you have any idea who I am, you mongrel?" Her pupils constricted.

She was trying to manipulate him.

Keahi tried not to clench his jaw at the mention of that word. The derogatory word high-borns used on mid-borns.

"No, Ma'am."

"Well, you will learn. You're coming with me." She gripped his collar.

"Mrs. Baskerville!"

Chardonnay retracted her hand as she turned around. A man stood there, shaggy black hair growing into his black beard. He looked half her age, and he pointed to the darkened passage to the Royal Sector. "We've been waiting for you."

"That won't be necessary, Mr. Wolfe." She gripped hold of Keahi's collar again.

"I've managed to catch one myself."

Mr. Wolfe's expression fell at the comprehension that he had just lost out on a sale.

Keahi tried not to let his amusement show on his face. He stuck his hands in his pockets. People weren't for profit.

Chardonnay yanked him forward and dragged him to the parking lot. She unlocked the trunk of the Chevelle and looked at him.

"Well, get in." When he didn't move, she screamed at him. "Now!"

He pretended to be startled by her sudden shout, though it echoed throughout the empty parking lot. Keahi was having trouble trying to be afraid of her.

He wasn't, not even a little bit.

"Yes, Ma'am."

Keahi climbed into the trunk of the car and Chardonnay slammed it shut. He felt her start the car and drive off. He turned on his side and ran his finger against the edge and scooted further into the car so that he could hear her.

"Mr. Wong? Yes, I got someone — yes, already. The best part is, I didn't purchase him — he bumped in to me like a wild animal. He wasn't even watching where he was going. You'd think he was mundane who accidentally stumbled across the Imperial Quarter."

Keahi curled his hand into a fist and smirked.

What an idiot.

Mundane. He supposed he'd need a cover story, should anyone ask, but pretending to be mundane was pushing it.

When they got back to the house, Mrs. Baskerville didn't waste a second. She opened the trunk and practically yanked him out of the car herself.

He was about to step into that house as a person, rather than a Dreamweaver.

Keahi knew who Mr. Wong was. He was the man who never seemed to talk to anyone except for the Baskervilles and Mrs. Hamasaki. He seemed to pretend as if the rest of the staff didn't exist, like he didn't even see them. Keahi's actually seen a few of them make faces at him and he had done nothing in return.

Mr. Wong stared down at him with the most condescending look. Keahi tried not to notice and looked at Mrs. Baskerville.

She yanked on his collar.

"You are not to leave this property unless allowed. You will follow orders without problem. Do you understand me?"

"Yes, Ma'am. I understand."

"He's all yours," she grumbled and pushed him toward Mr. Wong. "Now I have to change my shirt — and I still have appointments. That wretched boy." Mrs. Baskerville continued to mutter angrily to herself, though loud enough that she made sure he heard her.

Mr. Wong snapped in front of his face to get his attention.

"Your starting pay is nothing. You won't be getting a raise, so don't expect one. You will have meals and a place to sleep in exchange for your services. Do you understand?"

Keahi nodded.

"Then follow me."

He did as he was told, walking further into the house, they stopped at the edge of the stairs that seemed to descend down into a basement.

"Aren't you going to ask me for my name?" Keahi asked.

Mr. Wong just stared at him like he was looking through him.

"I don't care."

He turned on his soles and walked away. Keahi raised his eyebrows and shrugged before heading down the steps.

He fixed his sleeves as he observed the other staff move about their quarters.

"Are you new?"

He turned around to see a girl in a maid outfit standing behind him. She seemed to be the only one wearing make-up. Keahi frowned slightly. She was mundane.

"Uh, yeah. What gave it away?" he asked, scratching the side of his jaw.

She handed him a rubber band.

"You can't leave your hair down. Especially if you're going to work in the kitchen. Besides, I would've known if I've seen you before." A smirk spread across her face. "Would you like me to put your hair up for you?" She clasped her hands around his.

"I think I can handle it." He looked around as people passed him before he looked back at the girl standing in front of him. "How many of you are there?" he asked.

"Eleven — well twelve now— including you. Mr. Wong is the butler, Mrs. Hamasaki, head of the kitchen. There's about four others in there — you are going to work in the kitchen, right? I know Mrs. Hamasaki wanted more help. Hope you got some muscle under those sleeves," she said and poked his arm. She raised her eyebrows and poked his arm again. She then grabbed at his arm and gave it a squeeze. "I guess you do."

"Shouldn't you buy me dinner first?" he asked and she laughed. "I mean, I don't even know your name."

"Pia Accardo." She blew him a kiss as she stepped back. "See you around, Kitchen Boy."

"Finally, another dude." This worker was a little taller than he was, and his hair was tied back. Keahi looked down at the rubber band Pia gave him. "Welcome to the Baskerville Cave, brah! I'm Gentry Yoshimura."

"Keahi," he said as he tied his hair into a bun. Baskerville Cave?"

"Well, it's either that or Servant Quarters."

"Got it."

"I'm drowning in a pool of women. Mr. Wong, Min-Jae, Abbey, and I are outnumbered."

Keahi raised his eyebrows. "Most guys wouldn't complain about that."

Gentry shrugged. "They do when they're ace," he said, pointing to himself, before waving his hand in a circle, "and all the girls are bi and gay for each other."

"We aren't all gay," Pia said, poking her head into the room. "But like you said, you're asexual. Your loss."

"Not really." Gentry rolled his eyes. "Watch out for her," he said as she disappeared up the stairs. "Sooner or later, she's going to try to get into your pants."

"You think so?"

Gentry raised an eyebrow.

"Not that I'm — interested — or anything."

"Yeah sure, brah. Keep your snake in its cage."

The both of them laughed.

So far, this was a lot better than staying cooped up in Odette's bedroom all day. The social interaction was good.

Gentry showed Keahi around the Baskerville Cave. There were two dorm-like rooms, the bigger one belonging to the girls, and two smaller bedrooms belonging to Mr. Wong and Mrs. Hamasaki. They shared a bathroom, while everyone else shared another. There was a small kitchenette, a table and a couch. It wasn't much, but Keahi's seen worse.

Gentry opened the door.

"This is our dorm," he said. "Sup, Abbey."

"Is it time for work already?" he grumbled as he turned over on the mattress. There were two bunkbeds, and Abbey slept on the bottom bunk of the one to the right of the door.

"We've got fresh meat. Get up."

Abbey lifted his head from the pillow and opened one eye as he pushed his messy brown hair out of his face. "Oh, hey."

"This is Keahi," Gentry said. "New kitchen kid."

Abbey sat up and pushed his hair out of his face.

"Nice." He nodded toward the bunk across from his. "That bed's empty. Gentry and Min-Jae sleep on the top bunks. I don't mind," he said, laying back on his bed. "I can't climb up there after a long day."

"He works outside," Gentry said.

"I'm jealous already."

Abbey smirked. "Not gonna wanna lose that tan of yours, eh?"

"I don't look good in pale."

"Yeah, none of us do." Gentry laughed. He stepped into the room. "I should head to bed. I usually work nights but I'll see you around. The kitchen's right upstairs around the corner if you take the ones near the bathroom."

Keahi nodded. "Got it. Mahalo." He shaka'd, pinky and thumb sticking out with his index, middle, and ring finger folded down, and ran up the stairs.

He ran right into Odette once he went up. He caught her so she wouldn't fall and her eyes widened as she regained her stance.

Then she frowned at him.

"*What* are you doing down here?" she asked.

"What are *you* doing down here?"

"Stop repeating everything I say," she snapped. "Look, if you get caught —"

"Will you relax? I joined the staff. Are you worried about me now or something?"

"No, I'm worried about *me*. I told you that I need you and now you're running around the house playing servant boy."

Mr. Baskerville turned the corner.

"Odette, could you please bring me —" Ahren stopped talking when he noticed Keahi. He frowned slightly, before dismissing it. He returned his attention back onto Odette. "A glass of wine? My wife is giving me a headache so make sure it's *Chardonnay*."

"Yes, Mr. Baskerville."

He glanced at Keahi again before passing them.

"Why aren't you that nice to me?" Keahi asked.

"I tried once. Remember? You didn't want to be 'coddled'." She narrowed her eyes. "Don't get caught."

Odette grabbed his wrist and pulled him into the kitchen.

"Mrs. Hamasaki, this is Keahi," she said. She let go of his wrist and tried to push him forward, though she could barely move him. "And he's going to be helping you for a little while."

"Finally, another man." Mrs. Hamasaki grabbed his arm to give his bicep a squeeze, only her hand couldn't fully wrap around it.

"Why does everyone keep grabbing me?"

"Who else grabbed you?" Odette asked, raising her eyebrows.

"Wouldn't you like to know."

She rolled her eyes. "Please make sure he works hard."

"You won't be joining us?" Mrs. Hamasaki asked.

"Maybe in a few days. I don't want to get anyone else sick. I'm going to practice piano. Could someone please bring me some orange juice in a little bit?"

Mrs. Hamasaki nodded. "Smart girl. Lailoken's lucky, no?" she nudged Keahi.

"No —" he answered without thinking and Odette scowled at him. "I mean yes. Yeah, sure."

Odette turned away from him and Keahi reached for her wrist. She turned around. Odette glanced down at his hand before looking up at him. "*What*?"

"Are you going to be okay, down here, with these people?" he asked, his voice was low.

Odette raised an eyebrow.

"Oh, are you worried about me now or something?" she asked him in a mocking manner.

He let go of her wrist. "No, it's just, if something happens to you I won't get to go home."

Her expression faltered.

"Right. Well, I can take care of myself."

"They can't know that you —"

"I know." She pat his chest with her hand. She pulled her arm back down, becoming uncomfortable at her realization of how firm he was. Odette knew he was muscular, she had seen him without a shirt on. But seeing and touching were two very different things. "Relax."

When she had woken up that morning, she knew she'd have to go downstairs eventually. As much as she wanted to, she couldn't fake being sick forever. She wasn't stupid either. Odette knew she couldn't let Lailoken know she remembered everything.

That she knew everything.

It took her a while to mentally prepare herself that morning, but seeing Keahi downstairs gave her a boost of confidence.

She poured Mr. Baskerville his glass of wine and went to find him.

Odette found his study door closed and she knocked.

"Mr. Baskerville? It's Odette. I have your —"

"Please just put it on the floor," he answered without opening the door. "I'll get it later."

"Okay," she said. She put the glass down.

The days that Lailoken and Mrs. Baskerville both worked made her happiest. Mr. Baskerville rarely came out of his study and servants went up to give him his food; though out of the three of them, he was nicest to her anyway. In some ways, he reminded her of her own father.

Odette felt like she had the whole house to herself.

She sat at the baby grand piano and played Bach's Goldberg Variations. It made her miss home. The way she would sit on the sofa, listening to her mother teach her older sisters, and eventually teach her. Her mother often told her she had been the best, but Odette disagreed.

Not aloud, of course.

Kiko had just finished cleaning the dining room when she returned to the kitchen. She saw Keahi standing with her mother and raised an eyebrow. "Oh, pour me a cup of that." Kiko gave him a once over. "Hey, Hot Chocolate!"

Keahi looked up. He looked around and his eyes landed on Kiko. He pointed at the center of his chest. "Are you talking to me?"

She nodded as she hopped up on the counter. "Where did you come from?"

"Down, Kiko," Mrs. Hamasaki scolded her.

"Relax, Mama Bear. I'm just being friendly."

Kiko slid off of the counter and smacked Keahi's ass. He bumped into the cabinet.

"Whoa, Jesus Christ."

"Maybe you should be called Honey Buns instead."

"Kiko! Go bring Odette her orange juice."

"Why — is she thirsty too?"

"Kiko!"

"Okay, I'm going." Kiko grabbed the glass of orange juice her mom placed on the counter and disappeared out of the kitchen.

"Is everyone always like this?" Keahi asked.

"When the Baskervilles are away, the servants will play." He turned around. Someone else from the kitchen staff raised her eyebrows as she approached him. Her wavy brown hair was tightly pulled back in a ponytail. "Kiko and Pia are the worst, in different ways. I'm Jiyun." She nodded her head toward the door. "Come on, I'll show you around."

Jiyun gave Keahi a basic tour of the house and she showed him where all of the cleaning supplies were and went over the tasks Mrs. Baskerville usually had them do.

"Since you're new, expect her to pick on you more than the others."

"I can take it," he said with a shrug.

"Good." Jiyun pulled the dishtowel from her shoulder and draped it on his. "I'm done for the day and I need a nap. So — have fun. The kitchen's just through there." She pointed to the door. Keahi sighed at the sound of the piano coming from it.

"Problem?" she asked.

He shook his head.

"It's just Odette, she's a sweet girl."

"Yeah, I guess. Mahalo," he said, and she shook his hand.

"Have a good day."

When Keahi stepped into the room, Odette slid her foot and hit the glass of orange with her heel, knocking it over onto the floor.

He stopped and looked down at the traveling liquid as it spread across the tile from her glass. Keahi glared at her as she continued to focus on the piano.

"Are you kidding me?"

"Oops." She shrugged.

"You're enjoying this, aren't you."

"Of course not." She glanced at him as he got down on his knees to wipe up the mess. He pulled the rag off of his shoulder. "Besides, you're the one who wanted to work for the family. I'm just helping you do your job."

When he looked up at her, she smiled sweetly.

"Because you're a princess, who needs slaves to do everything for her."

"They're servants and I'm not a princess! In fact, I think you should call me Miss Thomsett and stop with this princess nonsense."

"Yeah, in your dreams."

Keahi put the wet rag in the glass and stood up.

"Do you want another?" he asked.

"Yes, please."

"Well, you know where the kitchen is."

She humphed. Odette crossed her arms and tried to slouch back as he walked off and she almost fell off of the piano bench.

Luckily, she caught herself, and he didn't see.

TOVALEY B. KYSEL

9   THROUGH THE FIRE

Mr. Baskerville requested the same thing of Odette the next few days as soon as she came downstairs from her bedroom. Though it was always morning still, she didn't question his habits. She was just happy to do things that involved being nowhere near Lailoken.

Odette went straight to the kitchen, and frowned when she spotted Keahi who was washing dishes at the sink. She glanced around. They were alone. She went right up to him.

"What's with the glasses?" she asked, acknowledging the black-framed spectacles that were sitting on his face. He shrugged and dried his hands before readjusting them.

"It's my Clark Kent look," he said, tucking a couple of loose strands of his dark hair behind his ear, while most of it was messily bound together by a rubber band.

Odette raised her eyebrows.

"So you're Superman now?"

"You said it, not me."

"Does that disguise really work on anyone?"

"You'd be surprised." He grinned.

He was pleased with himself.

"Well, I like it. It's cute." Her large green eyes scanned over his face before bringing her attention back onto his eyes. "It hides all the parts of your face that remind me you're actually an asshole." She smiled.

He narrowed his eyes as he leaned his lower back against the sink. "What a dirty mouth," he said as he took the glasses off and pushed his hair back. "For such a pristine little *princess*."

She pursed her lips together at the mention of that word.

"You'd be surprised." The corner of her mouth twitched in a subtle smirk as she gave him a once over. She licked her lips and raised an eyebrow. Odette grazed her teeth gently against her bottom lip before spinning on her heels as other kitchen workers started coming in. "I'll be in the pool, can someone, who's not Keahi, please bring me a virgin Lava Flow?" Odette asked as she got a wine glass from the cabinet and poured Mr. Baskerville his glass. "Thank you!" she said as she turned around and pressed her back against the door to leave. Keahi just shook his head and put his glasses back on. Pushing his hair back, he turned to the sink.

"I wasn't gonna be the one to do it anyway," he mumbled to himself.

Jiyun ran up to him as he turned the faucet on. She was still wrapping her hair up in a bun.

"Was Lailoken's fiancée just flirting with you?" she asked. Keahi barely glanced at her.

"What?" Keahi scoffed. "That was *flirting*? Here I thought she hated me."

She nodded, pinning her hair up. "That was a sexual innuendo, hello. You'd be 'surprised' what other dirty things she's capable of doing with her mouth. Come on, it's like when guys say they're good with their hands. They want you to think about it. She wants you to think about it! Her mouth, her lips. I saw her bite her lip. She was trying to get you to look at her mouth!"

Keahi rolled his eyes.

"One, you're ridiculous, and two, if that's how high-borns flirt then I understand this society even less than I thought I did."

"Odette knows she's attractive," Jiyun said as she grabbed a dishtowel to dry the dishes as he finished them. "Do you have any idea how much the Baskervilles paid for her? And girls who look like *that* in this society are only really useful for one thing. But as long as you don't do anything about her flirtations, it should be fine. Otherwise she'd get in trouble."

"What?" he asked, not that he intended to do anything. He could hardly wrap his mind around the fact she may or may not have flirted with him.

Not that he believed she did.

"Only the men are allowed to commit adultery," Jiyun said, leaning against the counter as she dried the pitcher. "Don't you know that? They go to brothels all the time. Men can sleep with any woman as long as she isn't married. It's in the Constitution."

"So, Lailoken could cheat on her —"

"She can't do anything about it. He owns her. The Baskervilles own all of us. But I won't tell."

He frowned. "For what reason would you have to keep it a secret?"

She just shrugged. "What reason do I have to tell any of them? I admit, I can't say I particularly like Lailoken anyway. Odette, on the other hand, is a nice girl."

"Is she?"

"*Yes*," Jiyun told him sternly. "She *is*. So don't hurt her — and don't get yourself into trouble. I can't imagine the punishment for the man who lays with another's wife. I assume it's even worse if you're a servant."

"Whoa, hang on, I'm not gonna sleep with her."

She shrugged.

"I'm just saying, you never know where things will lead. Attraction is a crazy thing."

"I'm not attracted to her."

"Maybe not. You're a little more difficult to read since anger seems to be your front emotion. But she's definitely attracted to you. I don't think she realizes it yet, though."

"How would you know?"

"Empathy," she whispered. He was about to ask and she nodded. "Yes, I am one." Jiyun put her finger against her lips. "I'm not a very strong one but — that girl's got some intense emotions. If I didn't already know she was a grot, I'd think she was an Empath too. Every time she looks at you, even I start feeling attracted toward you and no offense, but the only guy I've ever been attracted to is Min-Jae."

Keahi started to laugh.

"Why are you laughing?"

"Because it's funny."

She frowned. "Why is that funny?"

"You're trying to convince me that Princess Perfect has a crush on me. Do you know how ridiculous that sounds?"

"Why is it so ridiculous to you? Because you're part of the staff? It's not like Lailoken's a nice man, regardless of how charming he seems. Odette's not his first fiancée either."

"Wait, what? What happened to the others?"

"I'm not at liberty to say, but Odette's the third one. I guess we'll see what happens."

"Do you think she's in danger?"

"Aren't we all?"

Keahi felt a pang in his chest as someone turned on the blender.

Odette brought the glass of wine to Mr. Baskerville, and this time, his study door was wide open. Nonetheless, she knocked.

"I have your wine, Mr. Baskerville," she said, standing in the doorway.

He looked up from where he sat and raised his hand, acknowledging her to come forward.

"I appreciate you bringing this to me," he said, taking the glass from her. "I'm glad you've been feeling better. We've all been worried about you."

"Thank you," she said and smiled. "Me too."

She started to turn to the door.

"I almost forgot," he said and she turned around to face him again. "I'm sure you've noticed the lack of his presence, but Lailoken's been busy with work though things should die down within the week or two. He wanted me to let you know."

"Thank you, I appreciate that."

It only made being in that house easier to breathe in. She went to her room to change into her pale blue bikini and went back downstairs.

In the kitchen, Gentry made Odette's drink. He poured the pineapple-coconut blend in a glass, which was coated with strawberry puree, and slid it across the counter to Keahi.

He frowned.

"She said someone who's *not* me."

"Oh, is that what she said?   Because I heard, 'can no one but Keahi' —" Gentry shrugged his shoulders.   "None of us have a problem with her except you — and Pia — but that's another thing altogether. She's a nice girl. She's kind and helpful, why don't you like her? What's your problem with her?"

Keahi turned around and the rest of the staff looked away from him.

Jiyun just smirked to herself.

He groaned.

"Fine." He grabbed a straw and stuck it in the drink, that mixed with the strawberry, before heading toward the door.

"You can at least try to be nice!" Kiko shouted and he just waved his hand behind him. "He's not going to be nice, is he."

Kiko looked over at Gentry.

"Well, as long as he doesn't spill the drink on her, then it'll go better than I think it will."

Odette waited in the pool for someone to bring her the Lava Flow. She was at war with herself on whether or not she actually wanted *Keahi* to be the one to do it. Part of her didn't, but a stronger part of her did.

She waded in the water when she saw a shadow against the wall in the house, and then another. Odette put her arms up at the edge of the pool and narrowed her eyes.

It was Keahi — and Pia.

She scowled as she watched Pia push him up against the wall, running her hand against the front of Keahi's chest. Odette rolled her eyes and pushed away from the side of the pool.

A few seconds later, she heard the door open, but she didn't turn around.

"Here's your drink."

"You're not going to bring it to me?" she asked as she slowly turned to face him.

"I'm not your cabana boy."

"That's for sure, because a cabana boy would at least have some manners," she snapped. Odette wasn't sure what had gotten into her. She clenched her jaw and slowly moved toward him.

"Here's some manners for you, you shouldn't be drinking anything while in the pool anyway. What if you get stomach cramps and I'm going to have to —" Keahi put the drink down on the table. He narrowed his eyes. "Are you wearing my key in the pool?"

She looked down and then shrugged. Odette pulled the chain off and reached her hand out to hand it to him. "Sorry."

He stepped to the edge of the pool to grab it from her, but instead of letting him have it, she grabbed his wrist and yanked him into the pool with her.

Keahi broke the surface of the water and pushed his wet hair out of his face.

"What the fuck, Odette?"

She averted her eyes. She knew what had gotten into her. Keahi had been her secret, cooped up in her bedroom, and now she had to share him.

And she didn't like it.

"Can you please stop being so mean to me? Please?" She put the key back around her neck and returned her attention to his eyes. "I know you're annoyed with me but this could be easier — for the both of us — and would probably go a lot faster if you'd drop the attitude. I will let you go home, I told you that. But for now, I still need you. *Please*."

Keahi didn't say anything. He just got out of the pool and went back inside.

Odette sighed and got out too.

Kiko started to laugh as soon as Keahi came back into the kitchen. She clapped her hands together as she fell against Gentry.

"What happened to you?"

Keahi looked down at his wet clothes and at the puddle forming at his feet where he stood. "I — uh —" He clenched his jaw. "I fell in the pool."

Gentry cringed.

"You didn't spill the drink, did you?"

"No, I put it down."

Odette came in soon after, a towel wrapped around her body.

"I thought I said someone who's *not* Keahi?"

"The rest of us were busy," Kiko said as she turned around.

"I must have heard you wrong," Gentry said with a shrug.

Odette put her glass down on the center counter and looked at Keahi. She glanced down at the wet, white shirt clinging to his muscular body. Biting down on her bottom lip, she left quicker than she had come in.

Jiyun came up behind him. "She wants you," she whispered over his shoulder.

"Stop."

Later that evening, a few of the kitchen staff and some of the other servants, had gathered in the kitchen to tell stories, and listen to some of the many Mrs. Hamasaki had to tell about her life as a little girl, and her parents immigrating to Hawai'i.

When Keahi never came up to kiss her goodnight, Odette crawled out of bed and tiptoed down the stairs to the kitchen, where she ended up distracted by Mrs. Hamasaki's story about what it was like to fall in love with Kiko's father.

The way her eyes would light up at the mention of him, Odette could just tell the woman was truly in love. She knew she could listen to her talk about him all night.

"Love is beautiful," Mrs. Hamasaki said, "but it's soul crushing as well. Especially when you're in love with someone you can't have."

Odette glanced at Keahi, and looked away when he caught her.

Her cheeks reddened.

"Do you regret it, Mom?" Kiko asked. Mrs. Hamasaki didn't even take a second to ponder the thought. She just shook her head.

"Not one moment of it. I'll still believe he's the love of my life for as long as I live, and I could never be so selfish to ask him to leave his home for me. Love is about sacrifice, and that's putting their needs over your wants."

Keahi scratched his jaw. He glanced at Odette through his hair that curtained the side of his face.

Her voice bounced around in his head.

She needed him.

His gaze dropped to the chain of his key that was tucked into the front of her loose tank top.

He only *wanted* to go home. He didn't need to.

Keahi sighed and turned his attention back onto Mrs. Hamasaki.

Odette fell asleep on the counter and Keahi carried her back to her room. He put her down on her bed, and she slowly awoke. She grabbed his arm. "Wait," she said.

"Yeah?" He took a seat on her bed beside her as she sat up.

"Have you ever been in love?" she asked. "Is it like what Mrs. Hamasaki says? Is that how it feels? It seems so vulnerable — and sad."

"Isn't it?" he said. "You're trusting someone to not hurt you. To be gentle and to respect you. Hearts are in cages for a reason. But I wouldn't know if that's how it feels, or if it's worth it." He shook his head and scratched at his scalp. "I mean, she thinks it's worth it so I'll take her word for it, I guess. I've never been in love."

"I wanted to love him, you know. I wanted to love whoever bought me, but I wanted them to love me too. I thought, if I did everything right, it would work out the way I wanted. Then it didn't." She pursed her lips together. "Why do we get punished for being too trusting?"

"I don't know," he said, meeting her gaze. "But you didn't deserve this." He kissed her forehead. "Go to sleep."

He got up.

"Thank you," she said.

Keahi turned around. "For what?"

Odette fumbled with the key around her neck.

"Staying."

He nodded as she got comfortable in her bed. He could try harder to be nicer.

Odette often played with the radio while the staff worked in the kitchen. Whenever an eighties song came on, she would squeal happily and turn it louder. Mrs. Hamasaki would have to scold her to turn it down if Mrs. Baskerville was home, but when she wasn't, she allowed her to blast the music as loud as she could. It made Odette happy, dancing around the kitchen as she sang along.

Keahi thought it was a nightmare.

Every time she'd turn it on, he'd make sure to turn it off whenever he'd pass the radio. If he especially disliked the song, Keahi would go out of his way to turn it off.

Most times, Odette would turn it back on when he'd walk away from it.

Through the Fire by Chaka Kahn was the only tape in the stereo, and as soon as Odette had noticed, she played it almost every day.

He hated that song.

She would always start off singing along with the song and swaying her hips. As the song would continue, eventually she'd turn it into a playful dance. Mrs. Hamasaki mostly let Odette do whatever she wanted, as long as she didn't take anything off.

She ran her fingers through her hair as she leaned against the counter; her hands traveling down her body. Odette held everyone's attention.

Including Keahi's, and she noticed.

She was always most daring with him, probably because he had already nearly seen her in her underwear the first night she summoned him, and she didn't feel shy around him.

Keahi would just look at her and shake his head; a small smirk started to form, though never completely spread across his face. Nonetheless, he never took his eyes off of her.

She grabbed his hand and tugged him toward her.

"Dance with me," she told him.

"I can't dance."

"Everyone can dance," she said, and turned around to purposely bump him with her butt.

"Okay, I just don't dance."

"Boo! You're boring."

Whenever the chorus came on, Odette would lean back against the wall again. She'd slide one hand down the curve of her body and point at him.

Every time it happened, he hated the song a little less.

"You still think I'm ridiculous?" Jiyun asked in one breath as she came up beside him and he quickly averted his eyes away from Odette.

"I don't know what you're talking about. She's just having some fun. It's harmless."

"If it's so harmless, why don't you go dance with her?"

"Because I don't dance."

"I think you're scared."

"Oh, really?" he asked as he turned to her. "Of what?"

She leaned toward him and whispered, "liking her back and not being able to have her."

Keahi clenched his jaw as Jiyun walked away.

The lyrics of the song weren't helping either.

He moved around the counter and turned the stereo off.

"Hey!" Odette ran up to him. "I was listening to that."

"Can you stop fooling around? Some of us are trying to work."

"I was just trying to have some —"

He turned to face her.

"Work isn't supposed to be fun." Keahi's gaze dropped down to her lips and he turned away from her. "Why don't you go be a princess somewhere else?"

Odette didn't move from where she stood.

"What did I do?"

He didn't look at her again. "Mrs. Hamasaki, may I please take a break?"

Keahi was out the door before she could finish nodding.

Odette turned around to face the rest of the staff.

"Did I do something wrong?"

"I think Honey Buns is just moody," Kiko said. "I mean, sometimes it does get a little hot in here and trust me, Doll Face, that dance wasn't helping anybody." Kiko started pulling on the front of her own shirt to cool herself down.

Odette smiled at her, but she couldn't fully pull her attention away from the door.

When she finally managed to slip away from the kitchen, she came across Pia coming up the stairs from the servant quarters.

Pia didn't say anything, but fixed her hair and smirked as she passed Odette. She wiped the corner of her mouth and shook her head.

Odette frowned and went down the stairs. She found Keahi sitting on his bunk against the back wall, his head was tucked down in his hands.

She knocked on the open door.

"I'm sorry for what happened in the kitchen."

Keahi rubbed his eyes beneath his glasses and looked up at her. He shook his head and pushed his hair out of his face. "It's not your fault," he said. "I'm sorry. I — um — I know you're trying to enjoy your time here and I'm just —"

"Still being an asshole?" she asked as she took a seat beside him.

He forced a chuckle. "Yeah, that. But I swear, I'm trying not to be."

She nodded. "I know you are." She pursed her lips together and faced forward. "I should probably spend less time in the kitchen anyway. Mrs. Hamasaki doesn't need my help anymore."

"I didn't know."

"Didn't know what?"

"I didn't know Mrs. Baskerville made you work. I thought —"

"I know what you thought." Odette shrugged. "I had no intention of telling you."

"Why?"

"Because." She got to her feet and turned around. "I didn't want your pity, Keahi. You would've just pitied me, right? Felt sorry for me? Well, I can live without it."

He looked up at her and nodded. Keahi got up.

"You're right," he said.

"That you'd pity me?" she asked.

"You can live without it," he said. "You're stronger than I thought."

Odette chewed on her bottom lip.

"Can you stop wearing those glasses?"

He furrowed his brows. "Why?"

"They're deceiving."

"I thought you wanted me to be nicer to you. I don't — I'm confused."

"I thought I did too." She shrugged as she moved toward the door. "But the truth is, I don't really know what I want."

She turned to leave.

"Odette."

She stopped in the doorway and turned around.

"What's wrong?"

She sighed. Odette glanced back at the door and pulled it shut.

"I had this friend," she started, averting her eyes. Even though he kept his focus on her, she seemed to want to look everywhere but at him. "Well, we weren't really friends, but he was my secret. He didn't — doesn't — like me very much, but I knew that I could rely on him. I knew he would protect me and keep me from harm. He was my secret, something I had all to myself. My safe place. Now I don't have that anymore." Her eyes began to water. "I don't have anything in this house."

"I'm sorry — I —"

Odette closed her eyes and shook her head.

"It's not your fault. Maybe you wouldn't have needed to escape me if I hadn't made things so miserable for you."

"I'll be whatever you need me to be, Odette. You just have to ask."

"Lailoken's schedule returns back to normal tomorrow." She finally met his gaze. "I just — I need to know you'll be there."

"I'll never be too far away."

"Thank you."

She opened the door and froze when she saw Gentry standing there.

"Well, this is awkward," he said, raising his eyebrows.

Odette's eyes widened.

"It's not what it looks like."

"It looks like you two were talking and needed some privacy."

"Then it's exactly what it looks like?" Odette glanced at Keahi, then looked at Gentry again. "I'm gonna go."

Gentry nodded.

"Yeah, that's probably a good idea."

He watched her go up the stairs. Keahi tried to walk past him and Gentry shoved him into their dorm and closed the door.

"Are you out of your mind? That's Lailoken's fiancée!"

"All we did was talk. She just wanted to make sure I wasn't mad at her. It was nothing."

"She was in our dorm, Keahi. Do you know what people do on beds?"

"Sleep?"

"Besides that. You know what I'm talking about."

"People don't need beds to have sex, you know."

"That's — that's not the point!"

"What's the problem, Gentry?"

He clenched his jaw and sighed. "Lailoken's not the most *stable* type. Especially when it comes to his property."

"Odette's not property."

"I know, but." Gentry turned around and lifted his shirt to show Keahi the scar that lined the back of his body. "He hit me with a heated iron rod when his last fiancée stopped to help me with something," he said, putting his shirt back down as he turned around. "Odette's fond of you, and he's the jealous type. His last one — she trusted me because I know sign language. We both had — have — deaf younger siblings. All she did was help me with something, Keahi. Imagine if he knew of your alone time with Odette."

Keahi nodded. "Okay."

"You're a good guy," Gentry said, he pat Keahi's shoulder. "Just be careful."

"I got it." He nodded. "Thanks. Wait —"

Gentry stopped and turned around again.

"What happened to them?" Keahi asked. "The others?"

"I think you already know, man." Gentry opened the door. "We should get back to work."

Keahi followed him back upstairs.

10 RIGHT HERE WAITING

It had been easier to pretend that Lailoken was no longer a problem while he was hardly in the house, but as soon as he returned to his normal schedule, Odette found herself slowly returning to her old ways. She would shrink in his presence, and become the submissive girl she was supposed to be.

The one he purchased.

From the kitchen, she had been on her way to bring Mr. Baskerville his wine, when she bumped right into Lailoken, spilling it on the front of his shirt.

"Look at what you did!" he snapped, while the glass slipped from her hands and onto the floor. "You're so stupid."

"I'm sorry." She dropped to the floor to pick up the glass and started drying the spot with the hem of her skirt. "I'll clean this up right away — and your shirt, I'm sorry —"

Lailoken pulled her back to her feet. She was shaking, hands grasping tightly onto the glass. "Come here," he said, tugging her into his arms. "You'll be more careful next time."

She nodded.

Keahi came up the stairs, holding a towel in his hand.

"I'll get that," he said. He knelt down in front of the two of them to dry up as much of the spilled white wine from the carpet. He glanced up at Odette, who mouthed a 'thank you' to him.

He got back to his feet.

Lailoken didn't let go of Odette. "Would you like me to take care of your shirt? You can change into a new one and I can get it to Quinlan —"

"She can do it," he said, finally releasing Odette from his arms. "Come on, Odette. Give the kitchen boy the glass and let's go."

She slowly handed it to him and walked down the hall with Lailoken. Odette glanced back at him and Keahi clenched his jaw.

Nothing changed over the next few days, aside from Lailoken's temper that seemed to increase the more he was around her. If she didn't do something, she was in the wrong. If she did, she was still wrong. She could never win with him.

Keahi sat backward on her vanity chair, facing her, while she paced her bedroom mumbling to herself of all the things Lailoken wanted.

"Lailoken wants me to share a room with him soon. He's getting restless, that I've been here for so long and he doesn't get why I'm not ready." She twisted the engagement ring on her finger. "He wants me to —"

"Is that what you want?"

She stopped in her tracks and frowned at Keahi.

"What?"

"What do you want?" Keahi asked, resting his arms in front of him over the back of the chair.

Odette furrowed her brows. "I want —" She shook her head. "I don't know what I want."

Such a simple question, but she didn't know what she wanted. Odette wanted... what Lailoken wanted her to want.

"I want — what he wants — I guess."

"Do you? Because it doesn't sound like it. I don't blame you. I mean, he's —"

"My fiancé."

"Yeah but —"

"No."

"Okay."

Keahi wasn't going to argue with her.

But things with Lailoken didn't change, no matter how much she hoped they would.

"I told you not to do that, Odette," he'd snap. He'd always raise his voice and hit something. Usually the wall, or the table. "Look what happened! See what happens when you don't listen? I do so much for you and you never listen to me."

Horrified, she'd always find herself apologizing, even if she didn't want to. Her bottom lip would quiver and she'd try not to cry, but sometimes she couldn't help it.

He'd only get angrier.

"Why are you being so sensitive? What the hell wrong with you?"

"I'm sorry."

She was a broken record, full of apologies. Odette didn't even know what she was apologizing for anymore. She just did it. As long as he didn't touch her. When he put his hands on her, fear itself seemed to run through her veins, taking the place of her blood.

It was lucky for her that he hadn't gotten physically violent, but she was growing tired of being blamed.

She was filled with confusion; Lailoken, her fiancé, treated her a certain way that she thought was normal. He would tell her what to do, and punish her if she didn't listen.

That was what relationships were.

She didn't like it.

Even without Mrs. Baskerville hounding her to do chores or help around the house, Odette found herself spending more time in the kitchen again.

Keahi was there, and being around him made her feel safe. She just wanted to feel safe.

"Pia's fond of you, you know." She looked down at the bowl he was mixing and he didn't look up at her.

"I know," he said simply.

"Oh. Well, are you fond of her?" she asked.

"I don't know. I'm a little... confused right now."

"By what?"

He shrugged as he put the whisk down. Keahi stuck his finger in the whipped cream.

"You should try it," he said, raising his finger to his mouth as he nudged the bowl toward her. "I make a damn good whipped cream."

Odette glanced at the bowl and then at his finger. She wrapped her hand around his and leaned forward, sticking his finger into her mouth. Her lips pressed gently around it as she pulled it out, clean. Odette pressed her tongue to the tip and then licked up the side of his finger.

"That was good," she said, licking her lips. "Want me to try anything else?"

"N — no." His voice cracked and he cleared his throat. "No."

"What are you two doing in here?" Mrs. Hamasaki asked and Odette spun around, startled.

"Tasting dessert," she said with a sweet smile. "I have to say, I'm looking forward to it." She glanced at Keahi before letting herself out.

Mrs. Hamasaki put her hands on her hips. "Was she talking about the whipped cream or should I be concerned?"

Keahi looked at his finger and curled it into his hand as he got up from leaning against the counter. "What — what are you trying to say?"

She raised an eyebrow. "You tell me." She crossed her arms. "Falling for a high-born is not a lot of fun, Keahi. It's heartbreaking."

"Why does everyone think I like her?"

"That wasn't what I said. Maybe you should think about that." Mrs. Hamasaki reached for the bowl. "I'll finish the dessert. Why don't you take a break? Everyone's downstairs for Abbey's birthday. You should join them."

"All right, thanks."

When he left the kitchen, Quinlan stopped him in the hall.

She dropped the laundry basket.

"Quin? You okay?" he asked, and her eyes began to turn white. She grabbed his shoulder, and her grip tightened. "Quinlan?"

"I know what you are." Her voice came out low and raspy. It wasn't her at all. "Keahi! Save her! Don't let her — don't let her end up —" the voice faded. Quinlan released her grip on Keahi's shoulder and started coughing. She rubbed her eyes.

Quinlan frowned at him. "Where did you come from?"

Keahi looked around as he picked up the laundry basket and handed it to her.

"I accidentally bumped into you, sorry."

"You okay?" She frowned. "You look like you just saw a ghost."

"Saw one, heard one..."

He shrugged.

Quinlan's eyes widened and she slumped into the chair behind her, loosely grasping onto the laundry basket. "It happened, didn't it. I —" She groaned. "Damn it, you two."

"I'm sorry, what?"

"Well, you're going to find out sooner or later. The house is haunted."

"I'm sorry." He shook his head. " *What*?"

She nodded.

"There are at least two ghosts that I know of. I thought I felt a third about a month ago, but nope. Just the same two." She crossed her legs and readjusted the basket on her lap. "What did they tell you?"

"To save her."

"Who 'her'? There's a lot of hers in this house."

"Didn't specify."

"Hm."

"What's it mean?" Keahi asked.

"It means don't worry about it." Quinlan got up from the chair. "We'll just forget this happened, okay? Please. Mrs. Baskerville always wants to know if they make contact and I just — I don't want to talk about it." Quinlan held the basket with one arm and raked her fingers through her thick black hair.

"Of course," he said. "I won't tell anyone. You going downstairs?"

"I'll see Abbey later tonight," she said with a grin as she walked away.

Keahi chuckled.

When he turned around, he bumped right into Mr. Wong.

"Where do you think you're going?" he asked.

"Downstairs? I heard there's a party."

"Not for you," he said. "Mrs. Baskerville wishes to see you."

"For what?"

Mr. Wong shrugged. "I don't meddle in her affairs. Come with me."

Odette peered around the corner as she watched Keahi walk off with Mr. Wong.

"Where are they going?" she asked Amaris, who was wiping the dining room table. Amaris's eyes flickered to the doorway before a smirk crossed her face.

"You like him, don't you."

Odette crinkled her nose. "Mr. Wong? Gross. He's like in his fifties. Maybe sixties?"

Amaris threw the dishtowel at her. "No, Keahi."

She laughed nervously and threw the towel back. "I don't know what you mean."

"You're turning red."

"You're embarrassing me!"

"You wanna know a secret?"

Odette nodded. Amaris glanced over at Kiko. She was coming up the stairs with Gentry following close behind. "Guess who I like."

"Gentry?"

Amaris shook her head. Odette clasped her hands over her mouth.

"Scandalous. It's —"

"Forbidden, I know. I know high-borns think it's bad. But sometimes there are just people who bring out the best in you. You don't always get a say in who does that. I see the way you are when you're around him, Odette. I see the way you look at him. I've never seen you act like that around Lailoken, and he's your fiancé."

"Keahi and I just have a little bit of history. But we're friends. There's nothing romantic or — sexual — going on between us."

"You're blushing again."

Jiyun laughed as she walked past the two of them.

"What's so funny?" Odette asked.

Jiyun turned around.

"'Just friends'." She made air quotations with her fingers. "Girl, *please*. I can feel your attraction for him a mile away."

Mr. Wong announced Keahi's presence, and when Keahi stepped into the room, it wasn't just Mrs. Baskerville. He only briefly glanced at Pia before directing his attention onto the older white woman.

"You wanted to see me?" he asked.

Chardonnay continued to rearrange a few things on her desk.

"Yes, Pia has expressed some concerns."

"About what?"

"She thinks you could be doing more, and quite frankly, I agree with her." She finally looked up at him. "You are to do more around this house and you are to listen to any instruction she gives you. Do you understand?"

He frowned. He didn't bother to glance back at Pia. "I thought Mr. Wong was in charge outside of the kitchen?"

"I asked you a question, Keahi. Do you understand me?"

"I understand."

"Good. You may both leave." She waved her hand and Keahi turned around. Pia followed closely behind him.

When she closed the door, he turned to face her.

"What are you doing?"

Pia stepped back and pressed herself against the wall. She tilted her head to the side and her eyes widened. "What ever do you mean?"

"Don't play innocent with me."

"She said you have to follow my orders."

"Instruction."

"What's the difference?"

"You'll see." Keahi stepped back from her. "You're messing with the wrong person."

"So are you," she muttered under her breath. Pia turned her head, she could hear Odette and Amaris in the dining room, and decided to invite herself in.

Odette fell silent rather quickly, and didn't take her eyes off of Pia.

"Guess who just ran into me?"

"Ran into you? I'm sure you ran into them."

Pia's lip curled. "Oh shut up, Amaris."

"Don't tell her to shut up," Odette snapped as she stood up.

Pia tilted her head slightly. "Are you just protective of all the kitchen workers?" she asked her, looking down at Odette. Pia wiped the corner of her lips with her thumb. "I know of one you seem to have — misplaced. But don't worry, I'm sure he's forgotten all about you, now."

Amaris grabbed Odette's shoulder.

"Go away, Pia. Don't have a toilet to clean?"

"Oh, I have other things to do with these hands." Pia smirked as she turned on her heels, and headed out the same way she had come in.

Keahi came in through the other door and Odette scowled at him.

"What? I had to see Mrs. Baskerville —"

"You're a pig."

Odette pushed him out of her way and left the dining room.

He looked at Amaris, who pretended she wasn't paying attention as she started setting the table.

"What the hell was that?"

She glanced up.

"Oh, um. Pia." Amaris fumbled with her collar as she stood there awkwardly. "Did you want me to maybe serve dinner tonight? Maybe you should just stay downstairs."

"Yeah, maybe."

He looked up at the staircase Odette had ran up.

Keahi inhaled deeply. He walked out of the dining room, checked his surroundings for anyone else, and disappeared.

"What the — don't do that!" Odette threw a pillow at him when he appeared in her room. "Get out of my room!"

"Not until you tell me what's bothering you."

"I told you that you were my safe place and you just —" She turned away from him as her eyes began to well up with tears. "You just..."

"I just what?"

"You're an asshole. Those glasses don't hide that anymore."

"What are you talking about? What did she say to you?" He reached out to touch her shoulder and she shrugged his hand off of her.

"She didn't have to say anything."

"Odette, can you please look at me?"

"No."

"Please?"

But she continued to face her bed. He moved in front of her and she tried to turn away from him. Every direction she turned to, he followed.

"I don't know what she said, or what she implied, but I didn't do anything. I didn't do anything. I know what I want, and she's not it."

Odette turned to look at him.

"What is this?" she asked. "What are we?"

"I thought we were friends."

"Are we?"

"Aren't we?" He took her hand and tugged her to sit beside him on her bed. "Listen, I'm only here because of you. You come first. Some girl in a skimpy maid outfit isn't going to change that."

Odette frowned. "She looks good in that outfit."

"She does."

Odette hit him in the shoulder and he laughed.

Odette stood out in the hallway, fixing the picture frames that had shifted from the wind. Lailoken had turned the corner, and leaned against the wall.

"Come here," Lailoken said, but she didn't move from where she stood. She fixed the next picture frame in the hall and took a step back to make sure it was straight. "Maybe you didn't hear me. I said, *come here.*"

"No." She didn't even look at him.

"No? Did you just tell me 'no'?"

"Are you trying to manipulate me, Lailoken?" she asked as she turned to face him and frowned. "You promised me you wouldn't." She crossed her arms and raised an eyebrow.

"Odette," he said, softening his tone. "*Please* come here."

"No," she said again. She felt a sense of power in her words. In her choice. "I have things to do. I don't want to disappoint your mother."

"I don't care what my mother told you to do. You will listen to me." His nostrils flared. "You are my wife."

"Not yet."

He scowled and turned around, going back the way he came.

"I wouldn't — talk back to him like that."

Odette turned around and Keahi was standing there wiping down the top of the polished handrail. He threw the towel over his shoulder once she faced him.

"Why not? It felt —" She sighed in relief and smiled. "It felt good."

"You could be in danger," he said as he took a step toward her.

"I can take care of myself, Keahi. I'll be fine."

"No, it's — no. It's not that."

"Then what?"

Keahi inhaled deeply and glanced at the portrait of Lailoken hanging on the wall, hovering over them. He returned his attention back onto her. "You're not his first fiancée, Odette."

Her eyebrows knitted together. "Well, what happened to the others?" she asked.

"I don't know. But I'll find out."

She tilted her head. "Then you don't know if I'm in danger. Maybe they got away."

"And maybe they didn't."

"Oh, are you worried about me?" she teased, and pushed him playfully against his shoulder.

"Yeah," he said. He didn't smile, and he didn't take his eyes off of hers. "I am."

"Oh, I — oh."

"Just please be careful. Because if something happens to you —"

"I know," she said. "You can't get home."

"No, I'm going to lose it."

She frowned. "What are you talking about?"

"Just please be careful. Please." He gave her a quick kiss against her temple and walked past her. She turned around; he was gone. Odette frowned at his sudden disappearance, but took a step back when Lailoken returned.

"No," he said. "You don't get to say no to me."

Lailoken grabbed her by the arm and yanked her toward him. She stumbled and fell against him.

"Hey!" Keahi shouted as he came up the stairs, like he had never been up there at all. He stepped between the two of them. "Leave her alone." He was at least five inches shorter than Lailoken, but Keahi wasn't threatened by him.

"Stay out of this," Lailoken snapped. He released his hold on Odette's wrist to crack Keahi in the jaw. Caught off guard, he knocked him to the floor.

"You fucking haole," Keahi mumbled as he sat up.

"What did you call me?"

He got up.

"I said, you fucking —" Keahi glanced at Odette. She looked horrified — wide shining eyes; jaw dropped. He touched his bloody lip and looked at his hand. "Nothing," he said in a softer tone. "I'm sorry. I was out of line."

"That's what I thought." Lailoken ignored Odette and walked down the hall, trying to be subtle about the fact that his hand hurt.

When Lailoken disappeared into his room, closing the door behind him, Odette grabbed Keahi's hand and dragged him into her room. She closed the door and leaned against it. She hit the back of her head against the wood and got up. Odette grabbed him by the hand again and pulled him toward her bed.

"Here, lie down," she said, as she pushed on his shoulder, trying to get him to sit but he wouldn't.

"Are you okay?" he asked as she gave up and plopped down onto her mattress. Keahi took a seat beside her. She forced herself to look at him and her gaze fell to his bloody lip.

"I'm so stupid, I'm sorry."

"Whoa, hey, you're not stupid, Odette. Don't say that about yourself."

"I'll be better. I'll try harder — I'll do what he says."

She got up and began to head to the bathroom but Keahi gently caught her wrist.

"Hey, listen. It's not your fault," he told her as she turned around. "I don't care what he tells you. It's not your fault. Please, do whatever you need to do." Keahi rubbed at his jaw as his hand slipped from her wrist. "I can take a punch."

"I don't want you to get hit because of me." Odette pressed her hand against his cheek and softly rubbed beneath his bottom lip with her thumb. "Look what happened to your face."

"Oh, are you —"

"Yes," she said, cutting him off as she pulled her hand away. "I'm worried about you. I care about you."

She went into the bathroom and returned with a warm, damp washcloth.

"But this isn't about me," he said. "It's about you." Keahi ran his tongue over the split in his lip as she sat down beside him. She pressed her hand against his cheek and turned his head to face her so she could press the cloth against the corner of his mouth. "His punch was weak anyway. He's probably one of those guys who work out but can't fight for shit."

She laughed and looked down, her hands fell into her lap.

"There we go," he said with a smile.

"What?" she asked, glancing back up at him.

He shrugged. "I like it when you laugh."

"I like it when you're nice to me."

"I'm sorry."

Odette shook her head. She turned to him again and wiped his chin with the cloth before dabbing the corner of his mouth. "I get it," she said. "I took you from your home and wouldn't let you leave." She frowned, pulling her hands back into her lap. "I guess Lailoken and I have more in common than I thought."

He started to protest, but she changed the subject before he had the chance to speak.

"Would you win?" she asked. "In a fight against him?"

"We're not really fond of violence —"

"That's not what I asked."

"Yeah," he said. "I'd win."

"Good," she said as she leaned her head against his shoulder. "He'd deserve to lose."

"He deserves more than that," Keahi mumbled and wrapped his arm around her slender frame. He rubbed her arm.

"You have rough hands —"

"Oh, sorry."

"No," she said and grabbed his finger when he tried to pull back. She put his palm back against her arm. "You must use them a lot. Are you good with your hands?"

He chuckled and shook his head, remembering what Jiyun told him.

"Yeah," he said, looking at her through her reflection in her vanity mirror. "I guess I am." He looked down at her from where he sat as she nestled against him. "You're going to be okay, right?" he asked.

"Yeah, as long as you're here," she said. "You make me feel safe."

The corner of his mouth lifted into a smile.

"Will you stay in here?" she asked. "I don't know where you go at night, but I don't want to be alone."

Keahi nodded. "If you want me to stay, I'll stay."

"I want you to stay." She glanced up at him. "Are you ever going to stop wearing those horrible glasses?" she asked.

"A pretty girl once told me it was cute. Haven't wanted to take them off since." Odette blushed and averted her gaze. "Oh, I didn't mean you. I meant Pia —" he said with a grin and she hit his arm. He started to laugh. "Oh, jealous — ow! Okay, okay!" She pushed him over on her bed and pinned him down. "You win."

Odette took the glasses off of his face and put them on her own. She blinked as she tried to see out of them.

"How the hell can you see out of these — are you blind?"

"I'm — adaptable."

She narrowed her eyes, only able to see a blurry version of his face. "Good answer."

"You should give them back before you strain your eyes." Odette took them off and returned them to his face.

"Lailoken wouldn't like me in glasses. But I think I'd look cute, don't you?"

"Nothing in the world could make you ugly, princess." He frowned slightly. "I mean, because you know, you've got a great personality and I just — I don't see that changing.   And — people say, you know, a beautiful personality makes a beautiful person."

"Do I make you nervous?" she asked.

"What makes you think I'm nervous?"

"You're rambling."

"Well, you're sitting on top of me."

"Oh, I'm sorry."   Odette slid off of him and Keahi sat up from her bed.

"You know, you're surprisingly strong for your size."

Odette laughed.

"Don't act like you didn't let me do that.   I think you secretly wanted me to."

"Then I guess the secret's out."

He smiled while she laughed, and playfully pushed against his shoulder.   But the smile soon faded at the remembrance of the ghost that briefly spoke to him through Quinlan.

TOVALEY B. KYSEL

11   PLEASE FORGIVE ME

Instead of being in the kitchen, where he was actually needed, Keahi was out in the halls wiping down vases and cleaning the stairs. He knew every single decoration on every vase Mrs. Baskerville owned in the entire house.

"You know why you're doing that, right?"

He stared blindly at the wall while he wiped the vase for the thousandth time that he almost didn't hear the person talking to him.

"What?" he said as he snapped out of his daze and looked up at Kaeli. Kaeli Chen, Mrs. Baskerville's personal maid. Kaeli and Min-Jae were the workers of the house people almost never saw. Kaeli was rarely allowed to leave Mrs. Baskerville's room except to sleep during hours Keahi wasn't aware of, and Min-Jae was always off fixing something or another. He had moved from being a kitchen worker to the handyman.

She wasn't dressed like the other maids. Instead of the short maid dress, she wore long pants and a blue tank top. Her hair was down too, another special privilege he supposed.

"You know why you're wiping vases, right?" she said as she crossed her arms and leaned against the door frame.

"Why?"

"Because with you in the kitchen, that leaves almost no work for Odette."

"But I do other things too. I clean up around the house. I —"

"Yeah, which is why she took something away from you that she thinks you enjoy."

"She thinks I enjoy being in the kitchen?"

"She thinks you enjoy being around Odette, and that no work is getting done in the kitchen."

"There are other workers in there besides us," he said.

"Oh, she knows. She's not doing it because she wants to. It was Pia who voiced a complaint. Truthfully, Mrs. Baskerville just doesn't like Odette. In fact, I think part of her hopes you'll just take Odette and runaway with her. It's actually quite fascinating, how much she dislikes that girl. I haven't had the pleasure of really being around her, but from what I've heard from Jiyun, she seems sweet."

"Ah, Jiyun."

Kaeli laughed. "I'm guessing she told you about her suspicions?"

"Yeah, she was very open about that." Keahi then elevated his eyebrows. "Mrs. Baskerville thinks Odette likes me too?"

"No, but I think she hoped she would when she brought you home. She doesn't think she's right for her son."

"I agree."

"So why haven't you?"

"Why haven't I what?"

"Taken her and run away?"

"We're friends."

"How long are you going to keep up with that?" Jiyun asked as she came around the hallway. She gave Kaeli a quick peck on the lips and crossed her arms, leaning against the wall.

"For as long as it's true?" He frowned and threw the cloth over his shoulder. "Why are all of you guys pushing me? What aren't you telling me?"

"The house is haunted," Jiyun said.

"Yeah, I know —"

"By the ghosts of Lailoken's ex-fiancées." Jiyun and Kaeli exchanged glances. "If someone doesn't get Odette out of here — she's probably going to die like the other two."

"See, no one's good enough for Lailoken Baskerville."

"But he does seem to have a special attachment to Odette —"

"Which Mrs. Baskerville hates —"

"What's gonna happen?" he asked. "When?"

Kaeli shrugged.

"None of them seem to make it to Christmas. Mr. and Mrs. Baskerville always take a cruise around the Hawaiian Islands during the last two weeks of November for their anniversary and stay on the Big Island for another two. Then after that — well."

"You care about her, right?" Jiyun asked, frowning at him. "I still can't read any of your emotions but you do, don't you? Look, whatever you do, just don't get caught."

"Why hasn't anyone told her?"

"Because she's a scion bride. They're all raised the same way, Keahi. They want love, the Bridal Expo was romanticized for them. But sooner or later they all come to the same realization. They're property, and their feelings don't matter."

"How do I know this isn't a trap?" He looked at Jiyun. "You told me to be careful. You told me what could happen. How do I know you guys aren't trying to trick me?"

"You don't," Kaeli said.

Keahi clenched his jaw.

Jiyun quickly went back downstairs when Mr. Wong came around the corner. He stared at Kaeli and then at Keahi, before crossing his arms.

"What are you two doing?" he asked.

"I was just telling him he missed a spot," Kaeli said, pointing at the vase.

Keahi groaned and pulled the rag from his shoulder.

"Do I really have to keep doing this?" he asked Mr. Wong who turned to leave. "This is ridiculous and a waste of time. I could be doing something useful and helping Mrs. Hamasaki."

He shrugged.

"Mrs. Baskerville's orders. Unless she decides you can do otherwise, you will continue to wipe her vases." He glanced at the vase. "You should be happy, it's not real work."

"I want to work. I'm bored out of my mind —"

"Work is boring."

"Not if you're doing the right job."

"Well then, how unfortunate it is that you belong to the Baskervilles."

He turned on the soles of his shoes and left faster than he had come.

Keahi looked at Kaeli.

"One of the ghosts wanted me to help her. They told me, through Quinlan."

"Then maybe that's what you need to do."

That night, Keahi sat at Odette's bay window. It was easier now, to go back to her room instead of to the Baskerville Cave, now that he wasn't confined to kitchen duty. Still, he missed it. The work beat wiping down vases any day. He should've known what he was getting into when he decided to work there.

Odette came out of her bathroom, wearing her usual pajamas that were thin enough to be underwear, and she had her hair wrapped up in a towel. She was calm, unbothered by what she didn't know. He didn't know how he was supposed to tell her.

"Keahi, why are you staring at me? Oh my god, can you see —" She looked down at her clothes to make sure it wasn't damp enough to be see-through. Her hands cupped at her chest before she quickly crossed her arms.

"Sorry," he said. "I kind of lost my train of thought for a second there."

"Oh, well I'm sure you're gonna get to go home soon. Aren't you excited?"

"What do you mean?"

She shrugged. "Like you said, I haven't had a nightmare in a while. I stood up to Lailoken again — and no one got hurt this time. I think I'm going to be okay here."

He frowned. "Do you know about the ghosts?"

Odette rolled her eyes and shook her head.

"I was told about them, but I haven't seen or heard anything. Except for Pia scaring me on the first night. Other than that, it's been quiet. Especially since you stopped my nightmares. So I don't think the house is haunted at all. Besides, I'm not afraid of a ghost story." She pulled the towel from her hair and continued to rub it against her head.

"You should be."

She stopped. Her arms lowered and she raised her eyebrows. "Excuse me?"

"It's just — you don't know what's going on in this house."

"I don't care —"

Someone knocked on her door and Keahi faded from sight.

Odette huffed and answered the door.

It was Pia.

"What do you want?"

"Who are you talking to?" Pia asked and peered into her room.

"Myself." Odette blocked her from stepping inside. "What do you want?"

"Well, I suppose it doesn't matter. I just wanted to thank you." She tucked a few loose strands of hair behind her ear and smiled.

Odette raised her eyebrows. "For?"

"Lailoken."

She frowned. "What about him?"

"He came back to me since you've been a brat. It was fun."

Odette pressed her lips together and nodded.

"Great, you have fun being his mistress." She tried to close the door, but Pia stuck her foot in the crack and blocked her from shutting it.

"How does it feel?" she asked, shoving the door back open.

"What?"

"Being unwanted?" Pia pressed her lips together and gave Odette a fake pout. "By your fiancé, by the kitchen boy... How does it feel to be second — to me?"

"Get out of my face!"

As hard as she could, Odette shoved Pia out of her way and slammed the door.

Keahi appeared in the hallway and turned around the corner. He rushed to help her up. Pia shook her head as she rubbed her temple with her fingers.

"Are you okay?"

"What just happened?" She closed her eyes tightly and kept her hand against the side of her head. "Where am I?" Pia glanced at him and frowned. "Who are you?"

"I'm — wait — you don't recognize me?"

"Should I? I'm sorry. Are you a friend of my brother's?"

"What —" Keahi started hitting Odette's door with his palm. "Odette!"

She opened the door. Odette looked at him, then at Pia. "Ugh." She started to close the door again.

"Wait. She hit her head — I don't think she remembers anything."

Odette rolled her eyes. "Please."

"Odette."

Pia looked up at her.

"Who is that?" she whispered to Keahi. "She's pretty."

"On second thought, I like her better like this." Odette stepped to the side and let Keahi carry Pia into her room. "What happened? She was fine a minute ago."

"Depends. What'd you do?"

"Why do you think I did something?"

Keahi put her down on Odette's bed. "She was right outside your door."

"Okay — so I pushed her."

"Why?"

"She made me angry."

"How?"

"It doesn't matter." Odette swept her gaze over to Pia. "What are we gonna do about her?"

"I don't know. She's mundane."

"What did you call me?"

Keahi knelt down in front of her. "What's the last thing you remember?"

Pia furrowed her brows. "My father married a woman who called people that."

"Mundane?" Odette asked, sitting beside her.

"Yes!"

"Do you think her father married a high-born?" Odette asked Keahi. She turned back to Pia. "Where's your father now?"

Pia's gaze dropped. "Dead. He died, and my brother and I..." She furrowed her brows again. "I don't remember."

Keahi grabbed Odette's hand to get her attention and her heart fluttered. She tried to ignore it.

"Do high-borns marry mundanes and sell their children?" he asked.

She looked down at their hands.

"I don't — I don't know. Maybe? Poorer women who haven't married and are looking for easy money."

"Are you saying my stepmom killed my dad?"

Odette tried not to show the disgust on her face at the sight of Pia sitting on her bed beside her. Especially with Keahi there too.

This was something she never in a million years would have ever imagined to happen.

The three of them in her room.

"I don't know, Pia. I don't know your life. You don't even know your life." Odette rolled her eyes and fell back against her pillow.

"You don't like me?"

Odette stared at her as Pia leaned over her.

"I really don't — and I would appreciate it if you got out of my face." She pushed Pia away from her.

"I'm gonna get Gentry," Keahi said as he got up from his kneel.

Odette sat up. "You're going to leave her with me?"

"You pushed her, princess." He shrugged. "Just give me five minutes. I'll be right back."

"You better."

She fell back against her bed as Keahi let himself out.

"So who is that? Is he your boyfriend?"

Odette rolled her eyes. "If I didn't know better, I'd think you were messing with me."

"Why? Are we not friends?"

"No, Pia. We are not friends — and this is weird."

"Why is it weird?"

"Oh my god. You don't shut up, do you?" Odette sat back up. "You don't like me, Pia. You never did. You scared me the first night I came here and now you're just..." Odette grabbed her pillow. She pressed it against her face as she fell back on her bed and groaned into it.

Keahi came back after what felt like an eternity. Gentry was right behind him.

"Who's that?" Pia asked Odette. Odette groaned again, not bothering to remove the pillow from over her face.

Gentry looked at Keahi. "Wow, you weren't kidding."

"What should we do?"

Gentry took a step forward and Pia scooted back up against the wall.

"I don't know but I don't think she likes me."

"What is everyone doing in — why is Pinup on Doll Face's bed?" Gentry and Keahi turned around. Kiko stood there in the doorway.

Gentry grabbed her wrist and pulled her into the room before shutting the door.

"Pia doesn't know she's a — you know."

"A what?" Pia asked.

"You're a concubine, Pia."

"Excuse me?"

"Odette!" Gentry said. "Why did you —"

"Who's concubine?" Pia asked. "Any of yours? How did I get here? Where's my brother?"

"What else do you remember?" Kiko asked as she sat down beside her. "Anything about your family?" She looked at Gentry. "Maybe we can contact someone."

Keahi shook his head as Pia began to cry.

Odette pushed her pillow off of her and slipped off of her bed. With Gentry and Kiko distracted with Pia, she pulled Keahi to the side.

"Do it," she said quietly, glancing at Pia.

"Do what?"

"Consume her fears." Odette crossed her arms. "I know what it feels like. It hurts. Look at her, Keahi. I don't like her but — I know that look. I was her before you got here. I was a mess. I can't stand to see someone else like that. Not even her."

He nodded.

"Okay." He rubbed the back of his neck. "We need to calm her down first or it'll be obvious."

"You didn't bother calming me down."

"You knew what I was — and you were fighting with me. You were a little distracted anyway."

"Right. Good times." Odette huffed and shrugged. "Well, just do what you have to do. Just make it stop, please."

Keahi rubbed his hands together and Odette grabbed his wrist.

"Just remember there are other people in the room."

"*Meow.*" Keahi raised his eyebrows and chuckled.

Odette frowned and pushed him toward Pia.

He sat down beside her as Odette watched the them all in the mirror of her vanity.

"We all work for a family called the Baskervilles," he began, as he looked up at Gentry and then at Kiko who was sitting beside Pia. He put his arm around her, and she sank against him. "Most days, it's not so bad."

"I'm someone's concubine?" Her voice was shaky.

"Well, you're mostly a maid now," Kiko said. "I don't remember the last time Lailoken —"

"Today, apparently." Odette stared at them from her mirror. She turned around and leaned back against her vanity. "That's why she was at my door. To gloat about it."

"Who's Lailoken?" Pia asked.

"My fiancé."

Pia's eyes widened and she buried her face into Keahi's neck. Odette averted her gaze.

"It'll be okay," Keahi said. He rubbed her shoulder and kissed her forehead. "I promise."

"Thank you," she said softly. "You're very comforting." Pia looked over at Odette. "You're lucky."

"What makes you say that?"

"Well, aren't you two —"

Kiko raised an eyebrow and crossed her arms as she looked from Odette to Keahi.

"No," Odette said sharply. "We are not. Like I said, Lailoken is my *fiancé*."

"We should take her down to my mom. Maybe she'll know what to do." Kiko reached her hand out to Pia. Pia looked up at Keahi and he nodded at her. She took her hand and stood up.

"Not coming, Honey Buns?"

Keahi shook his head and turned his gaze to Odette.

"Odette and I have something to talk about."

"Okay, see you." Kiko led the way outside. As Gentry backed out of the door, he pointed at Odette and Keahi and then pointed at his eyes. At first, his expression was serious, but then it turned into a broad smile as he closed the door.

"What did you want to talk about?" Odette asked.

"That could've outed me, you know."

"I know," she said softly. "I just — I needed it to stop." Keahi pat her bed beside where he sat and she got up from against the vanity. Odette took a seat beside him and crossed her legs. "She just reminded me of me. Of that night." Odette glanced at Keahi. "Of everything you've done for me. I had to ask, I'm sorry."

"It's okay," he said. Keahi wrapped his arm around her and she leaned against him. "Like I said, you come first."

"What's gonna happen to her?"

He shrugged.

"Maybe she'll be able to fake it like I can."

"We can't just — release her?"

"*Odette.*"

"What?"

"We have no money to give her."

"But won't she just get manipulated again?"

Keahi shook his head. "I kissed her forehead. She'll be immune to a Pusher's manipulation for at least a week or two unless I do it again —"

"You're not —"

"— or she develops her own immunity." Keahi grinned. "This is a new side of you I haven't seen. Jealous much?"

"I told you," she said. "You were my secret, and I don't like to share. Especially with Pia."

"Don't worry," he said, rubbing her arm. "The only person I'll kiss is you — uh — the only forehead I'll kiss is yours."

"You talk too much."

"I know, it's my only flaw."

Odette scoffed. "Whatever you say, Clark."

"Are you ever going to stop making fun of my glasses?"

"When you stop calling me princess."

"Then I guess that's a never."

Odette grinned up at him. He kissed her forehead.

"You should go to sleep," he said. His hand fell from against her arm and he stood up.

Odette fell back against her bed and looked up at him.

"Since I'm the only person you'll kiss," she teased.

"You're never gonna let that go, are you."

She pressed her lips together and shook her head as she snuggled against her pillow. "Not a chance."

He just shook his head and turned off her light.

12 CARELESS WHISPER

Mrs. Hamasaki managed to convince Pia to play along with being a maid. Apparently she had been easily convinced to being attracted to Lailoken, since she already found him physically desirable.

Odette shuddered at the thought.

Pia seemed to work harder now too than she did while under manipulation, and Mrs. Baskerville didn't have much choice but to let Keahi go back to the kitchen when Amaris got sick.

Odette couldn't deny the feelings she knew she began to develop for him. During dinners, she often found herself drinking more water than she needed to, just so he'd come near her and refill the glass. She'd drop her napkin on the floor so he'd pick it up.

"You dropped this, Miss Thomsett," he'd tell her in that smooth voice of his, and she'd sit back so he could put it on her lap. His face always got close to hers when he did it. The corner of his mouth would curve into a subtle smirk that only she saw.

It wasn't because she enjoyed him waiting on her, but because of how safe she felt when he was near, and that was the only way to get him to come closer during the times she felt unsafe.

Every morning, after she'd bring Mr. Baskerville his wine, she'd often sit on the counter in the kitchen while Keahi worked. While he cleaned. While he cooked.

Though she pretended not to pay attention to him, and would help Mrs. Hamasaki whenever she would ask, she'd often catch herself gazing in his direction. It was worse when he'd decide it was too hot to work with his shirt on. Not that she or anyone else complained.

Aside from Mrs. Hamasaki.

"Put your shirt back on! You are not a stripper!"

"Let him leave it off! Take off some more, Honey Buns!" Kiko would shout.

"Kiko!" She glared at her daughter and turned to Keahi. "Clothes! Now!"

"But Mrs. Hamasaki, I'm dying. It's hot."

"No one else thought so until you took off your shirt! Put it back on!" she yelled and threw a dishtowel at him. "Imagine if Odette had taken off her clothes when she would dance around here?"

Keahi glanced at Odette.

She blushed and looked away.

He rarely listened to her though. Usually he'd just readjust his glasses and laugh, shrugging off her suggestions. Eventually, Mrs. Hamasaki would let it go.

Eventually.

It was after one of those days in the kitchen, that made Odette feel bold.

After a shower, she stared at herself in the foggy mirror as she wrapped a towel around her body. She inhaled deeply, and opened the door that led into her bedroom.

Keahi sat at her vanity, but he turned around when the door opened.

"Are you still feeling hot?" she asked.

His lips parted at the sight of her, but he didn't say a thing.

"The bathroom's still hot from my shower. Maybe you should take a cold one."

She moved to her dresser and his gaze followed. Odette tried to keep herself from blushing.

It was difficult though, now that his attention was on her. She dropped her towel and opened the dresser drawer.

"Keahi, are you going to take a shower?" she asked once silence filled the room.

"Huh? Oh." He shook his head and stood up, pushing his glasses up the bridge of his nose. "Right."

She cupped her hand over her mouth and laughed to herself after he closed the bathroom door. Odette turned back to her dresser and put on her usual pajamas.

She crawled onto her bed and continued to towel dry her hair as she turned on the television. Her hair was nearly dry by the time the bathroom door opened.

She looked up and he was shirtless again, with his towel draped around his neck and over his shoulders. His body was still wet from the water, and the glasses were now absent from his face. The only thing he wore was board shorts.

"What are you watching?" he asked.

"What?" She blinked stupidly. He was looking at the TV screen. "Oh, um The Breakfast Club."

"Never heard of it," he said as he turned away from it. She frowned.

"You know who Superman is but you've never heard of The Breakfast Club? It's a classic!"

"Superman came out in the thirties, and we don't have television in the Woolgathering."

"Will you tell me what it's like? After you put on your shirt?"

He laughed. "You sound like Mrs. Hamasaki."

"Oh, I'm not complaining," she said as she looked at his chest. "I just won't be able to focus on what you're saying if you're planning to keep it off."

"Well, I am in the presence of someone's fiancée, who isn't mine, so I'll obey." He pulled the shirt over his head, but didn't fully put it on. "You should go to sleep though, it's late." Keahi leaned forward and kissed her forehead. "Goodnight, princess."

"Are you ever going to stop calling me that?" she asked.

"If you can honestly tell me that you don't like it, then I'll stop."

Her lips parted, but no sound came out. She couldn't say that, because it grew on her.

Princess.

It no longer felt like an insult.

Keahi turned off her light and her television while she crawled beneath her sheets. He went to her bay window and put the towel down on the seat so he could put on his shirt.

"You have a nice back," she said and he turned around.

"Go to sleep."

"Fine."

He hung the towel up to dry on the shower curtain pole and she was asleep by the time he came back out. Keahi went back to the bay window, and sat down. Rain began to fall, increasing in severity as the night went on. Within an hour, his attention was drawn back to Odette.

She was dreaming about him.

About them.

He frowned slightly, then his eyes widened.

It was going to be a long night. He scratched his jawline and looked back outside, trying to concentrate on the flickering streetlamp.

But her dream was as clear as if he were having it himself.

His face flushed; lucky for him, it was dark, and he was the only one awake.

Keahi sat beside her on her bed while the two of them watched one of her favorite movies from the eighties. Her eyes kept wandering over to him; to watch his expressions, but primarily to see if she'd ever catch him looking at her. Most of his hair was bound by the rubber band, though several loose strands fell around his face, and those bulky black-framed glasses he insisted on wearing, hid too much of it. More than she liked.

He readjusted himself against the wall.

"Are you uncomfortable?" she asked. "You can lie down, if you want." She scooted forward on the mattress so that he could do so behind her.

"You sure you don't have a problem with that, princess?" he asked and glanced at her.

"No," she said, a smirk peeking at the corner of her lips.

Keahi lay down on the bed and made himself comfortable. He was lying on his back, his hand resting against his stomach as he turned his head to keep his attention on the television. Odette leaned back against him and fumbled with the remote. She bit down on her bottom lip, and looked at him again.

"Do you actually want to watch this?" she asked. "We can watch something else — or do something else."

"Like what?" he asked, his eyes remained locked on the screen.

She sighed. Keahi was hardly paying attention to her.

Odette twisted her body so that she could climb on top of him and he finally turned his attention onto her once she was sitting in his lap.

"What are you doing?" he asked, pushing some of his hair out of his face.

"What you're too afraid to do," she said as she pulled off her tank top. She dropped it

on the floor and returned her attention to him. "Some of us aren't scared to go after what we want."

"You think I'm scared?" He didn't take his eyes off of hers, despite wanting to let his gaze linger over the curves of her body.

Odette ran her tongue against her bottom lip. "What happened to that boy who came into my room with fire in his eyes?" she asked. "I didn't take him for the submissive type. It's... disappointing." Odette moved her leg and slipped off of his lap and back onto the mattress. "Chicken," she said over her shoulder as she got up from her bed.

"You're calling me names now?" he asked as he sat up. Keahi took his glasses off and put them down on her bedside table as she turned off the television and put the remote down on her dresser.

"Maybe," she said, without looking back at him. "I mean, sometimes a woman just wants to feel like she's... desired."

Keahi got off of the bed. He walked up to her and she turned around to face him.

"First of all," he said, looking down at her. "I'm not a boy. I'm a man."

Odette glanced at his mouth before leaning closer to him; hers now only inches away from his. She looked up at his eyes. "Prove it." Her lips brushed against his as she spoke.

"If that's what you want, Miss Thomsett."

Before she could say another word, Keahi's mouth crashed against hers. With such force and demand, Odette had to take a step back, and leaned against the wall for support.

She found her hands tangled in his hair while his were on her waist, pulling her hips against his. His hands slid down her back and he groped her butt. Their mouths parted as she lifted her leg, curling it against his body. She stared at him with challenge in her eyes as he ran his hand against her bare thigh. Keahi lifted her in the air and she wrapped her legs around him.

His mouth moved to her neck and she gasped softly when his teeth gently grazed against her skin. Odette giggled as the scruff on his face tickled her skin but she inhaled sharply when he made his way to her collarbone. One hand still knotted in his hair, the other found his shoulder. He pulled her away from the wall, and she pressed her hands against his cheeks so that her lips could meet his again. Keahi leaned in to the kiss, and then pulled away just before he threw her onto her bed.

She looked up at him and gripped at the hem of his shirt. "Take it off," she demanded as he got down beside her.

He reached behind him and pulled his shirt off, and dropped it on the ground. She ran her hand against his bare chest as Keahi leaned forward, his hand gently caressing her cheek.

He pressed his lips against hers. His coarse hand slipped beneath her bra and squeezed at her, before traveling down her figure.

He slipped his hand between her legs.

She gasped, and he smirked against her parted lips. He tilted his head and nibbled at her neck as she trapped his hand with her thighs. Odette arched her back, fingers gripping at his hair while her other hand gripped at her bed sheet. With every moan that escaped her lips, Keahi moved his hand a little faster. She dropped her knees against the mattress and he ran his fingers over the edge of her underwear before slowly slipping a finger beneath it, and into her; then another.

He curled them, and pressed in deeper.

"Fuck."

"What a dirty mouth," he whispered against her neck, "for such a pristine little princess."

"I hate you," she said between gasping breaths.

"Not yet you don't."

He pumped his hand harder while his mouth explored her body. Odette squeezed her thighs against his hand as her back arched again. Her chest rose and fell rapidly as her breathing increased. She let go of the sheet and grabbed his shoulder.

Keahi sat up when she swore at him again, with a smug grin plastered on his face. He got up from the bed and pulled her legs toward the edge of the mattress as he knelt on the ground. Odette sat up, holding herself up with her elbows as she watched him push her skirt back.

He looked up at her.

"Ready to hate me?" he asked, pushing her legs back against her. He ran his hands down the backs of her thighs. He leaned forward. His hair tickled her inner thighs.

Odette's arms gave out when she felt his tongue press against her and she fell back on the mattress. Her fingers tangled in his hair again as she pushed him against her. His lips and his tongue had her squirming beneath his hold; one hand tight on the sheets, moans lingering on her lips, and sweat beading on her forehead.

Keahi looked up at her as she tried to sit up. She tossed her head back, chest rising and falling as she struggled for air.

Her body trembled.

He planted a trail of kisses on her inner thighs. "How do you feel?" he asked, running his rough hands along her legs.

Her breathing was heavy.

Odette tilted her chin down to look at him.

"Like a princess."

Sleepily, Odette rubbed at her eyes and sat up in her bed. She lowered her hands and saw Keahi sitting at the bay window, looking outside. He was already wearing his work clothes for the day.

She remembered her dream so vividly, she could almost feel the material of his shirt against her fingers as she tugged at it, wanting to him take it off. Demanding him to take it off.

She blushed profusely and she turned away from him, trying to slip out of her bed unnoticed.

When she stood up, he was standing right in front of her.

"Sleep well?" he asked.

"Goodness, you scared me! Don't do that!" Her hand was over her heart while it beat rapidly in her chest. Odette fanned herself with her hand as she inhaled deeply and nodded; avoiding making eye contact with him.

She was still embarrassed by her dream, and he was standing right there. Inches away from her. "Like a princess," she said, finally bringing her gaze to meet his. Her lips parted slightly while her eyes scanned his face. Odette glanced at his mouth for no longer than a second before she realized what she was doing. She brought her eyes up to meet his again. "Very well," she said, correcting herself. "I slept very well."

"Great," he said. "Can I go home now?" he asked, and she looked down at his hand that was now extending out to her. He waited for her to hand over his key.

She didn't want to. Her hand curled around the skeleton key hanging over her chest.

"No," she said, a little disappointed by his question.

"Why not? You haven't had another nightmare since I got here. I should probably get going. I've been away for a while now."

She frowned. "Because if you leave, they'll come back."

"You don't know that."

"Neither do you." Odette sighed, fumbling with the skeleton key between her fingers. "Please," she said, looking up at him again. "Just a little longer. Why are you suddenly in such a rush to leave?" she asked. "I thought we were friends now. I thought you'd stay for me."

This time, it was he who found himself staring at her lips as she spoke, in such a way that she knew he longed to kiss them.

Odette was tired of waiting for him to make the first move. She stepped forward and pressed her body up against his, and lost herself when their mouths collided in a kiss. She grabbed his wrists and put his hands on her waist before draping her arms over his shoulders. Odette touched the back of his neck and pulled him closer to her, fingers knotting in his hair.

Her lips were softer than he imagined, and kissing her felt like the sweetest sin, but a sin nonetheless. He turned away from her, severing the connection their mouths made and any connection they made. He dropped his hands from her waist and grabbed her arms to pull them down from his neck. Keahi didn't say anything.

He didn't even look at her.

"Did I do something wrong?" she asked as he let her go.

He shook his head.

"No, it's me," he said, still averting his gaze away from her. He turned toward the window. "I can't do this — not with you."

She frowned, and though he seemed to want to look everywhere else but at her, she couldn't take her eyes off of him. "What's wrong with me?" she asked.

"Nothing —" he said and inhaled sharply. Keahi wiped his face. He glanced at the door and pretended to look back at her. "I have to — I should go — get to work." He awkwardly turned in a circle, like he didn't know which way to walk in, and headed for the door.

"Keahi."

He stopped in his tracks, but he didn't turn around.

"You like me, don't you?" she asked, even though at this point, she was unsure of what his answer might be. She still wanted to know.

He didn't answer her. Instead, he just vanished.

She bit down on her bottom lip and fumbled with the skeleton key that hung from around her neck as she dropped back down onto her bed.

Dream Keahi was a lot more cooperative. Odette crinkled her nose and forced herself to get out of bed.

Despite intending to, Keahi didn't go to the kitchen first. He went to the basement, where he sat on the bed he never slept in. He had his head in his hands, elbows propped up on his legs, as he tried to process everything that happened.

She kissed him, and if Lailoken ever found out...

Keahi sighed.

He couldn't find out.

Keahi lifted his head and smoothed out his pants. He'd just pretend like it never happened.

Easier said than done, when Odette beat him to the kitchen.

"Nice of you to finally join us," Mrs. Hamasaki said as he came in. Odette was standing right beside her, making bread rolls. "Is everything okay?"

"Just feeling a little hot." He glanced at Odette as he walked past her. "But I think I'll survive," he said.

"Are you sure?" Mrs. Hamasaki asked. She turned to face him and balled her hands before resting them on her hips. "You can go rest if you need to. I know you're young but I don't want you overworking yourself. Not with Amaris already sick, and Jiyun is coming down with something too."

He glanced at the back of Odette's head, considering she hadn't turned around to face him. He finally nodded.

"That might not be such a bad idea. It was a long night."

Mrs. Hamasaki nodded her head toward the door.

"Go," she said. "Because we're gonna need you rested and well for the Halloween party next week. Mrs. Baskerville will throw a fit if something goes wrong."

He nodded and left the kitchen without looking back at Odette. The kitchen door swung freely behind him. Odette stopped with the dough and turned to Mrs. Hamasaki.

"There's a Halloween party?" she asked curiously. "Why didn't anyone tell me?"

Mrs. Hamasaki made a line with her lips.

"Apparently Lailoken's not very happy with you," she said, dusting her hands off. "I wasn't sure if you were allowed to go, and I guess he hasn't invited you."

"Oh."

"Don't tell him I said this, and I don't mean to speak out of place, but you're better off. Lailoken's not a nice boy. I've known him since he was a small child, and he's always had such a temper."

"He's always been this way? So there's no chance of him changing?"

"He needs to get his way. No matter what. He's not above using manipulation. He seems like such a charming and charismatic man, but — unfortunately now days, those are the ones to be wary of."

"So how do you know who to trust?" she asked.

"You don't. But I'd go for the ones with skepticism in their eyes. Who think people are out to hurt them. Usually they're the ones who've seen the true horrors that life has to offer. But they're not easy to know, because they've been hurt badly before. They never let anyone in."

Odette glanced at the swinging door. She pursed her lips together and frowned as she brought her attention back onto Mrs. Hamasaki. "You don't think Lailoken's been hurt?" she asked.

"I'm not even sure that boy has a heart." Mrs. Hamasaki looked at Odette with her small, kind eyes. She forced a small smile. "But you do. Never lose it."

Odette inhaled deeply through her nose and slowly let it out through her parted lips.

"Mrs. Hamasaki," she started, unsure if she was ready to know. "Has Lailoken had other fiancées?" she asked. "If he has, what happened to them?" A look of horror spread across Mrs. Hamasaki's face as she turned back to face Odette.

"How do you know there were others?"

"So it is true." She dropped the dough in her hands. "Something bad happened to them. Please don't lie to me, Mrs. Hamasaki. You're the only person who lives here that I trust."

"I'm sorry, Odette. But those are matters I can't speak about."

"Why not? What happened to them?" She frowned and took a step back. "Are they dead? Mrs. Hamasaki — please tell me they aren't dead."

"Who's not dead?"

Odette froze at the sound of his voice. She turned around and Lailoken was standing there, as charismatic as ever. He picked a strawberry out of the bowl sitting on the counter beside the door and took a bite as his eyes landed on her.

"You aren't getting upset over the dinner we're having, are you? I promise, no one in this house killed the animals, Odette. And I'm sure they were put down rather humanely."

"I'm suddenly feeling rather faint," she said. She didn't have to lie about it that time. Odette almost fainted right there in the kitchen. She would've collapsed if Gentry hadn't been standing right beside her.

"Please help her to her room," Mrs. Hamasaki told him and he nodded. Lailoken frowned as Gentry helped Odette out of the kitchen.

He continued to eat his strawberry.

"I don't understand," he said. He finished the fruit and licked his lips, and stepped further into the room. "She's never had a problem with duck before. I wonder if she's getting sick again. She has one of the worst immune systems."

Mrs. Hamasaki didn't say anything as Lailoken dismissed the other workers from the kitchen. She just gripped at the dish rag in her hands.

"Mrs. Hamasaki," he said, taking the towel from her shaking hands. "What happened?" he asked. She only shook her head.

"Nothing," she said, averting her eyes to the tray. "We were just making bread rolls and Odette got upset that you didn't invite her to the Halloween party."

"Then what did she mean by, 'please tell me they aren't dead'?" he asked. "Mrs. Hamasaki, you know if you don't tell me, I will make you tell me."

"Nothing," she said. "We were talking about food, honest. I won't lie to you, Lailoken. Do not threaten me."

"I know you're lying!" he snapped, and flung the tray off of the counter. The dough fell onto the floor as the metal tray clattered loudly against the tile. Mrs. Hamasaki flinched from the noise. "Something's been happening in this house, and I intend to find out what it is."

Lailoken grabbed Mrs. Hamasaki's face and forced her to look at him.

"Now that I have your attention," he said, staring into her eyes. "Tell me, what did you tell Odette? Tell me the truth, Mrs. Hamasaki, and please, don't leave out a single detail."

Gentry brought Odette back to her room and laid her on her bed. Her eyelids fluttered, and she saw him turn to leave.

"Stop," she said, and he did. Gentry turned around and crossed his arms.

"Did you need something?" he asked.

"I need to know, Gentry. Will you please tell me?"

"Odette —"

"Please. Gentry, please. I need to know. Is something going to happen to me?"

Gentry sighed and clenched his jaw.

"I hope not," he said.

Odette fell back against her bed, hardly able to keep her eyes open. She rubbed her eyes and began shaking her head. This couldn't be happening.

13   DIDN'T WE ALMOST HAVE IT ALL

Odette woke up in her bedroom to find Keahi sitting on the chair near her vanity. He was facing her this time, not staring at the mirror like he usually did. He stood up once he noticed she was awake. She shifted on her bed to face the wall.

"Shouldn't you be downstairs?" she snapped. "Since I made you feel sick?"

"Technically, I am still downstairs," he said.

"Of course you can be in two places at once."

"Simple reality manipulation —"

She sat up in her bed. "What do you want? I don't understand what you want. Are you playing a game with me, Keahi? Because if you are, it's not fun."

She readjusted herself and pushed her blanket away from her.

"You said, the only person you'll kiss is me. Then when you finally get the chance, you push me away. I don't understand."

"I didn't mean it like that."

"What are you doing here? Why are you in my room?"

"I wanted to see if you were okay. I heard you were upset," he said and approached her bed. "If I hurt your feelings this morning, I'm sorry. But we — we can't do that."

"Why not?"

"You know why. You're a high-born. You're someone's fiancée. I'm from the Woolgathering. And if someone finds out, they'll punish you."

"I can handle it," she said, tucking her hair behind her ear. She stared at him intensely and he sighed. "I can, Keahi. I can handle whatever they try to do to me."

"Maybe you can, but I can't. The thought of anyone hurting you again — I can't handle that."

"So you do like me, right?" she asked. "Tell me I'm not imagining that. You like me." She reached out for his hand, and he took it within his own; their fingers laced together. Odette pulled him closer to her bed. "Right?"

She pressed her other hand against his chest and gripped at his shirt. Looking up from where she knelt on her bed, she bit down on her bottom lip.

"What are you doing?" he asked.

"Trying to seduce you," she said. She pulled away from him. She slipped out of her shorts and began to unbutton the front of her blouse.

"Why?" he asked. He didn't take his eyes off of hers, not even to see what she was doing.

"Why, what?" Odette pulled down on her blouse to expose her chest and sat up on her knees, reaching for him again. She ran her hands up against his chest and rested them on his broad shoulders as she pulled him closer to her.

"Why are you trying to seduce me?" he asked.

"Because I like you, and you like me, right? This is what people do, Keahi. This is the only thing I'm good for."

Odette gripped the front of his shirt and pulled him down onto the bed so that he was on top of her. But Keahi held himself up, his fists pressing against the mattress on either sides of her body, so his wouldn't touch hers.

"What are you doing?" he asked again.

"You ask too many questions," she said, fingers trailing up his arms. "You find me attractive, don't you?" she asked, tugging on his shirt. Odette pulled the hem of it out from being tucked into his pants and she began to unbutton the front. "Don't you?"

"I, uh." He looked away from her.

She stopped. "Are you actually hesitating?" she asked. "You find me attractive, right?"

"You're engaged, Odette."

"Exactly. I'm not married yet."

She unbuttoned his shirt and ran her hands against his bare chest. But still, he did nothing. Keahi just stared at her, eyebrows scrunched together. Look of concern.

She ignored it and looked down at his body.

Odette gripped onto his shirt, trying to get him to release his locked elbows, but he wouldn't budge. He was too strong. She narrowed her eyes as her gaze met his.

"My top is open, I'm practically throwing myself at you. Keahi, do something to me. I'll do anything you want me to."

He frowned.

"*What?*"

He quickly got off of her and sat beside her on the bed. He didn't look at her and he started to button his shirt back up. "I don't know what's gotten into you, but I'm going back down to the dorms. I think I should stay in there now, instead. I'll come back if you have a nightmare." He flipped a token in the air, that landed flat on the mattress.

"If you need me, you know what to do," he said.

"I don't understand." Odette sat up as he stood up. "Why are you doing this, Keahi? Don't you want me? Lailoken's never —"

Keahi scoffed at the mention of Lailoken's name. "I don't know what's worse," he said, cutting her off. "The fact that you think this is all you're good for, or the fact that you think I'm just like him." Keahi shook his head and headed for her door.

"You don't think I'm good enough for you. Is that it?" she asked. "Why? Is it because I'm not a virgin anymore? Am I not *pristine* enough? You'll flirt with me but I'm not good enough to actually do anything with, right?"

"That's not what I said."

"It's what you meant though, isn't it. There's no other reason for you to turn me away aside from the fact that I'm unclean. I'm dirty, right? No good. Well, I didn't have a choice, Keahi!"

He walked back to the bed and she got up on her knees. Keahi ran his hand along the waist line of her underwear before looking at her.

"Do you actually want to do this with me, or are you doing this because you think it's what I want from you?" His other hand touched the small of her back as he pressed her body up against his. "What do you want?" he asked. Odette stared at him and looked at his lips, but she didn't say anything. He leaned in to kiss her and she closed her eyes, but one never came. Even though she waited for it. "Sweet dreams, Odette," he whispered, and disappeared from where he stood.

She groaned and she fell back against her mattress.

Keahi avoided her after their squabble. He didn't bother coming back upstairs to kiss her goodnight, something she had grown accustomed to. It didn't really matter to her if he was technically feeding off of her fears every time he did it. It was the action. The fact that he had been doing it every day for months. The fact that he stayed because she asked him to, and now she pushed him away.

Odette didn't leave her room that night. She remained locked inside, lying on her bed, facing the wall. She hadn't bothered buttoning up her blouse and instead just slithered beneath her bed sheets for warmth. But it wasn't the type of warmth she craved.

Her room felt bigger without him. Emptier.

Scarier.

Every creak in the floor had her turning around to glance at the door, to see if there was a shadow lingering on the other side.

She just wanted him to come back, but at the same time, she didn't.

He didn't want her.

Odette fumbled with the coin he gave her but she didn't let go of it.

She fell asleep with it still in her hand.

A few hours later, she awoke to knocking on her door. Odette gripped the coin tightly and sat up, rubbing the sleep from her eyes.

"Odette?" She heard someone say from the other side of the door, but she wasn't sure she recognized the voice. "Please tell me you're awake." She climbed out of bed and buttoned her blouse. She went to answer the door.

"Odette! You have to come downstairs." It was Gentry, and she had never seen him so frazzled.

"What happened? What's going on?"

"It's Mrs. Hamasaki."

Her eyes widened. Odette turned around and put on her shorts. She quickly followed him down to the kitchen where they found her on the floor, surrounded by a few of the kitchen staff, including Keahi. Mrs. Hamasaki was bleeding profusely from her mouth. There was blood smeared on the floor, scissors, and a tongue.

Her tongue.

"We think Lailoken made her cut out her own tongue after dinner," Gentry said. "She dropped the scissors when I came back from cleaning the dining room, and it was already on the floor." He was panicked, breathing deeply, sweat trickling down the sides of his face.

Odette's eyes began to water as she dropped to her knees beside the older woman. She took her hand. "I'm so sorry."

Mrs. Hamasaki weakly shook her head and patted Odette's hand gently. She shook her head again, like she was trying to insist it wasn't her fault.

It didn't matter though, because Odette already blamed herself.

"Can anybody heal her?" she asked, looking at the kitchen workers, but none of them said anything. Most of them looked away from her, averting their eyes. Turning their heads. They couldn't do anything. "Anyone!"

Kiko was a mess beside her mom, she couldn't stop crying.

Keahi knelt down on the ground beside Odette. He covered her hand with his own.

"Look at me," he told her, and she shook her head. She shut her eyes tightly, which only forced more tears to roll down her cheeks. "Odette, please look at me."

Finally, she did.

Keahi leaned toward her. "We can help her," he said softly against her cheek. "She's in pain, and we can take it away. You and me. But I need you to tell me to."

"Consume her fears," she whispered back. "Please."

His grip tightened over their hands and he closed his eyes. Mrs. Hamasaki soon stopped crying, and the bleeding in her mouth seemed to stop too. Her eyes widened, and she stared at Keahi curiously. He opened his eyes. Odette was still in tears, if not crying harder than she was originally. One hand cupped over her mouth.

But he didn't do anything — it was her. She wasn't a grot after all.

Odette was an Empath, and she siphoned the pain from Mrs. Hamasaki to herself.

Keahi released his grip on their hands and wrapped his arms around Odette.

"She's okay," he whispered, rubbing his coarse hand against her arm. She shook her head, burying her face into his shirt. "It's okay."

"No," she said, her voice weak and muffled. "It was my fault. She didn't want to talk about it but it was my fault. I made her. It's my fault."

"You should probably take her upstairs," Gentry said to Keahi.

"Yeah, get her out of my sight!" Kiko snapped. "This is her fault!"

"Whoa, Kiko!" Gentry grabbed hold of her as Kiko tried to get up.

"I hate you!" Kiko screamed at her. "I wish you never came here!"

"Just go," Gentry said, struggling to keep his hold on Kiko. "She needs to get out of here."

"Yeah, I'm on it," Keahi said. "Come on, princess." Keahi put one arm around her body and the other beneath her knees.

"No!" Odette said when he lifted her in the air. She tried to grab onto something so he couldn't take her out of the kitchen, but her fingers seemed to just miss everything. "No! Mrs. Hamasaki! I'm sorry! I'm so sorry! Kiko! I'm sorry!"

"Get out of here!" Kiko screamed at her.

"Odette, you need to be quiet, or he's going to wake up."

She pouted at Keahi when he scolded her, but he didn't turn to look at her, and she did what she was told. She kept her mouth shut as he carried her up the stairs, and she rested her head against his shoulder, watching the kitchen door as they moved farther away from it.

Odette wiped her face after Keahi put her down on her bed. He closed the door and she just kept shaking her head. Her hands covered her mouth.

"That poor woman," she said, her voice was muffled by the cupping of her hands. They slowly slid down her face, fingers pressing against her jaw. "I tried to make her tell me about Lucien's fiancées even though she didn't want to. This is all my fault. None of this wouldn't have happened if it wasn't for me. Kiko's right."

She couldn't stop crying.

"Does your mouth hurt?" Keahi asked, kneeling down in front of her.

She glared at him.

"What kind of question is that? I just saw someone's tongue on the ground! Of course my mouth hurts!"

Keahi cupped his hand over her mouth.

"You need to be quiet," he said as she continued to glare at him. He pulled his hand down, away from her face, but her eyes remained fixed on his.

"Do not touch me ever again," she snapped, enunciating each word sternly. She turned away from him. "Leave. I don't want you here."

"Of course," he said. Keahi stood up and started backing up toward the door while she stared at her bed frame. "Whatever you want."

"I want to be alone."

"Do you want me to —"

"No," she said. "Leave." She twisted her body to face the door. "Get out!" she screamed.

But he was already gone.

There was a knock on the door, and it wasn't Keahi.

"Odette? Are you okay?" he asked, and started jiggling at the doorknob.

Lailoken.

The last person she wanted to see.

"I'm fine! Sorry — I had a — I had a bad dream. I'm okay now, I promise."

Even though she was far from okay. Her fiancé was a monster.

"Are you sure? You can spend the night with me, if you like."

"No, I'm okay! I'll see you in the morning."

"Odette —"

"Goodnight, Lai!"

Her heart beat wildly in her chest as she waited for him to leave. She hoped he would just leave without making a fuss, and the doorknob of her door finally stopped jiggling.

"Goodnight, Odette."

She listened as his footsteps walked back down the hallway.

Odette laid down on her bed. Her mouth stung like her own tongue had been removed from it.

What Lailoken was capable of scared her.

Was she just going to be another Baskerville tragedy? Her stomach churned.

It made her sick to think about, but she couldn't stop. It flooded every inch of her mind. Odette still didn't know what happened to them, but she didn't have to know. If Lailoken was willing to cut out someone's tongue to hide the truth, then it must have been something awful.

She hugged her pillow as she thought about what it felt like when all of her memories came back. How she wanted them to go away, for the pain to go away. How she wanted things to go back to the way they were, when she was ignorant.

Perhaps it was better if she didn't know.

She never should've insisted. Why couldn't she just listen?

Odette turned on her bed and sighed. All Keahi was trying to do was help, and again, she didn't want to listen. She groaned and pulled the covers over her body and listened to the rain as it poured heavily against the rooftop.

Maybe he had been right about her all along. She was nothing more than a high-born scion *princess*. She needed to get her way, and when she didn't, she took it out on everyone else.

Her bottom lip quivered and she turned her face into her pillow so her cries wouldn't be heard, but the rain only seemed to fall harder.

Maybe no one would be able to hear her anyway.

Her heart ached; and she was never going to forget the look on Kiko's face.

"I hate her," Kiko said to Gentry, down in the Baskerville Cave. "I never want to see her stupid face again."

Keahi came stumbling into the basement and plopped down on the couch beside Gentry. He didn't look at either of them and just pulled the rubber band from his hair.

"How is she?" Gentry asked.

"Who cares."

"She wants to be alone."

"Good. She deserves to be alone."

"How's your mom?" Keahi asked.

Kiko just crossed her arms and sank back into the couch.

"She'll live," she mumbled. "Mr. Wong is with her right now."

"You know, the real person you should be mad at is Lailoken, not Odette," Gentry said. "He's the one who told her to do it."

Kiko got out a pocket knife.

"You're right. Why don't I go cut off something of his." The fight in her was strong, but when Gentry grabbed hold of her wrist, she just fell back into the couch and cried. "My mom's never gonna talk again."

Gentry took the knife from her hand and closed it. "I can teach her sign language. I know it's not the same thing," Gentry said, "but at least she'll still be able to communicate with us. That's what matters, right?"

Kiko nodded as she roughly wiped the tears from her face.

"I'm gonna kill him." Kiko nodded as she hiccuped. "I'm gonna kill that bastard."

None of the staff slept that night, aside from Kiko, who finally fell asleep nestled against Amaris. It was dark and desolate in the quarters. No one said another word to each other.

The workers barely looked at one another.

They sat around, together, and waited out the night.

Morning would come, and they would have to act like nothing was wrong. That Lailoken hadn't just forced Mrs. Hamasaki to cut out her own tongue.

Keahi didn't look at anyone. He didn't move, he didn't get up. He frowned slightly at his realization. The monster of the house was never Mrs. Baskerville.

He turned his head and tried to catch Quinlan's attention.

When she looked up at him, she tried to ignore his motions to get her to come with him, but eventually she did.

They sat at the foot of the stairs, on the opposite end of the basement away from everyone else.

"What?" she asked.

"I need you to tell me about the ghosts," he said. "I need you to tell me how they died."

"Keahi —"

"I need to know, Quinlan. Did Lailoken kill them?"

"No," she said. "He didn't make it that easy. They suffered." Quinlan crossed her arms as she glanced back at Kiko, whose head rested on top of Amaris's. "But I can't say anymore. I think Lailoken did this as a warning, to all of us. To keep our mouths shut."

"That's another thing I don't understand. Why don't they just manipulate everyone to forget?"

"They want us to be afraid of them, Keahi. You can't be afraid if you don't remember what happened. They want us to be too scared to talk. Too scared to run. I think Mrs. Baskerville feeds on fear," she said. "Like Dreamweavers."

Keahi stiffened.

"Yeah," he said, rubbing the back of his neck. "She seems to enjoy it, doesn't she."

He sighed and leaned against the wall.

"I'm sorry I can't be of more help," Quinlan said as she scratched her arm. "But I don't wanna get my tongue cut out too."

He nodded. "Yeah, no, I understand."

"Autumn's spirit is very strong in the washer room. You could give it a shot, but don't say you heard it from me."

"Mahalo."

Quinlan got up and returned to join everyone else.

Keahi glanced up the stairs and got up. Quinlan was usually the only one who ever went into the washer room.

She was responsible for laundry, and no one else seemed to bother going in there.

Maybe it being haunted was the reason for it.

He opened the door and flipped on the switch as he headed down the dark steps. He had never made contact with ghosts outside of the Woolgathering before, but it couldn't be too hard.

The light flickered.

Keahi sat down on the steps and looked over at the washing machines and driers. Two of each. Quinlan kept it clean down here; it wasn't dusty and he couldn't see any cobwebs. The washer room sounded creepier than it looked.

The wood of the stairs had wailed with his steps, but aside from that, it was silent.

He waited, but Autumn never came.

The following morning, the staff tried their best to go about like nothing happened. Except Kiko.

Kiko tried to attack Lailoken the first time she saw him and Gentry carried her back down into the Baskerville Cave, where he kept her from making things worse.

Mr. Baskerville carefully watched the staff, who seemed to shoot glares at his son when they thought no one was looking. He sat back in his seat, and looked at his wife. She hadn't noticed anything had changed, and neither had Lailoken, who continued to look through his planner and scribble things down while he wrote. Ahren turned to Odette. She hadn't touched her food.

"Are you not hungry, love?" he asked.

She looked up.

"I'm fine, but thank you, Mr. Baskerville."

Lailoken looked up at her.

"Eat something, Odette. You look sick."

She looked at him and sighed. She grabbed her fork and slowly started cutting into the breakfast sausage on her plate.

"Is something bothering you, Dad?"

"Something's not right with the staff," he said. He looked at Amaris and she looked away. "One, why is Amaris out here? She never leaves the kitchen anymore now that we have Keahi. And where's Kiko now?"

Amaris raised her finger.

"Yes?" he asked.

"She's not feeling well. I think there's a bug going around."

Mr. Baskerville sat back in his chair.

"I see. Jiyun, too? Kaeli and Min were feeling sick also."

She nodded.

Mrs. Baskerville put her hand over her phone.

"Ahren, if you think something's wrong, why don't you just go check?" she snapped before returning to her call.

He put the newspaper down.

"I think I will."

Lailoken watched as his father got up and headed for the kitchen. He turned his attention back onto Odette.

"What's wrong now?" he asked, closing his planner. "You're... poutier than usual."

Odette traced her finger over the silver of her personalized necklace.

"I was just wondering where I got this," she said. "I can't remember."

"I got it for you as a Valentine's Day present after the expo. You don't remember? I gave it to you at dinner."

Liar.

"Oh," she said. "That's right."

"Are you feeling okay, Odette? Maybe you should go back to bed."

"You're probably right."

She started to get up and Lailoken reached across the table to grab her wrist. Odette stopped, looking at his hand gripping onto her.

She looked at him.

"Do me a favor," he said, pupils constricting. "Don't leave your room until I say so."

"I won't leave my room until you say so."

He let her go and she left the breakfast nook.

Mrs. Baskerville put her phone down.

"Are you ever going to stop doing that?"

"Our engagement is none of your concern, Mother."

"Chardonnay," Ahren said, poking his head out through the crack of the door. "May I have a word with you in here?"

She put her napkin down on the table and got up. Lailoken briefly watched his mother walk to the kitchen before returning to finish his breakfast.

"What is it?" Chardonnay asked as she closed the door behind her. She crossed her arms and stood in front of it.

Ahren stepped to the side and Mrs. Hamasaki stood there.

"What?" Chardonnay asked. "Is she pregnant with another one of your children?"

"No," Ahren said, clearing his throat. "She cut out her tongue."

"*What*?" Chardonnay walked past Ahren and grabbed Mrs. Hamasaki's jaw, forcing her to open her mouth. She looked at Ahren and let her go. "What happened?" She crossed her arms. "If she can't do her job — we can't keep her. No one outside of this house even knows that Kiko exists and we have to keep it that way."

"So it wasn't you?"

"Of course it wasn't me. Do you think I want people to know what you did?"

Ahren looked at Mrs. Hamasaki and sighed. "I'm sorry, Yumi."

There was a knock on the kitchen door and the Baskervilles turned around.

Amaris slowly swung the door open and Mrs. Baskerville waved her hand, telling her it was okay to come in.

"Perfect," Mrs. Baskerville said as she looked at Mrs. Hamasaki. "Amaris, can you please tell us what happened?"

"Um — I was actually downstairs yesterday, not feeling well. Maybe I should get Gentry?"

She nodded.

"Please do so, and hurry."

As soon as she left, Ahren turned to her.

"You know what happened, Chardonnay."

"Let's not blame Lailoken until we know the truth."

Amaris returned merely a minute later with Gentry following her. His hair was sloppily thrown up in a bun and he rubbed the sleep from his eyes. He woken up rather quickly though at the sight of the Baskervilles in the kitchen.

"Sir, Ma'am." He bowed his head to the both of them.

"Gentry, would you please tell us what happened?" Mrs. Baskerville asked. She put her hands together as she looked at Ahren. "You see, we can't keep Mrs. Hamasaki on our staff if she can't do her job. She is head of the kitchen, you understand."

"I'm going to teach her sign language. Me and Keahi can teach the rest of the staff."

"Please answer the question, Gentry."

"I don't know, really. Odette was talking to Mrs. Hamasaki, they were making rolls. Lailoken had already come into the kitchen by the time I returned and Odette almost fainted."

"From what?" Chardonnay asked.

"I don't know, maybe the heat was getting to her. It gets hot in here sometimes." Gentry inhaled deeply. "I helped Odette back to her room to rest and things seemed fine. Lailoken left the kitchen and we continued with dinner prep. Then after I cleaned up the dining room, I came back here and she dropped the scissors. She already —" Gentry stopped when he noticed Mrs. Hamasaki began to cry. "I'm sorry — I can't."

"I understand," Chardonnay nodded. "Go back to sleep, Gentry. You look dreadful."

"Yes, Ma'am. Thank you."

He nodded to Ahren, then at Amaris, who was washing the dishes from breakfast, before leaving the kitchen.

"Amaris," Chardonnay said as she turned around. "Is Lailoken still in the breakfast nook?" she asked, and Amaris shook her head.

"He's already left for work."

"Do you think he knows?" Chardonnay asked Ahren.

"He couldn't," he said. "I don't think this is about that. I think this is about Odette."

"Yes. She's not like the others."

"He likes that, though." Ahren rubbed his face with his palms and sighed. "What are we going to do, Chardonnay? You can't —"

"You know I can't." Her expression faltered. Chardonnay raised her eyebrows and turned to her husband. "I can't, but maybe you can."

"What am I supposed to do? I'm a Shield. I'm not like you two."

"That's precisely my point, Ahren. You're not like Lailoken and I. You're a Shield. So what do Shields do?" Chardonnay turned to Amaris. "Will you get me a cup of coffee to go?" she asked, and Amaris nodded. "We are not covering up another suicide for him again, Ahren. Lailoken needs to grow up."

14 FOREVER YOUNG

Halloween was Sophie's favorite holiday, and they always made sure the apartment reflected that. They liked Halloween decorations far more than Christmas ones, which always seemed too cheerful for their taste. Sophie put up fake cobwebs and fake spiders over the cabinets. They hung bats that would tremble and shake, screeching loudly when someone clapped. They spent all day making the apartment look haunted, though with Paisley in the building, in a way, the place already was haunted by the spirits that followed her.

Once they were pleased with their work, Sophie put the remaining boxes away and went downstairs, where Midori was helping a customer. Sophie dug through the bottom shelves and began to restock the higher ones and didn't say a word to Midori until the customer left.

Sophie let out a sigh of relief as they turned to Midori. "Was that a high-born?" they asked, and she nodded.

"I feel like they're coming in here more and more." She raked her fingers through her black hair and crossed her arms. "Do you think Lailoken knows?"

Sophie shook their head. "How could he?"

"Do you think they're gonna try to do something to us?"

Sophie sighed.

"We're both high-borns, Soph. Technically, we *could* get in trouble."

"I know." Sophie started to gather their mass of curly black hair, to bind with a rubber band. "We could get in trouble even if we were mid-borns. But I don't think that's it either. It's not as if we've been hiding our relationship, Green."

"Wow, Soph. I hate what you did with the place."

Sophie grinned where they stood, hearing Shiro's voice travel from upstairs.

"What's wrong with bats and spiders, Shiro?" Sophie yelled up the staircase. "You live in an attic, you should be used to it!"

"Hilarious!" he said sarcastically.

"Where's Paisley?" Midori asked as Shiro came downstairs, grasping something in his hand. He threw it against the wall as hard as he could once he stepped onto the floor. It hit the wall and fell on the ground, spinning to a stop.

An empty bottle of Hypnolin-Z.

"Hey! Watch it!" Sophie snapped as they gathered several jars that Shiro could've hit.

"She's still sleeping," he said and hopped up onto the counter. "She needs to stop taking that." Shiro twisted his body to face Sophie. "Do something."

Sophie put the jars down onto the counter and crossed their arms.

"I've tried! What do you want me to do? Spoon feed her my potions? She'd probably tell a spirit to possess me to get me to stop."

"I thought that tattoo you got was supposed to protect you against possession."

"From negative energies and lesser spirits! Not if a spirit is commanded to possess me. Then I'm S-O-L."

"You already seem like a negative energy to me," Shiro grumbled.

"Am I interrupting something?"

They all turned around to see Lailoken Baskerville in the Apothecary. He towered over all three of them. His blonde hair was pulled back and bound by a rubber band. He eyed each of them with his intense stare, narrowing his eyes as they moved from one person to the next.

Shiro instinctively moved toward the stairs and Sophie stared Lailoken down. Midori turned around to the shelf, pretending to rearrange the bottles and jars. She was afraid of Lailoken, and she had every right to be.

"What do you want?" Sophie asked, in a less than friendly tone. "Isn't it a little sunny for you to be outside? Don't want to get that pale skin burned."

"Well, don't you have terrible customer service," he said, rolling his eyes.

"Only toward people who think buying and owning others is okay," Sophie retorted.

"You were once apart of that society, Sophie. Don't forget."

"I haven't."

Lailoken took a step forward and stared at Sophie straight in the eyes.

"But now that you've brought her up, what did you give to Odette? My — sweet bride is somewhat — bitter now. Uncooperative."

"Nothing," Sophie said. "If she's bitter, then it's your own fault."

He glanced at Midori.

"A Shield... I should've known. No wonder you feel no reason to tell me the truth."

Lailoken walked around the Apothecary and stopped in front of Shiro.

"If she's not going to give me any information, what about you?" he asked, looking down at Shiro from where he stood. Lailoken put his hands in his pockets.

"They."

Lailoken turned around and raised his eyebrows. "What?"

"You use they or he when you're talking about my partner or you don't address them at all." Midori was glaring at him from where she stood. "You know that, Lailoken, and yet you just continue to be an asshole."

He narrowed his eyes. "I've never seen you so fired up, Midori." Then, he rolled his eyes. "Whatever, I don't have time for this." He turned to Shiro again. "What did Sophie give to Odette?"

"I haven't seen Odette in almost all year," Shiro said. "So I don't know what you're expecting me to say. How am I supposed to know what happened?"

Lailoken glanced down at Shiro's clothes. His nose started to crinkle in disgust.

"Why are you wearing a skirt?"

"Why are you still here, Lailoken?" Sophie asked. "Leave."

"I hate witches," he muttered under his breath as he left the Apothecary.

Sophie stuck their tongue out at him.

"This is bad," Midori said as she leaned against the table and crossed her arms. "He knows something."

"No," Shiro said, stepping down from the stairs. "I read his mind. Odette's not just being uncooperative. She's resisting his manipulation. If she's resisting him then —"

"She summoned a Dreamweaver," Sophie finished for him. "Cause my potion wouldn't have done that. It would've just brought her memories back. Dreamweavers are powerful. Once you're under their protection, it takes a lot for a Pusher to regain control. If ever."

"We have to tell Paze. She needs some good news."

"She's not going to like that Lailoken came to us, though," Sophie said. "You know how she is."

"Are you worried?" Midori asked.

"Lailoken doesn't scare me," Sophie said. "But he's smart, and he's not going to let this go."

"I'll go tell her," Shiro said.

"Stop," Sophie said. "I'll do it. I'll talk to Paisley and everything will be fine. Trust me."

Sophie walked past Shiro as he stepped back down onto the ground floor. They walked up the stairs and up to Paisley's room.

"Paze?" Sophie knocked. "Can I come in? Are you awake?"

The door opened. Paisley's hair was bright orange again, but she didn't say anything. She returned back to her bed. Her laptop was open, and she sat down, pushing it away from her.

Sophie stepped in and closed the door behind them.

"I have good news," they said, stepping closer, but Paisley didn't look at them. Sophie fumbled with her finger. "She summoned a Dreamweaver, Paze. She did it."

"But she's in trouble." Paisley's voice was monotonous.

"What do you mean?"

"That spirit I saw — the one that wouldn't fully form." Paisley glanced up at Sophie. "I saw her. Lailoken had two fiancés before Odette. They were both reported suicides." Paisley pushed her laptop to face Sophie. On the screen, was The Scion Advertiser.

Side by side in two different windows, were articles of reported suicides from two different years, one from 2010 and the other, 2012. "But she told me that he made her do it. He made her kill herself."

"But Odette can't be manipulated anymore though. She's not under his control."

"Neither was she."

Paisley closed her eyes and her whole body began to tremble.

Sophie took a step back and the lights flickered. "What are you doing? Paze?" Her nose began to bleed. "Paisley!" Sophie's eyes widened as a spirit began to manifest beside Paisley. She wasn't clear, but like white noise on a television screen.

"I was a Shield," she said, her voice sounded like an echo. "Being around Lailoken was like being exposed to a disease. He convinced me I was worthless and undeserving, that the only good thing I had in my life was him. I don't want the same thing to happen to your friend. She deserves better than this. Than him."

Sophie's eyes began to water and the spirit vanished. Paisley fell over on her bed.

"Paisley!" Sophie sat down on the bed beside her and tried to wake her.

Her lids fluttered.

Paisley wiped her nose with the back of her hand like she had done so a million times and sat up. She blinked a few times before looking at Sophie. "Did you see her?" she asked. "Did she tell you?"

"Jesus, Paisley, don't do that again!" Sophie shoved her in the arm. "Next time just tell me instead of trying to make them manifest."

"Sometimes you have to see things for yourself," Paisley said, leaning back against her bed frame. "All trauma is valid, Soph."

Sophie leaned back beside her and rested their head down on Paisley's shoulder.

"What are we going to do?" they asked.

"I don't know." Paisley rested her head against Sophie's mass of hair. "What are we going to do about Lailoken? I heard him downstairs."

"I'm not afraid of him," Sophie said.

"I know, but he's a Baskerville. They can really do some damage if they really want to. I mean, look what they covered up?" she said, acknowledging her laptop. "Neither of these suicides were linked to Lailoken. How is that possible? Why is he still allowed to buy brides? I know the Bridal Expo is fucked up, but I thought they wouldn't condone this? You aren't even supposed to be allowed to use your ability against your partner. That's grounds for punishment."

"Like you said," Sophie said as they inhaled deeply. "He's a Baskerville. Maybe I should be worried."

"I don't think any of us can afford not to be."

"How's the writing going?" Sophie asked, changing the subject. Paisley got up from leaning against the bed frame and glared at them. Sophie crossed their arms. "Hey, the world doesn't just stop turning for any one of us. It keeps going, and we have to keep going with it. Odette wouldn't want you to stop because of this."

"It's not just because of this. It's everything. It's me." She sighed, running her fingers through her orange hair. "Have you ever felt like you're only good at one thing, and even that thing, you aren't that good? But you suck at everything else — and there's just nothing else. I can't do anything else. I don't want to do anything else. I'm no good with people — I'm worse than you are. I can't even fake it."

"You're good with people, just not strangers. But I mean, strangers are annoying. They suck. I don't blame you."

"Unfortunately people being shitty isn't a viable excuse. But we both know life isn't about being happy. Sooner or later, I'm just going to have to suck it up and get over it."

"Life isn't about being happy but so what? Life isn't about a lot of things. Doesn't mean you can't want it. There's nothing wrong with wanting to be happy, Paze. People say not to make homes out of others, or to rely on someone else for happiness, but the thing is, it's not really about relying on someone else. It's about seeing things through the eyes of people who love you. About having a different perspective."

Sophie closed the laptop, not wanting to look at the articles any longer.

"I didn't love myself before I met Midori. Some days, most days, I still don't. But I'm learning to, because if someone like her can love me, if I can have friends like you and Shiro and Odette, then damn, there must be something great about me that I'm not seeing because I don't know what I did to deserve any of this. I will keep looking for it until I see it too."

Paisley smiled.

"Who are you and what have you done with Sophie?"

"I swear, you're the only one who can turn me into some kind of motivational speaker. And I'll always do that for you."

"But you don't have to."

"I never said I did. Paisley, you never make me do anything I don't want to do. You know me, I never do anything I don't want to do. You don't manipulate me and I hate that she villainized you. You know I'd hurt her for what she did, but you don't want me to and I'm gonna respect that. Friends respect the decisions we make. That's something she never did. You're not a bad person, Paze. You're not worthless. Stop straining yourself trying to prove that because you don't have to. Has anyone ever told you that? You don't have to. You don't owe anyone anything."

"Autumn's right," Paisley said.

"Who's Autumn?"

"The spirit. Being exposed to abusers is like being exposed to a disease. Even when they're nowhere near you, you just continue to suffer."

"And the people who love you will do their best so that you suffer a little less." Sophie nudged her. "Come on, we'll close up early and go out for sushi. We need to get out of here for a little while. I think it's driving us all crazy."

"You hate sushi."

Sophie shrugged. "So I'll eat udon. Go change and let's go." They slid off of Paisley's bed and turned around to face her. "Yes?"

Paisley finally nodded. "Okay, I'll go."

They spent hours out in the mundane world, for a moment, able to forget about the awful things that came with the society they didn't live in, but were heavily exposed to and influenced by.

A society ready to knock them back down in no time.

It was during the night when they came, while most of them slept upstairs above the Apothecary.

Paisley was awake; sitting at the table between the kitchen and living room, where she had promised she'd start working again rather than being cooped up in her room. Her hair was a faint blue color, and she had felt a little more at ease.

Until she heard a noise downstairs.

She rubbed her eyes beneath her glasses and got up from the chair. Paisley peered down the dark stairway that led to the Apothecary.

"Hello?" she said. But there was no response.

Paisley slowly descended down the steps and into the dark Apothecary. A hand slipped over her mouth before she could say anything, and she was yanked into the shadows.

It only took seconds before Sophie and Midori came down. Sophie was grabbed next, and held by their neck, shoved into the wall.

Someone finally lit a match.

It was Jac Valentine and some of her friends.

"*Sophie*," Jac said as she circled the man who held them against the wall. "Sorry to visit you like this, but Lailoken wasn't very happy with you."

"Are you doing his dirty work now?" Midori asked, struggling beneath the grip of another man. "He can't do anything himself?"

"He can do plenty himself," Jac said as she spun on her heels. "But he also has a fiancée to return home to. Can't have her thinking less of him." She returned her focus back onto Sophie. "So, what did you give her?"

Sophie couldn't speak beneath the grasp. The man was choking them.

"Hey! Loosen up a little." Jac hit the man in the arm and he obliged.

"I didn't — didn't give her anything," Sophie wheezed.

"I really wanted to do this without making a mess." Jac started grabbing bottles and jars from the shelves and throwing them on the ground. "But I guess losing valuables will be the only way you might talk — is this real Dreamweaver blood?" Jac said, holding the vial close to her face. She tucked it into her pocket. "That'll sell well." She knocked a few more things off of shelves and onto the ground but Sophie said nothing.

Shiro came down the stairs and the three guys released their holds on his friends. They started pressing against their heads with their palms as they dropped to the ground, groaning in pain. He made them feel like their skulls were shrinking.

He let them go and they scrambled to their feet. They couldn't get out of the Apothecary fast enough as they fought each other to get out first.

"I'll do the same to you if you don't leave. I've been practicing with Midori and I can affect Shields now." Shiro stared at her. "Leave, Jacinta."

"Don't call me that," she snapped. She looked around. "This was getting boring anyway." Jac looked at Sophie, then Paisley. "This isn't over." She left without another word.

Sophie leaned against the counter and dropped their head forward. They groaned. "I'm awake before noon. This is absurd." They pulled back and looked up, arms still on the counter.

"Sophie, you were nearly choked to death and that's what you're upset about?"

They continued to speak like a zombie while ignoring Paisley.

"I could still be sleeping right now," Sophie said, staring blankly at the wall. "I hate Jac and Lailoken and all of them."

"What's with her?" Midori asked, rubbing Sophie's back and shoulder.

"Lailoken's attack dog," Shiro said. He looked at Paisley. "Next time you hear a noise, don't investigate by yourself. You've seen horror movies, you know better than that."

Paisley rolled her eyes and seemed to look at nothing. "I wasn't by myself," she said. "But we're not safe here."

"Where are we supposed to go?"

"I have an idea," Paisley said.

"That's never good," Sophie said with a sigh.

Paisley glared at them.

"It's been a while since I last saw my mom. I'm sure we can crash there until we figure something out. Lailoken doesn't know where my mom lives."

"Okay so, good idea after all. I happen to like your mom," Sophie said. "I like both of your parents, actually."

"Yeah — speaking of — my dad wants to know when you're going to stop calling him 'Dad'."

"Oh, pfft." Sophie waved their hand carelessly and rolled their eyes. "What I want to know is why this couldn't have happened like two days ago before I decorated — Paisley — is your mom going to let me decorate?"

Paisley shrugged.

"I don't see why not. I'll give her a call."

They spent most of the day packing up what they needed, from both the shop and their apartment above. Midori pulled Sophie aside and pursed her lips together, but didn't speak right away.

"What is it?"

"I think Shiro and I should go stay with our aunty for a little bit."

"Why?"

"There's four of us — it's unfair to ask her mom to house all of us."

"But your aunty lives on the other side of the island," Sophie said and crossed their arms. "When am I supposed to see you?"

Midori put her hands on Sophie's shoulders. "I'll come by, all the time. We'll be there so much you'll think we live there. It's just — this whole thing is just making me a little homesick. I feel like we should spend some time with our family."

Sophie pulled Midori close. "Just don't let them steal you back."

Midori draped her arms over Sophie's shoulders and smiled. "I would never let them keep me from you," she said, and pressed her lips against Sophie's.

Shiro backed away from the two of them and sat down beside Paisley.

"I understand now why you think relationships are repulsive."

Paisley laughed. "Of course you think that's repulsive, she's your sister."

"Oh, I was talking about Sophie."

Sophie grabbed something from the counter without having to look, and threw it at Shiro. The water bottle smacked him right in the face.

"Hey!" he yelled and Sophie grinned into their kiss with Midori.

Shiro rubbed his nose and Paisley tried to contain her laughter.

"I think I'll be glad after all to have some time away from Sophie," he said, before dropping his hand into his lap as he redirected his attention onto Paisley. "But are you going to be okay?"

"I'll be fine. Honest."

"Are you sure? Because I feel like you haven't had much time to worry about yourself lately. Especially with what you found out."

"Sophie told you?"

He shrugged. "Midori, but one guess who told her. I'm gonna see if my cousin knows anything. He works at the expos. Maybe they don't even know about what the Baskervilles have done."

"Or everyone's in on it."

"Do you really believe that?"

"I really don't know what I believe anymore." She chewed on her bottom lip and pushed her glasses up to sit on top of her head. "But I met Mrs. Baskerville once, I was really young, but I remember something she told me. I remember her laughing at me. I don't know why, but she laughed and she said, 'silly girl, everything is for sale for the right price'." She scratched her shoulder and tugged on her sleeve. "I wouldn't doubt that includes loyalty. Those who can't be manipulated, can probably be bought." But Shiro didn't look entirely convinced. "You know I'm right."

"I know, I know. I just wish you weren't." Shiro tapped his fingers on the table. "Your sister — she's a Telepath, right?"

Paisley nodded. "Yeah, why?"

"It's just good to know you won't be so alone with the spirits, just in case."

"Yeah, she doesn't go into my head much since she first saw the spirits when we were younger. But I'll be fine, honestly. I'll be a little better now. Autumn actually said she's going to return to the Baskerville mansion and keep me posted. I feel better knowing Odette summoned a Dreamweaver. They aren't the easiest to get along with sometimes but they're very protective."

"You'll keep me posted?"

"Shiro, you're only nineteen. You need to relax. You worry way too much for your age."

"Odette's just as much a worrier as I am and she's younger."

"I know. You two need to leave that to us."

"I will, if you do me a favor."

Paisley raised an eyebrow. "A favor like what?"

Shiro put the empty bottle of Hypnolin-Z on the table between them.

"Stop relying on it." He stared at the bottle, not wanting to look up at Paisley, who most likely had a guilty look on her face. "I need to know you're going to wake up every morning."

She grabbed the bottle and tossed it into the trashcan.

"I can't make any promises, but I'll do my best. My mom doesn't keep that kind of stuff in her house anyway, and she won't buy it."

Shiro sighed. "I'll take what I can get."

He got up and gave her a hug.

Midori gave her a hug too and Sophie had to force Shiro to give them one.

They packed their necessities and loaded up the two cars they had, and were off in different directions. Sophie got to play what they wanted on the radio, while Paisley tried to concentrate on the road.

It was both easier and lonelier without Autumn hanging around her.

But Paisley was conditioned to miss what once annoyed her. Conditioned to believe they were constants she needed in her life, despite hating them.

She glanced over at Sophie and sighed quietly to herself.

The drive to her mom's house wasn't a long one, and it took less than fifteen minutes to get there. Fifteen minutes too long. Paisley had enough time to crawl back into her destructive thoughts, that the first thing she almost did once she parked, was text Jana.

Sophie snatched the phone from her.

"Don't — you — dare." They held the phone up away from Paisley's reach. "You got awfully quiet. You really thought I wasn't gonna notice?" Sophie looked down at the phone. The last texts between the two were on the screen. "Paisley, why do you still have her number?"

"I just — I want to apologize."

"For what? It wasn't your fault."

"I mean, for what my dad did."

Taliesin Eversley wasn't too happy when he found out his youngest daughter was trapped in an abusive relationship with a Pusher. She was a high-born, and he outed her. Taliesin was one of the few high-borns who didn't care who someone fell in love with, but if there was one thing he wasn't going to stand for, it was someone causing harm to those he cared about.

Paisley knew that. Paisley knew her dad would do anything for her.

She just wanted to feel safe again.

"You know I don't agree with how high-borns treat bisexuality and homosexuality," Sophie managed to say in one breath, "but it was the only way to get her away from you. If you hadn't told your dad, I would've. She trapped you, forced you to do things you didn't want to do. She abused you, Paisley. Invalidated you." Sophie started messing with Paisley's phone.

"What are you doing?"

"I'm blocking and deleting her number. I'm deleting these messages. You do not deserve to feel this way. You do not deserve to feel responsible for what she did to you. You do not deserve to feel bad for what she brought on to herself. This is no one's fault but hers. I just hope that one day you can understand that."

Sophie handed the phone back to her.

"I'm going to make sure you don't get dragged back into that, even if you end up hating me for it — no, please don't cry, Paisley — you know my eyes always water when someone else is crying!"

Sophie pulled her into a hug, and hugged her tight.

"I love you," Paisley whispered, and Sophie nodded.

"I know, and I love you too. Which is why I'm doing this. You know that, right?"

She nodded.

She sat back in her seat and wiped her face. She looked at Sophie.

"Does it look like I started crying?" she asked as she sniffled, wiping her face. "I know my mom will ask if she can tell."

"Honestly, it just looks like you have allergies or a congestion problem."

"Good excuse. I'm sick, she'll believe that. I used to always get sick."

The two of them got out of Paisley's van and left most of their stuff in the car, except for the necessities. Evaline Eversley lived in a two story house with a two quarter landing staircase on the outside.

"So what do you know about Dreamweavers?" Sophie asked, once they were settled in Paisley's bedroom. Sophie had their feet dangling off the side of the bed; not quite tall enough for their feet to reach the ground from where they sat.

Paisley raised an eyebrow at them. "Oh, you're curious now?"

"Well, ones watching out for Odette. Of course I'm curious. They're all we have to make sure she's safe... and doesn't end up like..."

"She won't."

Paisley got up and slid open her closet door, where she picked up an old, vintage trunk. It had a red Chinese dragon painted on the top; that looked like a long serpent with four legs. Much like the one tattooed on Paisley's side.

"What's the dragon for?" Sophie asked.

"It's a symbol for power, strength, and — good luck — I think."

"Good, because we're going to need all three of those."

Paisley unlatched her trunk and flipped it open. Inside, were stacks of books, rolled up parchments, and many old photos that were older than the two of them combined.

"What is all this?"

"My great grandmother's history," she said proudly. "She was a Dreamweaver. For a while, she could pass between here and the Woolgathering, but ultimately she decided to stay here. Most of those in the Woolgathering are of Hawaiian or Asian ancestry. They left for good once Hawaii became a state in 1959, but the Woolgathering's existed since the eradication. People say The Darkness, the father of The Time Lord, The Sandman, and The Angel of Death, created it with his sacrifice." Paisley flipped through the pictures. "This is the three of them."

"Who's that?" Sophie asked, pointing to another picture sticking out from the stash.

"The children of The Sandman — The Master of Midnight, The Dream King, and The Storyteller."

Sophie pointed at The Storyteller. "She's gorgeous. Have you met any of them?"

Paisley pointed to The Master of Midnight. "I met him once," she said as she slid her finger over to The Dream King. "Him, twice. I've mostly come into contact with their uncle though. The Angel of Death, he helps the Mediums, if we ask nicely."

"Can high-borns trick them?"

Paisley shook her head. "They're kupua. Demigods residing over the Woolgathering."

"I wish I was a Medium."

"You complain about me seeing dead people and now you want to be a Medium?"

"Well!" Sophie slouched against the bed fame. "You're like, connected to this whole other world. The other world I'm connected to, I'm running from."

"But I don't belong there," Paisley said as she put the pictures back and pulled out a thick book. "This is about the Dreamweavers. Everything we need to know about them is in this book."

"That looks like a lot of reading. I'm no longer that interested. What about Dreamweaver tokens? Do you have any in there? Maybe we can summon one instead."

"Sophie!"

"What? They're so alien to me. You know I'd summon an alien if I could."

"You'd summon a dinosaur if you could."

"Well, duh."

Paisley closed the book and sat down on Sophie's bed. "You have to be afraid of something to summon a Dreamweaver. What are you afraid of?"

Sophie shrugged. "Things."

"Are you having nightmares?"

They groaned. "No."

"Didn't think so. It wouldn't work then."

"Aren't you having some?" Sophie asked.

"Not while I'm asleep."

Sophie huffed as Paisley handed them the book. They brought their knees up to use their thighs as a book holder. Sophie flipped it open.

"So how do you come into contact with the Angel of Death?" they asked as they slowly scanned the pages.

"A looking glass."

Sophie looked up.

"You mean like a mirror?"

"Well, *he* calls it a looking glass, but yes. A mirror. They travel between worlds through mirrors." Paisley dug through the chest again. "Here." She got out a small black pocket mirror and handed it to Sophie.

"What does this symbol stand for?"

"Death, in Chinese."

"Oh, lovely." Sophie handed it back to her. "Are you going to summon him?"

"I don't need to and I sure as hell am not disturbing him for no reason." Paisley lowered her voice as she put the mirror away. "He scares me," she whispered.

Sophie laughed. "You hang around spirits all day but someone in another realm scares you?"

"He's a little intimidating, okay! I'm just definitely not bothering him unless I absolutely have to, and I don't." Paisley pointed at the book. "Are you going to read that or should I put it away?"

"I actually have a question," Sophie said. They lowered their legs and flipped the book around to show Paisley. They pointed at the text. "What's a Dreamweaver's Promise?" Sophie asked.

Paisley frowned. "There's no explanation?"

Sophie flipped the book back to face them and shook their head.

"Not that I can find. You don't know?"

"I'm like one-eighth Dreamweaver. It's not like I was just born with this knowledge." Paisley shrugged as Sophie closed the book and handed it to her. "We can ask my mom, though. She knows more about this stuff than I do."

Sophie chewed on her bottom lip, biting off pieces of dead skin while Paisley put the trunk back into the closet.

"Do you think if the Dreamweavers came back, they could help us bring back the dinosaurs?"

"We are not bringing the dinosaurs back."

"But —"

"They aren't gods, Sophie."

"Demigod has the word god in it."

"Yeah, good luck getting one of them to help you cause the end of the world. As if they aren't hated enough. That'd be a trip. Knock, knock." Paisley knocked against the bed frame. "It's the Dreamweavers. Open your world. We've come to destroy it with our numen powers... and resurrected dinosaurs." Sophie couldn't help but laugh as

Paisley got out her phone. "By the way, my mom said yes to the decorations as long as she doesn't have to buy any."

Sophie jumped up from their bed.

"What! Why did we leave my decorations in the car then? Let's go get them."

"You get them," Paisley said. She grabbed her keys and tossed them to Sophie. "I'm tired. I need to take a nap."

"Oh, right, you didn't get *any* sleep last night, did you."

Sophie wasn't even asking. It wasn't a question because they knew. Sophie knew Paisley, probably even better than Paisley knew herself.

Sophie ran out of the room and Paisley got into her bed. It was unusual, being at home again. In a bed she hadn't slept in since she was eighteen years old.

Paisley laid on her side and stared at the door while she waited for Sophie to come back. She couldn't stop thinking about Jana, and what she did to her. She couldn't stop thinking about what Odette might be going through.

Part of her didn't want to sleep.

She sat up in bed and stared at her sliding closet doors that lined the wall. For a second, she considered summoning her own Dreamweaver.

Paisley still had fears. She still had nightmares.

Abuse doesn't stop with the person, she learned the hard way.

Once she heard Sophie come back upstairs, Paisley quickly shut her eyes, knowing that if she were still awake by the time they came back to the room, surely they'd try to coax her into helping with the Halloween decorations.

As much as she loved the holidays, it just wasn't the same. She couldn't help but wonder if that's why Sophie was trying extra hard to make sure they were obviously celebrating them still.

But Sophie didn't run back down the hallway and try to enlist Paisley's help. They were just getting the box out of the car when Phoebe, Paisley's older sister, came home. The two girls barely looked alike. Phoebe was shades darker, and her hair blonder, naturally lightened by the sun. She was a lot skinner too, but shorter.

"Good! You're home just in time to help me decorate for Halloween."

"Halloween decorations? Really, Sophie?" Phoebe raised her eyebrows as she shook her keys in her hand. "You're probably the only witch I know who actually likes this holiday." Phoebe stared at the box. "And where's Paisley? Why isn't she helping you?"

"She's taking a nap," Sophie said. "Didn't get any sleep last night. Did you hear about what happened at the shop?"

Phoebe nodded. "My mom told me after she got off the phone with her. I'm glad you're all okay."

"You know us," Sophie said, slamming the car door shut with their foot. "Takes more than a few angry Shadow Crawlers to bring us down." Sophie grinned. "How's Dad doing?"

Phoebe laughed as she headed up the stairs with Sophie following close behind.

"He's not your dad, Soph."

"He is until I say otherwise. I mean, he might as well be. I used to practically live there."

"You did live there."

"Well, he should just adopt me and make it official."

"You're twenty-three, Sophie."

"Age is but a number," Sophie grumbled. "I'm a child at heart."

Phoebe just laughed as she shook her head. She opened the door.

"Come on, I'll help you with that," she said, acknowledging the decorations Sophie held in their arms.

15 ALL BY MYSELF

Pia sat beside Kiko, shaking her leg vigorously as she chewed on the side of her fingernail. She kept glancing around and Kiko grabbed her knee to make her stop.

"*What* are you doing?"

"Do you think he's going to ask me?" Pia asked.

"Do I think who's going to ask you what?"

"Lailoken! To the Halloween party his parents are having."

Kiko started to laugh. "You're joking, right?"

Pia pushed her.

"Okay, obviously not. Why would he ask you? He's not your boyfriend, Pinup. God, you were kind of whoreish before but at least you weren't stupid."

"Hey! I'm not stupid."

"I have half a mind to just march you up to Mrs. Baskerville and tell her the truth."

"I am not stupid!" Pia said.

Kiko jumped off of the couch when Gentry came back.

"Thank God, Mega G. Where have you been?" Kiko ran up to him and pointed at Pia. "We need to do something about her. She is driving me crazy."

"What now?" he asked, pulling the rubber band from his hair.

"She wants Lailoken to ask her to the Halloween party!"

Gentry scowled at the mention of his name.

"Why?"

"Because she's an idiot."

Pia stood up. "I'm right here!" She crossed her arms. "He's very nice to me. I don't know why you all don't like him."

Kiko walked up to her and crossed her arms as well. "Let's see, I don't know, maybe because he made my mom cut out her own tongue!" she snapped and Pia took a step back.

"Okay, that's understandable for *you*." Pia grabbed Kiko's shoulders and moved her to the side. "But I don't know why everyone else has a problem with him."

"You realize he has a fiancée, right?" Gentry said. "He's going to take Odette before he takes a concubine."

"Yes, I know that. But she doesn't wanna go with him. She doesn't even like him."

Kiko laughed and clapped her hands together.

"I always forget you're a mundane until something like that comes out of your mouth. The scion society doesn't care about love." Kiko put her arm around the back of Pia's neck. "Lailoken bought her to marry her. It doesn't matter how she feels about him. She belongs to him. She is his property."

"Well, so am I."

"Yeah, but not as important property." Kiko's arm slipped from Pia's neck as she reached down to grab the feather duster from the table. She handed it to her. "You're a maid, now. Go clean something."

Pia snatched the feather duster from Kiko's hands and muttered expletives to herself as she stomped up the stairs.

Gentry raised his eyebrows. He crossed his arms and leaned his shoulder against the wall. Kiko only glanced at him before looking away.

"What's gotten into you?" he asked as he moved to sit down on the armrest of the couch. "You've never been that mean to her."

"I just don't understand."

Kiko ran her fingers through her short hair as she turned away.

"How can she like him? How can she not think —" She clenched her jaw and sighed. "It's just, she's not even compelled to like him anymore and she still does. How did that even happen?"

"You know people think he's charming, Kiko. Even without manipulation."

"We should've just made her leave."

"With what? Rocks?" Keahi asked as he came out of his dorm. "We have no money to give her. You know that."

Gentry laughed and Kiko groaned.

"This does not concern you, Honey Buns." Kiko clenched her jaw again. "How's Doll Face?"

Keahi shrugged. "Wouldn't know."

"But you're like, her best friend."

"Well, she doesn't want to see me. I thought you didn't care, anyway?"

Kiko pursed her lips together. "I may have been a little harsh on her. I mean, Gentry's right. This was Lailoken's doing, not hers. If I was in her spot, I'm sure I would've done the same thing. I can't really blame her."

"Well then maybe one of you should just tell her." Keahi poured himself a cup of water and leaned against the counter.

"Why don't you?"

"She doesn't want to see me," he said as he raised the glass to his mouth. "Princess's orders." He drank from his glass while Kiko watched him.

"Maybe if you show up like that, without your shirt on, she'll reconsider."

Keahi nearly choked on his water. He laughed and wiped his mouth with his hand and Gentry shook his head.

"What?" Kiko said with a shrug. "We all know she liked it when he'd take his shirt off in the kitchen. That girl made herself look like a tomato. Poor girl." Kiko shook her head and tucked her hair behind her ear. "She'd probably burn if she went outside for too long, with a complexion like that."

Gentry looked at Keahi.

"Did you actually fall in the pool that one time or did she pull you in to protect her from the sun?" He raised his eyebrows.

"Okay but that was hilarious," Kiko cut in. "Do you remember the look on her face about sending Keahi out?"

Gentry started to laugh.

"Things have changed a lot between you since then."

Keahi shrugged. "Well —"

Kiko waved her hand. "I don't wanna hear it. She doesn't suddenly hate you now. What could you have possibly done to her to make her hate you?"

"It's complicated."

Kiko and Gentry exchanged glances.

"It can't be that complicated." Kiko raised an eyebrow. She crossed her arms and took a step forward. Keahi put his glass down on the counter. "She kissed you, didn't she."

He laughed.

"She did! Didn't she? Oh my god."

"You're ridiculous."

"You know, I did catch them in our dorm. Together. Alone."

"Hey, we were just talking."

Gentry shrugged "Talking can mean anything now days and sometimes it can lead to... things. I'm not judging."

"Okay, so you kissed. What happened after?" Kiko asked. "I want all of the dirty details."

"There aren't any dirty details."

"So you admit it! You kissed her!"

"I didn't say that!"

"Your ears turn red when you lie."

"No, they don't."

Kiko narrowed her eyes.

"How can someone who looks like you, be so boring?"

Keahi shrugged. He got his glasses that were hanging off a belt loop of his pants and put them on. "Looks can be deceiving. Maybe I enjoy a quiet, sedentary lifestyle."

"Okay, first of all. Do you even know what sedentary means? You wouldn't look like that if you were stationary and inactive."

Keahi rolled his eyes. "Working here has given me some muscle, I'll give you that."

"Oh, please. Don't play with me, Honey Buns. I felt you up the first day you got here. Did you forget?"

"How could I?"

Kiko smirked. "I'll see you boys later."

"Where are you going?" Gentry asked. "Are you gonna talk to Odette?"

Kiko shook her head.

"I have a job." She shrugged. "If my mom can go upstairs and keep working, then so can I. I have no excuse."

Kiko went upstairs without another word. Keahi looked over at Gentry as he got up from the couch.

"Can I actually talk to you for a second?" Keahi asked and Gentry slowly sat back down.

"Sure," he said, slightly hesitant. "What's up?"

"I tried to get in contact with Autumn, and I didn't have much luck. Quinlan won't tell me anything because she's afraid what happened to Mrs. Hamasaki is going to happen to her. I just need to — I need to know what's going on. I need Odette to be protected."

"So you do care about her?"

Keahi shrugged. "What can I say? She grew on me. Everyone's right, you know? She's a nice girl. Jiyun and Kaeli, they wanted me to —"

"What?" Gentry got to his feet again. "They wanted you to what?"

"Take her away from here." Keahi crossed his arms. "What exactly happened to Lailoken's other fiancées, Gentry?"

He sighed and slouched back onto the couch.

"Are you sure you're ready for that?" he asked.

"It doesn't matter. I need to know. I know you care about Odette, too. She's like a sister to you, right? You and Kiko seem to be the only ones who aren't really afraid of the Baskervilles. How long have you been here?"

"Since I was ten. But it's not the parents you need to worry about. It never was." Gentry sat back on the couch and sighed again. He rubbed his sweaty palm against the armrest and looked up at Keahi. "Lailoken's first fiancée's name was Stasi Malone. She was a very cute girl, Odette reminds me a lot of her actually, when she's playing around in the kitchen. Stasi was a feisty one. She challenged everything Mrs. Baskerville made her do and would challenge Lailoken too. He hated it."

"Well, I already knew he liked control —"

Gentry shook his head. "Not only that. Stasi was gay. I mean, it was pretty obvious she wasn't attracted to Lailoken, but then Mr. Wong caught her making out with Kiko, and it all kinda went down hill from there. Lailoken tried his best, apparently, not using manipulation on her, since you know, they aren't supposed to use their abilities on their spouses, but after that, he started to control her. Then he made her kill herself."

Keahi dropped down into the seat across from Gentry.

"Autumn was a little different. She was a Shield. She was more submissive and obedient than Stasi was. Very timid. Odette was like that before you got here, believe it or not. She was also very insecure, which was something Lailoken used against her. He couldn't manipulate her using his ability, but that didn't stop him."

"What do you mean?"

"Lailoken's charming on the surface. He's well liked by the high-borns. In their eyes, he can do no wrong. But let me tell you, no one's perfect. Lailoken, he... He made her believe that without him, she was worthless. That he brought meaning to her life. He took away her hopes and her dreams, and got her to hate herself so much, Amaris found her dead in the bathtub."

"Well, I understand why you guys didn't want to tell me."

Gentry just shook his head.

"And they say Dreamweavers are monsters."

"What?"

"The high-borns, they say the Dreamweavers are the ones who strip you of your hopes and dreams. In my opinion, they seem like saints in comparison to what I've seen in this house."

"Yeah but I mean, you can't know what a Dreamweaver is capable of."

"I do, though."

Keahi furrowed his brows. "How?"

"My older sister — she summoned one when we were kids. She took away her fears. She asked us to never speak of it, then disappeared through the mirror. My sister was sick, and she died a week later, but she wasn't scared anymore." Gentry shrugged. "Sounds like the opposite of what Lailoken does, if you ask me."

"You wouldn't be afraid of a Dreamweaver?"

Gentry shook his head. "I don't think so, no. I wasn't then, and after what I've seen in this house... well, it would seem more like a good omen to me than a bad one. Why?" he asked. "Got one hiding somewhere?"

"Yeah, if only."

"Are you going to do it?" Gentry asked after a minute or two of silence.

"Do what?"

"Take her away from here."

"That's not really my decision to make. She has to want to leave, and she doesn't." Keahi sighed. He rubbed his eyes beneath his glasses and pushed them up to rest on his head. "Even when she kissed me —"

"Ah, so there was a kiss."

"Yeah, but it didn't mean anything. She's still his fiancée. She didn't say anything about that stopping."

"Maybe she doesn't know she has a choice."

Keahi chewed on the inside of his cheek.

"So his ex fiancées both haunt this house? What's their unfinished business?"

Gentry shrugged.

"Quinlan thinks it might be saving Odette. Lailoken hasn't been to an expo in four years and they went quiet for a while. Then suddenly, he decided this year he wanted to go."

"Why? If he had Pia —"

"I think some of Mrs. Baskerville's friends were giving him shit about not being married yet. It's funny though, how no one seems to remember what happened to his previous brides."

"You think they made everyone forget?"

"I know they did." Gentry got up from the couch to grab something from the fridge. "Lailoken's manipulation is strong. He's one of the strongest Pushers. He can manipulate people without even being in the same room."

"What do you mean?"

Gentry poured orange juice in his glass as he turned to look at Keahi. "I mean like broadcasting, dude — oh shit." He looked back and saw the orange juice spilling from the cup.

"So if someone were to interview him or something — and stream it —"

"That's exactly what I'm saying." He wiped up the orange juice with a wet paper towel. "He's strong."

"Well, what's his weakness?" Keahi asked as he got up. "Everyone has a weakness."

"I don't know — Dreamweavers are the only thing Pushers are afraid of. I have hope because I know they still exist, and I'm going to keep hoping that maybe they'll come back."

"That's a lot to hope for," Keahi said.

"I know, but what's the point of living without hope? Hope keeps you going. The hope for things to get better, the hope that things will change." Gentry shrugged as he took a gulp of orange juice. "When you don't have that anymore, what's left?"

"Despair."

Gentry nodded, running his finger along the rim of his glass. "With despair, you just lose the will to live. So I keep hoping. I keep hoping because I don't ever want to feel like — I want to die. My parents used to say that happiness is a choice. But as I'm sure you know, choices aren't always easy to make. But with hope, they become a little easier."

The night of Halloween didn't take long to come. The kitchen staff catered to their guests, while Odette stayed in her bedroom, pretending she didn't exist. Or at least she would have, if Pia hadn't come up to bother her.

She laid on Odette's bed, crying onto her pillow while Odette tried not to make faces at her in the mirror of her vanity.

"I don't know why he didn't want to take me," she sobbed. "What's wrong with me? I'm beautiful too. Did you even see his date? She's not very pretty."

Her voice was muffled by the pillow, but unfortunately, Odette could still understand every word she said. "Of course I didn't see her," Odette told Pia's reflection. "I'm not allowed to leave my bedroom without permission."

Pia sat up and wiped her face.

"Still?"

"Still. Or trust me, as soon as you came, I would have left a long time ago."

"You still don't like me?"

Odette turned around.

"Why do you care whether or not I like you?"

Pia frowned. "You're Lailoken's fiancée. I've always cared what you thought."

"You don't even remember what happened to you."

Pia dropped her feet down onto the ground.

"Actually, I started to get some of my memories back, from when I was being manipulated." She inhaled sharply.

"Then why are you crying?" Odette asked, raising her eyebrows.

"I wanted him to like me. I wanted everything you have. I was jealous. Nothing but a concubine. I wanted to be more. You're his fiancée, and you don't even want to be."

"Listen to me, Pia. He's not a nice guy —"

"I'm not a nice girl. The things I said to you about Keahi. I only went after him because you wanted him."

"I do not want him."

"Oh please. Don't bother trying to lie to me. I saw you pull him into the pool. I've seen the way you look at him — and I've seen the way he looks at you. I just — I want to be looked at like that too. I want someone to care about me. To respect me as a person."

"And you think you're going to get that with Lailoken?" Odette scoffed, crossing her arms.

Pia shook her head.

"Not even close," she said. "But he's the only option I got. I thought — maybe if I made you jealous enough when it came to Keahi, you'd just go after him and I'd have Lailoken to myself again. But as you can see —" Pia raked her fingers through her dark hair and laughed at herself. "That didn't work out the way I wanted it to."

Odette sat down beside Pia.

"I can't believe you tried to make me jealous."

"I know you like him," she said quietly. "Lie to yourself all you want."

Odette ignored her.

"You deserve better than Lailoken, you know." She glanced at Pia out of the corners of her eyes, but she didn't turn to face her. "You deserve someone who isn't going to treat you like a plaything."

"That's a nice thought," she said, "but I've been his concubine for eight years. After a while, I think you just don't want anyone else."

Odette frowned and finally turned to face her.

"Pia, how old are you?" she asked.

"Twenty-three."

Odette's eyes widened. "You've been his concubine since you were fifteen?"

She shrugged. "He's the only person I've been with. He's the only person I know how to be with. I know what he wants, what he likes."

"Yeah, but you can find all these things with someone who actually cares about you."

She laughed and shook her head.

"Life isn't a fairytale, Odette. Some people don't get a happily ever after. Some of us aren't so lucky. But you are. He wants you."

"Well, I don't want him."

"Love isn't a feeling, Odette. It's a choice. You can choose to be happy with him, or you can choose to be miserable. But ultimately, it's up to you."

Odette thought about her words, even long after Pia had left her room.

Love is a choice.

She had wondered if that was why Mr. and Mrs. Baskerville were still together. Because they chose to make it work despite how unhappy and tired Mr. Baskerville seemed. Surely he could have divorced her and bought someone else if he chose to, but he didn't.

She sat up abruptly when someone knocked at her door. Odette climbed out of bed and went to answer it.

It was Mr. Wong. He had brought her food from downstairs.

Odette frowned slightly as she took the tray from him.

"How's Mrs. Hamasaki?" she asked. "And Kiko?"

"Fine," he said. "They're both doing just fine."

"What about the rest of the staff?"

"Everyone's fine." Mr. Wong always spoke to her in such a way that it seemed like she was bothering him. Odette put her food down on her vanity and turned to him again.

"You don't like me very much, do you?" she asked.

Mr. Wong finally made eye contact with her.

"If you want the truth, I don't see the point in caring about anyone in this house," he said. "Everyone is disposable, Miss Thomsett. Including you." He walked away without another word. Odette frowned and slowly closed the door.

She was disposable.

Since Lailoken had other brides before her, she believed it.

Odette didn't touch her food, and was more than thrilled when Gentry came to fetch her dishes.

"How are they?" she asked, knowing he'd give a better answer than Mr. Wong.

"Keahi and I are teaching the staff sign language so Mrs. Hamasaki can still communicate with everyone. We can — I can — teach you too — if you'd like."

"I don't think Mrs. Hamasaki — or any of them — want to talk to me."

"She doesn't blame you, you know."

"But I do." Her voice came out small.

Gentry glanced at her food tray.

"You're not hungry?"

Odette shrugged.

"I guess I didn't really see the point. I'm ruining everything and I just —" she shook her head. "Not really hungry." She sat on her bed and sighed. "Have you ever got more than you wanted, and felt ungrateful for it?" she asked, twisting the ring on her finger.

Gentry formed a line with his mouth and shook his head. "I've never gotten more than I wanted," he said. "So I don't know how that feels. What's up?"

"I just — I feel like I should want all of this." She looked around her bedroom and then at the diamond on her hand. "I should be grateful for all of it. But I don't, and I'm not. Growing up, this was all I wanted since finding out I was a grot. I had dreams about the expo. About finding the love of my life. But it's nothing like it seemed, and I just feel so bad. People have less than I do and I just don't appreciate it. Keahi's right. I'm a princess."

Gentry stepped into her room and closed the door behind him.

"You're allowed to change your mind, you know. Just because you wanted it once, doesn't mean you have to want it for the rest of your life. You're allowed to change your mind as you grow. Your choices are just that. Yours."

"But what if you want what you're not supposed to want? What if you want something you know you can't have?"

Gentry shrugged.

"You can either find a way to get it or you can move on and hope that the next time, you'll want something you can have." He started to open the door again. "But don't let anyone make you feel bad for what you want, or for changing your mind. You're allowed to change your mind, just as you're allowed to grow."

"What do you want, Gentry?" she asked.

"For things to get better."

"You remind me of one of my friends, you know." Odette tilted her head to the side as she stared up at him while he picked up the tray.

"Really? What are they like?"

"She's very kind, caring. Puts others before herself." Odette got up from her vanity seat and went to her dresser to dig out her Daruma doll. She turned back to Gentry. "She gave me this the night of the expo. He's very special to me." She looked up at him. "It just — it seems like something you would do."

"You're probably right."

"Maybe you can meet her sometime."

Gentry raised an eyebrow.

"Are you trying to set me up?"

Odette smiled.

"I'm asexual," he said.

"So is she." Odette put her Daruma doll back where it was safe in her dresser. "If there's anything I've learned from being here," she said as she turned back to him. "It's that sex doesn't make or break a relationship. It's actually something I wish I'd known sooner."

"You're a smart girl, Odette."

She took a step toward Gentry.

"Will you please tell him I'm sorry?"

"I can't," Gentry said. "I think it's something he needs to hear from you. Apologies aren't really the same when they're said by someone they aren't from."

"I'm not supposed to leave my room."

"Well, I can try to get him to come up here, but I won't make any promises, Odette. He doesn't really like to listen to anyone."

"Yeah, I know that all too well."

"But I'll see what I can do."

Odette chewed on her bottom lip as Gentry started to walk away.

"Wait," she said and he turned around. "Do you think Kiko's going to be mad at me forever?" she asked.

Gentry crinkled the side of his nose and shook his head.

"She's got some fight in her, I'll give her that, but Kiko loves everyone. Including you — and she knows what happened to her mom wasn't your fault. Do you want me to try to get her to come up too?"

Odette shook her head.

"I have hope she will when she's ready. But she knows I'm sorry?"

He nodded. "She knows."

TOVALEY B. KYSEL

16   I'LL STAND BY YOU

The Halloween party came and went; one she didn't attend. One Lailoken attended with someone else.

But Odette wasn't bothered by it. Not the way he wanted her to be. She didn't want to entertain him or any of their family's guests anyway.

The main thing that did bother her, was the fact that November was already coming to an end, and Keahi hadn't come up to talk to her.

Neither had Kiko.

Lailoken hadn't allowed her to come out of her room, having her meals delivered to her by Mr. Wong, and she was too scared to disobey him after what he had done to Mrs. Hamasaki.

His parents had gone on their annual cruise for their anniversary, and it was quiet without Chardonnay screaming about one thing or another. Though Odette did find it peculiar that it had decreased significantly recently.

Perhaps the fact that their cruise was coming up was enough to put her in a better mood.

Part of her wishes she had been able to go with them. At least it would've gotten her away from Lailoken, and out of this house.

She sat on her bed in her underwear watching Pretty in Pink when someone knocked on her door. Her eyes moved to the clock first — it wasn't time for food.

"Odette?"

Lailoken.

"Yes?" she called from where she sat, having no desire to get out of her bed. She didn't even bother to lower the volume of the television to hear him better.

"I'm having some friends over for Thanksgiving tomorrow," he said. "Please wear something nice — something short."

She rolled her eyes.

"Okay! Thank you for inviting me!"

A small part of her hoped that when the dinner came around, she'd see Keahi standing there. That she'd spot him and he'd raise an eyebrow at her after catching her gaze, and she'd smile while trying not to blush. She hoped she could go back to drinking too much water, and he'd protectively stand between her and Lailoken to refill her glass. Creating a wall, his body shielding her from that monster, even if for only mere seconds.

That things could go back to the way they were before she had tried to complicate it.

It had been nearly a month since she saw him last, and though she spent most of her time in her room, staring at the token he had given her, she never bothered to use it. She'd always put it back into the drawer of her nightstand.

Along with the key she wouldn't give back to him.

When Thanksgiving came, Odette forced herself to get up from her bed and get ready for dinner with Lailoken and his friends. She had hope that Jac wouldn't be there, but she doubted she would. They were friends, but far from being apart of the same crowd.

She took a deep breath and sighed while she rummaged through the dresses that hung in her closet. 'Wear something nice,' Lailoken had told her. 'Something short.' Odette stuck her tongue out and made a gagging noise as she continued to flip through the clothes.

"All of these are short. I don't know why he felt he had to specify."

She finally decided on a little black dress with a plunging sweetheart neckline. The flaring, pleated skirt ran a little short, and decided to wear black leggings underneath.

She curled her blonde hair into soft, loose ringlets that dropped against her shoulders.

She went to her dresser to dig for her leggings and her Daruma doll fell out of the drawer. She looked down just in time to watch it return to its upright position.

"Get knocked down seven times, stand up eight." She smiled as she picked up the Daruma doll and put it back in her dresser. "Thank you, Paze," she said softly. "I'm trying."

Odette stared at the vanity mirror once she was done getting ready, feeling slightly naked by the absence of the Dreamweaver key that usually hung flat against her chest. Her silver Odette necklace looked lonely by itself. But she wasn't about to wear it to dinner. She didn't want Lailoken trying to take it from her, fully knowing he hadn't been the one to give it to her.

When she went downstairs, Keahi was the first person she looked for.

He wasn't there.

Kiko stood in his place. She should've known better. She blew it.

Kiko smiled weakly at her, and she kindly returned it before she forced herself to turn her direction to the table and tried not to show the disgust on her face when she was greeted by men. None of whom were looking at her face.

"Don't mess this up," Lailoken whispered sternly into her ear once she took her place beside him. He introduced the four men who were standing at the table with the two of them. The one who sat toward the left to her was Castor, whom she recognized as the son of the man in charge of the scion guard. The one across from her, Declan, had a clean shaven head, and his eyes seemed to be buried in her neckline. Odette sat back in her chair and crossed her arms as brothers, Drake and Brent, were introduced to her next. The two boys looked exactly alike, except one had short hair and the other had his hair tied up.

"Hey princess, why don't you stand up and show us that dress of yours?" Declan said with a smug grin on his face.

"Do not call me that."

"Odette," Lailoken said from beside her. "Stand up." She picked up her napkin from her lap and threw it down on the table and stood up.

"Turn around!" Drake shouted at her. Odette looked at Lailoken and he nodded his head. She did as she was told and Drake whistled.

When she faced them again, Declan had slid his chair out and was patting his lap.

"You wanna sit here instead?" he asked her and puckered his lips. Lailoken laughed. He grabbed his wine glass and took a swig.

Odette slumped back into her chair and Declan groaned.

"Aw, come on, princess." He continued to pat his lap. "Don't be shy."

"I said not to call me that!" she snapped.

"Geez, Lai. I thought you had her under control."

"She's going through a bit of a rebel stage," he said, grazing her cheek with the back of his fingers. "Aren't you, love? She's rather feisty, if you know what I mean."

Odette did her best to harden her expression.

It's just like before, she told herself. Don't let it get to you, don't let it show on your face.

She inhaled deeply.

"You really want me to sit on your lap?" she asked, staring straight at Declan. A slight smirk appeared at the corner of her lips as she tilted her head to the side.

"Are you offering?" he asked.

Odette stood up from her seat without looking back at her fiancé. She moved from her chair and walked around the table to Declan, and brushed her fingers against his neck.

Lailoken didn't take his eyes off of her.

She arched her back and slowly took a seat, but not before Declan managed to grab her. Still, she didn't let her discomfort show on her face. Instead, she continued to readjust herself on his lap. "Excuse me," she told him over her shoulder. "I just — can't get comfortable."

"Oh, that's no problem, princess."

Odette had trouble resisting the urge to cringe every time he called her that.

Lailoken knew what she was doing.

"Odette, come here."

"Why? I think he likes — *Oh*, I'm sure he likes it."

"Honestly, Lailoken, if I had the kind of money you do, I would've bought her myself. But this works too." Declan put his hands on her hips and tried to push her down against his lap.

"That's enough, Odette!" Lailoken snapped.

"Isn't this what you wanted?" she asked him from across the table. "For me to entertain your friends?" Odette turned her head and reached over her shoulder to gently touch the side of Declan's cheek. "You're entertained, aren't you?" she asked him.

"Yes I am, baby."

Lailoken slammed his fist down on the table and stood up.

"I wanted you to entertain them, not act like a fucking slut!" he snapped.

Her eyes widened and she clenched her jaw.

"How am I supposed to know that things are only acceptable when you do them?" she snapped back. "I thought this was what you wanted!"

Lailoken's left eye began to twitch.

Odette slid off of Declan's lap and headed for the stairs.

"Where do you think you're going?" Lailoken asked her, but she didn't stop. Once she was in the hallway, she glanced at the kitchen door, but she didn't go inside.

Instead, she ran up to her room.

"Maybe she's going to cry," Castor said, rather unamused by the dinner that hadn't even started yet. "I hear expo brides tend to cry a lot. It sounds depressing."

"Do you have a boner?" Drake asked Declan before he broke out into laughter with his brother. Declan nearly shoved him out of his chair.

"You would too if she was rubbing her ass all over your dick." Declan grabbed his napkin and dropped it over his lap. He leaned forward and put his elbows on the table before acknowledging Kiko to fill his glass. "You were a little hard on her, don't you think?" he asked Lailoken. "We were just having some fun."

"She was baiting me."

"Why would she do that?"

"Well, you did take someone else to your own Halloween party," Brent said.

"Yeah," Lailoken said, not fully paying attention to the conversation at hand. "I'm sure she was just getting back at me. I'll bring her something to eat later. I'm sure dinner's getting cold." He turned his attention to Kiko. "Can you tell Mrs. Hamasaki we're ready to eat?" he asked. She nodded quickly before running out of the dining room.

"Well, now I know why Lailoken wanted an all-female wait staff tonight," she said as soon as she was clear of them. "They're pigs. You should've seen how they treated Odette. I feel terrible. I should go apologize to her."

Mrs. Hamasaki glared at the door.

"Is she okay?" Amaris asked, and Kiko nodded.

"She ran upstairs before it got worse — and I was positive it was gonna get worse. I don't even feel safe out there. They're disgusting." Kiko shivered where she stood. "Ugh, they were so gross!" She turned to look at the door and frowned. "I should really go apologize to her for the things I said."

"Later," Jiyun said. "We have to get this dinner out to them before Lailoken gets any angrier."

"Can we accidentally spill some hot gravy in his lap?" Kiko eyed the turkey and Jiyun shot her a glare. Kiko widened her eyes when she noticed and put her hands up in surrender. "It was just a suggestion."

Amaris grabbed the tray before Kiko could pick it up. "Hey!"

"I think I should take that out before you accidentally spill something on him — or try to carve something that doesn't need to be carved."

"She didn't deserve that — to be treated like that."

"I know, but we need to get through this dinner." Amaris gave her a quick peck on the lips before nodding toward Mrs. Hamasaki. "Go help your mom with the dessert."

Kiko pouted a little and nodded.

"Fine." She sighed. She walked over to her mom. "I would've made it look like an accident, you know. Drop some gravy on him, oh let me clean that up for you! Drop the knife — oops — there goes your penis, you dick."

Mrs. Hamasaki raised an eyebrow at Kiko as she gave her a disapproving glare.

"What?" Kiko shrugged her shoulders. "We both know he'd deserve it."

'*There is something I have to tell you,*' Mrs. Hamasaki signed to her as she finished layering the apple pie.

"What?" Kiko asked as her mom stuck it in the oven.

Mrs. Hamasaki dusted her hands and pulled Kiko over to the side. She took a deep breath and sighed as she sat down at the counter.

"What is it, Mom?" she asked, and Mrs. Hamasaki pulled her to sit down beside her.

'*He — he is your half-brother.*'

"What?" Kiko got up from the stool. She started shaking her head. "No — no. I can't be related to that piece of shit. Ahren Baskerville is my father? Mom!"

'*I'm sorry — I'm so sorry.*'

Kiko continued to shake her head as she backed away from her mom.

Her eyes began to water.

"I don't believe you," she said. "I can't believe you."

She turned around and pushed open the side door. Kiko ran down to the Baskerville Cave, unable to stay in the kitchen with her mother any longer.

"Hey, are you okay?" Gentry asked as she tried to push past him. He grabbed her arm and made her turn around.

"Ahren's my father."

Kiko broke down into tears as she collapsed to the floor. She shook her head and hid her face in her hands.

Keahi and Abbey came out of their dorm and Abbey mouthed to Gentry, asking what happened.

"She knows," he said, his voice was a little louder than a whisper.

Kiko looked up at him. "What do you mean, 'she knows'?" she asked as she got to her feet. "Gentry! You knew?" She hit him in the arm. "You knew? And you just let me think it was someone else? Who would one day save me and my mom and this whole time, you knew!"

She started to hit him and Abbey pulled her off of him.

"I'm sorry, Kiko. It wasn't my place to tell you and I didn't think you'd ever find out."

Kiko pulled herself free from Abbey's grasp.

"I'm a bastard child. My brother's a monster. My brother made my mom cut out her tongue. This is all just nice to know." She turned to Keahi. "Did you know about this too, Keahi?" she asked, raising her eyebrows. Kiko didn't bother wiping the tears from her cheeks.

Keahi shook his head.

"I barely know what's going on in this house. I'm still trying to keep up."

"I'm sorry, Kiko."

She looked back at Gentry and shook her head as she backed away from the three of them.

"I can't talk to you right now — I can't look at you right now." She scratched the back of her head as she continued to back up to her dorm. "I need to be alone." She slipped into her room and closed the door.

From out in the hall, they heard her throw things around her dorm for a few seconds, before stopping altogether. Min-Jae came from their kitchenette and stood in the hall.

"What's happening up there?"

The three boys exchanged glances and shrugged.

"Happy Thanksgiving," Gentry said.

Min-Jae scoffed, "yeah, really."

Upstairs, despite what was popular belief at the dinner table, Odette hadn't gone up to her bedroom to cry. She couldn't care less what they thought of her. Instead, she paced in her bedroom, trying to figure out how to apologize to Keahi for her actions. If he didn't want to go to her, she would go to him. He didn't owe her anything, and she should have known that from the start. But she didn't know how to apologize.

How would I want Lailoken to apologize to

me?

She frowned at the thought, fully knowing that she wouldn't accept his apology even if he was sincere.

Maybe Keahi wouldn't accept hers either.

Maybe that's why he hadn't bothered to come up to see her.

Maybe now he was just waiting to go home.

Odette slipped off her sandals and pushed them to the side with her foot. She went to her bed and plopped down on her mattress. As she crossed her legs, she opened the drawer of her nightstand and took out the skeleton key. The token he gave her sat beside it. She turned the key over in her hand and noticed the marking on the token was actually a key hole. Though she was curious, she didn't connect the two together in fear that Keahi might disappear. Instead, she lay back on her bed and traced the key with her finger.

"I'm stupid and I'm sorry," she told the key, even though she figured he wouldn't hear her. "God, I'm such an idiot."

She hit her head back against her pillow and groaned.

Odette repositioned herself on her bed and lay on her side, still holding the Dreamweaver skeleton key in her hand, not wanting to let it go. She wondered why it was a key, and how many things it opened. Or what it opened. She sat up a little to peer into her drawer. Even if she wanted to try it, the hole in the token looked too small to fit the key.

She sighed and fell back against her pillow again.

Odette smiled at the memory of when Keahi had first gotten there. How angry he had been, and the way it had faded so suddenly when he realized she needed him. It was like a switch he had flipped off.

No hesitation.

Maybe he would forgive her. He did say he cared.

She couldn't lose hope. Not now.

Odette hadn't realized how long she had been laying in bed, lost in her memories and daydreams, until someone rattled her doorknob. Odette quickly threw Keahi's chain back into the drawer just as Lailoken shoved her door open.

"What is your problem?" he asked her as she sat up. She scoffed and narrowed her eyes. Odette wasn't going to let him threaten her.

"My problem? They were vulgar and rude to me, and you did nothing. You just let them be disrespectful toward me and you laughed! I'm your fiancée! What are you — ow! Lailoken!"

He didn't say another word to her. He grabbed a fist full of her hair and yanked her off of her bed. She tried to reach for the Dreamweaver coin in the drawer of her nightstand, but she couldn't get a grip on the knob to pull it open.

Lailoken put his other hand over her mouth and dragged her down the hallway. He pulled her into his bedroom and slammed the door shut behind him with his foot.

"I don't know what that witch gave you," he told her as he shoved her face down against his bed. "But I'm going to teach you a lesson." He leaned over her, feeling his body press against her back. He whispered against her ear, "if you ever humiliate me again, I swear it will be the last thing you do."

She tried to get up. "Please don't. I'm sorry!"

Lailoken shoved her back down onto the bed as he started to unbuckle his belt.

"Don't make this harder than it is," he told her. His voice was calm as he pulled her hips up, forcing her onto her knees. She felt his hands run up her thighs and she buried her face into the pillow when he ripped open her leggings. The way he touched her made her skin crawl with disgust. "You did this to yourself. Remember that."

17 HARD TO SAY I'M SORRY

Keahi had spent many of his nights in the kitchen, cleaning anything and everything he could think to clean; some things, even twice. He hadn't seen Odette since that night with Mrs. Hamasaki. She didn't come down to the kitchen since then either. She didn't want to see him.

He knew he should be happy. Odette could be a brat, and this is what he wanted.

Or what he thought he should want.

The kitchen had been cleared earlier that evening so that only women filled the positions of the kitchen staff, and after Kiko had come down, he paced the floor of the basement until he was able to return upstairs, much to the annoyance of the other workers who were happy to have the night off. He could overhear ruckus happening upstairs, loud noises, but he wasn't allowed up. Not until dinner was over, and Lailoken's guests had left. Technically he could go up if he wanted, and no one would know.

But out of respect for Odette, Keahi stayed downstairs. He didn't hang around her bedroom unwanted. He didn't linger. Gentry had suggested a few times that he go up to talk to her, but for what purpose? Odette wanted to be alone.

Now she was.

It was late in the evening when a handful of them returned to the kitchen. Though it was nearly spotless, Keahi was the type to not know how to sit still so he decided to clean the ovens again. Considering he didn't need much sleep, there was a lot of work he could get done. Even Mrs. Baskerville had noticed how clean things had been since he started working there. She kept asking him to continue to clean her vases, but he rarely did unless she decided to try to manipulate him, then he had no choice but to play along.

He glanced over at Gentry, who sat with Mrs. Hamasaki as he continued with trying to teach her more sign language. Keahi kept his focus on the oven and started pulling the racks out from it.

Keahi felt a tug at his sleeve and he turned around.

It was Mrs. Hamasaki.

'*How is she?*' she asked him as he stood up from the oven and threw his dirty towel to hang over his shoulder.

He shrugged and shook his head before replying.

'*I don't know.*'

'*What do you mean?*' Mrs. Hamasaki tilted her head to the side and frowned at him.

'*She doesn't want to see me.*'

She grabbed the newspaper from the table and smacked him on the head.

"What was that for?" he asked in a grumble. Keahi rubbed the front of his head and pushed his hair back.

'*You are blind, if you think she doesn't want to see you. Don't be stupid.*'

Mrs. Hamasaki raised her eyebrows and pointed at the door.

"How are you feeling?" he asked, trying to ignore her insistence, but she ignored him and continued to point at the door. "Okay, after I'm done here." He pointed to the oven and grabbed at the towel that hung on his shoulder but Mrs. Hamasaki snatched it from him. "Or I'll go now. Okay. Okay!" he said as she tried to shove him out of the kitchen.

The rest of the house was dark. Keahi didn't bother with the stairs. He turned around in a circle to make sure he was alone, and disappeared from where he stood.

He reappeared right outside of her door, and from beneath the crack at the bottom, he could tell her light was off. Keahi raised his hand to knock, but he didn't.

He turned away from the door and heard something shatter behind him.

"Odette?"

He disappeared from the hallway and went into her room, but it was empty. His heart started to pound a little harder in his chest. "Odette?" he said again and noticed the light in the bathroom was on. "Odette? Are you okay? I'm — I'm going to come in." He grabbed the doorknob and covered his eyes with his hand as he opened it. "I just want to know if you're okay and I'll leave," he said. But there was no answer.

He lowered his hand and she stood there, naked, in front of her mirror. Her face was damp, flushed, and splotchy; eyes bloodshot. The glass he heard was the shattered jar of cotton balls she kept on her counter, broken in a mess on the floor. He tried to be respectful and not look at her, but once he saw what was on her, he couldn't look away.

Keahi tightened his fists at the sight of the bruises and scratch marks along her trembling body. Odette put something down on the counter: it was the Dreamweaver token.

"When he was done with me, I sat on my bed and I thought about calling you," she said softly as her hand moved away from the coin. "But I figured after the way I acted, why would you care? You never came to see me."

"I'm sorry. I should've — I'm sorry."

He felt a pang in his chest. He didn't know what else to say.

She closed her eyes and shook her head. She wasn't blaming him. Odette was positive he had to know that.

"This was my fault," she assured him, but she didn't make eye contact. She couldn't bring herself to look at him. She couldn't bring herself to look away from her reflection. "I deserve what I got." Her voice was hollow, like there was no life to back it up.

His balled fists tightened at his sides, knuckles cracking. He'd kill him.

Keahi exhaled deeply and reached for the bathroom door again.

"Please don't leave," she said in the quietest voice, looking at him in the mirror. "Could you stay?" she asked him in a whisper, so soft he barely heard it.

"I feel safer with you here."

Keahi retracted his hand from the knob and nodded, slowly and subtly. He turned his back toward the door and leaned against it to shut it again as Odette stepped into the bathtub.

She sat down on the floor of her tub and pulled her knees up as she wrapped her arms around her legs. He could easily still see the bruises and scratches on her skin and he forced himself to look away as he slid down onto the ground. The more he stared at them, the angrier he got. He clenched his fists again at his sides, and closed his eyes, telling himself to relax.

His eyes opened when she spoke, but he didn't look at her. "I'm sorry." Her voice shook nearly as much as she did.

"For what?" he asked, staring at the cabinet beneath the bathroom sink, then dropping his gaze to the broken mess on the floor. Keahi kept his focus away from her; he couldn't see her like that.

"Trying to pressure you," she said. "You don't — you don't owe me anything and it was wrong of me. I hope you can forgive me."

He finally looked at her. "Odette —"

"*Please*," she said, her voice broke. "I don't want you to be upset with me."

What he really wanted to tell her was that it didn't matter. That she was being too hard on herself for a mistake she made. For a mistake that didn't leave a mark on him. She apologized for something he "actually wanted to do, but knew it was the wrong thing to do. Odette was visibly broken though, upset with herself and her actions; who was he to dictate what she should feel sorry for?

"I forgive you," he said without further argument, with the hope that upon hearing those words, may make her feel even the tiniest bit better.

It didn't.

"I'm such a fool," she said, burying her face into her arm. "To think that he'd eventually love me — that anyone would love me." She was too overwhelmed by her own thoughts, and her actions. Her mind raced as fast as her heart. She swallowed hard as she looked up at her faucet. "I tried to pressure you into having sex with me and then I tried to make you feel bad about it," she continued, then frowned. "God, I'm just as bad as he is!"

She started crying again and hid her face against her knees.

"Whoa, whoa." He crawled over to the bathtub from where he sat, careful not to touch the broken glass on the floor. Keahi sat by the rug and pulled his knees up to drape his arms over them. "You're far from it," he said, glancing at her. "You're nothing like him. Nothing."

She didn't look at him, but she did lift her head to rest her chin again on her knee.

"You don't find me attractive, do you." Odette stared at the dripping faucet. "I mean, how could you."

Keahi reached to turn on the water, knowing they'd need it to drown out their conversation. He sat back down and pulled up his knees again.

"Me saying no had nothing to do with your appearance."

"It's all I have," she said, and looked to the side as the water began to rise around her. Odette ran her fingers in the warm water, keeping her attention away from him.

"That's not true."

"I'm not smart. I'm not strong. I couldn't get away from him — I let him rape me —"

"Okay, wait." He touched the side of the tub and she glanced in his direction, but she didn't make eye contact. "You did not *let* him rape you, Odette. If there's one thing I need you to understand, it's the fact that it's not your fault. It wasn't your fault. It was never your fault, princess — Odette — sorry," he said as she met his gaze. He looked away. "Force of habit."

"I don't mind," she said with a subtle shrug. "Call me whatever you want."

"What do you want?" he asked in a low voice when he looked back at her.

Her gaze dropped to the faucet, the water continued to flow into the tub. "You know," she said softly, her voice was barely audible over the running water. "You're the only one who's ever asked me that." Her bottom lip quivered as her eyes began to well up again.

"I'm sorry, Odette. I didn't mean to make —"

"No," she said, and made herself laugh a little. "Just — thank you."

"For what?"

"Staying."

She rested her chin on her knee and smiled weakly at him.

They sat in silence for a while. Keahi looked around her bathroom from where he sat on the floor while Odette sat staring blankly ahead. He got up to clean up the glass from the tile. He felt for a hole in his sleeve and tore it off his arm.

"A woman is supposed to clean up after the man," she said, realizing what he was doing.

"I disagree," he said as he glanced at her. He started to pick up the larger pieces and tossed them in the wastebasket. "My father has always told me that if a man can't take care of himself then he doesn't deserve a woman."

"He sounds like a good man."

Keahi stopped with the mess. "Yeah," he said, feeling for a weak spot in his other sleeve. "I guess he is." He tore it off and wiped up the rest.

She looked over her shoulder at him.

"You ready to take a shower?" he asked and she shook her head. "Why not?"

"I don't see the point."

Her gaze fell and she wiped her face with her hands. He pulled off his shoes, then his socks.

He nodded and stood up. "Okay, well... I do."

Keahi rolled the bottom of his pants up to his knees and stuck one foot in the water and sat down on the edge of the tub.

"What are you doing?" she asked as she watched him reach for her washcloth.

"What I need to do," he said as he put soap on the towel. "May I?" Odette averted her gaze and she gave him a subtle, weak nod.

He was gentle with her, using his bare hands against her bruises. For the first time, they felt soft against her skin.

Once he finished, he got her to stand up and he wrapped her towel around her. Keahi carried her out of the tub and brought her to her bed. He slowly managed to get her to put on pajamas.

"You don't have to do this, you know." She watched as he dried her legs and her feet with the towel.

"I know," he said.

Still, he did it every day.

When Odette wouldn't get out of her bed in the morning, Keahi sat with her, and would patiently try to get her to eat the food Gentry brought up, but she'd always tell him she didn't see the point.

He didn't give up though.

Every day.

It irritated her.

"Why are you doing this?" she finally snapped. "Why can't you just leave me alone?"

"I'm not just going to let you rot in your bed, Odette. And you have to eat."

"Why?"

"Because you need food to live?" He shrugged his shoulders.

"Don't get smart with me, Keahi." She turned over on her bed to face the wall. "Just go away."

"I can't."

She tossed something over her head.

It was his key.

Keahi picked it up and put it around his neck. He could walk away. He could go home and pretend that none of this had ever happened.

The only problem was, it did happen. He wasn't going to pretend it didn't.

He went into the bathroom and turned on the faucet for her bath. When he came back into her room, she was sitting up in her bed now; her eyes puffy and red.

"Why are you still here?" she snapped.

"I told you I'd stay until you no longer needed me."

"I don't need you," she said sternly.

"I think you do. You might not want me here, but that doesn't mean you don't need me. That doesn't mean you don't need — someone. Anyone."

She threw her pillow at him. "Leave."

He knocked it away with his hand. "I'm not leaving you again."

Odette climbed out of her bed and stalked toward him.

"Leave!" she screamed again. "Go home! You know you want to — so just do it!"

But he wouldn't.

He went to her dresser and pulled open the first drawer, taking out her Daruma doll. He held it in front of her face. "What about this?" he asked.

She whacked it out of his hand.

"Odette —"

Odette smacked him right across the face. She started hitting him. Punching against his chest as she broke down in tears. She fell against his frame and cried.

Keahi wrapped his arms around her.

"It's okay," he whispered. "It'll be okay." He rested the side of his face against the top of her head and held her close to him. She was shaking.

"I'm sorry," she said softly.

"I know," he said. "It's okay."

He held her in his arms until she calmed down. Keahi loosened his hold on her and took a step back. His hands rested on her shoulders. "Are you ready to take a shower?" he asked.

Though she was hesitant, she nodded.

She moved to the bathroom, and stopped in her tracks. Odette turned around.

"You're not coming this time?"

"I'll be right out here."

"You promise?"

He nodded. "I promise. I'm not going anywhere."

That night, he sat with her on her bed. He sat near the foot of her bed, leaning against the wall, while she sat at the head, resting back against the frame.

Odette stared at the key hanging around his neck.

"Why didn't you go home?"

He turned to look at her.

"Because I said I'd stay until you didn't need me anymore. Odette, if you really want me to leave, then I'll leave. But I need to know that you're gonna be okay."

She frowned. "Why? Stop pitying me."

"I'm not pitying you, Odette. I care about you."

"Why do you keep calling me that?"

"Because I'm worried, okay?" Keahi slid off of her bed. He pulled the rubber band from his hair and ran his fingers through it, brushing stray strands out of his face.

"You're not just saying that to make me feel better?"

He didn't turn around. He stared at the wall and crossed his arms.

"I wouldn't do that."

Odette got off of her bed. She wrapped her arms around him and hugged him from behind. "Thank you for caring about me," she whispered. "I'm sorry I'm weak."

Keahi pulled her arms down and turned around to face her.

"You're not weak, Odette. That's why it's hard to see you like this. Because I know how strong you are." Keahi picked up the Daruma doll and handed it to her.

"Get knocked down seven times, stand up eight." She looked down at the Daruma doll in her hands.

"You stood up," he said. She looked up at him.

"Because I care about you too." She looked down, staring at the key hanging from around his neck. Odette lifted her gaze to meet his.

"Do you want it back?" he asked, and she glanced back down to the key.

She nodded.

Keahi took it off and put it around her neck.

"It looks better on you anyway."

She smiled, and fumbled with the skeleton key. Taking him by his hand, she pulled him back toward her bed.

She nestled against his body, comforted by his arm that wrapped around her.

He just laid flat on her bed, with his arm wrapped around her frame and his thumb gently grazing her arm. Her head rested against his chest, that rose and fell while he breathed. Odette wasn't used to this kind of treatment. Gentle and kind. But she liked it. She liked laying there with him, listening to his heart beat. She looked up at him again and he kissed her forehead.

"Can I ask you a question?" she asked.

"Yeah."

"If it wasn't because you found me repulsive or dirty, why did you turn me down?" Odette tapped her fingers against his chest. "I'm just curious."

"Are you having dirty dreams about me or something?"

She could feel the blood rushing to her face. Odette frowned and averted her eyes.

"No."

"Short answer? I didn't want you to regret it."

She sat up, resting her hand against his chest. "Why would I regret it?"

"You told me it was the only thing you were good for, and that's not true." He shrugged and pushed his hair back. "I wasn't going to take advantage of you like that."

"But I wanted it."

"Did you?" He raised his eyebrows. "Because when I asked you, you couldn't tell me that."

"I thought it was obvious."

"Well, I needed to hear you say that. Too many people do things because they feel like they have to. Because that's what's expected of them, or the only thing they think people want from them." He put his arm behind his head. "I just wanted you to be sure. I mean, you're very beautiful —"

"You think I'm beautiful?"

He smirked a little. "I thought it was obvious."

She narrowed her eyes. "It was, which is why I was confused. I saw the way you watched me when I'd dance in the kitchen. You couldn't take your eyes off of me."

"It was — it was very captivating — *distracting*. I mean distracting. I was trying to do my job and you were being distracting."

"Yeah, yeah. Whatever." She inhaled deeply and sighed. "Well, you missed your chance."

"I'm okay with that."

"Really?"

"You're more than just your looks, *princess*."

"Finally! It's weird when you call me 'Odette' all the time. I feel like I'm in trouble." Odette dropped back down on her bed and nestled up against him. "You didn't have to, but thank you for being my friend."

"It was my pleasure."

Days passed, and she never left her room.

Odette sat on her bed, back pressed up against the wall and her head on Keahi's shoulder as she mindlessly flipped through the channels on her television.

"Thousands of channels," she mumbled. "And nothing to watch." She pursed her lips together and pressed harder and harder onto her remote, as if the harder she pressed, the better chance she'd have at finding something.

No such luck.

Keahi glanced at the clock sitting on her dresser.

"Well, it's almost midnight," he said. "You could try going to sleep?"

"Nah," she said, not bothering to lift her head. "There isn't even an old movie on for me to watch. This is ridiculous."

"You're not tired?" he asked.

She sat up finally and shook her head before running her fingers through her blonde locks. "I haven't really done anything the last week, except stay in here pretending to be sick." She pressed her lips together and formed a tight line. "Well, I guess I wasn't really pretending. I still feel... disgusting."

"Is there anything I can do for you?" Keahi asked while she shifted on her bed to face him. "Can I get you anything?"

Odette shrugged. "You've kept me company, doing your reality manipulation thing. Are you sure *you* don't need some rest?" she asked. "I'm sure that takes a lot out of you. You look tired."

"This is just how I look."

"Well, you look terrible."

"Thanks."

Odette pulled on his arm and tried to push him down onto her bed.

"Why don't you get some sleep? And I'll watch over you for a change." She frowned. "Do Dreamweavers even sleep?"

Keahi sat up and shook his head.

"We don't really need to. Are you sure I can't get you anything?"

"I'm fine," she said, and leaned against him again. "As long as I don't have to go downstairs for a while, I'm fine."

He glanced at the window. "Do you want to — maybe — can I — show you something?" he asked, turning his attention back onto her. She stared at her window.

"Out there?" she asked as she looked at him.

He nodded.

"How are we supposed to get out there?" she asked. "I haven't been allowed outside of the property since I wandered away from Lailoken at the Imperial Quarter. I think he's afraid he's going to lose me in the crowd or something."

"Was that before I — you haven't been off of this property at all?" Keahi slid off of her bed. He turned around and reached his hand out to her. "I'll take you, if you want."

She pursed her lips and looked at his hand before looking down at her pajamas. "Should I change?" she asked, looking up at him. "I'm kind of — in my underwear."

"I promise no one else will see you but me."

"Okay."

Odette took his hand and they dissolved into smoke.

The two of them manifested on the beach. Waves crashed upon the shoreline, and Odette staggered away from Keahi.

"Oh my god, what just happened?" She inhaled deeply. Odette had her hand over her chest as she bent forward like she was about to vomit.

"Are you all right?" he asked and she gulped.

"I'll be fine," she said.

"Sorry," he said, pushing his hair back. "That was my first time doing that with someone else."

"Well, I'm honored but slightly —" Her stomach did flips in her body and she turned away from him, fanning herself with her hand as she dry heaved.

"Are you sure you're gonna be okay?"

Odette closed her eyes as she stood up straight. She inhaled deeply through her nose and exhaled through her parted lips. She nodded.

"Beats being in that house," she said, taking another deep breath of the salty air. Odette curled her toes, feeling the sand come between them. She looked out at the rolling waves. "I don't remember the last time I've been to the beach."

"I can tell," he said. "You're pretty white."

She frowned at him.

"I don't tan, I burn." She looked at the water, and then looked back at him. "Could I —?"

"Be my guest."

Odette took a step forward and her feet began to sink in the wet sand. The water filled the pockets she made when it stretched up the shoreline, and washed her footprints away as it pulled back into the ocean.

"It's beautiful," she said. "Calming. Like a dream."

"There's one more thing," he said. He reached his hand out to her and she took it. But where he led her, wasn't what she was expecting. She followed him up the steps, away from the beach and to a house that sat on a low cliff. She looked around at the seemingly abandoned house he had brought her to as he let her inside.

"You didn't bring me here to kill me, did you?" she asked and raised an eyebrow.

"You don't trust me?" he asked as he closed the door behind her.

"At this point, you're probably the only man I do trust." Odette turned around as she looked at the old house. "But an abandoned house isn't very romantic, Keahi. At least not if you're trying to woo a girl — which is what you're doing — right?"

"I can make anything seem romantic," he said and grinned.

"Can you?" she asked, taking a step toward him.

"Are you challenging me?"

"Maybe." She turned around. "Where are we anyway?" Odette frowned as she stepped toward a few scattered photos on a table.

She picked up a polaroid and held it up. The boy in the picture looked just like Keahi; only now he wore glasses on his own accord. "This isn't your first time being in the mundane world, is it." She was asking without really asking. Odette already knew the answer. She looked back down at the picture as Keahi shook his head.

"My dad used to let my brother and I come here when I was younger. Just so we could see what it was like. But things have gotten worse recently, and now unless someone has a token and knows how to summon a Dreamweaver, well. No one leaves the Woolgathering."

"Sounds like a prison," she said, tucking the picture into her back pocket.

"Nah, it's not so bad. Beats being murdered by high-borns."

"My people."

"I didn't mean —"

"No, I understand. I'm supposed to hate you."

"And?"

She shrugged. "And I don't," she said, catching his gaze. "Not even a little bit."

He smiled. Odette reached out to graze his cheek with the tip of her finger.

"Do that more often," she said.

"I'll try."

She looped her arm around his.

"So what is this place?"

"This was the house we stayed in whenever we'd visit. Kinda like a vacation home, I guess. As you can see, we've abandoned it."

"I'm surprised there aren't any squatters in it." Her eyes widened. "Oh, look!" she squealed. "A stereo!" Odette clapped her hands as she excitedly ran over to it.

"Oh, no." Keahi closed his eyes, feigning discontent, even though he knew the stereo was there, and he knew she'd notice. He also knew what was still in it.

The song started to play.

Alone by Heart.

"Not another eighties song," he groaned, continuing with his façade.

"Aw, Mr. Grumpy Dreamweaver still doesn't like my choice in music?" Odette fake pouted at him. "Clearly someone in your family has the same music taste." She grabbed his hand and pulled him toward her. "You're dancing with me this time." She turned her back to him. Odette reached behind her for his hands and put them on her waist.

"Can't I just watch?" he asked, his hands remained still. He remained still.

"No, don't be boring. This is not a lap dance." She turned to face him. "Though I wouldn't be opposed to you giving me one." Odette grinned at him and tugged at his shirt. "You can take this off, actually."

She started to lift it and he stopped her.

"No, I'm shy."

"Oh, you're shy?" She laughed. "Mr. I-Take-My-Shirt-Off-In-The-Kitchen-So-Everyone-Can-See-My-Body."

"I take it off because it's hot in there," he tried to say without laughing.

"Yeah, it is." She grinned. "What was it Mrs. Hamasaki said?" She pressed against him, fingers clutching at his chest. "Imagine if I took my shirt off in the kitchen."

"You're so inappropriate," he said and she laughed.

"And you're not. It's the cutest thing. I'm not used to a guy being like this." She wrapped her arms around his body and looked up at him. "I bet all you want to do with me is hold my hand and tell me cute things, right?"

"I'd do whatever you wanted to do."

She pushed her hand against his chest and stepped away from him.

"Don't give me ideas," she said as she walked away from him. Odette spun on her heels to face him again. "You'd do whatever I want to do but you won't dance with me." The end of the first chorus came on. "Even though I got you here alone."

Keahi walked toward her and started rolling up his sleeves. He slipped one hand on her waist and when his other found her hand, he laced his fingers with hers and pulled her close to his body. He didn't take his eyes off of her beautiful green eyes. His hand slowly ran down the curve of her frame. She lifted her leg and locked it around his, the roughness of his coarse hand grazed the bare skin of her thigh.

His other pulled away from her hand and found the small of her back. He pulled her closer to him. Her body moved with his.

When his hands found her waist, Odette turned around. She pressed back against him and reached behind her to touch his neck and turned his face toward her. Though their mouths were centimeters apart, their lips didn't touch.

After her hands found his again, she let one go and slowly twirled out from him. Odette turned back in, her body facing his now. The back of his fingers softly brushed against her cheek and she looked up at him.

"I thought you said you didn't dance," she said as the song slowly came to an end. Odette grabbed his hands and took a step back. When she let him go, he crossed his arms.

"I don't," he said. "But if it makes you happy." He shrugged. "Well, I'd do anything for you."

Odette had come to know Keahi, and she knew he wouldn't say things just because he thought she wanted to hear them. She pursed her lips together and glanced away as These Dreams by Heart began to play. She turned back to him.

"Are you going to stop hating on my music?" she asked.

"Probably not," he said. Keahi didn't take his eyes off of hers. "But seeing you happy makes it easier to tolerate." He stuck his hand out to her. "Dance with me?"

She took his hand.

"I'd love to."

But this one wasn't like the last. She wrapped her arms around his neck and his hands remained on her waist. Odette rested her head against his collarbone.

"You know," Keahi's voice was low as he spoke. "I think I'm falling in love with you."

Her eyes began to water. She moved her hands to wrap his arms around her body, and returned her own around his neck; she wanted him to hold her closer. Keahi kissed the top of her head and a tear rolled down her cheek.

"We should go back." She subtly rubbed her cheek against his shirt before stepping away from him. "Before Lailoken realizes I'm gone and sends all of the high-born Shields after me."

"High-born Shields?" he asked; his arms dropped from her waist.

"Scion guard," she said. Odette rubbed her eyes and pretended to yawn. "You know, enforcers of the constitution."

"Right, so that's what they're called."

"What did you think they were called?" she asked.

He shrugged. "Assholes."

She laughed and twisted her hair around her finger.

"We don't have to go back, you know," he said. "We could stay here. You could stay here, with me, if you wanted. Whatever you want."

The smile faded from her face and she turned away from him.

Odette moved to the window and looked out. The house sat on a small rise, stairs led down to a private beach. The waves rolled in against the shoreline, and dragged back. Surface of the water, glistening from the moonlight.

"This feels like a dream," she said. She didn't turn around. "I would love to stay here. To fall asleep listening to the crashing waves. To wake up — beside you." Odette turned to face him. "But it's unrealistic."

"Why?" he asked. Keahi went right up to her. "What makes this so unrealistic? Because you might be happy? Because you could be happy?" He took her hand and placed her palm flat against his chest. "Feel that?" he asked. "I'm real, aren't I? I think I'm falling for you, and I think you're falling for me too. I think you've been — you're just scared."

She pulled her hand away from him.

"Please don't challenge what I say," she said and turned away from him. Odette crossed her arms. "Take me home, Keahi."

"Whatever you want," he said. He snapped his fingers and the stereo went dead. Keahi put his hand on her shoulder and they disappeared.

Odette went to bed without another word to him.

He just kissed her forehead and let her be.

TOVALEY B. KYSEL

18 ALL OUT OF LOVE

On South King Street, Lailoken sat relaxed in a bar known to scions as The Wise Mongoose. On the outside, the bar looked like most other scion shops; run down and abandoned. One of those places you'd pass while driving in your car. You know it's there, you've seen it, but you've never been there. The type of place you find yourself wondering, 'is it still open?' every time you pass, but are never intrigued enough to check it out yourself. Somehow, you always managed to forget about it until you see it again on your way to somewhere else.

Scions had places like that all over Hawai'i, and even all around the world.

Across from him, was Jac Valentine, who was dragging her dagger into the wood of the table. It didn't seem to matter how many times the waitresses would tell her to stop. She'd continue to carve things into the surface like she hadn't heard them.

"Odette's been very difficult lately." Lailoken ran his thumb against the edge of his beer mug. "My manipulation is no longer working. At all. You should've seen her at Thanksgiving. It was a fucking disaster. She was rubbing her fucking ass against Declan's dick."

Jac snorted.

"You think that's funny, Jacinta?" he snapped.

"Don't call me Jacinta!" Jac gripped her knife and threatened to throw it at him. But he didn't flinch. "How is that even possible?" she asked, spinning her knife on her fingers. "There's no potion strong enough for that. Are you sure it was even Sophie?"

Lailoken shook his head.

"Not anymore." He chewed on the inside of his cheek as his eyes scanned the pub. "I had an interesting nightmare a couple of months ago," he said, as he returned his attention back to Jac. "I didn't think anything of it at the time, but now, I'm not so sure. Part of my desk was broken... What is it your dad's obsessed with? What are they called?"

She raised an eyebrow. "Dreamweavers?"

"Dreamweavers," he repeated after her as he sat back in his chair. "I think it's a Dreamweaver. Not the result of some stupid potion. Maybe that witch was telling the truth. She was just the first one I thought of because Odette had come out of there."

"Dreamweavers are extinct, Lailoken. They were eradicated a long time ago because of that Thackery guy."

Lailoken ran his hand over his head, smoothing his hair back in the bun. "I don't believe that," he said. "Because if they were, why would we continue to take precautions? Have woven symbols on our bed frames? What are we so afraid of?" he asked, running his finger along the bottom of his glass mug. "We shouldn't be afraid of anything if they're no longer a threat."

"Well, no one's seen or found one in years. Decades, even. I would know. Like you said, my dad is obsessed with them. Obsessed with proving they're still around — hey, maybe you two should talk." He didn't react to her words. She was beginning to find this conversation to be rather pointless. "Who do you even suspect?"

"There's a new kitchen boy," he said. "Odette used to spend a lot of time in the kitchen back in September and October."

"Is Kitchen Boy spending a lot of time *in* Odette?" Jac laughed. Lailoken wasn't amused, though she expected that. She rolled her eyes and pressed her fingers against the braids that were tight on the side of her head. She raked her fingers through the loose hair on the opposing side. "Seriously, Lai? A kitchen boy? Christ, she's got low standards. Are you sure, though? I mean, didn't your mom want her to know how to cook and clean and all that shit that 'good wives' are supposed to know how to do?"

He shrugged, hardly paying attention to a word she was saying. She wasn't telling him what he wanted to know. "How can I tell if he's a Dreamweaver?" he asked.

"Tell him to do something he'd never do unless he didn't have a choice. Dreamweavers can't be manipulated. That's what makes them so dangerous. Because as strong as Shields are, even we have weaknesses that will let our guard down." Jac stabbed her knife into the wood and sat back, crossing her legs. "If you really want to be an asshole, tell the guy to rape her. She'll hate him, you can have him tortured and killed for sleeping with your fiancée. Problem solved."

"No," he snapped. "I don't want him touching her."

Jac yanked her knife out of the table. "Well then maybe you —" she pointed the tip of her blade at him — "shouldn't have manipulated her from the start, Lai. That girl looked at you like you were a god. She probably would've done anything for you, and you pushed her away because you were an impatient little horny boy. You did this to yourself. If she likes him, well, you're the only one to blame here."

"I thought you were on my side."

"You're an idiot. I don't side with idiots. You know the only reason why we're 'friends'." Jac held up her hands to make finger quotations. "Let her go. Just buy a new bride. It's not like your family can't afford it."

"They are not going to make a fool out of me."

"Your pride will be your downfall, you know. She doesn't like you. Get over it. This unrequited love shit isn't cute. It's creepy and it's pathetic. I can't believe you're actually stooping this low. Especially over some chick who's barely legal."

"It wouldn't be unrequited if he wasn't in the picture."

"I've told you. Countless times! You can't manipulate someone into loving you. You can convince them that they do, but that doesn't make it real. They have a word for that, you know. It's called abuse." She got up from her chair. Jac closed her butterfly knife and put it away. "Deny it all you want, but we both know how you are."

"Where are you going?"

"I'm tired of this conversation." She stepped away from the table. "Let me know when you grow up."

He scowled as she walked away. Lailoken sat back in his chair and when he looked up at the balcony level, he saw someone take a step back. He narrowed his eyes and finished his beer before leaving.

On the second floor, Shiro daringly peered over the balcony again and watched him leave. He got out his cell phone and quickly pulled up Midori's name.

"Hey, I'm at The Wise Mongoose and you'll never guess who else was here," he said as he pushed himself through the crowd. Shiro lowered his voice. "He knows she has a — you know what. He was talking to Jac about it — no, I don't know what he's — can you let me finish talking? Did you get back home from the Imperial Quarter yet? Okay, I'm going to leave soon." His voice dropped. "Midori, wait, don't hang up."

Shiro slipped his phone back into the pocket of his shirt as several men approached him.

"Hey guys," he said in a shaky voice.

"Look, Charles. It's one of those men who think the gender roles don't apply to him. Whatta you doing wearing a skirt?" he asked as he shoved Shiro.

Shiro shrugged.

"What's wrong with liking skirts? Or wearing them? Or wearing make-up?"

"You're wearing make-up too?" He leaned toward Shiro. "You fucking —" the man fell over, grabbing his head. The other two did the same and they groaned in pain.

"Leave me alone, please," he said as he walked passed them. Shiro got out his phone again. "All right, I'll be — shit."

"What?" Midori asked as Shiro slowly lowered the phone. "What! Shiro!"

Shiro nearly bumped into Castor Vanderbilt. Castor towered over him. He ran his hair through his short, thick black hair and looked down at Shiro with his dark, almost black, eyes.

He took one look at Shiro and he sighed.

"Shiro, Shiro, Shiro... Causing problems again?" he asked as he circled him like a shark. "You know, my father, who is —"

"I know who your father is," Shiro said, rolling his eyes. "Here's the thing. I don't care. If you want to fine me, go ahead. But if I want to wear skirts, then I'm going to fucking wear —"

Castor punched him so hard in the face, Shiro fell over backward. His lip was bleeding, torn against his teeth; one of which Castor cracked with the ring he was wearing.

"Put on the fucking pants, Shiro. Or next time we meet," Castor said as he stepped over Shiro's body. "We're not going to let you go. You'll be sold, and we'll see how you feel about being someone's little bitch." He kicked him once in the face, and then another time in the ribcage before Castor let himself into the bar without another look behind him.

Shiro groaned and rolled onto his back. He reached for his phone that had been knocked out of his hand. "Midori?" he said, "are you still there? Maybe you should come get me instead."

Midori went to pick him up as quickly as she could. She left the house without a word to Sophie or Paisley and found her brother at a bus stop almost a mile away from The Wise Mongoose.

"I don't want to hear it," he said as he got into the car.

"Well, too bad. I don't know why you need to wear skirts, Shiro. I'm trying to be supportive, I really am, and you know I love you, but look at your face!"

"Do you think Sophie can fix my nose?"

"How should I know? They aren't Luna Lovegood! Sophie can't just wave a wand and make it better, Shiro." Midori pulled over and stopped the car.

"Why did you stop?"

"Why can't you just wear pants?" she asked.

"Before Mom died, she told me to express myself. She didn't care that I wore skirts. Why do you, Green? why does it bother you?"

She started screaming at him in Japanese, but he couldn't understand a word of what she was saying.

"In English, please."

She glared at him.

"Mom doesn't have to see you get beaten up. Or worry that every time you leave, you might not come home." She gripped the wheel tightly and sighed in frustration. "I don't care about the *skirts*, Shiro. I care about your safety. You're my little brother and I care about what other people might do to you because they don't like what you're doing. I can't lose you." Her eyes began to water and she bit down harshly onto her bottom lip, fighting the tears. "You're the only family I have left. Don't do this to me."

"I'm sorry," he said, wiping the blood that began to drip from his nose again. "But we should be allowed to wear whatever we want to wear. If other people have a problem with it, that's on them."

"You're the one who's going to suffer for it."

"I'd rather suffer being who I am, than suffer silently, being someone I'm not." Shiro shrugged. "I don't wear them every day, I like pants too every now and then, but it's hot in Hawai'i, and I can't wear that every day. I don't know how Paisley does it. If I want to wear a skirt, I'm going to wear a skirt — but — I will try to pick where I go a little more carefully. And who I leave the house with."

"Okay," she said, and wiped her face with the sleeve of her shirt.

"Are we okay?" he asked her.

She nodded.

"Okay," he said. "Because my nose really hurts. Can we please go? I'm bleeding out over here."

"Right! Of course, oh my god, I'm sorry."

"Can you imagine Sophie with a wand, though?" Shiro asked, holding his shirt over his nose as he tried to contain the bleeding. "I bet they'd whip it out for everything."

Midori laughed, then stiffened her expression.

"Tell me more about what you heard Lailoken say to Jac," she said and Shiro nodded.

"He said they have a new kitchen boy, and Odette's been spending a lot of her time in the kitchen, and she's completely resistant to his manipulation. Sophie seems off the hook for now, but I don't think we're in the clear yet." He glanced at his sister. "Something bad is going to happen, Midori. I can feel it."

"You're being paranoid," she said.

"Do you really believe that? What about the ghost that's been haunting Paze? We know who she is now and you think I'm being paranoid? What if he kills her too?"

The car came to a screeching stop, right in the middle of the road. Cars around them began to honk and zoom past them, yelling expletives and sticking their middle fingers at them. Midori ignored them all.

"What are you doing!" Shiro shouted.

"Do not ever say those words again." Midori slowly turned to look at her brother. "Do you understand me?" she asked. "Never say that again. Never. I never want to hear those words leave your mouth ever again, Shiro."

"You can't just keep acting like nothing's wrong," he said, his voice was slightly muffled by his hand and his shirt; words coming out like he was talking through his nose. "I get we all have our own ways of dealing with things, but ignoring it and pretending like nothing's happening isn't gonna make the problem suddenly go away. No matter how much you want it to."

Midori started the car. She didn't say another word to him.

He was right. None of them were very good with handling serious issues, but Midori often felt the need to pretend they weren't as serious as they were, or that they didn't exist at all.

That they weren't problems at all.

She raked her fingers through her hair, not looking at her brother again. Her eyes were kept on the road, but her mind was elsewhere.

She couldn't stop thinking about what he said.

You can't keep acting like nothing's wrong.

With everything falling apart around her, how did she have a choice to act any other way? Midori turned on the radio and sank back in her seat.

It was the same when her mom died. She held it together while everyone broke down around her. Her mother's sister, her father. She had never seen him cry. Though it broke her heart, she didn't let it show on her face. She held it together. She greeted and thanked everyone who came to the funeral. There were no dry eyes except for hers.

She remembered the way Shiro would throw things at her, calling her names. Calling her heartless. She just pulled him close and hugged him tightly while he cried.

Midori tended to live her life in denial.

She cried over little things. She got upset over little things. Shiro would often tell her it was because she kept things in, though she never felt like she did.

If she wasn't strong, then who would be?

People needed someone to be strong. Or at least that was the mask she had convinced herself was her true face.

She didn't know how to deal with her problems head on, though she told everyone else to. She didn't know how to practice what she preached. She took a deep breath and told Shiro to call Paisley. To tell her they were on their way.

Midori didn't say anything else.

Not even when she was sitting outside in the backyard on the patio and Sophie came to join her.

"He's going to be okay," they said as they took a seat beside her. "Paisley's — well — Phoebe's going to make him something to eat. Paisley would burn the house down."

Midori didn't even look up.

Sophie sat forward and nudged her arm with their fingers. "Hey, what's wrong?"

For a moment longer, Midori kept her focus fixed on the blades of grass that waved in the wind. "Am I heartless?" she finally asked, slowly bringing her gaze onto Sophie. "Am I — bad at dealing with things?"

Sophie sank back in their chair.

"What makes you think that?"

"I don't know. I just —"

"What did that little punk say to you?" Sophie started to get up. "I will break his nose again —"

"Nothing," Midori said as she grabbed the front of Sophie's shirt. "Just stay with me."

Sophie slid into Midori's chair with her and scooped her into their lap. They wrapped their arms around her, and rested their chin on her shoulder.

"What's wrong, Green?"

"I didn't cry at my mom's funeral." She stared blankly ahead. "I don't know how to deal with loss, Sophie. What if Odette dies?"

Sophie hugged her tighter.

"She's not gonna die."

"How do you know?"

"I don't," they said. "But if Dreamweavers are as good as Paisley tells me they are, then I have a reason to believe she's gonna be okay."

"I'm sorry for what I said."

"When?"

"When I questioned why you did what you did. I never should've done that. You're right — Paisley's right. It was the right thing to do." Midori turned around and faced Sophie. "I was just scared I could lose you." She looked down at Sophie, and her eyes began to water. "It scares me every day. I know you do what you need to do and deep down I know you're going to be okay but — it still scares me."

Sophie wiped Midori's face.

"Do you want me to stop?" they asked. "Just say the words, Midori. You know I'd stop for you."

Midori pressed her lips together. She closed her eyes and shook her head. "Because then you'd stop being you — and I can't have that."

"Why is everyone being so emotional." Sophie wiped their own eyes before kissing her girlfriend's face. "You're all making me cry like a damn baby."

Midori laughed as she turned to lean back against Sophie again. Sophie wrapped their arms around her, and laced their fingers together over her stomach.

"You loved your mom, Midori. Just because you didn't cry at her funeral, doesn't mean you loved her any less than anyone else there."

Midori put her hands over Sophie's.

"I almost forgot. Shiro overheard Lailoken and Jac at The Wise Mongoose place. He knows about the Dreamweaver, Soph. He's gonna try to manipulate him into doing something." She got off of Sophie and leaned against the table. "What if it doesn't work?"

Sophie got up.

"Let's go ask Paisley."

"Ask her what?"

"If Dreamweavers know they are unaffected by a Pusher's manipulation. I mean, they must know. I think that was part of the reason they were supposed to be killed off." Sophie reached their hand out for Midori's. "Come on, let's go talk to the Eversleys and laugh at Shiro's bruising face."

"You're such an ass." Midori laughed as she took Sophie's hand.

"Yeah, but you love it."

"Do I really, though?"

Sophie narrowed their eyes and nudged her with their elbow.

The Dreamweavers knew, but that didn't stop the worrying.

Phoebe crossed her arms as she stared at the four of them sitting at the dining table.

"Why don't you call Viola over here?" she asked, raising her eyebrows at Paisley. "She has Foresight. She can tell you guys if something bad's gonna happen."

"That might not be such a bad idea," Shiro said. He still held a towel to his face.

"But do we really want to know know?" Midori asked.

"It beats not knowing." Paisley got out her phone. "I don't think I can stand not knowing anything anymore. I can't stand all of this maybe this, maybe that. I need to know something."

"Even if it's bad?" Sophie asked.

Paisley stopped fumbling with her phone. She nodded and looked at Sophie. "Even if it's bad."

It didn't take long for Viola to arrive. Once she got off of work, she came straight over. She was very petite, small in stature and under five feet.

"This is your cousin?" Shiro raised his eyebrows and Viola glared at him as she tied her hair up in a ponytail. "Okay," he said as he took a step back from her.

"You guys aren't decorating for Christmas?" Viola asked as she looked around the house. "Your house is looking a little bare."

"Nope," Phoebe said. "We never do anymore. Sophie's still trying to convince Mom to let them do it but she hasn't budged yet so we're definitely not getting a tree again this year but at least Dad's got one."

"I miss Dad," Sophie said absentmindedly.

Phoebe and Paisley both shook their heads.

"So which of you saw Odette last?"

Sophie raised their hand. "I gave her a potion a few months ago."

"Give me your hands."

Sophie put their hands out, palms facing the ground. Viola put her hands beneath theirs, but they didn't touch. She closed her eyes. Within seconds, she jumped away from Sophie and turned around, running her hands through her hair, pulling the rubberband out.

"What?" Paisley asked. "What happened?"

"I saw the house," Viola said, not making eye contact with any of them. "And I saw Death."

"You mean —" Phoebe started and Viola nodded.

"I saw him — the Angel. He was there to collect." Viola looked at the rest of them, each of them individually. "I'm sorry," she said as she took a step back.

Paisley pushed her bright orange hair out of her face. "We have to get her out of there."

"How?" Midori asked. "They're Pushers, Paze."

"And you're a Shield."

"I could barely take on Lailoken in the Apothecary! I can't take on him and his mother too. Are you out of your mind?"

"Hey," Sophie said, taking hold of Midori's hand. "Don't yell at her."

Midori slipped her hand out of Sophie's and walked to the door. "I'm sorry, Paze, but I can't do that. Shiro, let's go."

"But —"

"Now."

Midori only glanced at Sophie before letting herself out of the house.

"I'm sorry," Shiro said as he got up from his seat. "I'll try to talk to her. I'll text you." He ran to follow after his sister.

Viola turned to Phoebe.

"Can I get a drink? I need a drink."

Paisley sank back into her seat while Sophie stared blankly at the front door, still seeing the ghost of Midori's presence as she left.

"I can't believe she did that."

"I was asking too much. She's right." Paisley looked up at Sophie.

"You know what she was thinking?" Phoebe asked as she poured Viola a shot of vodka.

Sophie and Paisley both looked at her.

"If she let her guard down while you guys were at the Baskervilles, and Lailoken convinced you all to commit suicide, she wouldn't be able to live with herself. That's what she couldn't do. She couldn't be responsible for causing you all to die."

Sophie narrowed their eyes.

"How do you know?"

"She let her guard down as soon as she got scared — at the thought of losing you."

"We all want to be strong on the outside," Viola said, swiveling on the stool she sat on at the counter. "But the truth is, most of us just aren't. We'd like to be, you know? We like to think we'd play the hero in tough situations, but most of us are just deer in headlights."

"You said you saw Death," Sophie said as they took a step toward Viola. "Is it possible what you were sensing

— they were already dead? That house is haunted —"
Sophie's words wavered off as Viola shook her head.

"Someone dies in that house." Viola glanced at the
calendar hanging on the refrigerator. "Before the year is
over."

"But that's in ten days," Sophie said as they looked
back at Paisley. "Even if I could make a potion, that's not
enough time. I don't have enough time."

But Paisley didn't even look up at them. She sat there
in her own daze, lost in her thoughts. She sank back
in the chair and pulled her feet up on the edge as she
wrapped her arms around her legs. Sophie looked back
at Phoebe, who just shook her head, acknowledging that
they just leave her be.

"Is she going to be okay?" Sophie asked.

Phoebe nodded. "After a while." She pushed a shot
glass across the counter to Sophie. "Are you?"

Sophie tore their attention away from Paisley. They
looked at Viola then at Phoebe.

"Do I have a choice?"

TOVALEY B. KYSEL

19 THRILLER

Since leaving the bar, Jac had gotten on her dirt bike and went straight home. She lived deep in Manoa Valley in an old redwood house. What set her home apart from many others, was the bridge connecting to the biosphere treehouse built in a banyan tree that stood near her home. Her father, Gerard Valentine, was a very private man, and they lived in the middle of many trees, with the sound of the waterfall faintly running in the background. He wasn't above spying on others though, especially people who tried to venture onto his property.

Her father often used the treehouse to scare the teenagers who thought it was funny to trespass on his property. He'd sit up there with his crossbow and shoot arrows at their feet.

Luckily, of course, he always managed to miss.

Jac dropped her bike and ran up to the wall and pulled on the chain, that raised the bamboo curtain. Gerard thought it was important to be open and one with nature, so there was a whole wall missing from their house, covered by nothing but a curtain, of thin bamboo strung together. She tied the chain and went inside.

"Dad!" she shouted, but there was no response. Jac ran to the bridge that lead to the treehouse. It was mostly concealed by the surrounding trees, but the overpass was unsteady. She hadn't gone across it since she nearly fell off of it a few years back. "Dad! Are you pretending to be Indiana Jones again?" she called, but there was no response.

"He's not home yet," said a voice that came from behind.

Jac turned around.

"For Christ's sake, Rosie, you scared me."

"No, I didn't. Nanaue couldn't scare you, Jac."

Rosie was Jac's younger sister, but nearly a head taller. She always wore her thick hair down, while Jac had insisted in keeping at least half of her own in tight braids.

"But you were shouting in the house and I couldn't focus on my book." Rosie held up the book in her slender hands.

"That book is almost as big as your head," Jac said as she pushed past her sister and went for the kitchen. "So where's Dad then? He never leaves the house and I've got something important to tell him." She opened the refrigerator and pulled out the orange juice.

"Weren't you with Lailoken?" Rosie asked, closing her book. She wrapped her arms around it as she held it against her chest as Jac drank straight from the bottle. "What could you have possibly gotten from that conversation that you'd feel the need to tell Dad?"

"You just don't like him," she said, wiping her mouth with the bottom of her top.

"Of course I don't like him. He's vile. It isn't as if you care for him much either."

"It's Dreamweaver stuff," Jac said, and capped the juice before returning it to the fridge.

Rosie rolled her eyes as she climbed onto the bar stool. She put her book down on the counter. "You aren't really feeding into Dad's delusions, are you? He's bad enough without you supporting this."

"I don't support it. But Lai thinks he's got a Dreamweaver in his house and I think it's something worth looking into. He seemed kinda freaked out by it."

"Oh my god, you're out of your mind." Rosie slipped off of the stool and turned away from the counter. "Just like he is. Dreamweavers are extinct, Jac!" she said as she spun around.

"I never said they weren't, I just think it's something to look into. Lailoken's getting all fussy about his bride."

"Poor girl."

"Eh, she's not so great."

"How would you know? You don't know what her life was like. Maybe she would've been different if she hadn't been raised to be a submissive bride."

"Maybe she would've, but so what? This is life — that's her life — and it's not our problem. What parents want to do with their children is not our problem."

"And Lailoken's supposed Dreamweaver is our problem?"

"God, Rosie, that's not the point!"

"Then what is the point?"

"I would just like to believe, for a damn second, that Dad isn't as crazy as everyone thinks he is. You think I enjoy being the daughter of 'Crazy Old Gerard'? No! I'm sick of it!"

"Maybe you should stop caring about what society thinks of you. I didn't even think you did care."

"Everyone cares. You can put on a brave face and tough it out, but that doesn't take away the fact that it hurts. We're conditioned to care. Conditioned to believe that what society tells us is right. People think Dad's crazy, Rose. I know that bothers you too. You might not care if people think you're weird, but it's different when it's Dad, isn't it."

"Yeah, I guess. But Dreamweavers, Jac?" Rosie tapped her fingers against her book that remained on the counter. "This is going to make him freak out."

"I know, so I promise to ease into it, okay?"

Rosie nodded. "Okay," she said, and pulled her book off of the counter, just as Jac made her way around it.

"So where'd he go?" she asked.

"He went to the market."

Jac grabbed her sleeve and made her turn around.

"Like a scion market or a mundane one?"

"A scion one, duh." Rosie ripped her sleeve out of Jac's grasp. "Like I'm going to let him go to a mundane market, especially by himself. The neighbors think we're weird enough." She had her book in one hand, and used her other to flatten her skirt as she sat down. "I don't need him out in a mundane market where he could just expose the scion society and we'd get in trouble again." She crossed her legs and looked up at her sister.

"We have trees for neighbors, Rosie."

"Exactly," she said and sat back in the chair.

"Well when's he coming back?" Jac asked, pacing back and forth. "Did he say?"

"I'm sure it shouldn't be too long. Will you please sit down? You're giving me anxiety."

"Wouldn't want that."

The two girls turned around. Their father stood there cradling a brown paper bag in his arm. Gerard was an older man with short gray hair, with a matching mustache and goatee. His skin was weatherbeaten, particularly on his face, around his eyes and mouth. There were wrinkles by his eyes, even when he wasn't smiling.

"Well, it's about time, Dad," Jac snapped as she reached for the bag he was holding. "What'd you buy?" she asked and he moved it out of her reach.

Gerard simply had to hold the bag over his head. Jac was too short to reach it.

"Nothing," he said. "Were you waiting for me or something?"

"Uh, yeah," Jac said. She glanced at her sister who tried to bury herself beneath her book. Jac turned her attention to her father and stuffed her hands into her back pockets. "What exactly — uh — do Dreamweavers —"

"Dreamweavers? Where? Did you see one?"

Rosie lowered her book and twisted her body to look at her sister. "That was your idea of easing into it?" she asked, while their father ran to the counter and put his bag on the surface.

"Did you have a better idea?" Jac asked.

"Yes!" Rosie snapped. "Not telling him!"

"Where was it, Jac? What did you see?"

She turned on the soles of her boots.

"I didn't exactly see anything, Dad." She walked over to the counter as he rummaged through the cabinets. "Someone I know, might, well, they think they might have one in their house. But —" she tapped her fingers on the edge of the counter. "They aren't entirely sure."

Gerard turned around and leaned against the counter.

"Well, what'd you tell them?"

"They asked me how they can tell if it's a Dreamweaver, and so —"

"And?"

Jac stomped her foot. "I'm trying to tell you, Dad!"

"Right, okay, sorry." He stood up straight and twiddled with his thumbs as he waited.

"And so I told — them — that Dreamweavers can't be manipulated. So I told them to just command them to do something they wouldn't normally do. If they don't listen," she said and shrugged.

Gerard hurried around the counter and grabbed Jac's shoulders.

"Are they going to tell us what happens?"

Jac shrugged. "I'm sure they will. The only reason I'm not telling you who it is, is because I don't need you barging into their homes like Mom said you used to do when we were little."

"Fair enough."

Gerard dug into his pocket for his keys. "Come, girls. I'm going to show you both something you've never seen before." He grabbed the paper bag from the counter and headed down the hallway.

Jac and Rosie exchanged glances. Rosie got to her feet and put her book on her seat and followed Jac. "Where exactly are we going?" Jac asked.

Gerard led them to a large, iron door at the very end of the hallway. It had their metal coat of arms hanging on it. The entire thing had rusted.

"Do you remember this door?" Gerard asked as he turned to face his daughters.

"You mean, do I remember you yelling at me when I was twelve and tried to open it? *Yes.*" Jac crossed her arms.

Gerard grunted.

"This door is forged with iron from the blood of Dreamweavers. Made by your great-great granddaddy after the eradication. What's behind it — well. You'll see."

Gerard got out his old matching rusty key and unlocked the bolted door.

He flipped on the light switch and led them down the wooden, creaky stairway.

"What the hell is this place?" Jac asked as the dark, dusty room came into view. There were large iron cages, iron posts and shackles. The two girls turned around, observing the room they had lived over their entire lives and had never known existed.

"This... den will hold a Dreamweaver," Gerard said simply.

"Hold one or torture one?" Rosie asked. She stared at a large, rectangular wooden frame with rollers at both ends. There were cuffs at the top and bottom. She caught sight of another device. It appeared like a sawhorse, only the top piece was triangular in shape, and weights were at the bottom near the feet. She looked away from it. "Why do you have torture devices, Dad?"

"You wouldn't hold a Dreamweaver to keep it as a pet, Rosalina. You don't domesticate them. They're savages. Your great-great-granddaddy used to harvest them."

"For what?"

"What's it matter, Rosie?" he asked. Gerard leaned against the rail of the stairs and crossed his arms. "According to you, there's no more Dreamweavers. You've nothing to worry about."

She looked at the torture devices again.

"They're just barbaric," she said. "I know what these are for — and I know that's a Spanish donkey. Please tell me you've never used them, Dad. It's wrong."

"Maybe, but so is stealing one's will to live."

Jac came around and kicked one of the iron cuffs on the ground. "You're really serious about this stuff, aren't you, Dad."

"Jac!" Rosie shouted and Jac shrugged her shoulders.

"Listen to me, both of you." Gerard put the bag down and reached for their wrists and pulled them by the foot of the stairs. "You have to understand that what I do, I do it to ensure the safety of you both. If anything were to happen to either of you — you're all I have left." He looked at his youngest daughter. "I'm not a monster, Rosie. But I will do what I need to do to protect my family."

"But you can't just —"

"If they harm one of you, I can, and I will."

She wiggled her wrist free from her dad's grasp and pushed past him, running up the stairs. Gerard sighed and turned to Jac as he released her wrist. She was staring up at the entrance as her sister's footsteps faded.

"Maybe I should go talk to her," he said, rubbing his temples.

"I'll talk to her." She started up the stairs.

"Jac —"

She halted and turned around. "Yeah?"

"You'll keep me posted, right? About the Dreamweaver?"

She pulled her gaze away from her father and looked at the room. Inhaling deeply, she nodded as she exhaled and turned to him again. "Of course."

"That's my girl," he said and nodded toward the door. "Go talk to your sister."

Jac went upstairs and looked for Rosie. Her book was gone from the chair she sat in when their dad came home so she figured she'd try her room next.

Her door was closed.

She raised her hand to knock with her knuckles.

"Rosie? It's me." Jac jiggled the doorknob. "Let me in." She pressed her ear up against the wood to see if she could hear movement.

The door opened and she stepped back.

"Rose — wait, are you crying?" Jac pushed herself into the room and grabbed her sister's wrist. She sat down with her on her bed. "Why are you crying?"

Rosie rubbed her red, puffy eyes and pressed her lips together. She shook her head.

"How can he be okay with those things? Did you see what's down there? And you! You're just condoning it."

"Dad's not going to listen to me. Besides, they're monsters, Rosie. You can't possibly feel bad for a monster."

"How do we know they're all monsters? I've never seen one. Have you? How do we know how bad they are, considering how the scion society treats its own people? How the high-borns treat each other — treat grots — and treat mid-borns? How do we know, Jac?"

"We don't! Okay? We don't." Jac got to her feet and rubbed her face. She got out her butterfly knife and started playing with it over her fingers. "But guilty until proven innocent, right? We don't know what they'd do. We have to be wary."

"How would Mom feel?"

"It doesn't matter how Mom would feel, Rosie. Okay? Mom is gone. She left Dad, she left me, and she left you. Why do you care what she thinks?"

"She's still our mom, Jac." Rosie stood up too, towering over her sister. "Please get out of my room."

Jac raised her eyebrows and closed her knife. "You're kicking me out?"

"Well, you came here to... what? To try to make me feel better, tell me I'm being ridiculous, convince me Dad's right, or to just yell at me? I'm not sure what your intentions are." Rosie went to the door and put her hand on the edge, holding it open for her. "Please," she said. "I promise I won't be fussy about whatever may or may not happen, but I'd like some time alone."

Jac sighed and nodded finally.

"Whatever happens," she said as she walked to the door. She turned around and looked up at her sister. "He's still Dad, and I'm still your sister."

"I know," she said quietly as Jac left.

Jac roamed through the house again to find her father. He was locking up his prison cell and she stopped in the hall, crossing her arms.

"Did you really have to bring her down there?" Jac asked. She raised her eyebrows as Gerard sighed. He avoided making eye contact with her.

"It was something you both needed to see."

"You might've scarred her for life, Dad."

"At least she'll be safe!" he snapped.

Jac's eyes widened.

"Please don't raise your voice at me."

"I'm sorry," he said. He averted his gaze again. "I just can't stand the thought of something happening to either one of you. I need you both to be safe, and I need her to know that if she's not gonna protect herself, I'm gonna protect her. I'm always gonna protect her."

"She can't know that without you showing her torture devices?" Jac's fell against the wall as she sighed. "Dad, honestly. That was even a little much for me to see." She ran her fingers through her loose hair and sighed. "I understand if I have to kill something for my safety — for her safety — but torture?"

"We have to know where they've been hiding, Jac. Can you imagine what they could do for our family? We could rise to power. Have a place among the high-borns."

"I don't care about being around the high-borns,. All I care about is Rosie's safety. I need you to guarantee me that. I need you to promise me that these delusions you have aren't going to get the better of you that you'll risk her safety. I need you to promise me."

Gerard leaned back against the iron door.

He rubbed his hand through the short gray hair on his head.

It took him a while, but he finally nodded.

"You hesitated."

"I still nodded, didn't I?"

"You can't keep blaming them for Mom," Jac said and scoffed. "You can't be blaming the Dreamweavers for everything that you do wrong as a father."

Gerard scowled and stalked toward his daughter. "You think you're so tough, Jac?" he asked, pushing her against the wall. "You don't even know the truth about what happened to your mother."

"She ran away," Jac said. "I wish she took us with her."

Gerard shook his head.

"She died in her sleep. I took care of her body, because I couldn't let the two of you see her like that. Eyes wide, frightened to death. No one was going to believe me anyway. Not even you two. Do you think I'm stupid?" Gerard pushed her against the wall again. "You act all tough, but do you actually have what it takes to get things done? I do what I do to protect you both. Don't question me again."

Jac looked at the ground as Gerard stepped away from her. He walked away, keys dangling on a ring in his hand.

She caught her breath and her bottom lip quivered.

Jac wiped her eyes before any tears had the chance to fall from them. She pressed her head back against the wall and took a deep breath as she closed her eyes. Quickly, she put her hand over her mouth as a soft whimper escaped.

'Do not cry, Jac!' she could hear her father shouting at her through all the memories. 'Crying is a sign of weakness! You aren't weak! Stop it! Stop being a fucking baby!' he would scream at her.

She opened her eyes and shook it off.

The semi permanent scowl she always seemed to have on her face returned and she got up from the wall. Jac walked down the hallway as she looked for her father.

She stared out at the bridge that swayed in the wind, and she could barely see him in his biosphere treehouse, but he was there.

Jac turned around as she inhaled deeply again. Part of her hoped that whatever was in Lailoken's house, wasn't a Dreamweaver.

She hoped he wouldn't call, even if it was. She plopped down on the couch and reached for the remote, but she didn't turn on the television. She sat there, trying to comprehend what her father had told her. Her mother hadn't run away from them. From her father. From she and her sister.

Her mother was dead.

Her mother's been dead; and she had spent so much time being angry with her.

Jac got up from the couch and the remote clattered to the ground as she ran to her room. She slammed the door shut and leaned against it as she broke down in tears. Her hand cupped her mouth when sound escaped; she tried to muffle it before it happened again. Her knees gave out and she sank to the floor, hand still over her face.

Rosie stepped to the side of her room. She pressed her ear against the single wood wall and could hear the quiet sobs coming from Jac's room beside hers. She backed away from the wall and frowned.

Jac didn't cry.

She turned around in her bedroom. She had calmed down, but she had little interest in leaving. Rosie crawled back onto her bed and hugged her legs. She sat back against her bed frame, and listened to what she believed to be Jac's crying.

She didn't go to her, offering comforting arms or a shoulder to cry on. She knew her sister.

If she so much as knocked, Jac would pretend like nothing was wrong. Like she hadn't been crying. She'd make an excuse. Something got stuck in her eyes. She did that a lot after their mom had left. Come out of the shower, eyes puffy, claiming she got soap in them.

After a while, Rosie stopped believing her.

Jac wasn't soft. She supposed she didn't have room to be soft either. Not after what apparently was now in their world.

She didn't want to believe it, but she knew her father. And she knew he would stop at nothing.

20 TEARS IN HEAVEN

Keahi spent most of his time with Odette, nearly disappearing from everywhere else in the house. There were a few moments when he'd make appearances, just so no one would worry, but he primarily stayed with her. She came first.

He walked around the house late at night, wiping down the vases to keep Mrs. Baskerville happy.

"There you are. Shit."

Keahi turned around as Gentry approached him from the kitchen; the door swung freely behind him. Keahi frowned as he threw the towel over his shoulder. "What?"

"Lailoken's looking for you," Gentry said quietly as he looked around to make sure they were alone in the hallway.

"What?" Keahi crossed his arms. "What for?"

"I don't know." Gentry shrugged. "But he doesn't seem very happy." His voice remained just a little louder than a whisper. "I'd avoid him as much as possible. Stay out of the kitchen, if you know what's good for you. I don't know what he wants, but it can't be good. Maybe it's got something to do with Odette?"

"We're just friends," Keahi said with a shrug. "I mean, she can get playful and all, but it doesn't mean anything. Really."

"Just be careful. I don't want anything bad to happen, you know?"

Keahi clenched his jaw and nodded. When Gentry left, he waved the towel away and disappeared.

Reappearing in her room, he noticed she was no longer in her bed.

"Odette?" he whispered as he walked to her bathroom. "Are you okay?"

The water was running.

"Odette?"

There was no answer.

Keahi disappeared from where he stood and went into the bathroom only to find her on the floor. He dropped to his knees and pushed the bottle of bathroom cleaner away from her.

"Odette!" Keahi picked her up and held her close to him as his eyes began to water. "What did you do?" Air caught in his throat; she was limp in his arms. Keahi let her go and he turned around to punch the cabinet door, splintering it with his knuckles. He sat back against the wall of her tub, burying his face in his hands.

He looked up, and though his vision blurred, he could still she the outline of her body perfectly. Keahi viciously wiped his face as he crawled back over to her. He clenched his jaw and put his hands over her chest. He took a deep breath, trying to calm himself down. Keahi closed his eyes and his key began to hover between her and his palms.

His eyes shot open, pure white, and a small but violent tornado began to form around them. His fingers outstretched and his arms began to shake. He slowly raised his hands and her chest began to rise with it. Keahi pushed down and her body dropped back to the floor. He fell back against the tub, blacking out for no more than a second.

The tornado began to dissolve.

He blinked a few times before he crawled back over to her. Keahi lifted her in his arms again and sat against the tub. "Baby, please wake up."

Her lids fluttered.

His heart nearly skipped a beat.

"Was I dreaming it — or did you call me 'baby'?" she asked. Keahi just gently pushed her hair out of her face as he forced a smile. Odette slowly opened her eyes and then she frowned. She brushed her fingers against his cheek. "No, you're crying — why — don't — I'm sorry —"

"I'm never leaving you alone again." Keahi shook his head. She wiped his cheek with her thumb. "Never."

Odette wrapped her arms around his neck and hugged him.

"I'm sorry," she whispered. "I'm so sorry." She could feel him crying beneath her arms, his chest pushing against hers as he struggled for air. "I never wanted to see you cry. I just wanted to be free. I can't live like this."

Keahi picked her up and carried to her bed.

He put her down, and at first she wouldn't let go of his neck. Odette kissed his cheek as she slipped away from him. His eyes were still red, and her eyes began to water when his bottom lip quivered. Odette took his hand, but her grasp was weak. When he took a step back, he slipped right from her fingers.

"Please don't," she said. She scooted over as much as she could. "Please lay with me. Please."

Keahi clenched his jaw as he turned away from her. He ran his fingers through his hair as he tried to steady his breathing.

"Please," she said weakly from behind.

He swallowed hard and nodded as he turned back around. But he avoided making eye contact. Keahi crawled into the bed beside her and pulled her close to him.

Odette looked up at him. She gently pushed his damp hair away from his face and wiped his face again.

Neither of them said another word that night, and he didn't let her go. She fell asleep, nestled in his arms, and every now and then, he'd run his hand against her neck to check her pulse.

To make sure she was still with him. He kissed her forehead, despite knowing it wouldn't help. Odette no longer had fears.

She didn't feel anything.

But she did feel his love, cradled in its warmth. When she briefly awoke, she tried to move closer to him, but she'd already filled any gap while still asleep. Her palm rested flatly against his chest, and she fell back to sleep listening to the rhythmic beating of his heart.

He didn't care about Lailoken, or what he wanted. Keahi wasn't curious. He stayed with Odette, just as he said he would. He never left her alone.

There were days when he got her to laugh, and days when he couldn't get her to stop crying. Sometimes, she'd lay in his arms, sullen. Eyes dry. Unmoving. She'd stare blankly across the room, intently, but not looking at anything.

"Make it stop," she'd plead with him.

"I can't," he'd tell her. His hand would brush against her cheek as he held her close. "I take away fear, Odette. You don't — you don't feel anything."

Odette closed her eyes when he kissed her forehead, and he was right. Nothing changed.

She didn't suddenly feel better. She didn't have the energy to argue with him, or the will to try. Odette just laid there, unmoving, as he gently ran his rough hand against her neck. His arms were comforting, but still, she didn't feel safe anymore.

She watched a few movies with him, sad romances, where the couple you're rooting for doesn't end up together. She didn't want to see happy, not when it was something she couldn't have.

Someone knocked on the door.

Odette looked up at Keahi, who had fallen asleep for what was probably the first time since his arrival. She tried to slip out of the bed unnoticed, but he reached for her wrist and woke up suddenly.

"I'm sorry," she said. "Someone's at the door. I didn't want to wake you."

"No, it's fine." He rubbed his eyes beneath his glasses and sat up. He got up to stand behind the door as she went to answer it.

It was Kiko.

Her eyes were puffy and red, cheeks damp.

Odette frowned at the sight of it. She thought the worst.

"Did something happen to —"

Kiko lunged at her, arms wrapped around her neck. She cried against Odette's shoulder as she buried her face. "I'm so glad you're okay," she said. "I'm so sorry, Doll Face. I'm sorry. It wasn't your fault."

Odette wrapped her arms around Kiko and pulled her into the room as Keahi closed the door.

"I never should have blamed you, and I'm sorry." Kiko took a step back, and Odette had started to cry.

Odette shook her head as she wiped her cheeks with the backs of her hands.

"She's your mother," Odette said as she sniffled. "I'm just — I can't apologize enough for what happened."

Kiko grabbed Odette's hands and pulled her over to the bed, managing to get her to sit down beside her.

"Gentry and Keahi have been teaching everyone sign language," she said. "My mom's okay — and she's not who I'm worried about right now."

Odette glanced at the door. Kiko turned around and jumped.

"Jesus Christ, I didn't know you were in here!" she snapped as she stood up. "What the hell!"

Odette couldn't help but laugh at Kiko's outburst. Kiko turned back to look at her and she smiled a little.

"I've missed hearing that laugh."

"Me too," Keahi said.

Kiko, Gentry, and Amaris started coming up to her room more often. They each took turns bringing up her food so that they could check on her and see for themselves how she was doing.

The interactions, though a bit overwhelming at first, turned into something she knew she needed, even if she hadn't realized it at the time.

One night after Gentry had brought her dinner, she sat on her bed, leaning against Keahi. Her soft hands traced his calloused ones.

"Can you teach me sign language too?" she asked. "I'd like to see Mrs. Hamasaki one of these days."

He nodded as she wrapped her hand around two of his fingers.

"I'll teach you anything you want to know."

She spent the next few hours trying to learn the basics, but grew frustrated with her inability to grasp the language.

"You're doing fine," he insisted, and she shook her head.

"I'm terrible at this."

"You're not going to learn it all in one night —"

"I haven't learned anything!" she snapped.

"Why don't we just go see her?" he asked. "I think you're just stressed out, and it's not easy to learn something when you can't focus." He got out of her bed and reached his hand to her. "Come on," he said. "I'll tell you everything she says."

Odette was hesitant, but she nodded.

She hadn't been in the rest of the house since Thanksgiving, and she kept her arms tightly wrapped around one of Keahi's as she walked with him down the steps of the Baskerville mansion. Her eyes were wide open, observing their surroundings, and every time her gaze landed on a painting, she forced herself to turn away from it. Especially the ones with Lailoken in them. She felt like their eyes followed her everywhere. That they could whisper to one another, signaling the real Lailoken that she was out and about.

She turned in toward Keahi and he slipped his arm out of her death grip to wrap it around her body while she wrapped her arms around his chest.

He pushed the door open and Mrs. Hamasaki was in the kitchen alone, drinking a hot cup of tea. She looked up when the door opened, and her eyes lit up at the sight of Odette. She smiled.

Mrs. Hamasaki quickly slid off of the stool she sat on and ran to hug her. Odette let go of Keahi and wrapped her arms tightly around Mrs. Hamasaki. When they parted, Mrs. Hamasaki noticed that Odette's eyes had begun to water.

She signed something to her, and Odette looked up at Keahi.

"She wants to know why you're crying," he said.

Odette turned back to Mrs. Hamasaki and smiled. "Because I'm happy," she said, a tear rolling down her cheek. "I'm happy to see you — and that you're okay."

Mrs. Hamasaki wrapped her arm around Odette and rubbed her shoulder. She then looked at Keahi and pointed at the door.

'*You are not supposed to be down here*,' she told him.

He nodded, knowing that.

Odette turned around.

"What did she say?" she asked.

Keahi looked from Odette, to Mrs. Hamasaki, to back to Odette.

"Uh — she's just telling me how pretty you are."

Mrs. Hamasaki hit him in the stomach with the back of her hand and frowned at him.

"Keahi."

"She thinks we should go back upstairs."

"But —" Odette turned to Mrs. Hamasaki who nodded at his words.

"Fine." Odette took her hands within her own. "I'll come back to see you, okay? I promise."

Mrs. Hamasaki pulled one of her hands back to gently touch Odette's cheek. She smiled and nodded. She gave her another hug, before opening the door for them to leave.

Odette wrapped her arms around Keahi's again and went with him back up the stairs.

"I'm glad she's doing okay," Odette said once they were back in the safety of her room. She sat down on her bed. She pulled her feet up on the mattress and crossed her legs.

He leaned back against her door, and nodded. "Yeah, everyone's adjusting pretty well. It was hard at first, but they're making it work. They all care about her, and they all care about you."

Odette nodded subtly. "I know," she whispered. He almost didn't hear her. Odette laid back on her bed and pat the mattress beside her. "Coming, *princess*?"

He raised an eyebrow.

"Are you calling me a princess now?"

She shrugged her shoulders and smiled.

He climbed into the bed beside her and she snuggled up against him for his warmth.

"Do you miss your dog?" she asked. "Your family?"

"I think about them sometimes," he said, putting his hand back behind his head. "But I'm okay. I'm sure they're all getting on just fine without me."

"I wanted to apologize for being so needy," she said. "You've been here for months but — I'm not sorry you're still here. I'm just — sorry for taking you from your home for as long as I have. I'm sure you didn't even get a chance to say goodbye."

"I'd be surprised if they even noticed I was gone."

"I'll notice." Odette fumbled with the key hanging around her neck, knowing he wouldn't stay forever. She sat up and pulled on his arm for him to sit up too. She reached her hands back to unhook her silver necklace. Odette leaned forward and latched it around his neck.

"My parents gave this to me when I was little," she said. "They wanted to make sure I never forget them." She stared at her name hanging from around his neck. "You won't forget me, right?" she asked, and lifted her gaze to meet his.

"I could never forget you."

She smiled.

21   AGAINST ALL ODDS

Keahi managed to cleverly avoid Lailoken for a while, who, in Keahi's opinion, was nowhere near as smart as everyone gave him credit for. Not wanting any of them to meet the same fate as Mrs. Hamasaki, he decided to continue to lay low. Not bothering to show up in the kitchens, or anywhere in the house for work, not even at night. Not anymore.

When Lailoken came asking and compelled them into telling, all they had to say was that he seemed to have disappeared.

Odette didn't say anything about what happened. But the very few moments he wasn't around, she would take out the picture she stole from his old house, and trace his jawline with her finger against the image. He was smiling in the picture, reaching for the camera. Caught in the middle of a laugh.

He rarely smiled like that.

At least not that she saw. The image of his tearful eyes had burned itself into her memory. She couldn't shake what she had caused.

She broke his heart.

Odette quickly blinked her forming tears away and stuffed the picture into her drawer when he reappeared in her room.

"Where did you —"

He pressed his finger against his mouth. Keahi stayed by the door and listened in the hallway. Someone was coming.

There was a knock on the door and she froze.

"Odette?"

It was Lailoken.

"May I talk to you for a quick second?"

Her eyes widened and she stood frozen in fear.

Keahi went over to her. "It's okay," he said softly. "I'll be with you the whole time."

She looked up at him, and nodded.

Odette closed her drawer and tried to shake the nerves from her trembling hands. She went to the door and unlocked it, opening the door slowly while Keahi stood behind it.

"Yes?" she asked.

"Oh wow, you do look awful."

She frowned.

"I know you're sick but —" Lailoken took a step back, like he didn't want to catch whatever she had. "I'm looking for one of the workers. His name is Keahi, long hair, about this tall —" he held his hand up in the air and Odette shrugged.

"I don't know why you'd think I would've seen him, Lailoken. I've been in here. I haven't left. Literally. Gentry has been bringing me my meals."

"I know, I just thought —"

"You thought what?"

"Don't interrupt me!" he snapped and she took a step back behind the door, using the door as a barrier between him and her. Keahi gently touched her arm. "I just wanted to check." Lailoken rolled his eyes and stormed off.

Odette closed the door and locked it before leaning back against the wood.

"Are you okay?" Keahi asked her.

She took a few seconds to breathe and nodded. "I'm fine," she said in a hushed tone. "But why is he looking for you?" Her gaze slowly wandered up his face until she met his eyes.

He averted his. "I don't know. Gentry told me a few nights ago —"

"Nights? Keahi, why didn't you tell me?"

"I didn't — I didn't want —" He sighed and turned away from her.

She grabbed his chin and made him look at her.

"To worry me?" she asked. Odette knitted her eyebrows together and let go of his chin. She reached her hand out to him. "Take me to the beach," she said.

"Really?" he asked. "Are you sure?"

"Yes," she said, waiting for him to take her hand. Odette gave him a reassuring smile. "I need an escape. Take me away."

Keahi placed his hand against hers and she laced their fingers together and they faded from her bedroom.

Her landing was easier that time. She kept her eyes closed and the world didn't feel like it was spinning beneath her feet. She felt the sand between her toes and she curled them in as she peeked, opening one eye at a time.

"Not bad," he said, there was a very subtle trace of a smile on his face.

Odette was determined to change how desolate he had become. Because of her.

She frowned.

"What do you mean, 'not bad'? That was way better than — wait." Odette let go of his hand and pressed her hands against her stomach. She closed her eyes and inhaled deeply. "Okay," she said, steadying her breathing. "Not bad."

She peeked at him.

"You all right, princess?" he asked.

"Better now," she said. Odette extended her hand out to him again. "Can we go for a walk?" she asked.

He took her hand again. But Odette didn't hold his hand for very long. Eventually, she found herself looping her arm around his instead, and walking closer to him. She didn't look at him though, her gaze remained fixed on the ocean, and the rumbling of the waves.

At first, Keahi suspected she wanted to leave the Baskerville house so that she could ask him about Lailoken, and why he was looking for him. But the question never came. She didn't bring him up at all.

He could breathe a little easier.

The truth was, Odette didn't want to talk about him. She needed to escape the suffocation of that house, for even just a moment longer. Even if it was a moment she knew wasn't going to last.

The beach was barely lit, most of the light coming from the moon and distant light from porches of houses that were nearby.

"Oh my god!" Odette squealed as she jumped away from him. "What was that?" she looked down at the sand.

"What was what?" he asked as she lifted her foot in the air and started brushing the top of it off. "Probably a crab. There are sand crabs all over the place over here."

"What?" Her foot slowly returned to the sand. Odette pressed her hair down against her chest as she looked at the sand. "Where?"

"Hang on." Keahi dug into his pocket and pulled out a mini flashlight. He shined it at the ground, then clicked it off, and shined it again.

"You keep a small flashlight in your pocket?"

"It's a keychain."

She laughed.

"There!" he said, and she looked at where he shined the light.

"Where? I didn't see it!"

"Okay, I'll catch one for you." Keahi stuck the flashlight in his mouth so he could tie up his hair in a knot. He readjusted the glasses on his face.

"Maybe you should take those off. I mean, do you really need them?"

"Yes," he said. He took the flashlight out of his mouth and shined it at the ground again. As soon as he spotted one, Keahi took off after it. Sliding against the ground, he grabbed a handful of sand and sat back up, not bothering to dust himself off. Keahi sifted through the sand in his hand as Odette skipped over to him.

"Did you get it?" she asked.

Keahi brushed the sand off of his hand and got up, holding the small white crab between his fingers. It was hardly bigger than his thumb nail. "I think they're also called ghost crabs. Ah! Fucker —" he shook his hand to shake the crab off of his finger. "Pinched me."

He cleared his throat.

Odette clasped her hands over her face as she tried to suppress her laughter. She grabbed his hand and kissed his thumb. "All better?" she asked.

His smile grew a little wider.

"All better," he said after her.

Odette didn't let go of his hand as she looked down at the sand again. "It was so cute though," she said, trying to find another. She looked up at Keahi. "I want to catch one!"

"Okay," he said. "When you see one, just go after it. Don't be afraid to get dirty."

"I'm not."

He cleared his throat again.

"Right, okay."

She smirked as he shone the light on the sand, avoiding making eye contact with her again. She hoped he was blushing. She looked at the sand and narrowed her eyes trying to focus on any movement. The second she spotted one, she did what he had told her to, and knocked him over in the process.

Odette sat up and felt for the crab in her hand.

Gently pinching it between her fingers, she held it up to show Keahi who was getting up from the ground. "It's bigger than the one you caught — ow!" She flung the crab off of her hand and waved her hand in front of Keahi's face. Odette still had a frown on her face and she pouted.

He looked at her hand and then at her. Keahi just shook his head as he took her hand within his own and kissed her finger.

"All better, Miss Thomsett?"

"Yes it is, thank you."

They moved to sit against one of the scattered trees, where sand met the grass. Keahi sat down between the roots and Odette sat on his lap. Her fingers were laced with his again, as one hand rested in her lap with hers, and his other, flat against her stomach.

"I think you know more about my world than I do," she said. "There's so much about Hawai'i that I haven't even seen. I've never seen a waterfall, though apparently O'ahu has some. I've barely been to the beach. I've been a pampered princess my whole life."

"Not by choice," he said. He stared out at the ocean as the waves crashed against the sand. The reef was poking through the surface from the low tide. "You're daring and adventurous, which is something that can scare people."

"Why?"

"Because you're a force to be reckoned with. Hard to control. Restless under control. Sound familiar?" he asked, fumbling with the hem of her tanktop.

"I've learned so much about myself these last few months... I'll never forget. I promise." Odette crinkled her nose. "I used to love those movies, you know, where a girl would meet a guy, and suddenly she'd become this better person because of it. I thought it meant that true love solved all problems. That true love gave life meaning. But I think I've been misinterpreting it. I don't think it was ever about meeting the boy at all."

"What do you mean?"

"I think it's symbolic. I don't think it's about the boy or their relationship. I think it's about how people can impact us, and the way we see ourselves. If someone we care about, causes us pain, we're conditioned to believe we deserve it. Because why would they hurt us if we didn't? But if we're shown love, and kindness, it makes us look at ourselves a little deeper. Maybe I'm just tired, but I think that romances are about self-discovery. I think the boys are metaphors. Look how much better you could be, if you allowed yourself the self-love you deserve."

She sighed and looked down at his fingers intertwined with hers, and traced a heart against the back of his hand.

"People thinking, 'the girl is nothing without the boy', is a result from what society has tried to drill into our minds. But I think it's 'we're nothing without self-love', and our hearts are closed to it until we see that someone else could love what we can't. I just wanted you to know — when I saw you — in my bathroom — I —I didn't think anyone would ever cry over me. I never meant to hurt you." She wiped her face.

Odette turned to look back at him and reached up to kiss his cheek.

"I told you that I care about you."

She nodded, watching his lips move as he spoke. Odette lifted her gaze to meet his eyes.

"I know," she said. "I believe you." She turned to lean back against him again. "Will you tell me about the Woolgathering now?" she asked, tracing the protruding veins in his hand with her finger. "I want to know what it's like — where you came from. I wish you could show it to me."

"Maybe I can," he said. "One day." Keahi glanced down at her but she was now focused on their clasped hands, still tracing the back of his hand. "Compared to here, there's nowhere near as much sunlight, especially at the dreamscape." He shrugged his shoulders. "But I don't go there often."

"What's the dreamscape?" she asked.

"The home of the kupua kings."

She frowned. "Kupua?"

"Demigods. There's three kings, The Time Lord, The Sandman, and The Angel of Death. The middle one, The Sandman, also has three children, The Master of Midnight, The Dream King, and The Storyteller. The Master of Midnight and The Dream King are assholes, if you ask me. But The Storyteller, she's something else. There's also —"

"Your girlfriend?"

He laughed. "No, not at all. As far as I know, she's not allowed to date."

"But you'd date her?"

"I told you, Odette. I'm falling in love with you."

"You told me you think you are."

"Maybe I just didn't want to look like a dumb ass in case you didn't say it back — which you didn't — but I mean — I know it was a bad time — I mean — you don't have to like me back. I probably shouldn't have said it to begin with. I'll survive — so anyway, moving on. The Woolgathering —"

Odette turned around. "You're cute when you ramble." She slipped out of his lap and sat against the root of the tree before climbing into his lap and faced him. She grabbed his face, her palms pressing against his cheeks, and made him look at her. "Do you want to kiss me?" she asked. She made him nod with her hands. "Yes, princess," she said for him and he started to laugh.

"I knew you liked being called that."

"Only when you say it. I also like it when you ramble." She didn't let go of his face. Not yet, at least. Odette knew if she did, he'd look away, and she didn't want him to. "I like it when you get protective, and that you give me choices. I like that you ask me what I want, and you care about what I want. I like the way you look at me — like nothing else in the world matters. That you look at my eyes when you talk to me and when I talk to you. I like that you respect my decisions, even if you disagree with them. I like that you keep your promises. I like to think about us, and what it'd feel like to kiss you again. I like to think about the way your hands feel when you touch me." He started to smile, and she couldn't help but smile too. "I like to think about the love you'd give me and the way you've made me feel it. But it doesn't matter how I feel, Keahi. Because I'm *his* fiancée and I belong to him."

He tried to look away. "People belong to no one but themselves."

"Only the lucky ones," she said. "I just want to know you'll be happy when you go home. I want you to be okay too." He didn't say anything. Odette inhaled deeply. "In another life," she continued, and her eyes started to water, "I would've loved you, in all the ways I know how."

Keahi sighed and closed his eyes. Odette leaned forward and pressed her lips against his.

"I'm sorry," she whispered once their lips parted.

Keahi opened his eyes and shook his head, the little that he could, since his face was still her prisoner. "You have nothing to apologize for," he said. Odette let her hands drop and she turned around, slipping into his lap again. Keahi wrapped his arms around her. She rested her head back against his shoulder. "Maybe you'll dream of me," he added.

"I know I will."

When he didn't say anything else, Odette tilted her head back to look at him and found him looking at her. "Can I kiss you?" he asked.

She glanced down at his lips and nodded. She closed her eyes and tilted her chin up until her lips found his.

They stayed in the same spot, sitting between the roots with Odette on his lap, for what seemed like hours. Sometimes they talked, and sometimes they sat in silence.

Sometimes they clumsily kissed, hands traveling, touching, feeling. But nothing came off. Despite what she wanted, and the desire she swore she saw in his eyes, she didn't push him.

She faced him again and her arms draped over his shoulders; his hands resting on her thighs. Odette had his glasses perched on the bridge of her nose and she planted soft kisses on his face and his jaw. Soft pecks against his lips, sometimes tugging on his bottom one gently with her teeth. Her mouth found the sharpness of his jaw, and she tenderly kissed his neck.

"You're putting me through hell," he told her. His voice, low.

"I know," she said as she sat up, taking the glasses off. Odette put them down between the roots beside them and leaned forward as she grabbed his hands. She rested them on her waist before slowly pushing them to slide over the curve of her butt. "Love is a kind of hell," she whispered against his lips and silenced herself with his mouth. Her fingers tangled in his hair as she managed to release it from the knot he had tied.

Odette broke their kiss and sat back on his lap. She smiled a little as she watched him lean forward. He wanted more.

"I changed my mind," she said softly. She met his gaze once he opened his eyes. "He might own me, but I belong to you. I think I've belonged to you for a while." Odette's gaze dropped to his lips.

"Can I —" he began to say, and this time, she silenced him with her lips.

Keahi didn't protest.

There was a pain in her chest. A sharp feeling knowing this wasn't going to last. A feeling — a feeling that would fade. A moment that would fade from her. In her desire to hold onto it, she refused to let him go. She feared he would slip through her fingers, the same way he could slip into the shadows, and dissolve into smoke.

She could feel him now, beneath her and pressed against her, but for how much longer?

She broke away from his lips to catch her breath.

Odette wrapped her arms around his body and nestled her head against his shoulder. The fit she had with him felt perfect, leaving no spaces between their bodies. Between the comfort his arms gave her and the soothing sounds of the ocean, she fell asleep snuggled up against him.

At first, Keahi didn't want to disturb her, but then she shivered against his body. He ran his hand against her arm and he could feel the bumps forming on her skin.

Keahi brought her back to her room, the journey was easier for her and she hardly stirred.

She didn't wake up.

He covered her with her blanket and disappeared from her room, reappearing downstairs like he had done so many times before fully knowing it was time he showed face to someone. To show that he was in fact, still around. So no one thought Lailoken got to him. Someone was always up late working.

Gentry, usually.

Usually.

Only this time, it wasn't Gentry. It was Lailoken who was still awake. It was Lailoken who he ran into, not another coworker of the house.

Keahi grabbed the rag on the table as he came around the corner.

"There you are," Lailoken said. "I've been looking everywhere for you."

"Have you?" Keahi asked, pretending to barely notice he was standing there. "I apologize, I've been a bit busy lately," he lied. He wiped down the vase that sat on the table, not bothering to turn to face Lailoken. Keahi didn't want to look at him. He had trouble trying to stop himself from punching him in the face. For now, he had to continue trying to resist that urge. For now.

"Really? Doing what?" Lailoken asked, tucking his hands into his pockets. "Everyone I talked to said you practically disappeared."

"Cleaning," he said with a shrug, barely managing a glance at him over his shoulder. "Like everyone else. It's a big house. Decided to work night hours so some of the other workers could get more rest. You know, with the seasons changing, people get sick." Keahi shrugged. "I don't know what anyone's talking about. I've been here the whole time — out back more than usual though to help Abbey, but still here."

Lailoken raised an eyebrow, but he had no reason to not take his word for it. Just because he hadn't personally seen him, didn't mean he wasn't there. The Baskerville house was, in fact, on the larger side.

One could get lost, and never found.

"Well, may I have a word with you?" he asked, and stepped back to the wall, just beneath one of his own portraits, to allow Keahi entrance into the living room.

"Yeah, of course."

He threw the towel over his shoulder and walked past Lailoken without so much a glance. He closely followed Keahi out of the hallway. There was a fire still burning brightly in the fireplace, like new wood had been added to it. Keahi raised an eyebrow, considering it was nearly three in the morning, but he said nothing of it. "What's up?" Keahi asked Lailoken as he turned around to face him.

Lailoken pulled his hands from his pockets and crossed his arms as he leaned against the frame of the doorway. "Stick your hand in the fire," he commanded, though his voice was calm. He only glanced at the fireplace to acknowledge it, in case Keahi hadn't noticed, though Lailoken was positive he had.

Keahi raised his eyebrows. "What?"

"I said to *stick your hand in the fire*. Leave it there until I leave, and don't make any noise." Lailoken stepped forward, not taking his eyes off of Keahi's. "Do you understand me?" he asked, narrowing his eyes. His pupils constricted.

This was a test. Keahi knew exactly what he was doing. He was testing him. Dreamweavers couldn't be manipulated. If Lailoken suspected him, he couldn't blow it now.

Keahi had too much to lose now.

"I understand," he said as monotonously as he could manage; like he hadn't a choice in the matter. Keahi turned around to face the fire that burned brightly in the fireplace. He could hear it crackling, and he could imagine the way it would feel, burning against his skin. He knelt down in front of it and removed the iron guard and screen from the front. Keahi set it down beside him, careful not to touch the poker that stuck out from the fireplace.

He started to roll up his sleeve as he inhaled deeply.

TOVALEY B. KYSEL

Don't make a sound, Keahi, he told himself.
Not a sound.

He closed his eyes as he made a fist and slowly reached his arm into the flames. The fire scorched his skin and Keahi bit down on his bottom lip, roughly, so roughly he began to draw blood, trying to keep himself from groaning. His whole body began to tremble, feeling the fire burn off layers of his skin. His eyes began to water while his skin charred. Crispy, leathery. Keahi clenched his jaw. Sweat trickled down the sides of his face and overcome by pain, he could hardly smell the burning of his own flesh.

Dissatisfied, Lailoken left the room.

Keahi looked back and yanked his arm out of the fire. He fell back on the floor and groaned. His arm was crisp from his fingertips to his elbow.

Skin, brittle, tender and black.

He looked toward the hallway and saw Odette standing there.

Eyes shining and red.

She ran right toward him and fell to the floor beside him. She pulled his head into her lap and started shaking her head.

"No —" he tried to tell her, "go back up — upstairs."

"No!" she shouted at him. Tears began to spill from her eyes before she could stop them. "I'm so sorry." Odette ripped his necklace from her neck and put it in the palm of his other hand. She closed his fingers around the skeleton key. "Please," she cried. "Take it and go home. I'm sorry, Keahi. I'm so sorry."

"No." Keahi dropped the key on the ground and grabbed her hand. She gripped onto his so tightly that her own hand began to shake. "I'm not — I'm not leaving you here, Odette. I'm not leaving you alone. Not with these people. Especially not with him."

"This is all my fault."

"Hey, listen to me." Odette slowly met his gaze. Her eyes were puffy and red, and her bottom lip quivered. "I'd walk through fire for you."

"I know," she said through her tears. She roughly wiped her face with the back of her other hand. "We have to — we have to soak your arm. Can you — can you get us to my — my bathroom?"

Keahi closed his eyes.

She felt him tighten his hold on her hand and they disappeared from the living room.

He fell forward against the counter of her bathroom and Odette quickly turned on the faucet of her tub. She dug through her closet for a step stool and put it down beside the tub.

"Please sit," she said.

"Odette —"

"Keahi, please. Let me help you, please."

Keahi did as she asked. He dropped his arm in the bathtub as the water level began to rise, but he couldn't feel it.

Odette collapsed on the tile beside him.

"Does it feel any better? Please tell me it feels better."

"I don't — feel anything," he told her honestly. Odette tightly held his other hand as she continued to cry. She kissed his fingers and held it between her palms, unwilling to let him go.

"I'm so sorry," she said. "But you have to go home. You have to leave." He didn't say anything, which caused her to look up at him.

"I already told you," he said. "I'm not leaving you."

Odette let go of his hand so that her fingers could brush against his face. She leaned forward and pressed her lips against his.

"I'll come with you," she whispered against his lips. "Please."

She kissed him again.

The more she kissed him, the faster he began to regain feeling in his hand. She was siphoning his pain into her. Once he realized it, Keahi turned his head, breaking the kiss.

"What are you doing?" she asked.

Keahi looked into the tub.

"Look," he said. He had little movement in his fingers, and they slowly wagged in the water. The charred, leathery looking skin began to loosen.

"How — are you healing yourself?" she asked.

He looked at her and frowned.

She still had no idea she was an Empath. She had no idea she was doing it.

"You'll really come with me?" he asked. "You'll leave here, with me?"

"I'll go anywhere with you," she whispered. She looked away from him, unable to look at his suffering any longer. "Do you know what it feels like," her voice trembled as she spoke, "to see someone you care about, in so much pain?

And there's nothing you can do?" She sat back, letting go of his hand and cried. Odette sniffled violently, unable to stop the tears that continued to flow. Her face, flushed, splotchy and damp.

A look she was getting used to. Odette hardly bothered to wear make-up anymore.

Keahi sat forward and gently wiped her cheek with his thumb.

"I do," he said. "It feels like this." He held his arm out as she looked up at him. "Come here. I could use a hug." She crawled over to him and leaned against his body while he draped his arm around her frame.

"I'm so sorry," she whispered.

"It's not your fault." He rubbed at her arm gently with his thumb. "It has never been your fault."

The longer he kept his charred arm in the water, the more the damaged skin began to loosen until it fell off completely. He slowly started to feel the coolness of the water as he continued to regain feeling in his hand and arm. Beneath the flaking black skin, were severe scars running up his arm from the burns, but Keahi could fully move his hand.

He took it out of the water and opened and closed his fist.

"Is it because you're a Dreamweaver?" Odette asked, staring at his hand. She was calmer now; but she didn't take her focus away from his scarred arm. "I saw those burns — and your arm when you pulled it from the fire — I don't know how you could've —"

"Yeah," he said for now. Keahi kissed her forehead. He got up and helped her to her feet as he dried his arm against his shirt. "But we have to get out of here."

"Is he going to try to kill you?"

"I don't know."

Keahi took her by the hand and led her into her room.

"If there's anything you want to take, you should get it now, and I'll —" he stared at her neck; staring at the absence of his key hanging against her chest. He pressed his free hand against his own. It wasn't hanging from his neck either. "My key," he said. "I have to get my key." He let go of her hand and she scrambled to grab hold of it again.

"No," she grumbled, one hand on his wrist and the other grasped tightly to his hand. "Please don't leave me," she begged him. Odette pouted at Keahi, and though her pouts usually worked, large shining eyes and plump bottom lip, he was insistent.

He had to get the skeleton key.

"I'll come right back," he told her.

She grabbed his face between her palms and their mouths collided.

"You better," she whispered once their lips parted. Odette tried to kiss him again, but he had turned into smoke before she could catch him.

The second he faded from her sight, she ran to her closet and started digging for the bag she had brought with her to the Baskervilles. There wasn't much she wanted to keep, considering Lailoken had bought her almost everything she owned. The things she threw in her purse were of little monetary value; primarily the

Dreamweaver coin and her Daruma doll. She left her cell phone on her desk, and searched through her many wallets for any money she might have. It wasn't much, aside from a few scripts and some mundane coins.

She stuffed a few clothing items that would fit in her small bag and quickly changed out of her pajamas. Odette looked at the clock on her dresser as she impatiently waited for Keahi to return, but he didn't.

Her stomach began to flip. Something was wrong, she could feel it.

She got to her feet and ran to her door.

TOVALEY B. KYSEL

WAITING FOR A GIRL LIKE YOU

Keahi walked around the ground floor unseen and found Lailoken in the living room with his skeleton key. He watched as Lailoken picked it up from the floor and glanced at the staircase. Keahi clenched his fists. He had no choice but to face him.

He stepped into view.

Lailoken's gaze fell to Keahi's arm. It wasn't charred from the fire. Not burnt, leathery, or crisp. In fact, it looked completely healed. Like an old wound, something he had gotten years ago. Nothing more than what seemed like a minor irritation now.

"What the fuck are you?" Lailoken asked, his hand curled over the chain.

Keahi ran his fingers along his new scars. "Your worst nightmare, probably."

Lailoken frowned. "Probably?"

Keahi shrugged. "I'm not really big on theatrics," he said, fixing the cuffs around his elbows as he took a step into the living room. "You did make me burn my shirt, though — which does piss me off a little. But now that my secret's out," he said, acknowledging the key in Lailoken's hand, "I no longer have to pretend like I'm your little bitch. Or your mom's." Keahi knocked the vase off of the table like a rude and disrespectful cat, and it shattered on the ground. He knocked it over for the sake of knocking it over. "I hate that vase — and all the stupid vases in this god forsaken house." He outstretched his hand to Lailoken. "Give me my key."

"Oh, you want this?" Lailoken asked, dangling the skeleton key from the chain. He dropped it into his palm and tossed it into the fire behind him.

Keahi sighed.

"Why do you high-borns always have to insist on making things difficult?" he asked. "You could've just handed it to me and we would've left quietly. No one would get hurt."

"You aren't taking her anywhere." Lailoken tightened his fists at his sides. The side of his nose twitched. "What happened between you two? What did you do to my fiancée? Do you have no respect for the high-borns? She's mine!" he shouted.

The vein that ran down the center of his forehead protruded with his anger.

"She's not property!" Keahi snapped.

"Yes, she is!" Lailoken shoved him. "I paid for her! She belongs to me!"

"You know," Keahi started as he rubbed his nose and pushed his glasses up the bridge. "I'm trying really hard here to not get angry. But if you shove me again —"

Lailoken tried to punch him this time. Keahi stepped out of the way and cracked Lailoken in the neck. He coughed as he fell against the couch.

"Fuck," Keahi said as he cracked his knuckles. "I've been wanting to do that for a while. now"

"I'm not afraid of you," Lailoken said, he rubbed his neck as he stood up.

"No?" Keahi asked, tilting his head slightly. "Because I remember you being pretty afraid of me the first time we met. For a second there, I understood why my brother enjoys scaring people." Keahi circled Lailoken. "Do you remember? Should I refresh your memory?"

The moisture seemed to drain from his skin and Keahi turned into a black winged demon right before Lailoken's eyes as the glasses fell from Keahi's face. The same one he had seen in his nightmare.

"It was you. You're a Dreamweaver! Help! Hel —"

Keahi didn't say anything.

He grabbed Lailoken by the throat and shoved him against the wall. He slammed his head back against the stone, hard enough that the pictures hanging up began to rattle.

"I warned you." His claw began to dig into Lailoken's neck. "Do you remember what I said? I will rip your skeleton right out of your body." Lailoken clawed at his hand, trying to get him to release his hold. But Keahi wouldn't. "You raped her."

"Rape?" He gave disbelief a voice. Lailoken laughed through his wheezing. "I didn't rape her. She wanted it."

Keahi snarled. He tightened his grip; his talons began to draw blood beneath Lailoken's jaw.

"Just because you compelled her to want it, doesn't mean she actually wanted it."

"Go ahead," Lailoken said between struggled breaths. "Show her what kind of monster you really are." His gaze moved past Keahi.

Keahi dropped Lailoken and turned around. Odette stood there in the doorway, hand clasping onto the strap of her bag that hung on her arm. She stared at him in horror.

"Keahi?" she stared at him, and he started to return back to his human form. "Keahi!"

Lailoken grabbed a chair and broke it against Keahi's back. He dropped to his knees as the bone of his broken wing stabbed into his back, and fire seemed to glow in his dark eyes. Keahi got up and turned around. He waved his hand. Lailoken flew across the room and knocked against the wall.

Keahi followed him.

Odette ran toward Keahi and she grabbed hold of his arm. "Keahi, stop!" She moved in front of him as he continued to stalk toward Lailoken like predator hunting pray. "You're not a murderer, Keahi," Odette said, standing in front of him; still half changed into a demon. Her heart was pounding. She put her hand against his cheek when he turned to her; her eyes glinted as she stared into his dark cold ones.

"Come back to me," she whispered. "I love you."

He tilted his head, as though he were trying to comprehend what she was saying to him. "Do you understand me?" she asked. "I love you." Odette shook her head. "Don't do this."

The demon slowly shrunk back fully into his human form and Keahi dropped to the floor. Workers began appearing in the hallway; Kiko stood with eyes wide, having seen Keahi in his true form.

She was speechless.

"Thank you, Odette." Lailoken started to get up from the ground. But Odette pursed her lips together and shook her head as she got up too.

"I didn't do it for you." She walked over to the fireplace and grabbed one of the iron pokers from the fire. She turned it in her hand as she stared at the hot glow.

"What are you doing?" he asked, staring at the tip too. "What are you going to do with that? Put it down before you hurt yourself."

"No," she said.

"I said, put that down!"

"You want to know what happened between me and him? I kissed him," she said as she approached him. "Again and again and again. I also tried to get him to have sex with me a few weeks ago. I didn't realize at the time why he told me 'no', but I get it now. See, I didn't know, because he did something you never did." She pointed the poker at him. "He gave me a choice. He respected me as a person. I didn't even know what it felt like to be respected because no one's ever respected me. No one has ever asked me about what I want."

Lailoken tried to get up and Odette burned him with the rod.

"What the fuck!" Lailoken fell back, gripping onto his shoulder, rocking back and forth in pain.

She ignored him.

"He thinks I would've regretted it," she continued, looking at the glowing orange of the iron. "He's probably right. Because even though they were his hands, I would've felt yours. I would've been disgusted with myself, all over again, and it wasn't even my fault." Odette smacked him in the face with the heated part of the rod. "I hate you," she said over his groan. "You ruined my life!"

She stabbed the poker into his leg as hard as she could. Lailoken hissed in pain and tried to reach for the iron rod protruding from his thigh as Odette turned around and ran back to Keahi. "We should go," she told him.

"Probably," he said, glancing at Lailoken. He returned his attention back onto Odette and smiled. "You're amazing."

She couldn't help but smile back and grabbed his hand. "Come on, we have to get out of here."

Keahi let go of her hand as he walked up to Lailoken. "Usually I'm above hitting a man when he's already down." Keahi furrowed his brows slightly, and without hesitation, he cracked Lailoken in the face. "Of course," Keahi said, stretching out his hand. "That's far from what you deserve."

Odette grabbed Keahi's hand again and started pulling him to the hall. It took him a while to turn his focus away from Lailoken. Odette stopped at the sight of the kitchen workers. She looked back at Lailoken, then back at Kiko.

"I had to —"

"Go," Kiko said.

"Come with us," Odette said.

Kiko looked over at her mom and shook her head.

"My place is here." She grabbed Odette's wrist and pulled her into a hug. "Be safe," she whispered, and kissed Odette's cheek. Kiko looked up at Keahi. "You take care of her, Honey Buns."

"It'd be my pleasure." Keahi reached his hand out to Odette again and she took it with her own and smiled. "How are we leaving?" he asked her. "Do you want me to take you out of here? Just focus on me and you won't feel sick after."

"No," she said and frowned. "You're too weak right now, Keahi."

"I'm strong enough —"

"Keahi, don't."

"Okay." He glanced back at the living room. "Then what are we gonna do?"

"We'll take a car." Odette caught the keys just as Kiko tossed them to her. She turned to Keahi again.

"Can you drive?" she asked.

"We don't have cars in the Woolgathering."

"That isn't what I asked."

"No, I can't."

"Well, good thing I actually paid attention when my dad was trying to teach me how to drive." She twirled the keys around her finger and dragged him toward the garage. She pointed at the Chevrolet Chevelle and she unlocked the driver's side. "Get in, babe." She climbed in and unlocked his door from the inside.

Keahi opened the door. Resting his hand against the hood, he leaned into the car.

"Babe?" he asked, raising his eyebrows. Odette had her hands on the steering wheel as she turned to face him. She frowned.

"I'm sorry — was that weird? Do you prefer Keahi?"

"No," he said, slipping into the car. He slammed the door shut. "Everyone calls me Keahi, aside from the few nicknaming me Kitchen Boy and Honey Buns..." He clenched his jaw at his rambling. "I'll be your babe." Keahi awkwardly ran his fingers through his hair and turned to face forward, trying to ignore the blood rushing to his face.

"Good." She started the car and pressed the button to open the garage door. "And I like it when you ramble." Odette glanced at him out of the corners of her eyes. "It's cute." She focused on the road as she pulled out of the driveway.

"Where are we going?" he asked, scratching at the scars on his arm.

"I don't care. Anywhere's better than here." She glanced over at him. "How are you feeling? Do you want me to take you to a hospital? Wait — no."

He laughed. "I'm fine. Are you?"

Odette gripped the steering wheel.

She nodded. "I'm... free." She frowned and looked at him. "What do I do now?"

Keahi shrugged. "Whatever you want." He sat back in the seat and looked out of the window. "I would've killed him, you know."

"I know." Her voice came out small. She reached out her hand to him and nudged him gently with the back of her fingers. Keahi looked down at her hand before taking it within his own. "You're not a killer, and you weren't going to turn into one because of me. Besides, I want him to suffer. He deserves to suffer. His pain would've ended with his death."

"Not necessarily."

"What do you mean?"

"The Angel of Death," he said. "I'm sure he would've given him a punishment he deserves." She smiled at his words. "Why are you smiling?"

Odette shrugged.

"It's nice," she said. "Knowing that eventually, bad people will get what they deserve."

Odette turned on the radio just before she turned the car around the corner. Don't You (Forget About Me) by Simple Minds started playing. "You can change it," she said, acknowledging the radio.

"Nah, it's good." Keahi started tapping his thumb against the door of the car.

"I thought you didn't like anything from the eighties?" He glanced at her.

"I've found new appreciation for it."

"This song is in The Breakfast Club, you know."

"I know," he said and paused. "I... watched it."

"You watched it? Without me?" She clicked her tongue in her mouth as she shook her head. "Unbelievable."

"I'll watch it again with you."

"Nope. Once we get to my friend's Apothecary later, we are having a Brat Pack marathon. We're also going to watch The Goonies — oh — and The Princess Bride. I think you'll love Inigo Montoya." She continued to shake her head. "I can't believe you."

"Are you upset because I watched the movie without you or are you upset over another reason?" he asked, raising an eyebrow.

"What other reason would there be?"

He shrugged. "You tell me."

She furrowed her brows and returned her attention back onto the road.

Then, her eyes widened. "Oh my god!" She pulled the car over and turned it off. She slowly turned to face him. "You know, don't you? You know — you knew about the dream I had of you — and me — didn't you? You knew! This whole time."

"What dream?" he teased. Keahi raised his eyebrows and grinned.

"No, don't — don't smile! Don't — oh my god — I am so embarrassed." Odette's face flushed and she turned as red as a tomato. She fanned herself with her hand. "Is that why you wanted to leave that morning? Did I make you uncomfortable? I'm so sorry."

"No, it was complicated. I didn't — I mean — I did want you to act on it but." He laughed awkwardly. "I didn't want you to regret it, and I didn't want you to get in trouble. I didn't want him to hurt you again — and he did." Keahi scratched his jaw as he looked away from her. "And I didn't stop him."

"I'm going to tell you something someone very special told me." Odette grabbed the back of his hand and squeezed it. He looked at her. She smiled. "It's not your fault."

"You're not mad?" he asked. "I feel like I — I invaded your privacy. I mean, that dream —"

She cut him off. "I'm embarrassed, yes. Definitely. Mad?" She shrugged. "You did everything I asked you to, and more. How could I be mad? You saved me, Keahi. You got me out of a really bad situation. How could I be mad at you?"

He shook his head. "I didn't save you, Odette. I won't take credit for it. You saved yourself, and you saved me."

"So am I the princess or the hero?"

"I don't see why the princess can't be the hero. Princesses are pretty heroic, after all."

She smiled at his words.

"I've been thinking about something Lailoken said. About him owning me." She pursed her lips together as she turned to face him. "If you had the money, would you've bought me?"

Keahi pondered the thought for a moment, and then he shook his head. "No," he said, and her heart sank. She averted her eyes and he took her by the hand. "I would've stolen you." She looked back at him. The way he said it, he wasn't saying it to be romantic. Keahi wasn't... romantic, really.

Least not with words.

He said it so casually, the way people ordered the same dish at their favorite restaurants. Automatic, and without thought. He didn't say it because he thought that's what she wanted to hear. He said it, because it was honest to him. That's what made him special. He didn't tell her things for the sake of trying to please her. He just spoke from his heart, until his head started to overthink.

"You just, you can't put a price on human life," he continued. "I'm not — I'm not saying you aren't worth the money or that I think you're worthless — I swear you aren't worthless. I just mean — someone else shouldn't benefit off of — I don't know. You aren't property."

She smiled as he tried to explain himself, tripping over his own words. She found it charming. "I know what you meant," she said. "And you did."

"Did what?" he asked, still confused by his own words.

"You stole me."

A small smile formed on his face.

She fumbled with his scarred hand beneath the gentleness of her fingertips.

"When I saw your hand in the fire, I realized, for the first time in my life, I really did matter to someone. I mean, I know you told me so, but I've grown so used to people telling me things I wanted to hear, that part of me still believed it was fake. But you didn't do that to prove anything to me. You didn't even know I was there. And you can deny it all you want, but you were gentle with me, patient with me. You reminded me that even though the world is cruel, people can be kind." Odette looked up at him. "No one else would've done for me all that you've done. I'm sorry that it took me so long to fully believe it. Part of me is still surprised you didn't go home."

"Nothing worth having is ever easy to get." He turned his hand over and laced his fingers with hers. "You really thought I was going to give up that quickly?"

"I was difficult."

"You're worth it." He sighed and averted his gaze. "But there's something you need to know," Keahi said, watching her fingers trace his scars. "I got these scars because of *you*."

She frowned and pulled her hands away from him. "*What*?" She sounded horrified.

"That came out wrong. My arm healed quickly, because of you. Mrs. Hamasaki's pain went away, because of you. Odette, you're an Empath. A really strong one, too. You can siphon away the pain of others. That's why your mouth hurt that night. You felt what she felt. I didn't heal her. You kind of — beat me to it. I wouldn't be surprised if you felt like your arm was on fire."

"That's why you pulled away from me."

"Well, it certainly wasn't because I didn't want you kissing me. I'll never oppose to that again."

She laughed and pushed him in the shoulder. He pulled her hand down from his arm and kissed the back of her fingers. "You're meant to be so much more than you were told you could be."

Odette pursed her lips together. "But what if I disappoint people? Myself — or you." Odette shook her head. "I can't."

"You won't. The only thing anyone can ask of you is your best effort. Even if that's just getting out of bed in the morning." He grinned then. "Though I can help you do that, Miss Thomsett."

Odette rolled her eyes. "You're lame." She laughed. "I hate you."

"Not yet you don't," Keahi teased as he wiggled his eyebrows.

"No!" Odette pushed him in the shoulder again. "Don't you bring that up!"

He laughed, unable to hold it in.

"Stop laughing at me," she said and pouted.

"That pout isn't gonna work on me, princess. Not this time."

Odette frowned at him and started the car.

"Where are we going?"

"Somewhere with a little more privacy," she said and grinned. Odette changed gears and stepped on the gas pedal.

"Privacy for what?" He ran his fingers through his hair, pushing it back out of his face, as he looked out the window.

"You'll see."

He ran the back of his fingers against her arm as she drove. His touch was comforting. Coarse, but gentle. He was gentle.

Odette bit down on her bottom lip as she drove to the beach and parked in an empty lot nearby.

"An empty parking lot?" Keahi looked around. He raised an eyebrow at her. "Not very romantic if you're trying to woo a guy."

"Oh, shut up. I don't have to woo you." She pulled the key out of the ignition as she turned to look at him. "Besides, I thought you said you can make anything romantic."

"Yes, I can, but can you?" he asked. His gaze fell to her lap when her hands reached to unbuckle her seatbelt. "What are you doing? Why are you taking that off?"

"I'm going to make you pay for teasing me," she said. Odette crawled out of her seat and into his lap. She reached down by the door and pushed his seat back and unbuckled his seatbelt.

"Here? It's so... public."

Odette pulled her top off and dropped it on the driver's seat.

"No one will see you but me," she said with a grin and he caved.

"Can I kiss you?" he asked, his eyes traveling down her body. She leaned forward and pressed her lips against his. She tugged on his bottom lip, gently with her teeth as she pulled away.

"Where?" she asked, fumbling with the buttons of his shirt.

Keahi put his hand on her back as he sat up. His lips lingered near hers. "Everywhere." He pressed her body up against his and kissed her hard.

TOVALEY B. KYSEL

23   SMOOTH CRIMINAL

"Well, don't just stand there! One of you help me!" Lailoken snapped at the staff that stood around in the hallway. Kaeli and Min-Jae went into the living room and helped him onto the couch.

"Do you want me to —"

Lailoken yanked the iron rod out of his leg and threw it on the floor.

"Never mind."

"Should we call your parents?" Kaeli asked and Lailoken shook his head. He pushed his hair out of his face and leaned back against the couch, tenderly touching the burn on his face.

"Jac," he said. "Call Jac Valentine. Right now. Mr. Wong!" Lailoken shouted from where he sat. "Get Mr. Vanderbilt on the phone."

"You got what you deserve, in my opinion."

Kiko crossed her arms as she leaned against the wall, staring at Lailoken.

He glared at her.

"I don't want to hear anything out of you," he snapped. "You let them leave!"

Kiko scoffed. "Are you blaming me? This is your fault," she said as she stepped into the room. "Big brother. You disgusting, pig-headed asshole."

"What did you call me? Did you just call me 'brother'?"

"Yeah, it's unfortunate." She sat down on the couch. "I was upset about it too, knowing I'm related to the scum of the planet."

He started to laugh.

She raised an eyebrow. "You know, only psychopaths start laughing after being stabbed with an iron rod."

"I don't believe you."

"No? Call your father — wait — call Dad."

"Won't be necessary," Mr. Wong said as he stepped into the room, his hand over the phone. "I was here ten years before your mother arrived." He looked at Kiko. "I remember the details of her agreement." He then turned to face Lailoken. "She's telling the truth. Yumi Hamasaki used to work at your grandfather's brothel. Ahren spent a lot of his time there during the early years of his marriage to Chardonnay."

Lailoken clenched his jaw.

"I'll just make you forget."

"No, you won't."

"And why is that?"

"Because you don't care about me. Not when the 'kitchen boy' has your fiancée." Kiko shrugged as she got up. "Kitchen Boy who's not really a kitchen boy. Good luck finding him." She patted Lailoken's shoulder and laughed. "They got away from you so easily, it was great. The way Doll Face beat your ass? Hilarious."

Lailoken tried to stand up and he fell back against the couch, groaning as he grabbed his thigh.

"I'm going to make her pay for that."

"Sure," Kiko said as she left the room. "Whatever you say."

Lailoken looked up at Mr. Wong.

"It's Mr. Vanderbilt," he said, his hand still over the phone. "What would you like me to tell him?"

"I want Odette's picture on the front page of the Scion Advertiser. This will be bad publicity for the Bridal Expo. I want everyone looking for her and that piece of shit. Where's Jac!"

As soon as Jac got the call from Kaeli, she went to her father's door. She could hear him groaning at her knocking.

"My friend called about the Dreamweaver," she said finally, and she heard him fall out of his bed. "That's what I thought."

She walked to her sister's room and knocked on her door. "Rosie, do you want to come with us?" she asked. "We're going to the Baskerville's."

Rosie answered her door and wiped the sleep from her eyes. "For what?"

"He called about the Dreamweaver."

Rosie's eyes widened as she stepped back from her door.

"No, don't worry. He's not there. We're just going to check out what happened."

Rosie sighed and nodded. "Okay, I'll get dressed."

Gerard couldn't stop talking about the dreamweaver in the car. Jac rolled down her window to get some fresh air while Rosie read her book.

"Can you shut up, Dad? For like five minutes?" Jac snapped while he continued to ramble. "Kaeli said he got away and kidnapped Lailoken's fiancée."

"So? We can track him, Jac. You and me."

She rolled her eyes. "Why don't we get there first and see what happened?"

Gerard nodded, gripping onto the steering wheel.

"Yeah, yes, good idea."

He focused on the road, the only lights coming from the street lamps and the headlights of Gerard's rundown car.

Mr. Wong was there to open the door when they arrived.

Jac couldn't help but laugh when she spotted Lailoken on the couch, ice and a cloth over his leg and the burn on his face.

"What happened to you?"

"Odette stabbed me with a iron rod."

"That little girl beat you up?"

"She's your size, Jac."

"I didn't know she had it in her. I'm surprised. Good for her."

Lailoken narrowed his eyes.

"She wasn't alone —"

"Precisely!" Gerard said, clapping his hands together. "Which is why we're here."

Jac rolled her eyes and Rosie plopped down on the couch across from Lailoken. She crossed her legs and sank back, opening up her book.

Lailoken frowned at her before looking back up at Gerard. "So what happens now?"

"Tell me everything about him."

Jac rolled her eyes again and walked around his living room. She stepped over the broken chair as she tried to visualize what happened. But she couldn't get the image out of her head of Odette going after Lailoken with an iron poker. She did her best to hide the amusement on her face and pursed her lips together.

She glanced at the dying fire in the fireplace and noticed something shiny and blue. She raised an eyebrow as she looked around, Gerard was consumed in his conversation with Lailoken, while Rosie focused on the book she brought with her.

Jac grabbed the poker and dug it out of the fire. She looked at the key, wiping the ashes from it. Glancing up at Lailoken and her father, she stuck it in her pocket as she stood up.

"Are we almost done here?" she asked.

But more company arrived.

"Mayor Mendoza," Gerard said and Rosie looked up. She closed her book. His second wife, Nina, stood at his side. She was hardly older than Jac and Rosie. The mayor was at least twice her age. She stood with elegance though, hands clutching her bag in front of her, plump lips pressed together; red against her pale skin.

"What are you trying to put on the front page, Lailoken?" he asked, stepping into the room.

"My bride was kidnapped by a Dreamweaver, Mayor."

Nina raised one of her perfectly waxed eyebrows.

"A Dreamweaver?" Her voice was smooth. "*Really?*"

Jac and Rosie exchanged glances. It was obvious she didn't believe him.

"So what do you expect me to do then?" Lailoken asked. "Just let him have her?"

"No," Nina said as she looked up at her husband. "We'll put her picture out on the front page and say she was kidnapped but not by a Dreamweaver. Don't be silly."

"Silly?"

Nina handed her purse to her husband and sat down beside Lailoken.

"Love, if he's a Dreamweaver, the mundane world will destroy him all on its own. She'll probably come crawling right back to you once she realizes what kind of monster he really is. Just let nature take its course."

"I want him to suffer."

"He will," she said. "And your fiancée will realize she made a terrible mistake." She turned to face her husband. "Tell Colonel Vanderbilt of the change and to prepare his guard. Though I doubt it will be hard to find one little girl." She faced Lailoken again. "Is anyone else missing from your home?" she asked.

Lailoken sank back in his seat.

"She took my father's car, so yes. Gentry. Gentry Yoshimura. He was part of the kitchen staff too."

"Kidnapped by two kitchen boys. Well," Nina stood up. "We all know how boys can be. The public will be all over that. Saving a girl from them. We're done here." Nina walked up to Gerard and looked up at him. "Your services are no longer needed." As Nina passed Rosie and Jac, she stopped to turn to her. Her eyes glanced down at Jac's pockets, before she curiously met her gaze. "Hm." When Nina stood by her husband again, she kept her eyes on the Valentines. "I hope you all have a good evening," she said.

Gerard clenched his fists. "But Mayor —"

Mayor Mendoza didn't turn around, though Nina did. She stopped in her tracks and turned to face Gerard again.

"Do you have a problem, Gerard?"

Gerard looked away from her, keeping his focus on the mayor. "Mayor, why do you just do everything she says?"

Nina stepped toward him. "I assure you, that's none of your business. We have an arrangement, you see. And you, have a job, Gerard. What is it you do? You're a Shadow Crawler. You do not chase Dreamweavers."

"We used to."

"Well, not anymore. Go find a child to kidnap." Nina turned away from him and left with her husband without another word.

Jac turned to Lailoken, who just shook his head.

"Wait till my mother hears about this."

She stuck her hands into her pockets, and felt along the key that sat safely in confinement. She glanced back at the hallway. There was no way Nina had known. "What's your mother going to do?"

"Yeah, you heard the lady." Gerard sat back on the couch beside Rosie.

"You mean you aren't going to bother?" Lailoken asked.

Gerard turned to face him. "Just give the order."

Lailoken narrowed his eyes and his pupils constricted. "I want you to find that Dreamweaver, and I want you to bring him to me. Alive."

"I will find him and I will bring him to you, alive." Gerard got up and headed for the door. Jac frowned as Rosie stood up too.

"What'd you do that for?" Rosie snapped.

Jac grabbed her wrist.

"Come on, before he leaves without us."

She pulled her sister toward the door and glared back at Lailoken, who sank back into the couch again before he shouted for Mrs. Hamasaki.

24 KEEP ON LOVING YOU

"Mele Kalikimaka," Keahi said.

Odette smirked and kissed his lips. "Joyeux Noël," she said back. "Best. Present. Ever."

He grinned.

She slipped out of his lap and he zipped up his pants. In the backseat, she leaned against him and he wrapped his arm around her. They cracked the windows and watched as the sun rose over the water. Odette wore his shirt, she fumbled with the front as she buttoned it and crossed her legs.

Keahi sat shirtless, his sweaty back pressed against the seat, the wound in his back had healed. His fingers touched the cuff of his shirt and it restored like new. No blood, no burn marks.

Odette sat up to straighten her skirt and Keahi peeled himself off of the leather, rubbing his back from the burn. He shifted on the seat and leaned against the side of the car.

She tucked her hair behind her ear as she turned to face him.

"You look beautiful," he said.

She blushed.

"How do you feel?" he asked.

"Like a princess." Her gaze dropped to her necklace he wore around his neck. "My name looks good on you."

Keahi felt for it with his fingers.

"Was this your way of claiming me as yours?"

"People don't belong to people," she told him.

"I wouldn't mind being yours."

Odette couldn't help but smile at his words.

Keahi felt a sharp pain in his abdomen and he quickly slid his hand over his stomach.

"Is something wrong?" Odette asked. She moved closer to him. "Keahi?"

He didn't look at her.

He inhaled deeply, still rubbing the front of his body. "No, I'm — ah, fuck." His breathing grew jagged, and his eyes turned black for just a second.

"Keahi, what's wrong?"

"The Woolgathering," he said. "It calls for me. Look." He pointed down at his feet; his boots were beginning to disappear. Keahi looked back at her. "You're not scared anymore, princess. You don't need me anymore."

"What about what I want?" she asked, moving closer to him. She grabbed his hand. "What about what you want? I want you to stay. Don't you want to stay? With me?"

He gingerly touched her cheek. "Can I kiss you?" he asked, looking down at her lips.

"Why do you keep asking me that?"

"Because I want your permission."

Her heart fluttered. Odette's gaze dropped to his mouth. "Well?" she asked, looking up at him. "What are you waiting for?" With both hands, she grabbed his face and passionately pressed her lips against his.

When their mouths broke apart, he started, "if you don't like it when I ask —"

"No." She shook her head. "I love it when you ask." She closed the space between their mouths. But Keahi began to disappear from right under her.

She had no choice but to stop.

Odette sat back on her shins as he slowly faded from her sight. "You said you wouldn't leave again! You promised me!"

"I —"

"Keahi!" Tears began to slide down her cheeks as she cupped her mouth with her hand.

She reached in front seat for her bag and started looking for the token he had given her. When she found it, she held it tightly in her hand and looked in the rearview mirror.

"Dreamweaver, consume my fears."

She waited, but nothing happened.

Odette sank back against the seat in the Chevelle and dropped her bag. The polaroid of him fell out of the opening. She reached to grab it. "You promised me," she whispered, tracing his jawline with her finger. Odette turned toward the leather seat and cried.

Almost an hour had passed and her face was now dry and sticky from crying. Odette rubbed her eyes and turned around when she felt something hit against the backseat. She grabbed the keys and slowly got out of the car as she approached the trunk.

She unlocked it.

Gentry sat up and she screamed.

"Were you in there the whole time?" she shouted, her hand over her heart. "Jesus Christ."

His eyes were wide as he climbed out of the trunk.

"I think I'm scarred for life — were you guys having sex? You guys were having sex in the car. While I was in the car."

"We didn't know you were in the trunk! Besides, you didn't see anything."

"But I felt every —" Gentry pushed down on the car with his hand, again and again and again. "Yeah. That. And you. I heard you." He pointed an accusing finger at her face. "Keahi's my friend and all but there are some things I could've lived without hearing. What the fuck."

Odette covered her face and turned away from him. "Oh my god," she mumbled, her voice muffled by her hands.

"Where is Keahi, anyway?" Gentry asked as he turned around. "Where are we?"

"He left — wait. Gentry, why were you in the trunk?"

"Lailoken put me in there last night. Thought I was covering for Keahi. Said he was gonna deal with me later and didn't want me getting in the way. but apparently things didn't go according to his plans."

Odette pulled him into a hug.

"I'm so glad to see you."

Gentry hugged her back before frowning. He stepped away from her. "Wait, but what do you mean he left? Where did he go?"

"Keahi was a Dreamweaver, Gentry," she said as she turned away from him. "He went home."

"He just... left you? He wouldn't just leave you. That's not —"

"He didn't want to." She pushed her hair out of her face and sighed. "When I first summoned him, he told me he'd stay for as long as I needed him." She shrugged. "I guess the Woolgathering or something decided that I didn't. Anymore."

"That's a good thing though, isn't it?"

"Is it?" Her eyes started to water again.

Gentry averted his eyes. "I mean — Dreamweavers are supposed to consume fears and then they're done. So — you're not scared anymore."

"It didn't matter if I was scared. He made me feel safe."

"I'm sorry, Odette." He rubbed her shoulder. Gentry realized she was wearing Keahi's shirt. She was wearing worker's clothes; he was dressed in the same one. "But maybe now it's about making yourself feel safe. Dreamweavers are supposed to teach us things about ourselves. I think you're braver than you realize." Gentry closed the trunk.

Odette stared at the car.

"Why didn't you say something about being in the trunk?" she asked as she looked up at him. "We would've gotten you out sooner."

Gentry raised his eyebrows.

"What — was I supposed to interrupt you or something? Doubt you would've heard me anyway..."

She shoved him in the shoulder. "Gentry!"

"Felt like someone was using a jackhammer in here."

"Oh my god, please stop."

"No, but I'm glad."

She furrowed her brows. "About what?"

"You both got away from Lailoken."

"If you haven't realized it yet, you did too, Gentry."

"You're right." He frowned. "Shit."

"You're not happy?"

"We don't have any money, Odette. At the Baskervilles, I had food to eat and a place to sleep. What are we supposed to do?"

"Well, we should get rid of the car — I could call my friends! We have to find a payphone. I have a few mundane coins in my bag." She walked around the car. "Get in." Odette pointed at the passenger side as she opened the door.

Gentry opened the door as Odette got into the car. She threw her raveled top into her bag as she looked over at Gentry, who leaned into the car.

He stared down at the front seat.

"Did you —"

"Will you just get in?" She frowned at him. "Gentry, get in the car. Right now."

"All right, all right." He slipped onto the seat and closed the door. He rolled down his window. "It smells like —"

"I don't want to hear it."

Odette started the car and drove away from the parking lot. It was no longer an empty lot, now filled with cars from all the people who went to the beach early in the morning. Local surfers, primarily.

At a stoplight, Odette glanced at Gentry, who was looking out the window. "You weren't surprised when I told you he was a Dreamweaver."

Gentry shrugged and glanced at her. "I knew something was different about him. I mean, I didn't think he was a *Dreamweaver*, but it makes sense now. He kind of just always showed up out of nowhere when someone needed him. Like he could sense it or something. Couldn't have just been good intuition or whatever bullshit he claimed. Do you think he'll come back?"

"I don't know. He said unless summoned, no one leaves the Woolgathering."

"Depressing. Have you tried again?"

"Of course I did," she snapped.

"Okay, easy."

Odette clenched her jaw and sighed. "Sorry, he just. He promised me he wouldn't leave."

"Maybe I should drive."

"Do you know how to drive?"

"...No."

"Don't worry, there are normally payphones in front of markets and stuff. I think there's one in front of this one."

Odette pulled into the parking lot, not looking at Gentry again. Her face was sullen and expressionless. She closed her eyes and inhaled deeply, trying to pull herself together.

She left the keys on top of the car and dragged herself to the payphone outside of a grocery store with Gentry following close behind. She dug into her bag for the mundane coins she had and inserted them into the machine and picked up the phone.

She closed her eyes and dialed the first number she could think of.

"Hello?"

"Paisley?" she asked. "I'm so happy you answered."

"Oh my god, Odette? Is that really you?"

"Can you please come get me?"

"Yes — yes! Where are you? I'll come now."

Odette went silent, cupping her mouth with her hand; she tried to muffle the sobs that were trying to force their way back out. Gentry furrowed his brows and looked away from her while he seemed to stand watch.

"Odette? Are you okay? What's wrong?"

"Just — please hurry." She sniffled violently and wiped her face. "I'm at the grocery store in Māewa."

"I'll be right there."

Odette put the phone back on the receiver and crossed her arms over her chest as she turned around. She didn't look at Gentry.

He touched her arm and acknowledged the car they had come in. Some man circled the Chevelle and eyed the keys she had left sitting on the roof.

They watched as Mr. Baskerville's car got stolen.

"How angry do you think his parents are going to be?" Gentry asked.

"Whatever happens, I hope they blame Lailoken for it."

Odette leaned against the wall and tilted her head down. Keahi's shirt still smelled like him, and it was all she had left. She inhaled deeply.

Her eyes lit up at the sight of Paisley's van nearly twenty minutes later. She'd recognize that car anywhere. Paisley practically drove around in an asexual flag. She started hitting Gentry's arm.

"That's her!"

He raised his eyebrows.

"Nice car."

Paisley jumped out of the driver's seat and ran straight to them. She wrapped her arms around Odette and hugged her tightly. "I'm so glad to see you again." She gave her another tight squeeze before she stepped back. "How are you? How are you feeling? How did you get away from him?" She glanced at Gentry and frowned slightly before turning back to Odette.

"It's a long story," she said. "But I could really use a nap. Can we go back to the Apothecary?" Odette tucked her blonde hair behind her ear. "Oh," she said as she turned to Gentry. "This is Gentry, he worked for the Baskervilles."

Paisley looked him up and down and raised an eyebrow. "Nice to meet you," she said. She looked down at his hand as he stuck it out to her, but she didn't take it. "Paisley."

"Okay, pleasure." He curled his hand into a ball and crossed his arms.

Paisley turned back to Odette. "We actually aren't at the Apothecary anymore."

Odette frowned. "What?"

"I'll tell you in the car."

The two of them started walking and Paisley turned around to see Gentry still standing awkwardly at the pay phone.

"Are you coming, or what?"

"Oh, I didn't know — okay."

Gentry ran after them and the three of them climbed into Paisley's van. Odette in the front seat and Gentry in the back. She told Odette about the visit Lailoken had paid them. Paisley told her everything, including the ghost she had seen after Odette had gotten sold at the Bridal Expo.

Gentry hit the back of Odette's seat.

"So that's where Autumn's been going."

Paisley frowned and turned around in her seat.

"You know her?"

He nodded. "Well, I knew her. While she was alive. Quinlan, the Medium of the house, said that Autumn kept leaving, but she didn't know why or where she was going. Guess she was going to see you."

"I'm glad she did," Paisley said as she looked back at Odette. "Sophie and I are staying at my mom's house for now but..." Paisley pressed her lips together and made a line. "He got them to commit suicide. We were so worried about you." She reached over to hug her again. "I'm so glad you're okay."

"Thank you," Odette whispered. When she pulled away from Paisley, she watched as her hair changed from bright orange to a light shade of blue. "What's going on with your hair?"

Gentry was staring at it too.

"Sophie," Paisley grumbled. "They 'accidentally' spilled a potion on me." She used finger quotations and all. Her gaze fell.

"Hey, looks like your wish came true."

"What?" Odette asked.

"Your Daruma doll, he's got two eyes," Paisley said, looking at the small figurine peeking out of Odette's bag. She looked up at Odette. "What'd you wish for?"

Odette looked down and took it out of her bag. She was right, he had two eyes. "For the one I end up falling in love with, to love me back," she said softly. Her eyes began to well up again and she swallowed hard. Trying to blink them away. She glanced out the window and inhaled deeply.

"So who was it?" Paisley asked. "Was he cute?" She looked back at Gentry. "It's not him, is it?"

Gentry frowned. "What's that supposed to mean? I'm adorable."

"Paisley!" A smile peeked at the corner of Odette's lips; her face flushed. "His name was Keahi. My Dreamweaver — and he was very cute."

Paisley frowned. "Keahi? Are you sure?"

"Positive. Why?"

"Keahi's the name of — you used that token I gave you? The one you got from me at the shop? Right?"

"Paze, why are you acting all weird? Weirder, than usual."

But Paisley was hardly paying attention to a thing Odette was saying.

She was too caught up in trying to figure it out on her own. "I mean, something brought you two together. Keahi's not a Dreamweaver."

"He's not?"

"Oh —" Odette shook Paisley from her own thoughts. "So, you didn't know that."

"He said I'm an Empath. I'm not a grot."

"That would make sense then."

"What do you mean?"

"I think when Sophie gave you that potion, well, it unlocked *everything*."

"What are you saying? That my parents did something to me?"

"Well, grots go for more money, Odette. If you're an Empath, then it's likely your pain was too strong for a *Dreamweaver* to handle."

"If he's not a Dreamweaver, then what is he?" Gentry asked. Paisley almost forgot he was even in the car.

"Boy, are you in for a surprise." She started her car. "But where is he?" she asked as she glanced out her window. "Why wasn't he with you?"

Odette glanced away from Paisley as she drove out of the parking lot.

"He left," she said quietly. "Because I didn't need him anymore. He said he'd stay until I no longer needed him, and I guess that's what he did." Odette let out a small laugh. "Why am I not even surprised I'd end up falling for someone I can't have? It's like I'm not allowed to be happy. I feel like I'm already being punished by the scion society and they haven't even come after me yet." She sank back in her chair. "What's going to happen then?"

"Nothing," Paisley said. "Because you're here now, and we'll protect you. No matter what it takes. We'll protect you."

"But he bought me."

"So? People aren't property, Odette."

"Keahi told me something like that too."

Paisley turned the car back off. She sighed, looking forward, and let her hands slip from the steering wheel.

"A little while before you and I became friends, I knew this girl. She was a high-born girl, and she seemed to idolize me so we got to talking. I thought she seemed kinda cool. She gave me her number, and we went our separate ways. One day, I decided to text her. I liked making friends, and I felt like I could always use more. But the more we talked, the more controlling she got. I had no time to myself, I had no time for my friends. I rarely saw everyone. She wouldn't leave me alone, and she convinced me to believe I was okay with that. Convinced me to be her *boyfriend*. Whenever she'd loosen the leash, she only did it to make me into a bad guy. She'd wait for me to get upset with her, so she could guilt me into things. 'No' wasn't an option."

Paisley chewed on the inside of her cheek as a tear rolled down her face.

"There are days when I still wonder if it was my fault. When I still question whether she was the victim, or was I. She had convinced people she was, she even had me convinced at one point, and I crawled right back to her. I was putty in her hands, for her to control and manipulate into what she wanted. Sophie helped me see that what this girl was doing to me, was wrong. She invalidated me, and she violated me. And still, I question myself every fucking day on whether or not it was my fault. On whether my anger was misplaced. I thought I belonged to her because she told me that I did. I thought it was my fault, because she insisted that it was."

"What happened?"

Paisley inhaled deeply. "I realized something. Abusers don't take responsibility for their actions. They'll hurt you, and condition you to apologize for making them do it." She wiped her face and turned to Odette, whose eyes had begun to water too. "Remember when we met, and I told you I didn't like people? I especially didn't like new people? She's why. It was so hard for me to be your friend because I was scared. Because even though she's out of my life, her presence haunts me every day. But I'm so grateful that I didn't let her ruin what became of our friendship before it had even started. And I'm so glad, that whatever Lailoken did to you, didn't keep your heart from falling for someone else. Because you deserve to be happy."

Odette leaned over and hugged Paisley tightly. "So do you," she said softly.

"I am," Paisley said. "I am happy, knowing that the people I care about are safe."

Gentry glanced down, awkwardly picking at his finger, fully knowing this wasn't a conversation he should be hearing.

"Does it ever go away?" Odette asked.

"It hasn't yet — but that doesn't mean I don't have hope that it will. I was a victim of abuse, and it took me a long time to accept that. I still don't, not fully at least, but I'm working on it."

Odette hugged her tighter.

"You aren't a victim, Paisley. You're a survivor. We both are." Odette pulled away from her and grabbed Paisley's shoulders. "You're your own hero, okay? And you saved the part of you that needed to be saved. Friends are just reminders that we're worthy of being saved. If we weren't, they wouldn't be our friends." Odette picked up her Daruma doll. She flicked it so it knocked over and it returned to it's upright position. "Get knocked down seven times —"

"Stand up eight." Paisley smiled.

"I wouldn't have remembered my strength if it wasn't for you."

"You're not the same girl," Paisley said, wiping her face. Odette looked down at the Daruma doll in her hand.

"I'm not. I'm stronger now." She sat back in her seat and took out the Dreamweaver token Keahi had given her. "I wish I could tell her what I know now."

"Which is what?"

"That I'd learn to love myself, and realize I deserved more than what I was getting. That I could be more than what society tried to make me." She laughed, running her finger along the hole in the center of the token. "If there's one thing I am happy about," she continued as Paisley started the car again. "Is that they can't hurt him. He's home and he's safe, and Lailoken can't touch him. But I'm going to miss him. A lot. I already do."

"I think I can help you miss him a little less."

Odette frowned and looked at Paisley. "What do you mean?"

"You'll see." she said and glanced back at Gentry. "You both will." Paisley smirked at Odette. "Just wait till we get to my mom's house. I have something I need to show you. I'm about ninety-five percent positive that it will make you feel better."

When they got to Paisley's mom's house, Odette jumped out of the car. Paisley closed her door and started for the stairs.

"Hey," Gentry said as he reached for Paisley's shoulder. Odette was already half way up the stairs to the front door. "Can I talk to you for a second?"

"Sure."

"I couldn't help but overhear what you said in the car. I just wanted you to know that I think you're strong. I know it's not my place, and I'm sorry, I don't know you, but I know that abuse isn't easy to get over. Some people never bounce back from it. I guess I just wanted you to know that whatever you can manage, it's good enough."

She stared at him for a moment, then reached her hand out to him. "Paisley Eversley," she said.

He cracked a smile and shook her hand. "Gentry Yoshimura."

"Can I call you Yoshi?" she asked.

He shrugged, shoving his hands into the front pockets of his pants. "Yeah, why not. I could use a new nickname."

She smiled and nodded toward the stairs.

"Come on."

They followed Odette up the stairs and Sophie stared at her when she walked through the front door. They raised an eyebrow. "You look like you just had sex."

"Wow, no hello first?" Odette asked as Sophie hugged her.

"You smell like you just had sex too." Sophie stepped back from her and frowned, crossing their arms. "Who are you having sex with?" They looked over at Gentry as he stepped into the house after pulling off his boots. "Him? Was it him?" They glared at him, pointing an accusing finger. "I will kill you if you hurt my Odette."

"Okay, *Dad*, relax." Odette patted Sophie's shoulder. "No, this is Gentry." She pursed her lips together. "He's... long gone."

"He? Who is he?" Sophie looked at Paisley for some kind of explanation.

"Don't look at me. She was like this when I picked her up."

"Whose shirt are you wearing?" Sophie demanded.

"Okay, so maybe I do know. He was from the Woolgathering," Paisley said, wiggling her eyebrows.

Sophie's jaw dropped. "You went and did your Dreamweaver? Odette! You dirty girl." They pointed at Paisley. "I hope you realized you basically handed him to her on a silver platter. That's like giving someone a sex toy."

"I did no such thing!"

Gentry burst out into laughter and Odette couldn't help but laugh awkwardly as well, as she raked her fingers through her blonde hair. "I can't believe this is happening right now."

"I can," he said between laughs.

"I'm sorry, I don't mean to be vulgar — oh wait, yes I do." Sophie pressed their finger to their chest, pointing at their heart. "I'm *me*."

Paisley rolled her eyes.

"Where's Midori and Shiro?" Odette asked. "I haven't seen Shiro in ages."

"At their aunty's," Sophie said. "But I'll text Midori to give her an update and maybe we can have them over for dinner?" Sophie looked at Paisley and she shrugged.

"Sounds fine with me, it's not like I'm cooking."

"You never do."

"Nothing's changed," Odette said with a smile. "I'm glad."

"You have though," Sophie said, slipping into the chair as Paisley walked down the hallway to her bedroom. Sophie looked up at Odette and crossed their legs. "You're different — but it's a good different."

"Mom!" Paisley shouted from her bedroom and Sophie glared down the hallway.

"Hey! I'm trying to have a moment here with my friend!"

"Mom!" Paisley shouted again as she came out of her room, ignoring Sophie and Odette laughed.

"What?" a disembodied voice shouted back from another room.

"Come here, Mom! I have a question!"

A little Chinese-Japanese lady emerged from a far bedroom, sweeping the floor as she walked down the hallway. "What?" Evaline asked, not looking up at any of them.

"Mom, where is the trunk Grandma gave me? With all the old books and scrolls in it? The one with the dragon on the top?"

"I gave it to your father. I thought it was his."

"Mom!" Paisley groaned. Her hair started to turn orange again.

"How was I supposed to know? You leave your things all over the place."

"Ask! You're supposed to ask before you just give my things away."

"It's just at your father's! I didn't throw it away. Don't be so dramatic." Mrs. Eversley stared at Paisley's hair as it changed to blue. "At least know I know when you calm down," she said as she went back to sweeping the floor. "I could have thrown it — WHY ARE YOU WEARING YOUR SHOES IN THE HOUSE?"

Paisley quickly kicked them off. Using her foot, she pushed them behind her.

"Oh, don't try to hide it now I already saw it."

She slipped her shoes back on.

"Maybe it's because I have to go to Dad's house now so I saw no reason to take them off!"

"Oh, you don't have Foresight."

"Ugh, I was literally just in that area." Paisley rolled her eyes as she grumbled to herself and her mom went back down the hallway with her broom. "Okay, so who wants to come with me to my dad's house real quick?"

"I do!" Sophie said, shooting their hand up in the air. "He has a pool and it is fucking hot today."

"You could've turned the air conditioning on!" Evaline said from down the hall.

"Oh! You let Sophie turn the AC on but I can't!" Paisley shouted back.

"You're surrounded by spirits! You should be cold enough!"

"Hey! That's mean!"

Paisley glared at Sophie who couldn't stop laughing at her. "I love your mom, Paze," they barely managed to say between laughs. "So much."

She frowned and pushed Sophie's shoulder.

"Go change!"

"There's no need for that. I have a suit at your dad's house."

"Of course you do." Paisley looked over at Gentry, who had a grin on his face. "What are you grinning about?"

"It just —" He shrugged. "It reminds me of my home."

"Asian moms, huh?"

He laughed.

25 ETERNAL FLAME

The four of them piled into Paisley's van and she drove to her father's house, which was only minutes away from where she had picked up Odette and Gentry. Country music played in the car, and Sophie spent the whole time begging Paisley to change the station. They even asked Odette to take pity on them, but she just shook her head and laughed.

Sophie turned to Gentry, who sat beside them, and crossed their arms. "So if you aren't Odette's lover boy, then who are you?"

"I — uh — I was another kitchen boy at the Baskerville mansion. I'm —" he paused and glanced up at Paisley. "Yoshi. Gentry Yoshimura."

"How did you guys get out?"

"Well, I was in the trunk. I'm technically... not supposed to have left. I mean, I hadn't intended on leaving —"

"Wait," Sophie said as a grin spread across their face. In the front seat, Odette closed her eyes.

"You were in the *trunk*?" Sophie hit the back of Odette's seat. She refused to open her eyes. "Did you have sex in a car, Miss Thomsett?"

"Gentry!" Odette snapped.

"I'm sorry! She asked me a question!"

"Oh, hey." Sophie pat Gentry's shoulder with the back of their hand. "I'm non-binary. Please don't use 'she'. Please use literally anything else. Anything else."

"Oh, I'm sorry. What do you prefer?"

"'They', or 'he' works too. But I can't believe this." Sophie tried to suppress the amusement. "You were in the trunk while they —"

This time, Gentry closed his eyes.

"Please. I'm going to have flashbacks. I don't want flashbacks."

Sophie couldn't contain their amusement any longer and broke out into laughter.

"Odette, you naughty girl!"

"I didn't know he was back there!" She didn't turn around. Odette didn't want to see the look on Sophie's face.

"If I did, I wouldn't have climbed into Keahi's lap in the first place!"

"Okay!," Gentry said. "I don't need visuals, either."

"Why is this happening..." Odette hit the back of her head against the seat.

"You know Sophie likes to talk about this kind of thing," Paisley said, barely glancing away from the road to look at her.

"Yeah, but I didn't think I'd ever be the topic of discussion!"

"Well, who knew you could be so naughty," Sophie said.

"You'd be surprised," Odette muttered.

"What was that?"

"Nothing!" Odette slouched into her seat and kept her focus ahead.

Paisley's dad lived up on a mountain side. He had a pool to the side of his house, and a deck that overlooked Waikiki.

When she opened the front door, Taliesin Eversley was sitting on the couch in the breakfast nook reading the scion newspaper.

"Merry Christmas, Padre!" Sophie said, following Paisley into the house.

"I'm not your dad, Sophie." He didn't even put down the newspaper he was reading.

"You're so funny." They walked past him to head to the bathroom. "Bye, Dad!"

Taliesin turned his attention onto his daughter. "Are they ever going to stop calling me that?" he asked her as she put her palms down against the edge of the table.

"No, but that's not why we're here —" Paisley's voice trailed off when she noticed what was on the front page of the newspaper he was holding. Her father glanced down, then the three of them looked at Odette. She stood on the welcome mat, still as the dead.

Her picture was on the front page.

EXPO BRIDE: MISSING!

"Does that say 'possible kidnapping'?" Odette frowned as she pointed at the article. "Keahi did not kidnap me."

"This is weird," Gentry said.

"What do you mean?" Paisley asked.

He shrugged. "Lailoken's never cared this much about his other brides — they both committed suicide and their pictures were never on the front page." He crossed his arms and looked at Odette. "No offense, and I really mean it, don't take this the wrong way but what makes you so different?"

Odette shook her head.

"I'm not sure it's about me at all. I think he's using me as an excuse. Last night, when Lailoken found Keahi, he told him to stick his hand in the fire. I think he already knew."

"So that's why he was looking for him."

Paisley frowned. "Dad, if a Dreamweaver was here in the mundane world, is that something the society would put in the paper?"

Taliesin shook his head as he put the paper down on the table. "No," he said, "they'd want to keep that under wraps. A reported sighting would cause chaos, and you know how much the high-borns hate that. They hate doing damage control. They'd probably want the Shadow Crawlers to take care of it silently."

Gentry picked up the newspaper and read aloud from the text, "The Baskervilles have reason to believe that two kitchen boys have kidnapped expo bride, Odette Thomsett. All three were last seen Christmas Eve. 'We

fear for her safety and just want to see her returned' —
Lailoken Baskerville. What kind of bullshit is this? He
fears for her safety? Since when?"

"What happened?" Taliesin asked, noticing Odette's
eyes began to water.

"He — he was —"

"It's okay," Paisley said.

Taliesin looked at his daughter and she nodded.

"What was it you needed?" he asked.

"Right — my trunk. Mom said she gave you my trunk.
The one with the dragon on the top?"

Taliesin furrowed his thick brows. He got to his feet
and Gentry took a step back.

"Wow, Paisley, your dad's tall."

"He's only like — six feet, six inches?"

"Only?"

She laughed and the three of them followed him down
the hallway. He grabbed it from the office and brought it
out to the dining room table. She was about to open it,
but then Paisley slowly turned back to face her dad who
was still in the dining room with them.

"Yes, *Father*?" She widened her eyes at him. Taliesin
widened his eyes right back at her before backing up into
the kitchen.

"I'm leaving, I'm leaving," he said, fully knowing when
his presence was no longer wanted.

Paisley opened her trunk and dug through the many
loose images and parchments before pulling out the old
photograph she had been looking for.

"Is this him?" she asked, pointing at the man to the left of the picture. Odette took the photo from her and nodded. She showed Gentry.

"Yeah," he said in agreement. "That's him, all right."

"So what does this mean?" Odette asked while Paisley continued to rummage through the trunk. She pulled out an old book and flipped it open to show them a center page that depicted a family tree of the kupua family in the Woolgathering.

"He's not a Dreamweaver, Odette. He's a kupua prince, one of the children of The Sandman himself. Haunaele, Keahi, and Aulani. He's The Dream King. You summoned The Dream King. It makes sense that you aren't a grot because of it. Not just anyone can summon someone from the royal family, especially not a grot. They're practically gods. They're weaker in the mundane world than in the Woolgathering, but still very powerful."

"He brought me back to life," she mumbled.

Paisley slammed the book shut.

"Excuse me? What?"

Odette sighed. She pulled out one of the chairs at the table and took a seat.

"Things were just so bad with Lailoken, and with Keahi, I had this glimpse of what I could have. What I wanted. I knew I was never going to be happy — and I couldn't live like that. I know it was selfish of me, but I —"

Paisley opened her mouth to speak, but Gentry cut her off.

"It wasn't selfish." He knelt down in front of her. "When you're in that place in your head, you aren't really thinking your actions are gonna affect anyone else. You aren't thinking that anyone cares, or maybe you wouldn't feel as bad as you do. You want the pain to stop, and you'd do anything to make it stop."

"He's right," Paisley said. "Anyone who calls you selfish for it, can't even begin to understand what that kind of pain feels like. People always say, what about all of the people who love you? Why would you hurt them like that? But it's not about them. It's about you, and the last thing anyone should do is guilt trip you." Paisley frowned. "He didn't do that, did he? Keahi?"

Odette shook her head.

"He just — cared. I tried to push him away but he wouldn't leave me." Odette dug into her purse and pulled out the polaroid she stole. She handed it to Paisley. "I — stole this from his house."

"His house?"

Odette nodded. "He said that he and his brother used to come here until they stopped allowing it and now no one leaves the Woolgathering." Odette pursed her lips together. "I don't know how you expected this to make me feel better, Paze."

"Don't you get it?" she asked. "He's the Dream King —"

"Which means he'd be a lot harder to reach, don't you think?"

"Not at all, quite the opposite actually. If he was just a regular Dreamweaver, he'd be way harder to track down. There's just so many of them. But I know exactly who he is. I really don't think you've seen the last of him."

"You really think so?"

She nodded.

"He's the Dream King, Odette. Have faith." Paisley picked out the Daruma doll from her bag and handed it to her. "He loves you."

26 IT MUST HAVE BEEN LOVE

Keahi manifested on the ground in the Woolgathering.

The sky had a faint yellow glow with no clouds, which meant it was still day time in the mundane world. When it was night, dark clouds would cover the sky, and shield the Woolgathering from any light. The Woolgathering was just like Hawai'i, though a thin veil seemed to cover the sky, which lightened the impact the sun could have. It was a darkened O'ahu without street lamps, cement sidewalks, and cars. Torches lined the dirt roads, standing out in front of homes build of wood, clay, and stone.

He sat up and looked down; he was still shirtless, and still wearing the same pants he wore while at the Baskervilles, with his loosely (carelessly) tied boots. His father wasn't going to like that. He got to his feet and quickly dusted himself off.

Other Woolgatherers stared and whispered to one another as they passed him. He knew what they were talking about. He had been gone for months; and his attire showed where he had come back from.

They all knew.

He clenched his jaw and disappeared.

Keahi reappeared in the central hall of the dreamscape palace. He looked to the left, and turned away as soon as he spotted his brother.

"Oh, look who's back. How was the mundane world?" Haunaele asked, grinning from ear to ear as he adjusted the black sarong wrap tied around his hips. Keahi walked past him and Aulani stood up. She wore a red and yellow feather lei on her head like a crown; made with an inner fiber core, where bundles of very small bird feathers were attached to create a continuous feathered cord.

"What happened, Brother?" she asked, pulling her long, brown hair over the front of her shoulders. She wore a short yellow pareo, which wrapped around her chest and tied behind her neck, and a matching pa'u skirt over her waist.

He stopped in his tracks.

"I'll tell you both after," he said, hardly looking over his shoulder.

He continued walking before either of them could speak again. Aulani looked at Haunaele, and the two of them trailed after him down the steps and to the throne room.

Keahi didn't bother knocking on the door and instead, he just let himself in. There were three men sitting on large thrones at the very end of the room. They wore feathered capes, with matching feathered helmets at their sides, all as bright as the clothes Aulani wore.

He headed straight for the man in the middle. He was burly, they all were, but only he had his hair cut short. The man to his left had long, dark and frizzy hair that covered his shoulders, while the eldest man to the right, had long, straighter hair. Much like Keahi's.

The Sandman sat in the middle. His brothers, The Angel of Death to his left, and The Time Lord, to his right.

Keahi crossed his arms when he stopped at the foot of his father's throne.

"I want to go back," he said.

"Why?" The Sandman sat back in his seat. "Because you think you love this scion girl?"

"I know I love her."

He scoffed. "Love is strong, but it won't protect either of you. Who's to say she won't fall out of love with you? Did you not learn from what happened the last time this happened?"

"It's different."

"People often claim that, but it never really is. You're never to see her again."

"You can't just —"

"I am The Sandman," he said as he rose from his throne. His voice grew louder as he spoke, roaring through the throne room. "And you will do as I say if you want her to continue waking up every morning."

"She's not a grot or mundane... You can't control her, Dad. Not from here."

"Shall we test that theory?"

Keahi clenched his jaw.

"Now stop running around pretending to be a dreamweaver and do your damn job, Keahi."

Keahi scowled as his father returned to his seat. He turned around and walked back out, barely noticing his siblings standing in the hall, who had listened at the doorway. The two of them exchanged glances, but neither of them moved to follow him.

He found himself downstairs, deep in the ground in the hidden chambers, where dreams roamed freely. Where imaginary friends would manifest once they were long forgotten. Where he and his siblings would perform their work. He walked through rows of orbs that sat on shelves, colored of horn or ivory, depending on their dream. Some were blackened by nightmares that haunted them. Personal nightmares, not given by his brother.

Keahi continued to walk through the seemingly endless rows of shelves and cases holding the orbs like he were looking to get lost in a maze he knew his way out of. He nearly tripped on his shoelace and kicked his boots off in frustration.

"You may not be able to be there with her, but dreaming is a powerful thing."

He turned around to see his uncle standing there. Mauli, The Angel of Death. Mauli towered over him, and was nearly twice his size. But the only person he ever felt threatened around, was his own father.

"What are you saying?" Keahi asked.

"You're a kupua prince, Keahi. You're The Dream King. I'm saying, do your job."

"But she's a scion. We're not supposed to —"

"Rules... We all break them every once in a while. Some for wrong reasons, some for right. What's right, is all about perspective. Isn't it? She loves you, Keahi."

Keahi frowned. "How do you know?"

A small smile appeared across his face. A smile that would likely scare anyone who didn't personally know Mauli. Despite his intimidating appearance, he was rather friendly. If not the friendliest of the three Woolgathering Kings.

"Because you gave her hope. I'm the Angel of Death. People die without hope." His uncle turned around, looking at the orbs that glowed around him. "When despair has hooked them and dragged them deep into the depths of their own personal Hells," he said as he clenched his fist and turned to face his nephew again, "not many are strong enough to climb back out. You gave her something to believe in. You made her do something she never knew how to do."

"What?"

"You got her to love herself. You got her to realize she deserved better, and that, is the best thing one can do for someone."

Keahi glanced away. "And I left her."

"You weren't given a choice. You did what you said you would do and then it was time to leave. You know the rules, for those who are... difficult with the keys. A Dreamweaver's Promise."

"I wouldn't have said that if I knew I was gonna fall in love with her."

"Love is unforeseeable. Even you know that. When you got there, I'm sure the last thing you felt in your heart was love." Mauli patted his nephew's shoulder with a heavy hand. "Considering how you were before you left." He raised an eyebrow. It had a slice through it. "I know you'll make the right decision," he said. "Even if it's one others would disagree with. You should talk with your brother and sister. They missed you — or at least — Aulani did. Maybe you should ask her to tell Odette a story if you don't want to appear to her yourself."

"You know her name?"

Mauli's expression faltered.

"I almost collected her soul, Keahi. Like I said, you gave her hope. People who suffer, suffer silently. They're always in more pain than they want others to believe. You never gave up on her, and sometimes, that's all a person needs. Someone to believe in them. Someone, to show that they care. You wouldn't have been able to bring her back if she didn't want to come back." He began to turn around so that he could leave, but Mauli stopped in his tracks. "You have to forgive your father. It's been... a while since he's allowed himself to feel anything for anyone."

Keahi didn't turn around.

"I don't have to forgive him."

"You're right, but holding a grudge will do nothing for you. It certainly won't faze him."

Mauli walked away, disappearing into the darkness of the many crevices in the chambers. Keahi clenched his jaw as he glanced at the clear orb he had stopped in front of.

Odette Thomsett.

Keahi found Aulani in the music room, blasting her phonograph, which only ever played vinyl records from the eighties. She loudly sang along to Roxette's It Must Have Been Love as she danced around in the room by herself.

"Aulani, may I ask a favor?"

She spun around, hand over her heart. "Keahi! You frightened me!" She wagged her finger at the phonograph. "Normally you remove the needle first so you at least give me a warning, for goodness sake. What happened?"

He glanced at the machine.

"I guess it doesn't bother me anymore."

"Well, that only took —" she stopped to count on her fingers. "Almost four decades." She stopped the song. "What favor?"

He brought her down to the dream chambers and led her to Odette's orb. Keahi nodded toward it. "Can you tell her a story? For tonight?"

Aulani raised her hand and let her fingers linger beside the orb, but she didn't touch it.

"She's sad."

"She's not the only one."

"This is her?"

He nodded.

"Where's Haunaele? We have to find out how many scions are having nightmares about masked people. Now that I know for sure he's not the one inflicting it. To think I thought he was lying to me all these years."

"Why?" she asked, folding her arms over her chest.

"Because I finally know what it means. We have to send Dreamweavers to help them."

"But Dad said — you can't override what Dad says. We're not supposed to help scions. We're barely allowed to help mundanes."

"I can't negate Dad's orders myself, but I can do it with your help. Will you not help me?" he asked. "You've been curious about scions your entire life, Aulani. But you were never allowed in the mundane world, only Haunaele and I. You're going to listen to Dad now? We could help these people."

"What did that girl do to you?"

"She inspired me." He shrugged and glanced at the orb. "Sometimes, you just meet someone who reminds you of why people get up every day, despite the weight of the world pushing against them. When you come across someone who has the strength to keep going, based on something as small as hope. Even though they have nothing good in their lives. You want to be better for them. Sometimes, you meet someone who just makes you want to be a better you. So that maybe one day, you deserve to have their light in your life."

"You don't think you deserve her?"

"No," he said. "I know I don't. I don't think I ever will, but I can still try to be better, in spite of that. I hated her, Aulani. I loathed her. I thought she was a dull, vacuous and shallow woman, the most narcissistic high-born I ever had the displeasure of meeting. But then she opened herself to me and I realized — I was the fool. I was vain, I thought I was better by default without even knowing her." He looked at the orb. "I just want to make sure she knows that I didn't leave because I wanted to. I wanted nothing more than to stay."

"You're not happy to be home?"

"I am," he said. "But I didn't want to leave her behind."

"I'll do it," she said.

"Thank you." He turned around and began to leave.

"Wait, what do you want me to tell her?"

"That I love her — and I'm coming back."

"Dad's going to kill you."

Keahi shrugged. "I don't care. Dad doesn't scare me."

But he should.

TOVALEY B. KYSEL

Tell Her

Tell her about a lonely son, caught in the middle.
Between a black sheep and the innocence of a young girl.
The focus point; with a light shining bright.
He was youthful, ambition caught in his eyes.
Meant to rise over the failures of his older brother.

Show her he became a lonely child, destroyed at the core.
Who broke under a pressure too strong for him to fight.
The blood on his knees, coating his palms.   Fingertips.
The salty smell of iron led the way.
Leading to disappointment.

She'll see how he became a dead man.
He dug his own grave with those hands.
The blood had dried around his nails.
There was nothing left but a shell of what he was.
A void, the absence of what could have been.

Bring her a mirror, and show her herself.
Let her see the way nature swayed in her eyes.
The flowers that grew from the beauty of her heart.
Rays of the sunlight that danced in the locks of her hair.
Touch bringing him from the decay he's called home.

Let her fall in love with her reflection.
Let her fall in love with what I see.
Let her fall in love with herself.
Let me believe —

She fell for me.

RHYTHM OF THE NIGHT

Paisley and Sophie spent some time moving into Taliesin's house, where Gentry and Odette had room to sleep. Gentry shared a room with Sophie, while Paisley and Odette shared the other. She often still wore Keahi's shirt, usually over her other clothes. The only time she ever seemed to take it off was when Sophie insisted it needed to be washed.

At first, Odette refused, not wanting the smell of him removed from the fabric. But luckily for her, it seemed to linger.

"How are you doing?" Paisley asked, sitting on Odette's bed beside her.

She shrugged where she lay.

"I miss him," she said, "but I'll manage."

"Anymore dreams about him?" Paisley asked, and Odette nodded.

"Every night. He visits me in my sleep," she said with a smile, but it faded soon after. "I think it only makes me miss him more because I know it's just a dream, and that when I wake, he won't be there anymore."

Paisley inhaled deeply and clasped the back of Odette's hand with her own.

"Well, what if Sophie and I figured out a way for you to see him while you're... awake?" she asked, and Odette sat up. "You won't be able to communicate with him all the time, he is the Dream King and he has a job to do, but we think it's better than nothing?"

"Well yes, of course. What is it?"

Paisley handed her the pocket mirror from her trunk. "I've used this to contact his uncle in the past. The Angel of Death. He's strict, but rather — sympathetic. I mean, he does deal with the dead, you kind of have to be, right? Anyway, I think he might allow the communication if you ask nicely."

"Thank you!" Odette threw her arms around Paisley and hugged her as tight as she could.

"Just don't be like — gross — or anything. Yoshi's gonna want to talk to him too. Let's not give him bad memories."

Odette's cheeks turned red.

"Oh god, once Keahi sees him, he's going to know. He's going to know Gentry was in the car with us. He's already shy enough."

Paisley scoffed. "The Dream King is shy?"

Odette nodded.

"I don't think it's about being shy."

"What do you mean?" she asked and frowned.

"I think it was about vulnerability. When he was here, he wasn't Keahi, The Dream King. He didn't have his title attached to him. He couldn't just be anyone in the blink of an eye. He couldn't morph, he couldn't change. He was just himself. He was just Keahi." Paisley shrugged. "I'm sure that frightened him on some level. I doubt he's ever been just Keahi. In front of anyone. That family, they've always been who they are. He let his guard down for you. That would scare anyone." Paisley smiled. "Look at you, growing up and snagging kings."

"Who's shagging kings?" Sophie asked as they came into the room.

Paisley twisted her body to face the door. "That is not what I said."

"Like it's not true though."

A large man began to manifest right in her room. He was nearly as tall as Paisley's dad, and covered in muscle. The Angel of Death was a rather robust man. Thick curly hair covered his bare shoulders. He wore nothing but the same thing Keahi had worn when he first appeared in her room. A pareo wrap tied around his hips.

"What now, Paisley —" Mauli said as he turned around. He tilted his head and furrowed his thick brows at the sight of the small blonde girl. "Odette?"

"You know me?"

"You died, remember?" Mauli said.

She furrowed her brows. "Right." She hated thinking about it. When she thought about it, she was reminded of the look on Keahi's face. Reminded that she made him cry. Though it was in the past now, thinking of him like that broke her heart all over again.

"And — my nephew told me a lot about you. I assume that's why you're contacting me."

Odette smiled a little. "Could I please speak to him?"

"It's against the rules —"

Her smile began to fade.

"— but I am known to break them every now and again."

"Thank you so much, Sir."

"Please," he said with a broad grin. "Call me Uncle Mauli." He turned away to look at someone she couldn't see. "Hey, you. Bring me Keahi."

Odette's heart began to beat faster. She turned to face her mirror and wiped the corner of her lip as she fixed her hair.

"You already look perfect, you know."

She turned around. Keahi stood where Mauli once was, wearing the same pareo wrap she remembered. His feet were bare, as was his chest. From his neck hung her necklace, and a shark tooth tied to a leather cord.

"I've missed you!" she said as she threw her arms around him. She pulled away just enough so she could put her hands against his face. She kissed him. "I've — missed — you — so — much," she said between each kiss she planted on his lips.

Keahi smirked. He rested his forehead against hers.

"Wow, I should've found a way to get here sooner."

"Are you trying?" she asked, her hands resting on the back of his neck. "To come back?"

"I promise you that I am." Keahi kissed her forehead. "I've missed you too, princess."

"I can't believe you're The Dream King and you didn't tell me." She took a step back and gave him a once over. "But I can get used to this look." She smirked, and bit down on her bottom lip.

"Don't look at me like that," he said, a grin forming on his face.

"Don't worry, I'll behave." She pat the front of his chest. "Someone actually wants to talk to you."

"Who?"

"Gentry." Odette moved to the door and opened it. Gentry, Sophie and Paisley all fell into the room. "Or all three of them."

Sophie was the first to stand up.

"So it was you!" Sophie said. "You had s —"

Paisley slipped her hand over Sophie's mouth.

"We'll be back later," she said as she pulled Sophie out of the room.

Gentry raised his eyebrows at the sight of Keahi.

"So this is you?"

"This is me. Gentry, how did you —" His expression faltered. Odette buried her face in her hands at his realization. "Were — were you —"

Gentry nodded.

"I was in the trunk. Worse two hours of my life."

"It wasn't that long —" Keahi frowned and looked at Odette. "Was it?"

"Well, we did kind of fool around a lot before we actually —"

"Stop!" Gentry closed his eyes and shook his head. "I'm just glad to see that you're doing okay."

"How are you guys?" Keahi asked. "Odette and I don't really talk when —"

She slapped his arm. "Shut up!"

"Hey, they're your dreams, princess."

Gentry rolled his eyes. "You two are disgusting. I'm leaving."

"Hey Gen, I miss you too." Keahi was serious now. "You're one of the best friends I ever had."

"Come back soon, man."

Keahi nodded. "I'm trying."

Gentry headed for the door. "I'll leave you two alone —" he opened the door and Sophie came right back in.

"Not alone time yet," they said. "I have a few things to say to you, *Dream King*."

"Good luck," Gentry said as he slipped past Paisley, who stood in the doorway.

"So you just had sex with her and abandoned her in a parking lot?"

"Whoa, okay, it wasn't like that."

"Really? Do you know how much she's cried over you?"

He looked at Odette and she started to shake her head. "Keahi, I just —"

"Odette, shh." Sophie held up their hand.

"Sophie just wants to know if you love her," Paisley said. She leaned against the frame of the doorway and had her arms crossed over her chest, one of her feet pressing flat against the wall.

"I do," he said, he didn't take his eyes off of Odette. "And if it was up to me, I never would've left."

Sophie looked back at Paisley, and she shrugged her shoulders. They turned to face Keahi again. "Fine, but if you hurt her, I swear, Paisley and I, we'll find a way to kill your kupua ass."

"I would never hurt her."

"I'm watching you, Dream King. You don't scare me."

"Come on, Sophie. See you, Keahi."

"Nice to see you again, Paisley."

Odette pursed her lips together. "You know Paisley?"

"I've met her a few times. My uncle tries to maintain a good relationship with the mid-born Mediums, and she's got Dreamweaver blood flowing through her veins. She's a special one."

"Hey." Odette tugged on his pareo wrap. Keahi grabbed her hands.

"Don't, you might pull it off of me."

"I'm the only special one," she said, she didn't loosen her grip.

"I know," he said. "You're my princess." He smirked. "Are you getting jealous?"

"No, I just haven't been around you in days and I — okay, yes. Maybe a little."

"I only have eyes for you."

"Good."

His gaze dropped down to what she wore around her neck. "You made a necklace out of my token?"

"I wanted you close to my heart."

Keahi raised his eyebrows. "You're actually being corny with me? You? What happened to Princess Vulgar?"

"She's waiting for her prince to come back. Impatiently." She gripped at his pareo wrap. Keahi averted his eyes and watched something like he was looking at someone who walked past them. "You're... not alone there, are you."

"No, I'm not, but I'd like you to meet someone."

Odette loosened her grip on the knot of his pareo wrap and held his hand instead. Her face flushed. "Who?"

"The girl you wanted me to date — my sister — The Storyteller."

She turned redder as a girl stepped into view. Odette recognized her from the picture Paisley showed her. She was beautiful then, though more beautiful in person. She looked like Keahi, it was the facial structure. High cheekbones. Beautiful brown eyes.

"This is Aulani," Keahi said.

"Wow," Odette said. "You're so beautiful."

"Told you." Aulani smirked as she looked at her brother. She returned her gaze to Odette. "As are you, Odette. Much lovelier than my brother has led on. He tells me you like the eighties?"

"I love the eighties. The movies, the music — are you the one who enjoys it too?"

"I love it."

Odette looked at Keahi. "I think I should be dating your sister instead," she teased.

He frowned and Aulani laughed.

She stopped suddenly and looked around.

"I think I heard Dad."

Keahi's gaze shifted too.

"Don't worry, I'll go distract him." Aulani's focus returned to Odette. She reached out to touch her arm. "It was a pleasure to meet you."

Odette smiled as Aulani stepped out of view.

"Are you going to get in trouble?"

"Nah, but I should probably get going." Keahi took off the shark tooth he wore around his neck and fastened it around hers.

"Are you claiming me now?" she asked, looking down at it now hanging beside his token.

Keahi shook his head.

"This is me — promising myself to you." He gently touched her cheek, brushing his thumb against her skin. "I miss you."

"I miss you too." She looked down at his mouth. "Can I kiss you?" she asked.

He smiled. "Always."

Odette kissed him goodbye and when she faded from his sight, he saw his brother standing there. Watching.

"Why didn't I get an introduction?"

"I didn't know you wanted to meet her," Keahi said as he turned to the door.

"Of course I want to meet the high-born who has my brother wrapped around her little finger."

"Can we not do this right now?"

"Yeah — I just came to tell you that you were right about the masked people. Women, and even men, are having those nightmares all over the world. You think they're all being manipulated?"

Keahi nodded. "When I first got to Odette, she had those same dreams and they were revealed to be her fiancé. They're manipulated to forget the abuse, so the person haunting their dreams is seemingly faceless and without identity. They know something is happening to them, they just don't know who's doing it."

Haunaele groaned. "But why should we help them? They're scions. Their own community did this to them, not us. If you forgot, they're our enemy. They're the reason we don't live in that world anymore. And what about this girl? You think she's going to wait for you?"

"Just because a high-born broke your heart, doesn't mean one's going to break mine."

Haunaele clenched his jaw as Keahi walked away from him..

28 TIME AFTER TIME

Jac Valentine laid on her bed, staring at the key she got from the Baskerville mansion. The blue gem in the center started to glow, and it tugged against her grasp. "What the hell?"

Sitting up, she let it go and it dropped to the ground, sliding across the floor as though it were being pulled by a magnet.

She got up from her bed and grabbed her jacket from the hook in her room and put it on before grabbing the key. Slipping on her boots, she tiptoed around her house, careful not to wake anyone up, staying as quiet as she could manage until she reached the front door.

The blue gem of the key glowed brighter now.

Frowning, she went around the side of her house. Jac rummaged through her father's belongings in the back and picked up a lantern from the table. She ventured into the forest, following the pull of the skeleton key, keeping her eyes peeled for any movement that came around her.

Nawao lurked amongst the trees, hidden from scion and mundane civilization. Among them, Menehune.

She didn't want to run into either of them.

She stopped in her tracks when the pull of the key ceased. Jac looked ahead as the key led her further and further into the forest.

There stood a mirror, encased in the trunk of a tree. She stepped forward and circled it. It had rusted, and she could hardly see her reflection in the glass. Holding the key out in the flat of her hand, the wings started to unfold, outstretching against her palm. It shot out of her palm and latched itself into a concealed key hole. She took a step back and the mirror began to ripple, like the surface of water in a disrupted pond.

Extending her arm toward the mirror, fingers out, she reached to touch the soft reflective waves, and the tips of her fingers went through it as it brushed against it. She leapt back and glanced down at her hand, before returning her gaze to the mirror.

Jac stepped forward and pressed her face against her reflection. Slowly, another world, a mirror world, began to manifest in front of her eyes. It was darker, dreary. Instead of street lights, dirt roads were lined with crossed torches.

The Woolgathering.

sequel coming soon.

About the Author

Tovaley B. Kysel was born and raised in Honolulu, Hawai'i and has nothing remotely interesting to say about herself. She's half Asian, half Caucasian, and has a desperate need to understand people. Tovaley believes she's the most disorganized writer on the planet and will occasionally (accidentally) lose her dog in all of her mess. Sometimes it's amazing that she gets any writing done.